Vampire Game

JUDAL

ALSO AVAILABLE FROM TOKYOPOP®

MANGA

.HACK//LEGEND OF THE TWILIGHT*
@LARGE (December 2003)
ANGELIC LAYER*
BABY BIRTH*
BATTLE ROYALE*
BRAIN POWERED*
BRIGADOON*
CARDCAPTOR SAKURA
CARDCAPTOR SAKURA: MASTER OF THE CLOW*
CHOBITS*
CHRONICLES OF THE CURSED SWORD
CLAMP SCHOOL DETECTIVES*
CLOVER
CONFIDENTIAL CONFESSIONS*
CORRECTOR YUI
COWBOY BEBOP*
COWBOY BEBOP: SHOOTING STAR*
CYBORG 009*
DEMON DIARY
DIGIMON*
DRAGON HUNTER
DRAGON KNIGHTS*
DUKLYON: CLAMP SCHOOL DEFENDERS*
ERICA SAKURAZAWA*
FAKE*
FLCL*
FORBIDDEN DANCE*
GATE KEEPERS*
G GUNDAM*
GRAVITATION*
GTO*
GUNDAM WING
GUNDAM WING: BATTLEFIELD OF PACIFISTS
GUNDAM WING: ENDLESS WALTZ*
GUNDAM WING: THE LAST OUTPOST*
HAPPY MANIA*
HARLEM BEAT
I.N.V.U.
INITIAL D*
ISLAND
JING: KING OF BANDITS*
JULINE
KARE KANO*
KINDAICHI CASE FILES, THE*
KING OF HELL
KODOCHA: SANA'S STAGE*
LOVE HINA*
LUPIN III*
MAGIC KNIGHT RAYEARTH*

MAGIC KNIGHT RAYEARTH II* (COMING SOON)
MAN OF MANY FACES*
MARMALADE BOY*
MARS*
MIRACLE GIRLS
MIYUKI-CHAN IN WONDERLAND*
MONSTERS, INC.
PARADISE KISS*
PARASYTE
PEACH GIRL
PEACH GIRL: CHANGE OF HEART*
PET SHOP OF HORRORS*
PLANET LADDER*
PLANETES*
PRIEST
RAGNAROK
RAVE MASTER*
REALITY CHECK
REBIRTH
REBOUND*
RISING STARS OF MANGA
SABER MARIONETTE J*
SAILOR MOON
SAINT TAIL
SAMURAI DEEPER KYO*
SAMURAI GIRL: REAL BOUT HIGH SCHOOL*
SCRYED*
SHAOLIN SISTERS*
SHIRAHIME-SYO: SNOW GODDESS TALES* (Dec. 2003)
SHUTTERBOX
SORCERER HUNTERS
THE SKULL MAN*
THE VISION OF ESCAFLOWNE*
TOKYO MEW MEW*
UNDER THE GLASS MOON
VAMPIRE GAME*
WILD ACT*
WISH*
WORLD OF HARTZ (November 2003)
X-DAY*
ZODIAC P.I. *

For more information visit www.TOKYOPOP.com

*INDICATES 100% AUTHENTIC MANGA (RIGHT-TO-LEFT FORMAT)

CINE-MANGA™

CARDCAPTORS
JACKIE CHAN ADVENTURES (November 2003)
JIMMY NEUTRON
KIM POSSIBLE
LIZZIE MCGUIRE
POWER RANGERS: NINJA STORM
SPONGEBOB SQUAREPANTS
SPY KIDS 2

NOVELS

KARMA CLUB (April 2004)
SAILOR MOON

TOKYOPOP KIDS

STRAY SHEEP

ART BOOKS

CARDCAPTOR SAKURA*
MAGIC KNIGHT RAYEARTH*

ANIME GUIDES

COWBOY BEBOP ANIME GUIDES
GUNDAM TECHNICAL MANUALS
SAILOR MOON SCOUT GUIDES

080103

VAMPIRE GAME

Volume 3

by

JUDAL

Los Angeles • Tokyo • London

Translator - Ikoi Hiroe
English Adaptation - Jason Deitrich
Associate Editor - Tim Beedle
Retouch and Lettering - Jennifer Nunn
Cover Layout - Aaron Suhr

Editor - Luis Reyes
Managing Editor - Jill Freshney
Production Coordinator - Antonio DePietro
Production Manager - Jennifer Miller
Art Director - Matt Alford
Editorial Director - Jeremy Ross
VP of Production - Ron Klamert
President & C.O.O. - John Parker
Publisher & C.E.O. - Stuart Levy

Email: editor@TOKYOPOP.com
Come visit us online at www.TOKYOPOP.com

A  Manga

TOKYOPOP Inc.
5900 Wilshire Blvd. Suite 2000
Los Angeles, CA 90036

ISBN: 1-59182-371-4

First TOKYOPOP® printing: October 2003

10 9 8 7 6 5 4 3 2 1
Printed in the USA

VAMPIRE GAME

This is the tale of the Vampire King Duzell and his quest for revenge against the good King Phelios, a valiant warrior who slew the vampire a century ago. Now Duzell returns, reincarnated as a feline foe to deliver woe to... well, that's the problem. Who is the reincarnation of King Phelios?

When last we left our menagerie, the search for Phelios had led them to La Naan, home of Princess Ishtar's Aunt Ramia and her three cousins, Seiliez, Laphiji and Vord. Realizing any one of them could be the reborn king, Ishtar enrolled Duzell into La Naan's famous martial arts competition, a brazen show of brutality, brawn and, of course, blood. Since our fearless antihero can only recognize the reincarnated Phelios by the taste of his blood, it would seem to be a perfect plan. There's just one problem. Never one to leave well enough alone, the princess has promised her hand in marriage to whichever prince wins the tournament. With the throne of Pheliosta as the prize, a prince would do just about anything to guarantee victory. And three princes whose lineage is now in question are liable to behave in the most unprincely of fashion...

Table of Contents

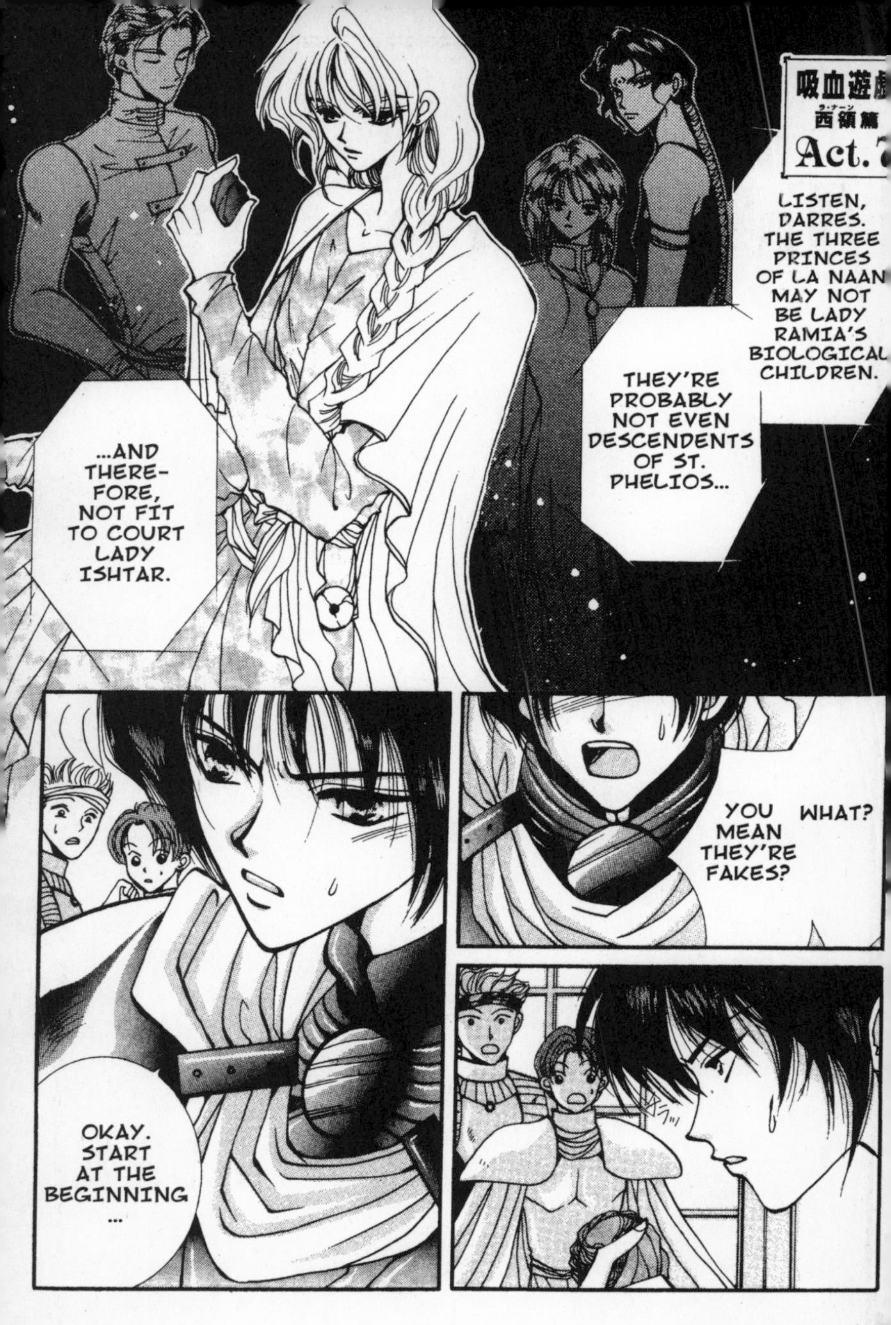
吸血遊戯
西領篇
Act. 7
LISTEN, DARRES. THE THREE PRINCES OF LA NAAN MAY NOT BE LADY RAMIA'S BIOLOGICAL CHILDREN.
THEY'RE PROBABLY NOT EVEN DESCENDENTS OF ST. PHELIOS...
...AND THEREFORE, NOT FIT TO COURT LADY ISHTAR.
WHAT?
YOU MEAN THEY'RE FAKES?
OKAY. START AT THE BEGINNING...

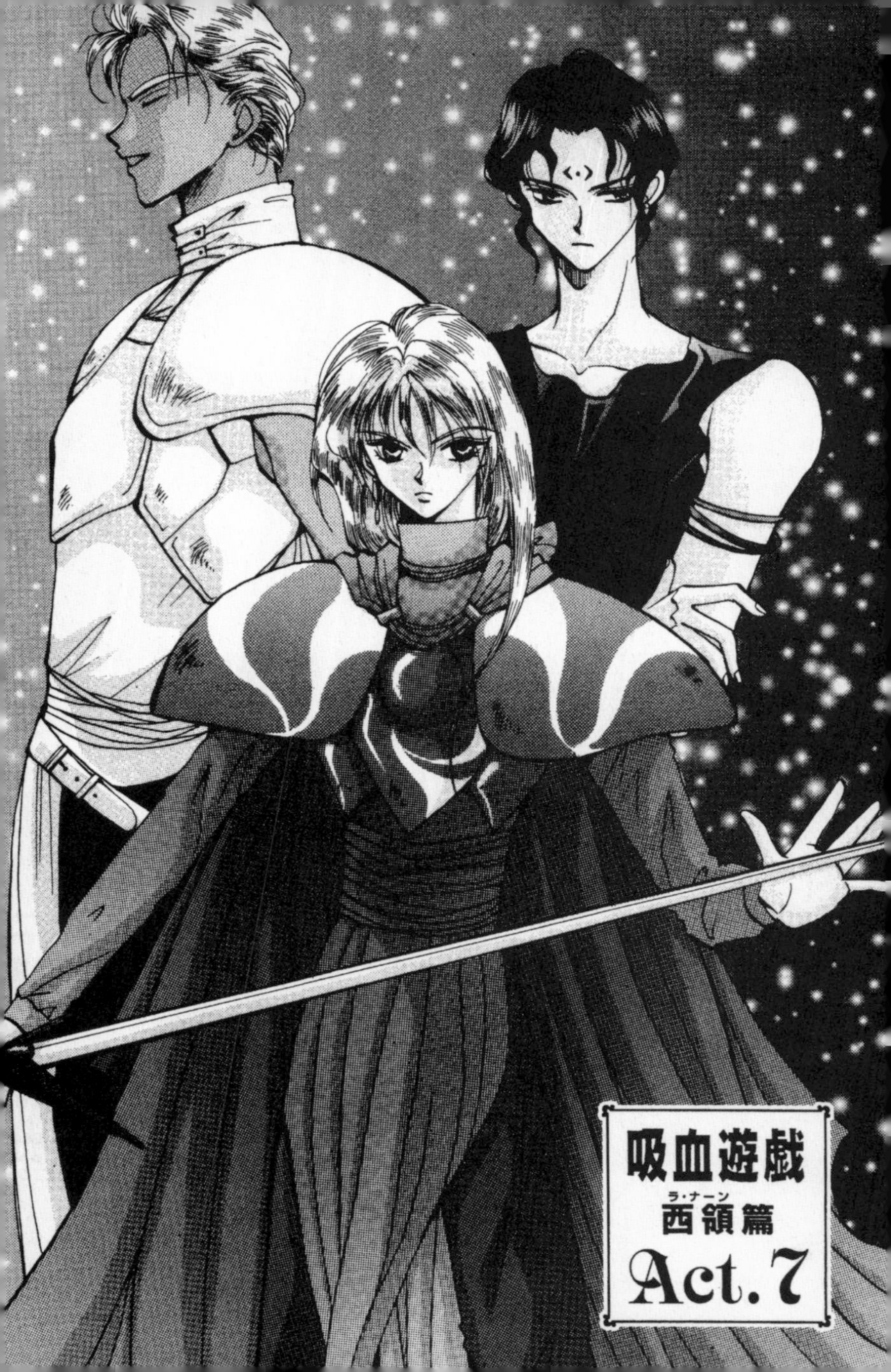
吸血遊戯
ラ・ナーン
西領篇
Act.7

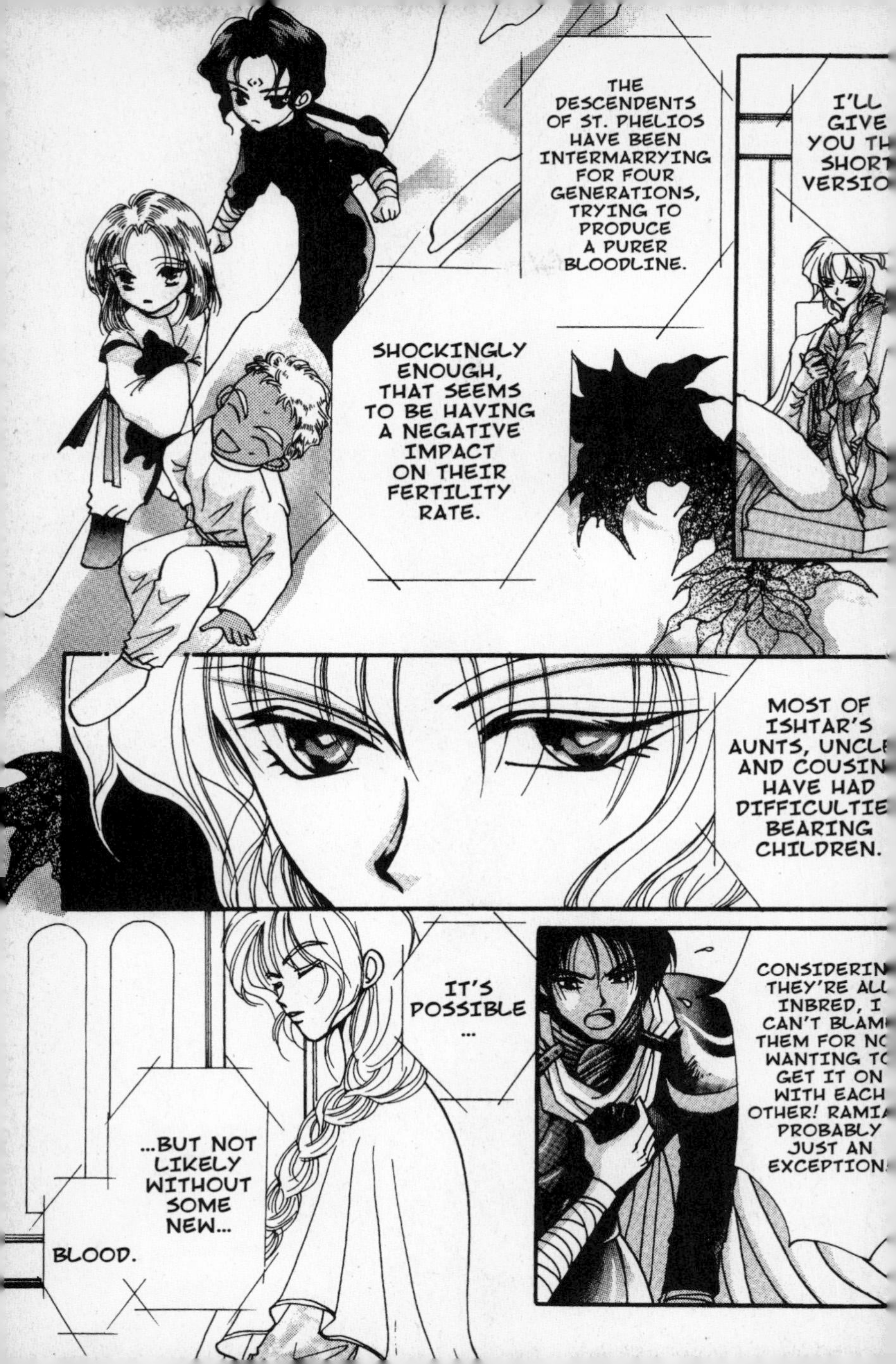
I'LL GIVE YOU TH SHORT VERSIO
THE DESCENDENTS OF ST. PHELIOS HAVE BEEN INTERMARRYING FOR FOUR GENERATIONS, TRYING TO PRODUCE A PURER BLOODLINE.
SHOCKINGLY ENOUGH, THAT SEEMS TO BE HAVING A NEGATIVE IMPACT ON THEIR FERTILITY RATE.
MOST OF ISHTAR'S AUNTS, UNCL AND COUSIN HAVE HAD DIFFICULTIE BEARING CHILDREN.
CONSIDERIN THEY'RE ALL INBRED, I CAN'T BLAM THEM FOR NO WANTING TO GET IT ON WITH EACH OTHER! RAMIA PROBABLY JUST AN EXCEPTION
IT'S POSSIBLE...
...BUT NOT LIKELY WITHOUT SOME NEW...
BLOOD.

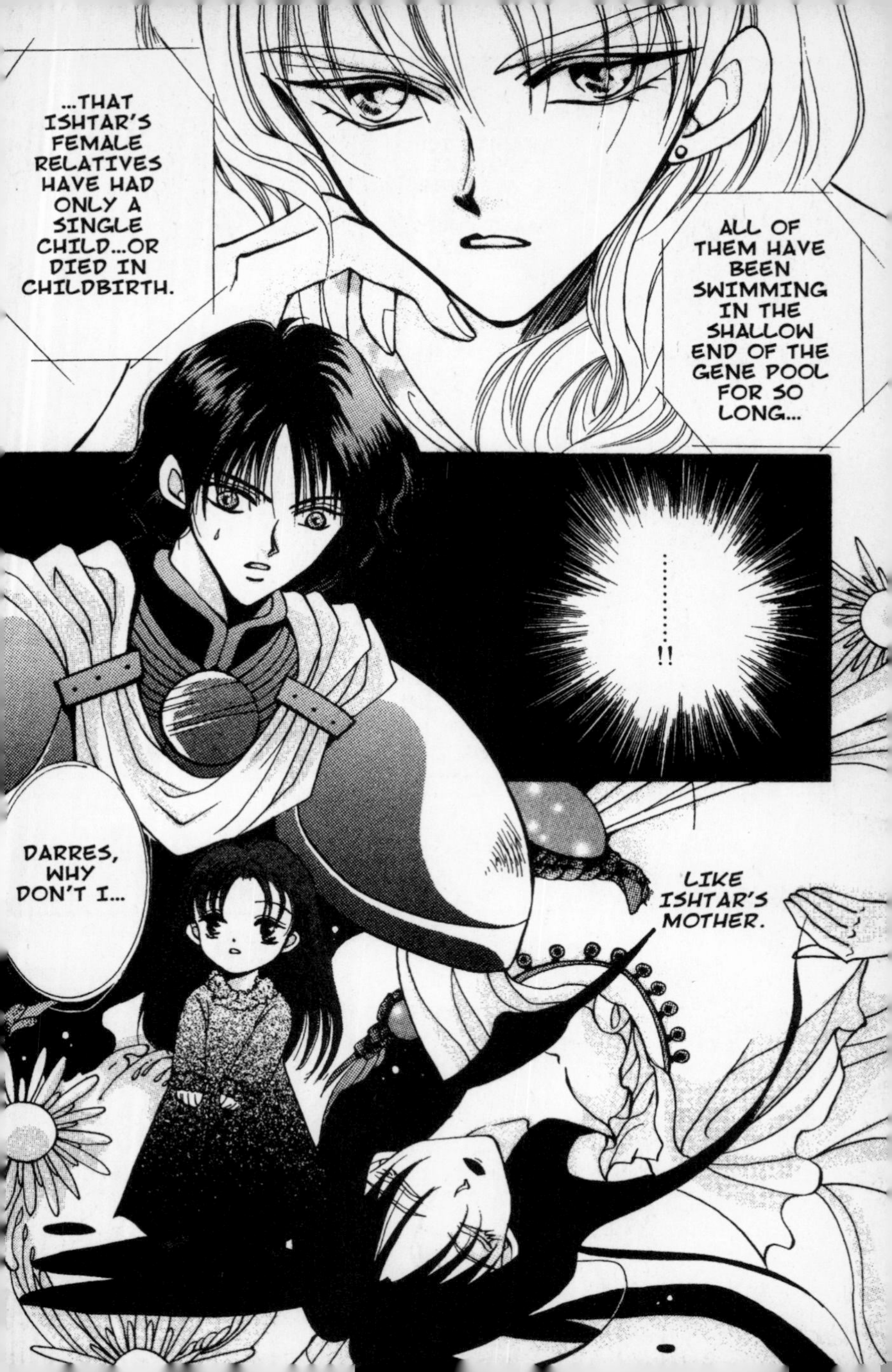
ALL OF THEM HAVE BEEN SWIMMING IN THE SHALLOW END OF THE GENE POOL FOR SO LONG...
...THAT ISHTAR'S FEMALE RELATIVES HAVE HAD ONLY A SINGLE CHILD...OR DIED IN CHILDBIRTH.
......!!
LIKE ISHTAR'S MOTHER.
DARRES, WHY DON'T I...

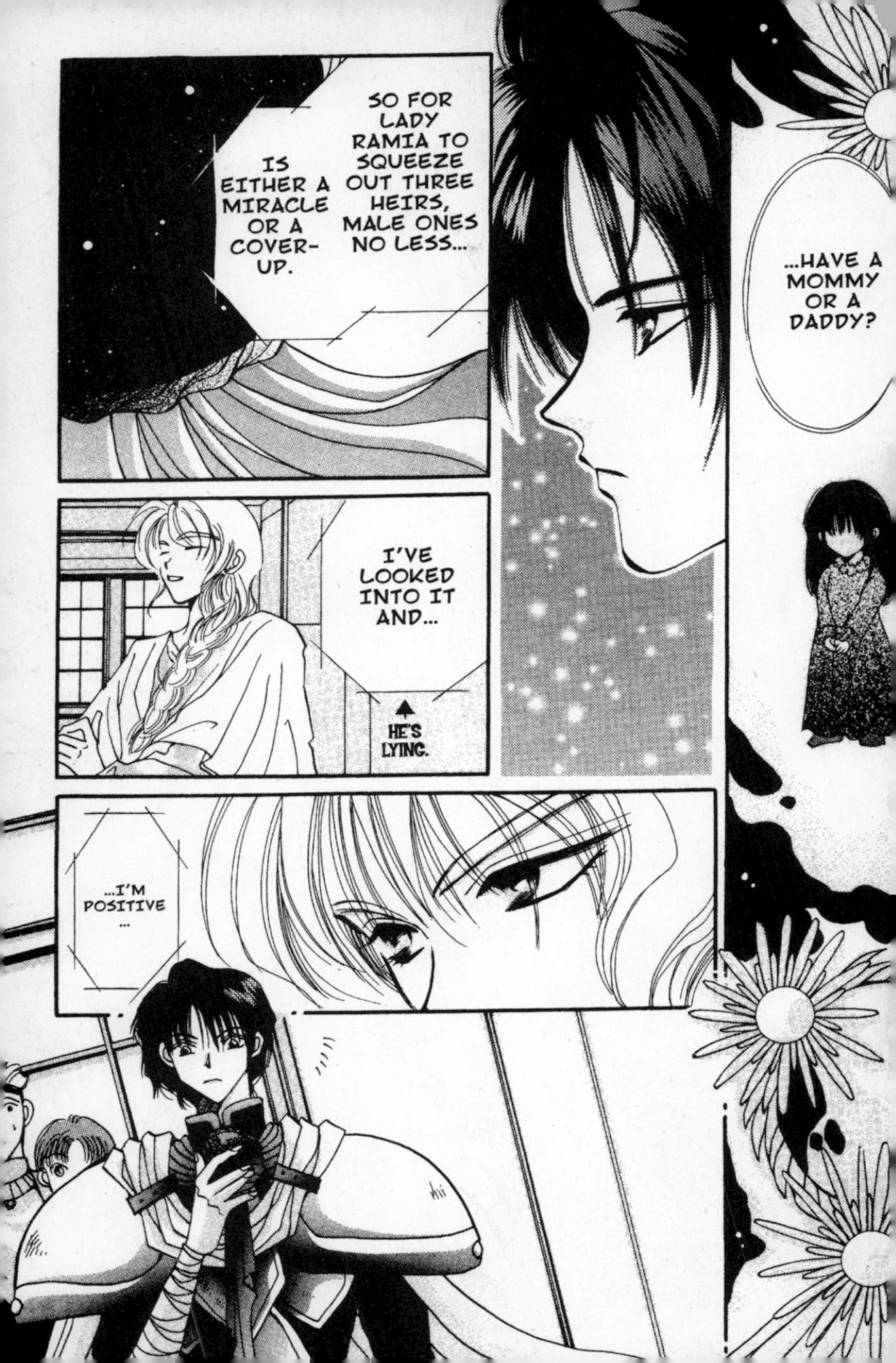
...HAVE A MOMMY OR A DADDY?
SO FOR LADY RAMIA TO SQUEEZE OUT THREE HEIRS, MALE ONES NO LESS...
IS EITHER A MIRACLE OR A COVER-UP.
I'VE LOOKED INTO IT AND...
HE'S LYING.
...I'M POSITIVE ...

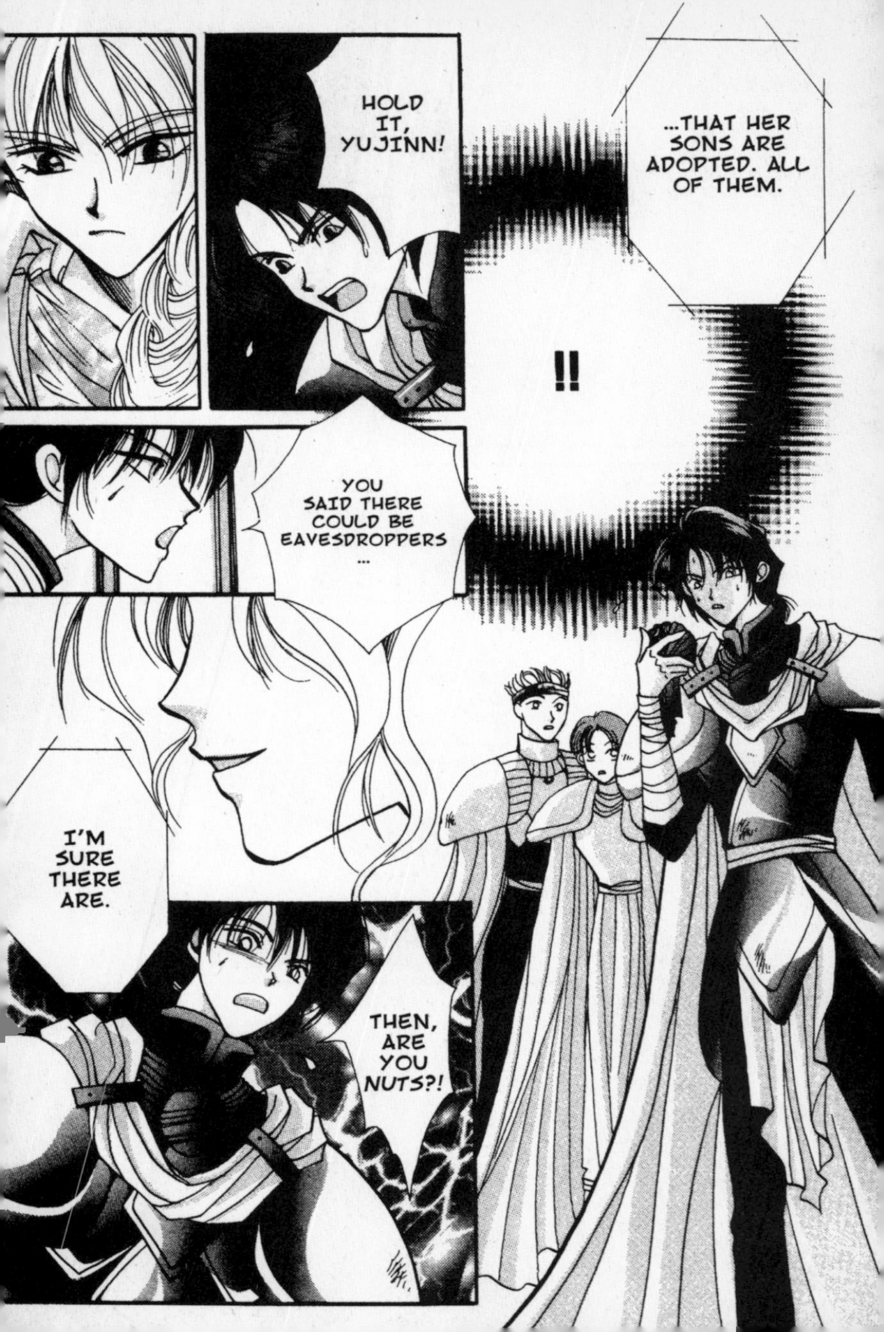
...THAT HER SONS ARE ADOPTED. ALL OF THEM.
!!
HOLD IT, YUJINN!
YOU SAID THERE COULD BE EAVESDROPPERS ...
I'M SURE THERE ARE.
THEN, ARE YOU NUTS?!

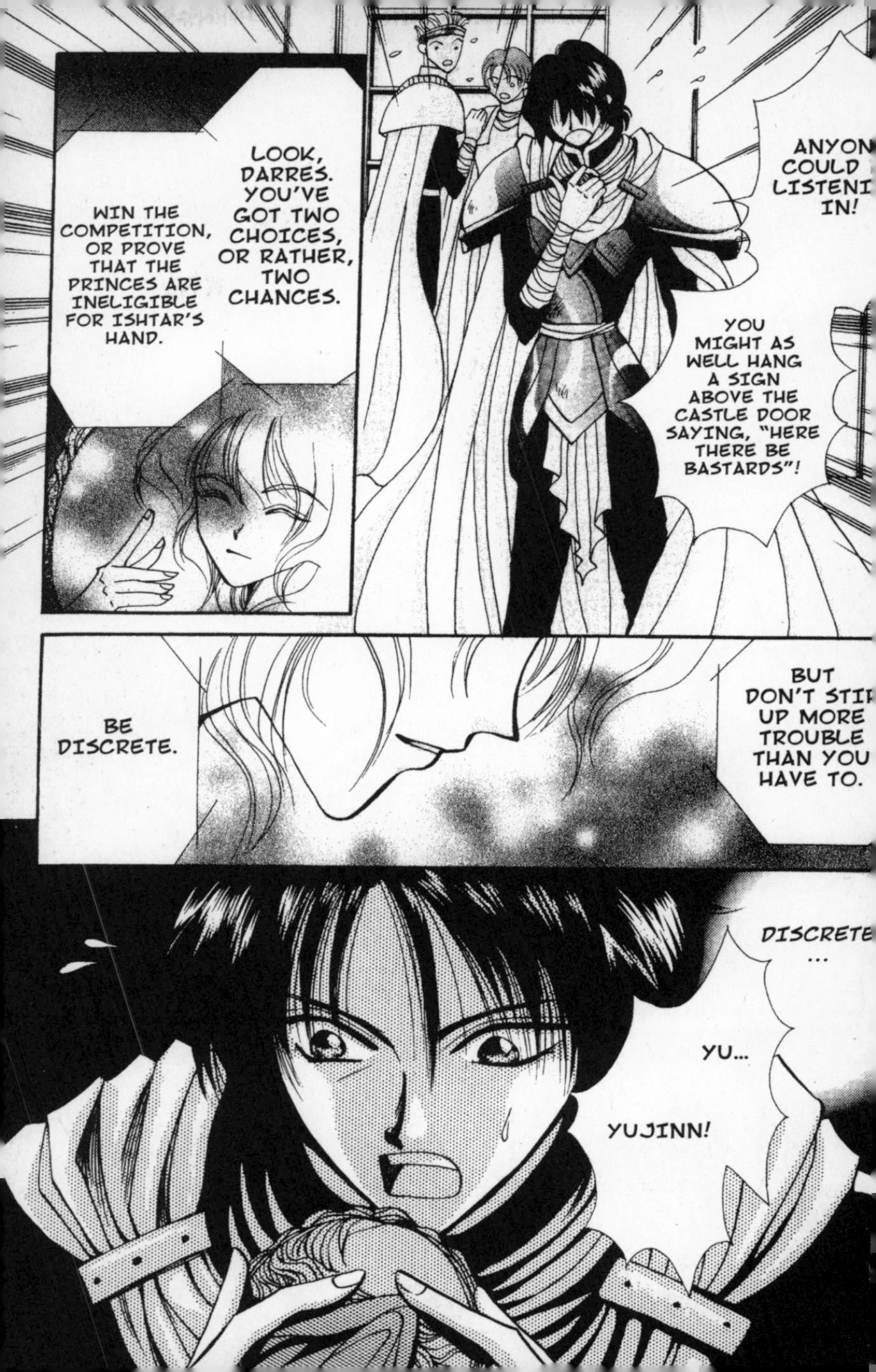
ANYON COULD LISTENI IN!
YOU MIGHT AS WELL HANG A SIGN ABOVE THE CASTLE DOOR SAYING, "HERE THERE BE BASTARDS"!
LOOK, DARRES. YOU'VE GOT TWO CHOICES, OR RATHER, TWO CHANCES.
WIN THE COMPETITION, OR PROVE THAT THE PRINCES ARE INELIGIBLE FOR ISHTAR'S HAND.
BUT DON'T STI UP MORE TROUBLE THAN YOU HAVE TO.
BE DISCRETE.
DISCRETE ...
YU...
YUJINN!

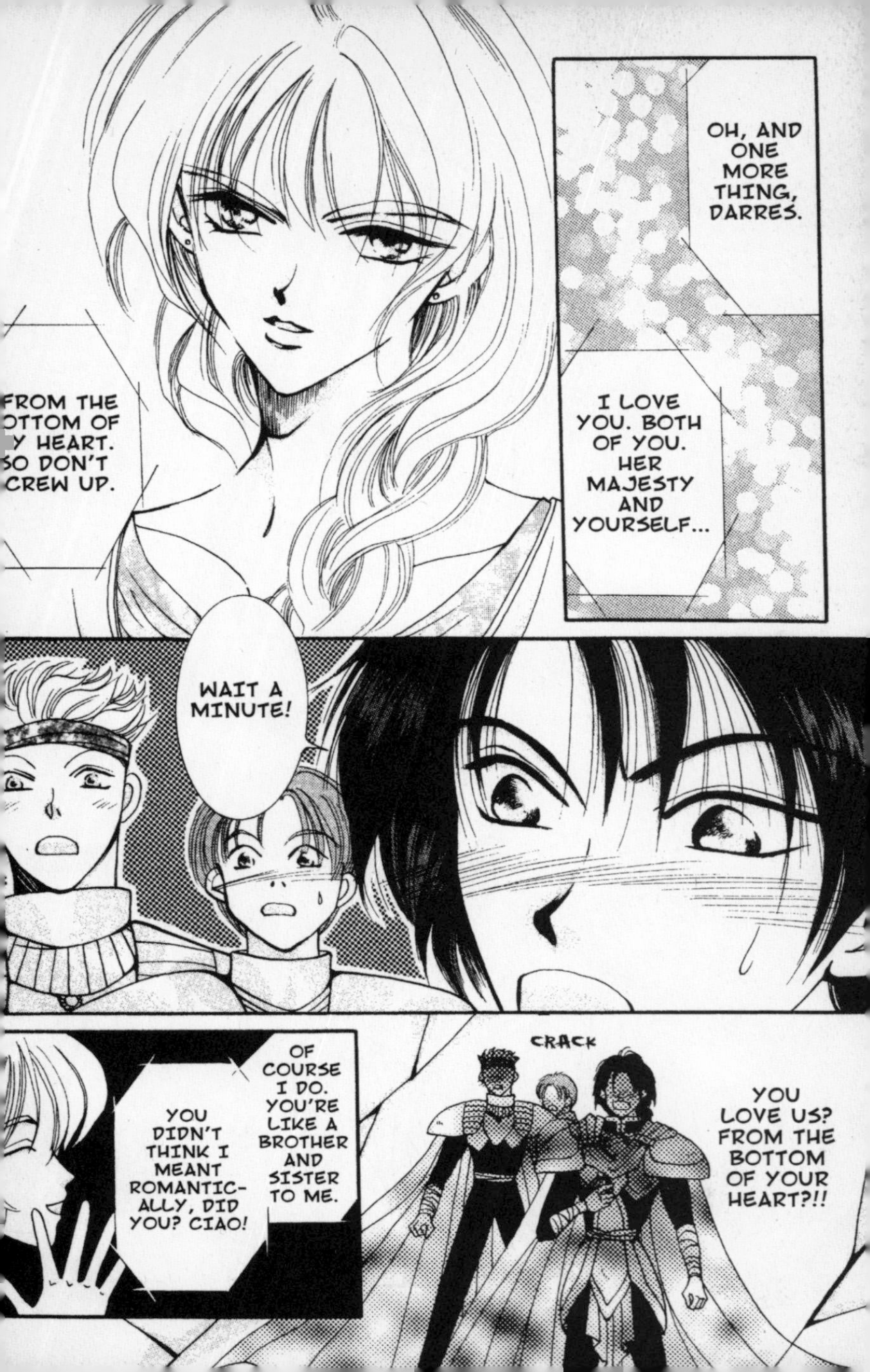
OH, AND ONE MORE THING, DARRES.
I LOVE YOU. BOTH OF YOU. HER MAJESTY AND YOURSELF...
FROM THE OTTOM OF Y HEART. SO DON'T CREW UP.
WAIT A MINUTE!
YOU LOVE US? FROM THE BOTTOM OF YOUR HEART?!!
CRACK
OF COURSE I DO. YOU'RE LIKE A BROTHER AND SISTER TO ME.
YOU DIDN'T THINK I MEANT ROMANTIC-ALLY, DID YOU? CIAO!

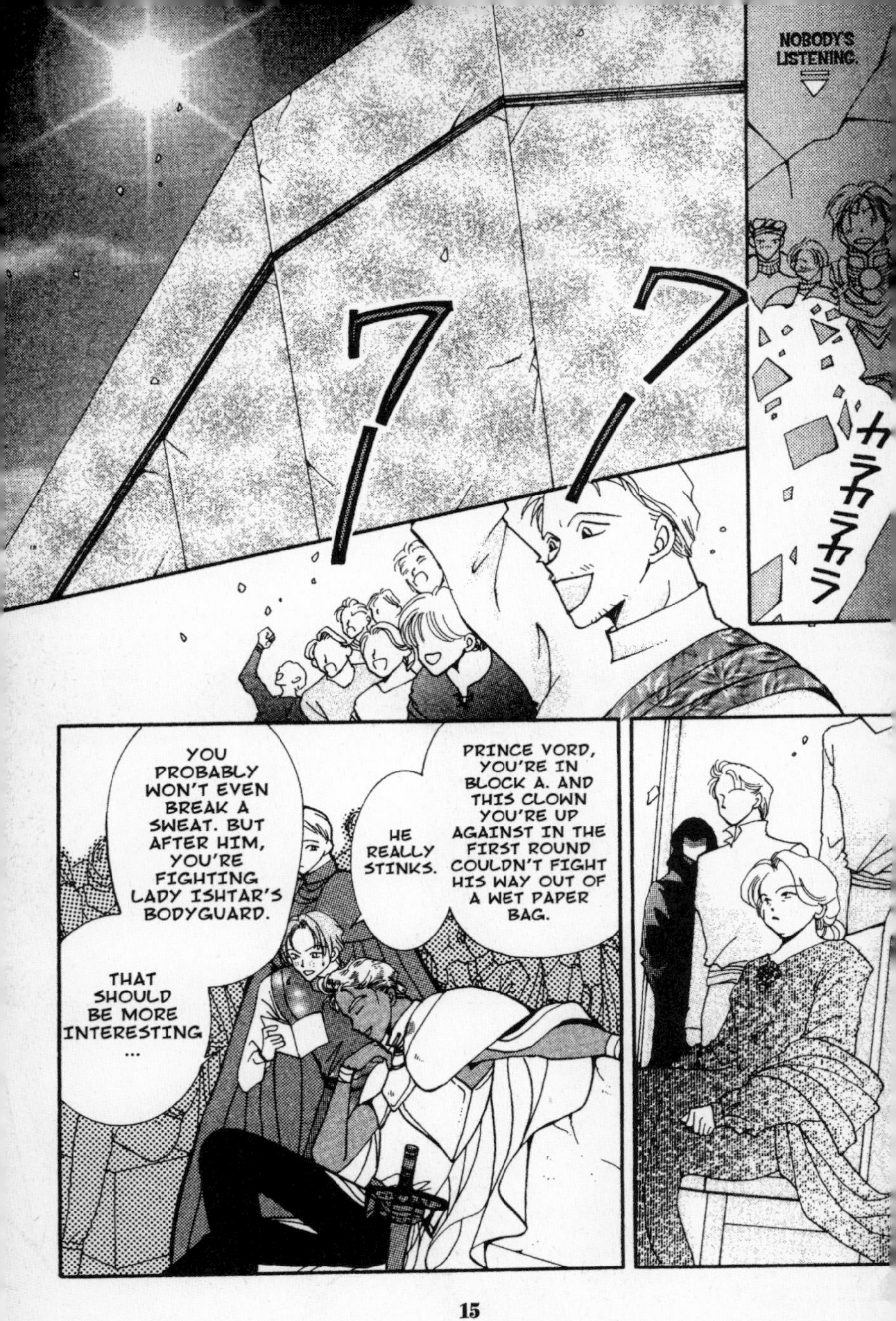

NOBODY'S LISTENING.
カラカラカラ
PRINCE VORD, YOU'RE IN BLOCK A. AND THIS CLOWN YOU'RE UP AGAINST IN THE FIRST ROUND COULDN'T FIGHT HIS WAY OUT OF A WET PAPER BAG.
HE REALLY STINKS.
YOU PROBABLY WON'T EVEN BREAK A SWEAT. BUT AFTER HIM, YOU'RE FIGHTING LADY ISHTAR'S BODYGUARD.
THAT SHOULD BE MORE INTERESTING ...

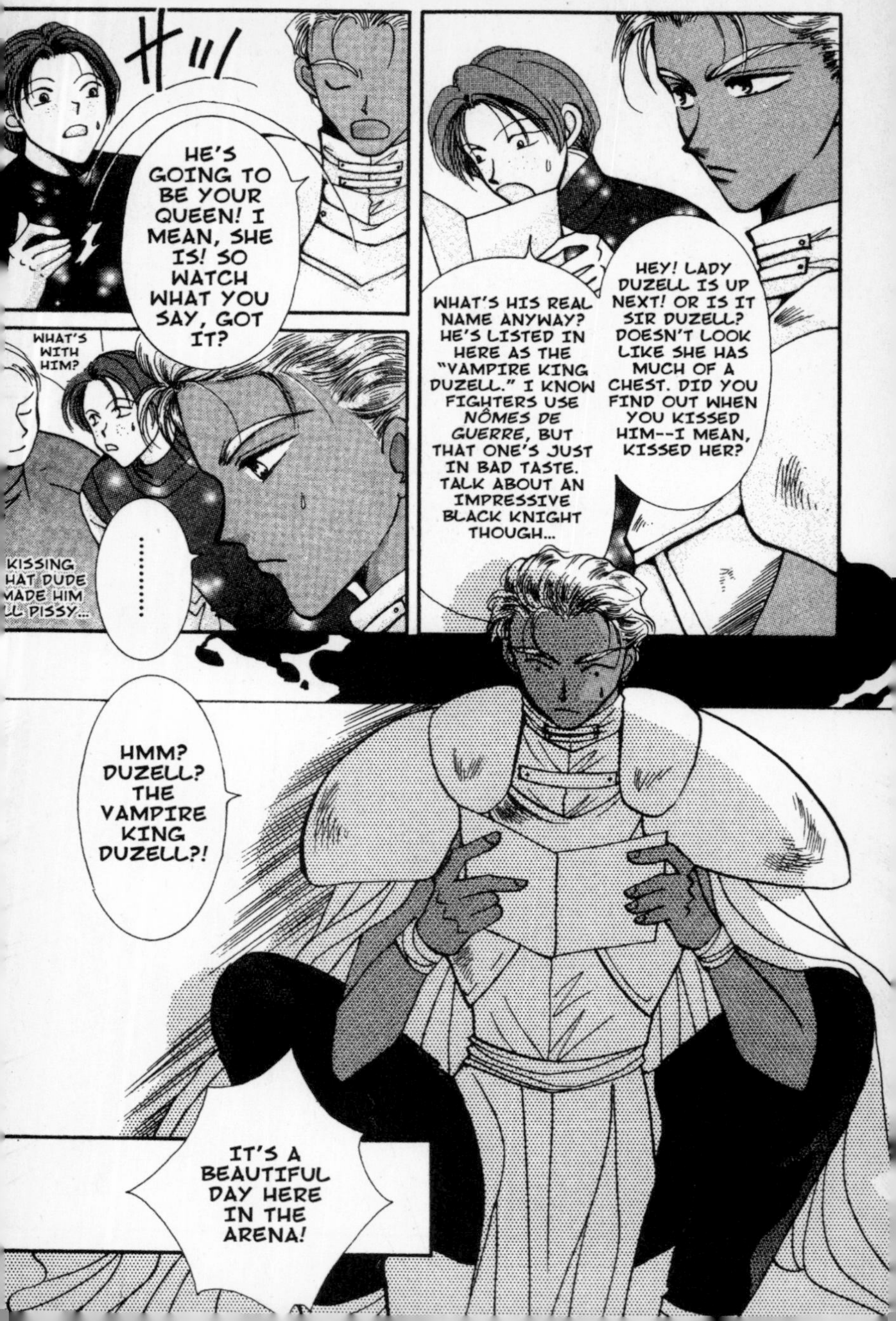
HEY! LADY DUZELL IS UP NEXT! OR IS IT SIR DUZELL? DOESN'T LOOK LIKE SHE HAS MUCH OF A CHEST. DID YOU FIND OUT WHEN YOU KISSED HIM--I MEAN, KISSED HER?
WHAT'S HIS REAL NAME ANYWAY? HE'S LISTED IN HERE AS THE "VAMPIRE KING DUZELL." I KNOW FIGHTERS USE *NÔMES DE GUERRE*, BUT THAT ONE'S JUST IN BAD TASTE. TALK ABOUT AN IMPRESSIVE BLACK KNIGHT THOUGH...
HE'S GOING TO BE YOUR QUEEN! I MEAN, SHE IS! SO WATCH WHAT YOU SAY, GOT IT?
WHAT'S WITH HIM?
......
KISSING HAT DUDE MADE HIM LL PISSY...
HMM? DUZELL? THE VAMPIRE KING DUZELL?!
IT'S A BEAUTIFUL DAY HERE IN THE ARENA!

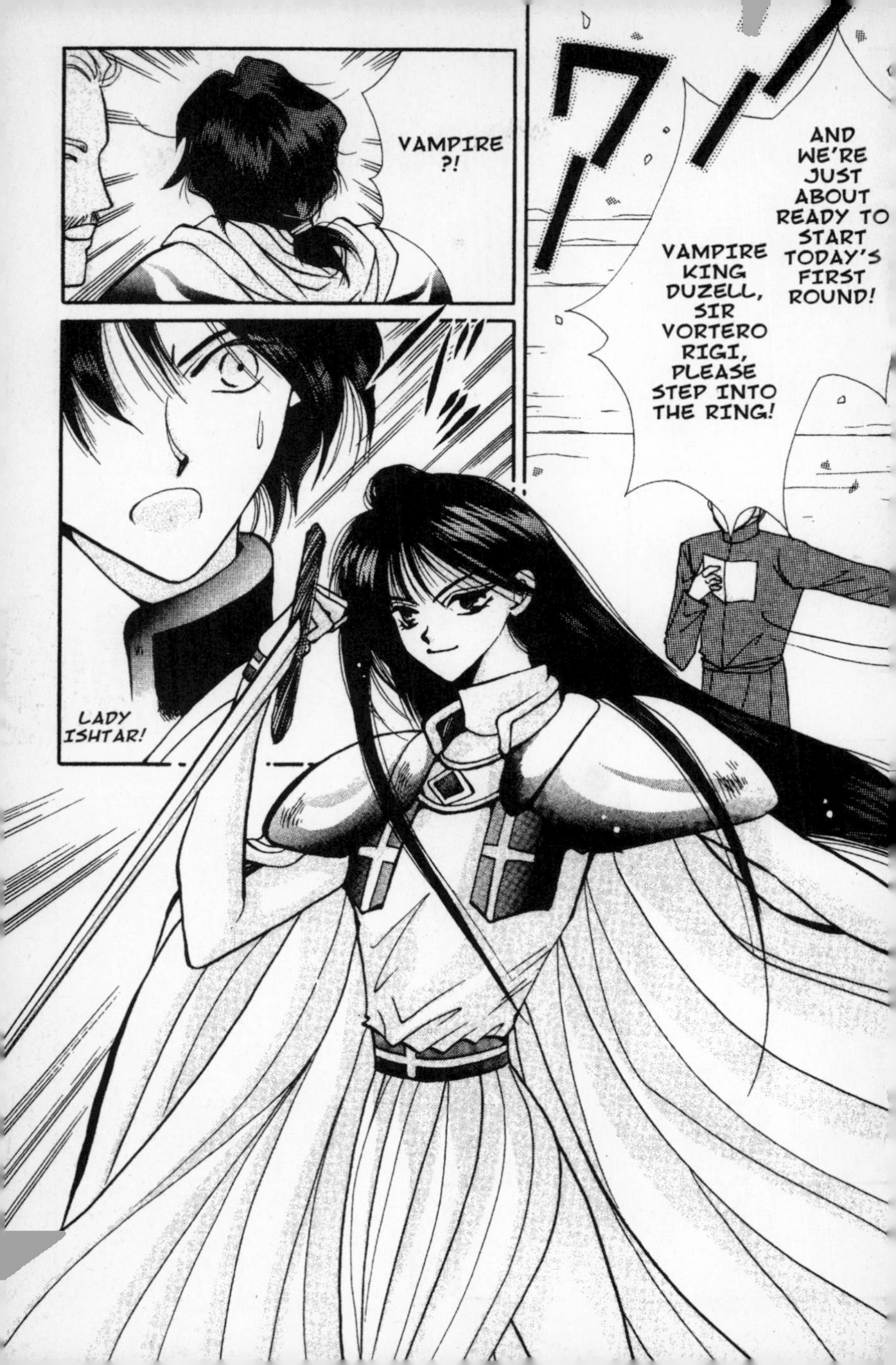
AND WE'RE JUST ABOUT READY TO START TODAY'S FIRST ROUND!
VAMPIRE KING DUZELL, SIR VORTERO RIGI, PLEASE STEP INTO THE RING!
VAMPIRE ?!
LADY ISHTAR!

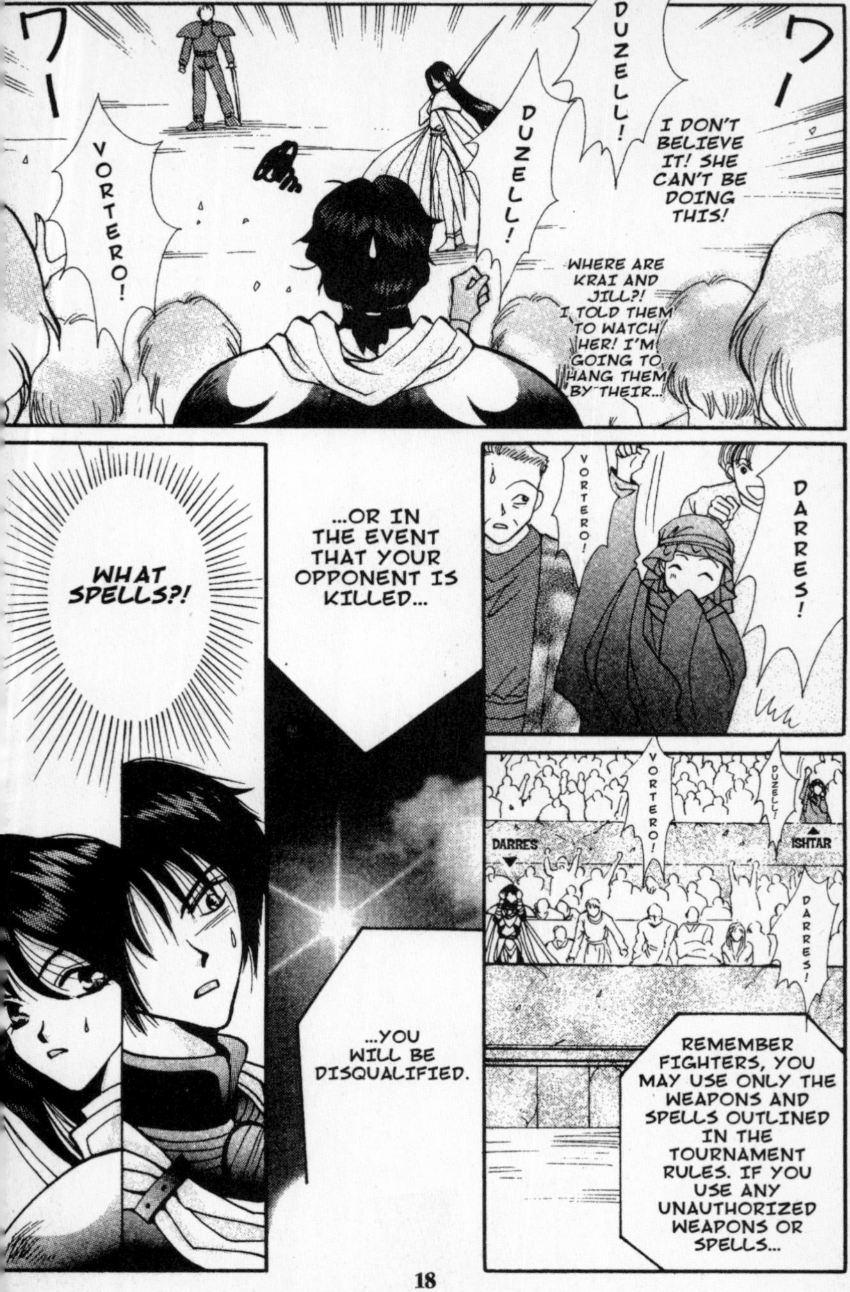

ワー
I DON'T BELIEVE IT! SHE CAN'T BE DOING THIS!
DUZELL!
DUZELL!
WHERE ARE KRAI AND JILL?! I TOLD THEM TO WATCH HER! I'M GOING TO HANG THEM BY THEIR...
VORTERO!
ワー
DARRES!
VORTERO!
DUZELL!
ISHTAR
VORTERO!
DARRES
DARRES!
REMEMBER FIGHTERS, YOU MAY USE ONLY THE WEAPONS AND SPELLS OUTLINED IN THE TOURNAMENT RULES. IF YOU USE ANY UNAUTHORIZED WEAPONS OR SPELLS...
...OR IN THE EVENT THAT YOUR OPPONENT IS KILLED...
...YOU WILL BE DISQUALIFIED.
WHAT SPELLS?!

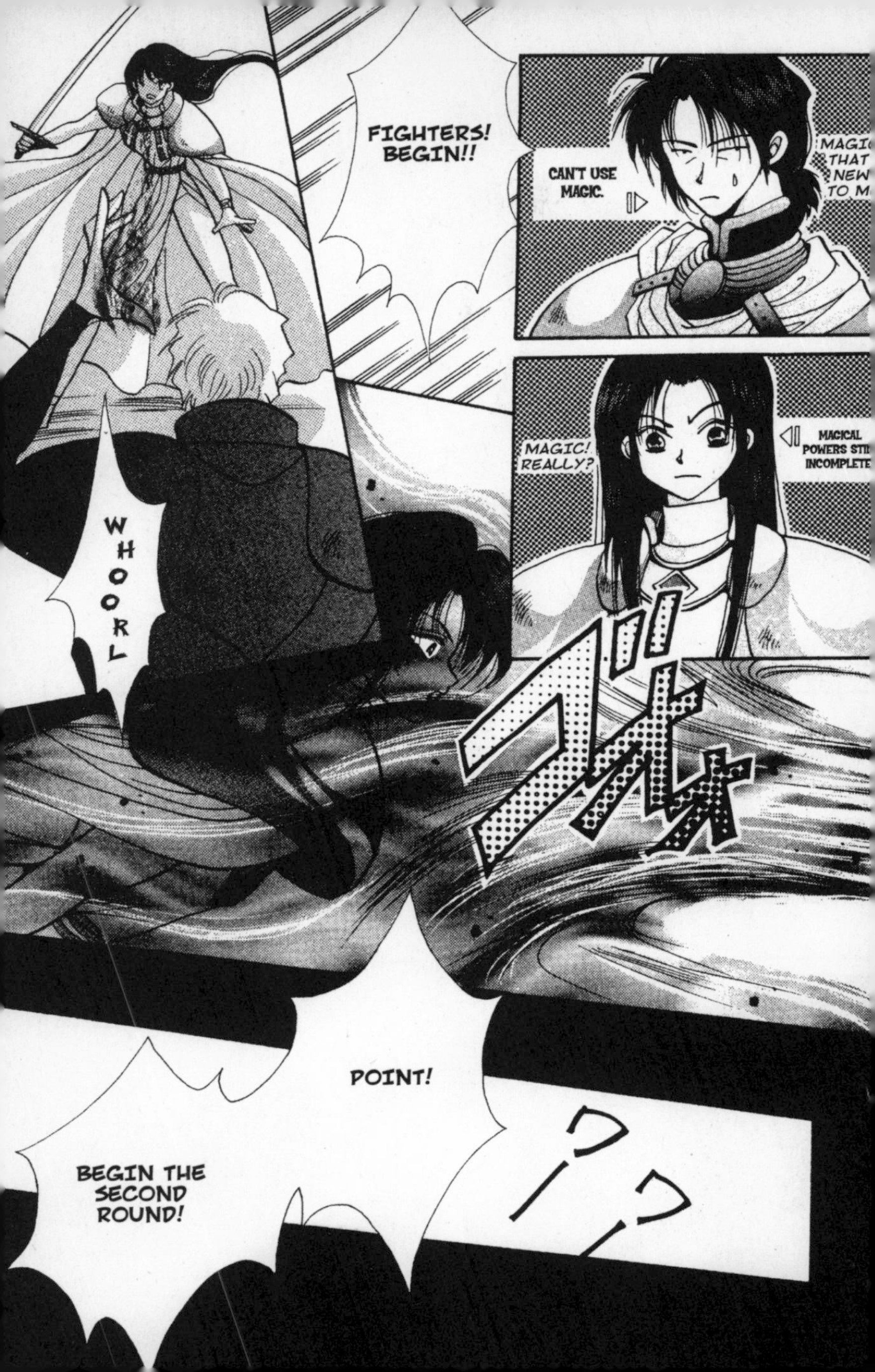
MAGIC THAT NEW TO M
CAN'T USE MAGIC.
MAGICAL POWERS STI INCOMPLETE
MAGIC! REALLY?
FIGHTERS! BEGIN!!
WHOORL
ブォッ
POINT!
BEGIN THE SECOND ROUND!
!?

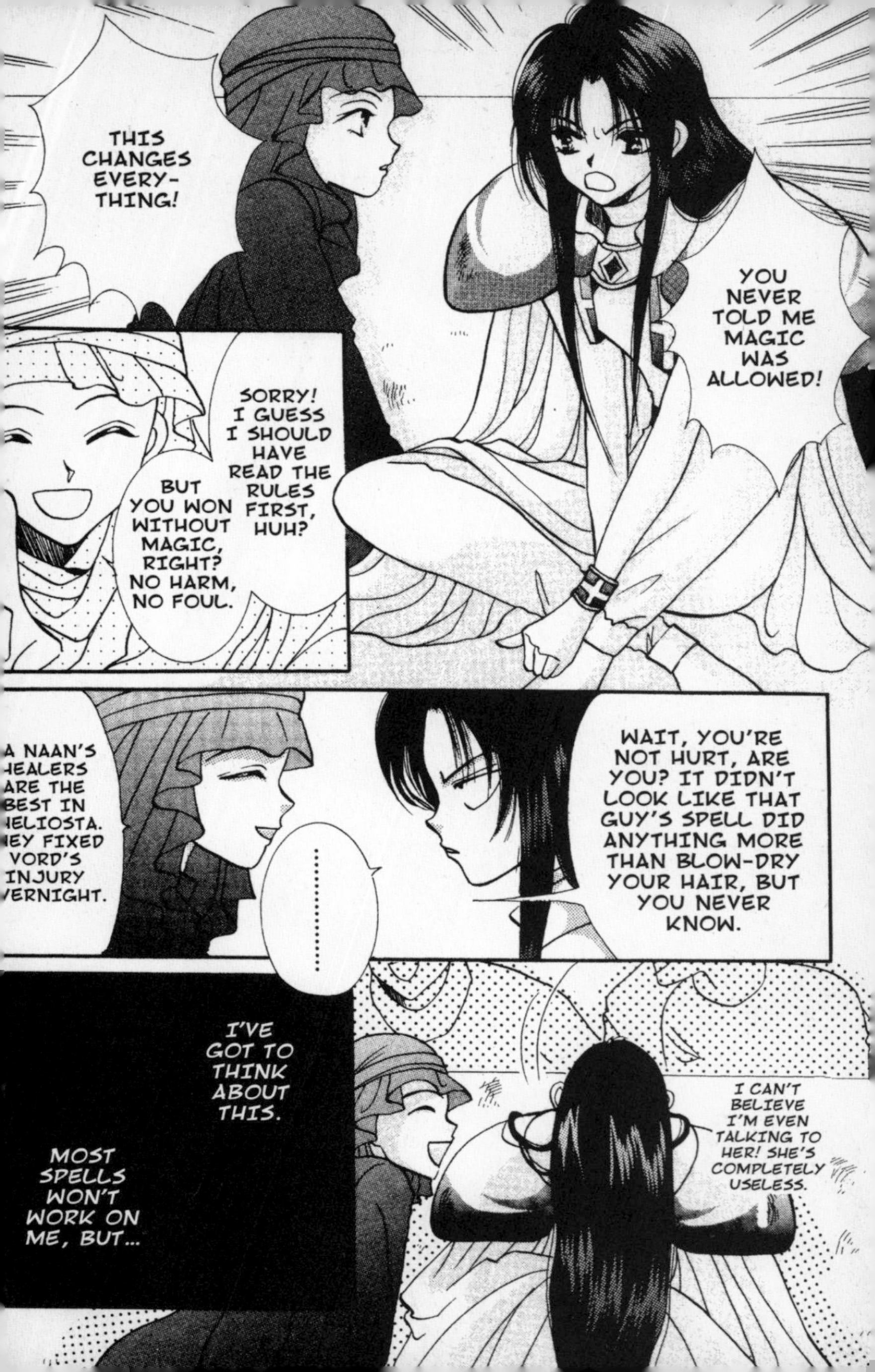
YOU NEVER TOLD ME MAGIC WAS ALLOWED!
THIS CHANGES EVERY-THING!
SORRY! I GUESS I SHOULD HAVE READ THE RULES FIRST, HUH?
BUT YOU WON WITHOUT MAGIC, RIGHT? NO HARM, NO FOUL.
WAIT, YOU'RE NOT HURT, ARE YOU? IT DIDN'T LOOK LIKE THAT GUY'S SPELL DID ANYTHING MORE THAN BLOW-DRY YOUR HAIR, BUT YOU NEVER KNOW.
......
A NAAN'S HEALERS ARE THE BEST IN HELIOSTA. HEY FIXED VORD'S INJURY VERNIGHT.
I CAN'T BELIEVE I'M EVEN TALKING TO HER! SHE'S COMPLETELY USELESS.
I'VE GOT TO THINK ABOUT THIS.
MOST SPELLS WON'T WORK ON ME, BUT...

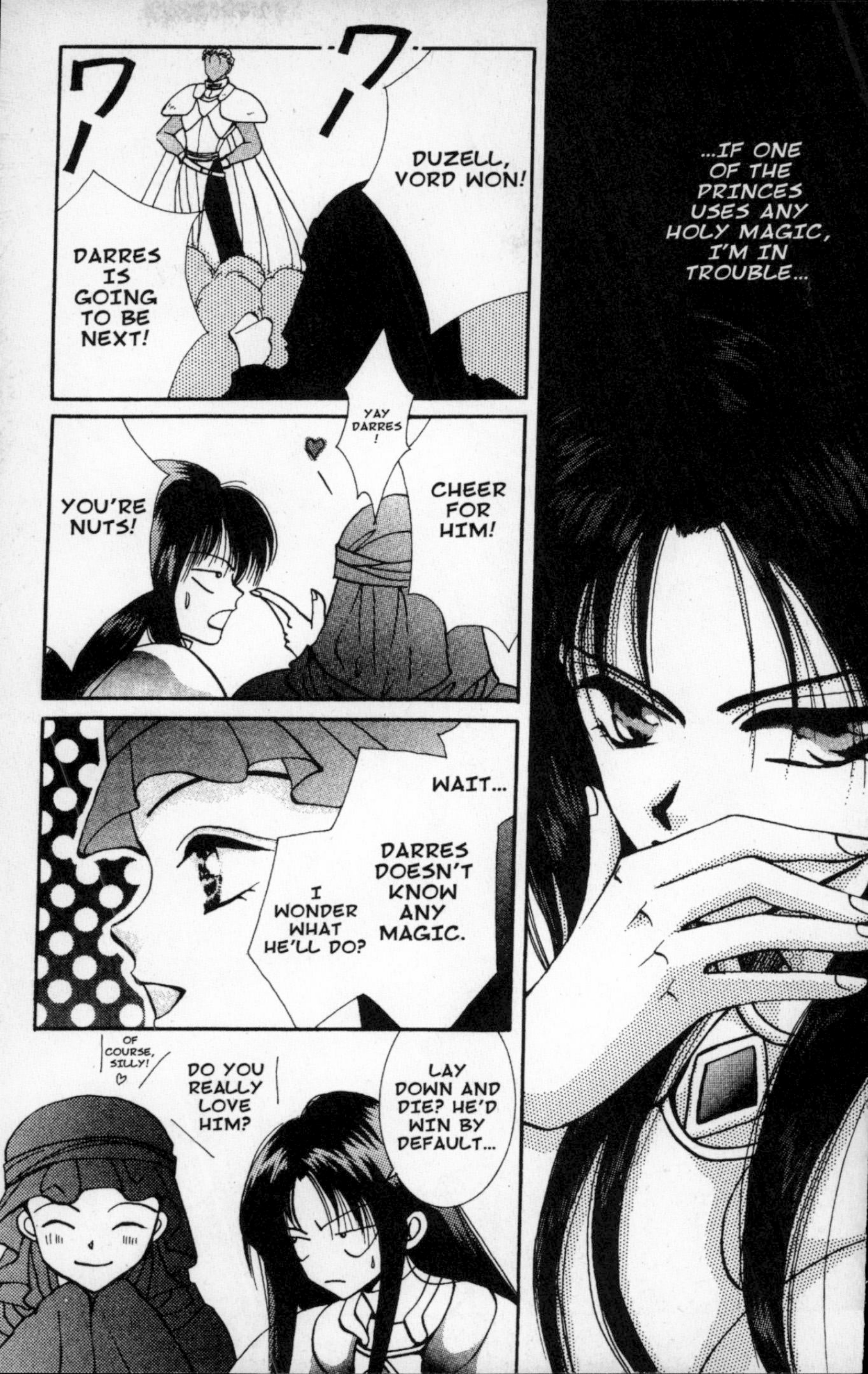
...IF ONE OF THE PRINCES USES ANY HOLY MAGIC, I'M IN TROUBLE...
DUZELL, VORD WON!
DARRES IS GOING TO BE NEXT!
YAY DARRES!
CHEER FOR HIM!
YOU'RE NUTS!
WAIT...
DARRES DOESN'T KNOW ANY MAGIC.
I WONDER WHAT HE'LL DO?
LAY DOWN AND DIE? HE'D WIN BY DEFAULT...
DO YOU REALLY LOVE HIM?
OF COURSE, SILLY!

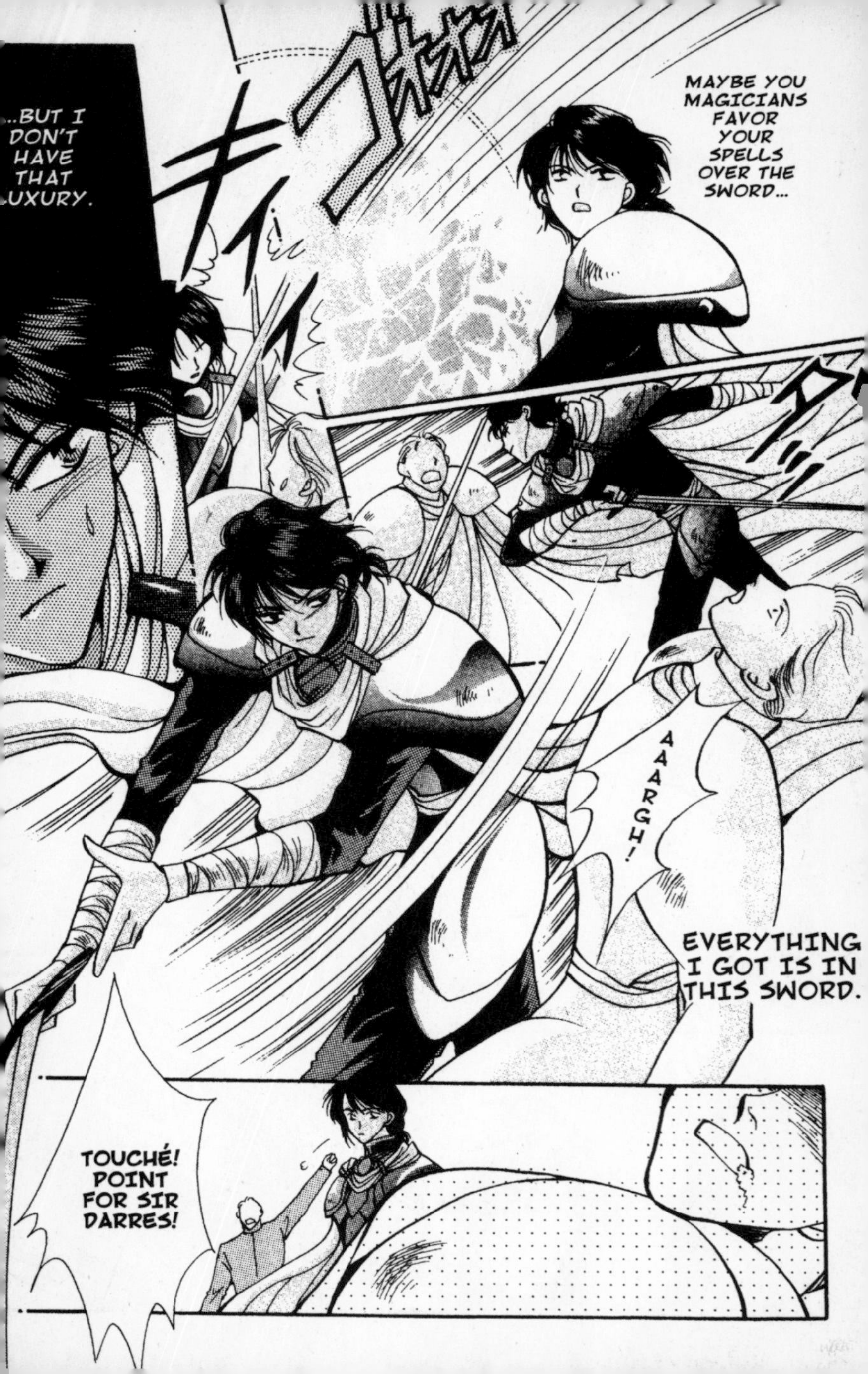
MAYBE YOU MAGICIANS FAVOR YOUR SPELLS OVER THE SWORD...
..BUT I DON'T HAVE THAT UXURY.
AAAARGH!
EVERYTHING I GOT IS IN THIS SWORD.
TOUCHÉ! POINT FOR SIR DARRES!

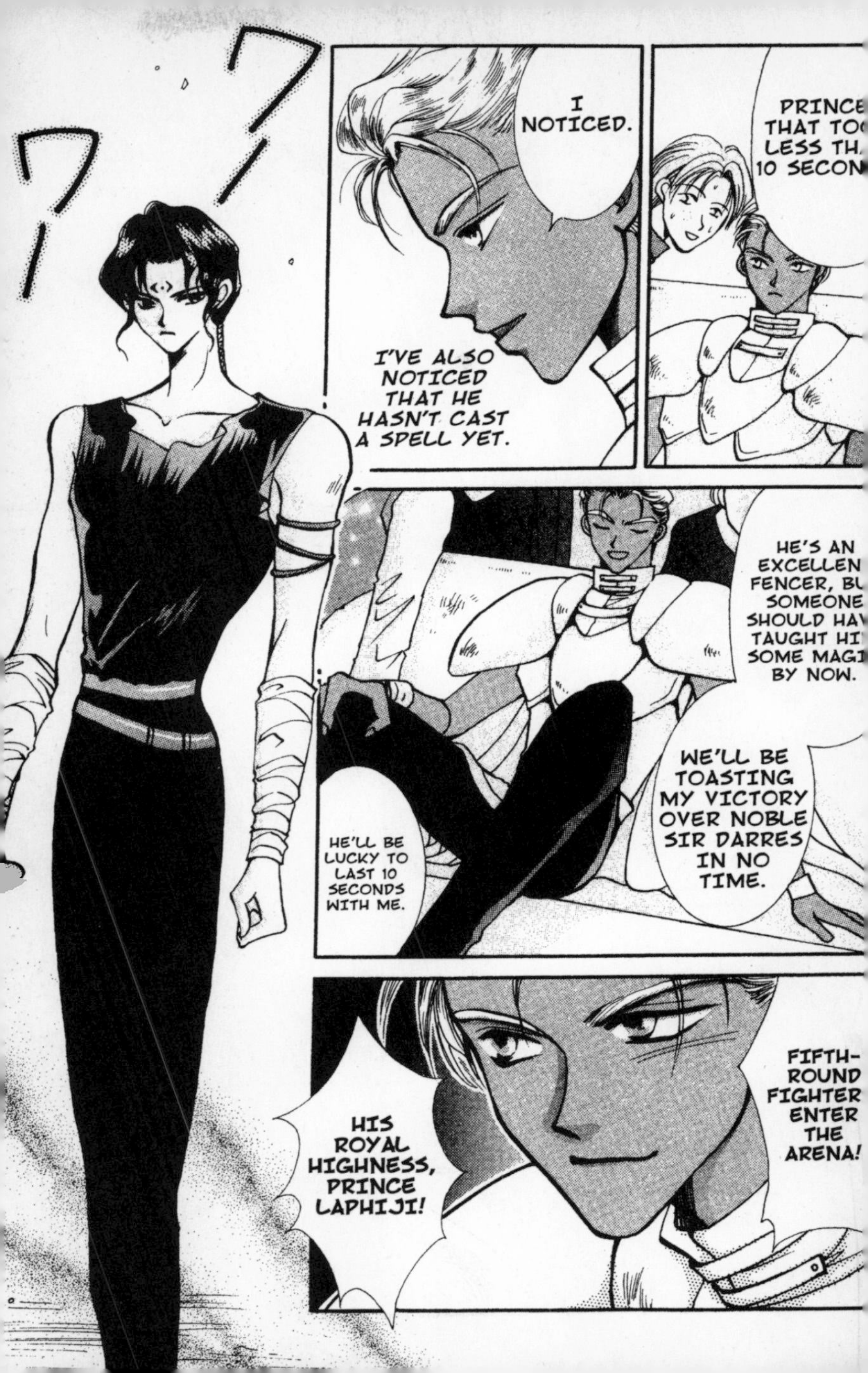
PRINCE THAT TO LESS TH 10 SECON
I NOTICED.
I'VE ALSO NOTICED THAT HE HASN'T CAST A SPELL YET.
HE'S AN EXCELLEN FENCER, BU SOMEONE SHOULD HAV TAUGHT HI SOME MAGI BY NOW.
WE'LL BE TOASTING MY VICTORY OVER NOBLE SIR DARRES IN NO TIME.
HE'LL BE LUCKY TO LAST 10 SECONDS WITH ME.
FIFTH-ROUND FIGHTER ENTER THE ARENA!
HIS ROYAL HIGHNESS, PRINCE LAPHIJI!
??

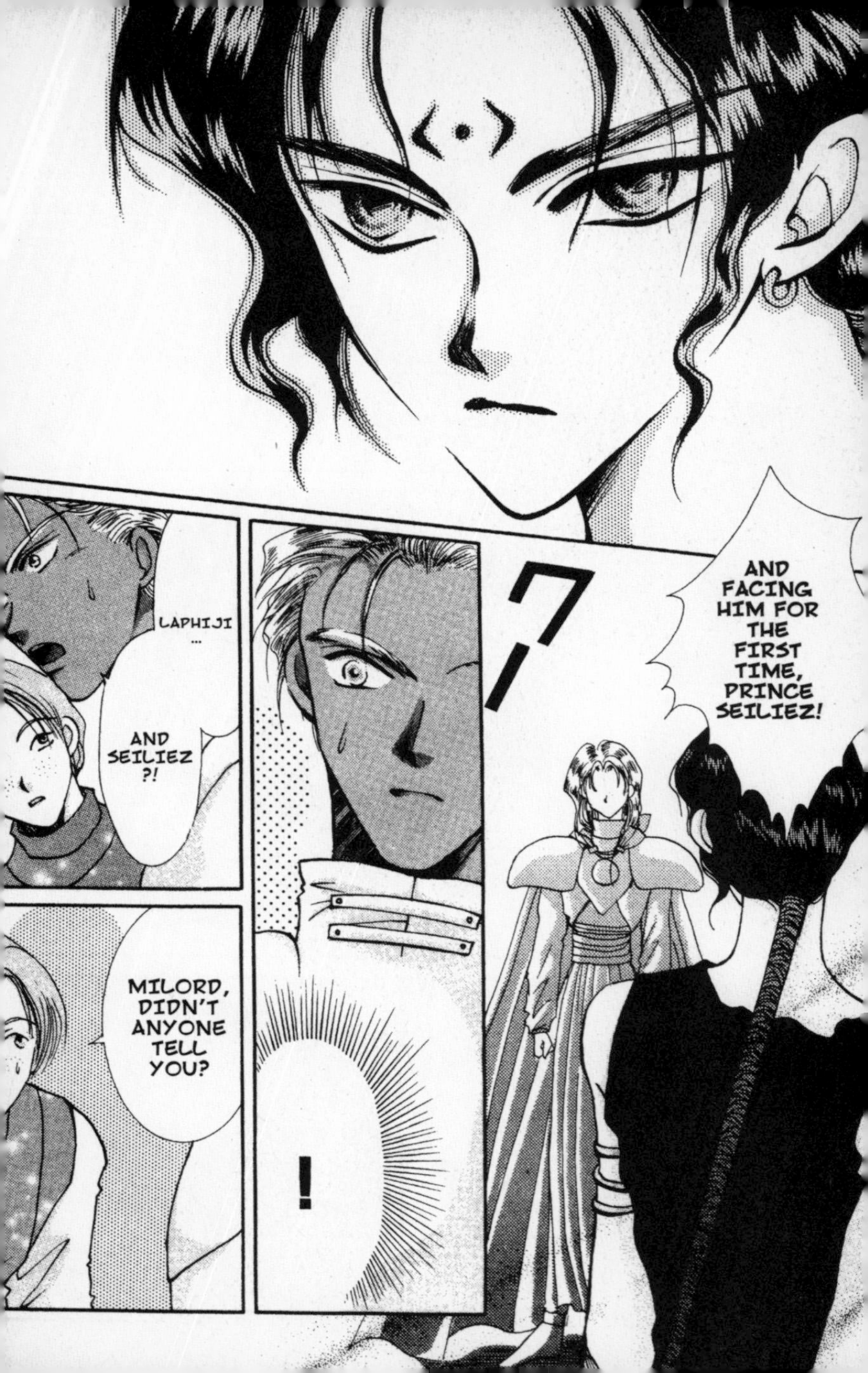
AND FACING HIM FOR THE FIRST TIME, PRINCE SEILIEZ!
!
LAPHIJI ...
AND SEILIEZ ?!
MILORD, DIDN'T ANYONE TELL YOU?

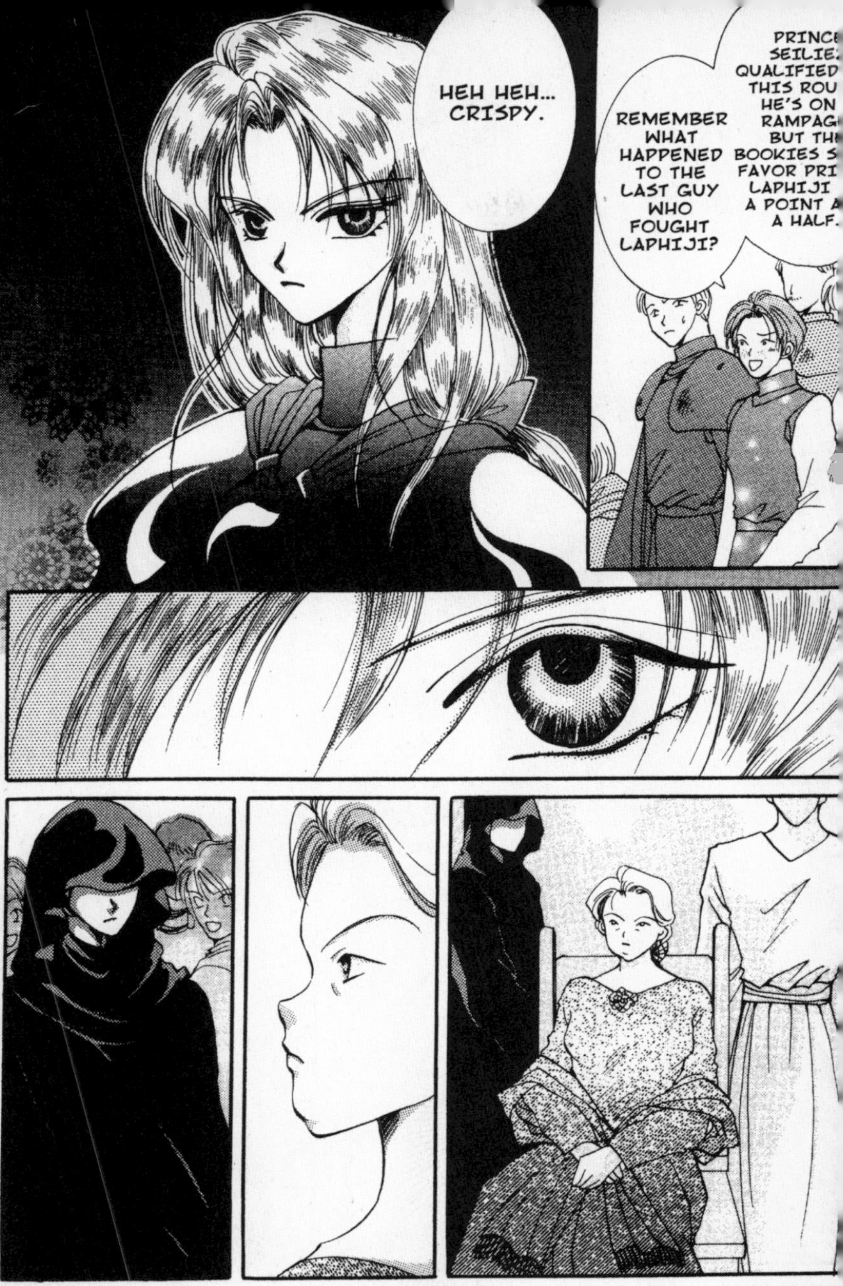
PRINCE SEILIE QUALIFIED THIS ROU HE'S ON RAMPAG BUT TH BOOKIES S FAVOR PRI LAPHIJI A POINT A A HALF.
REMEMBER WHAT HAPPENED TO THE LAST GUY WHO FOUGHT LAPHIJI?
HEH HEH... CRISPY.

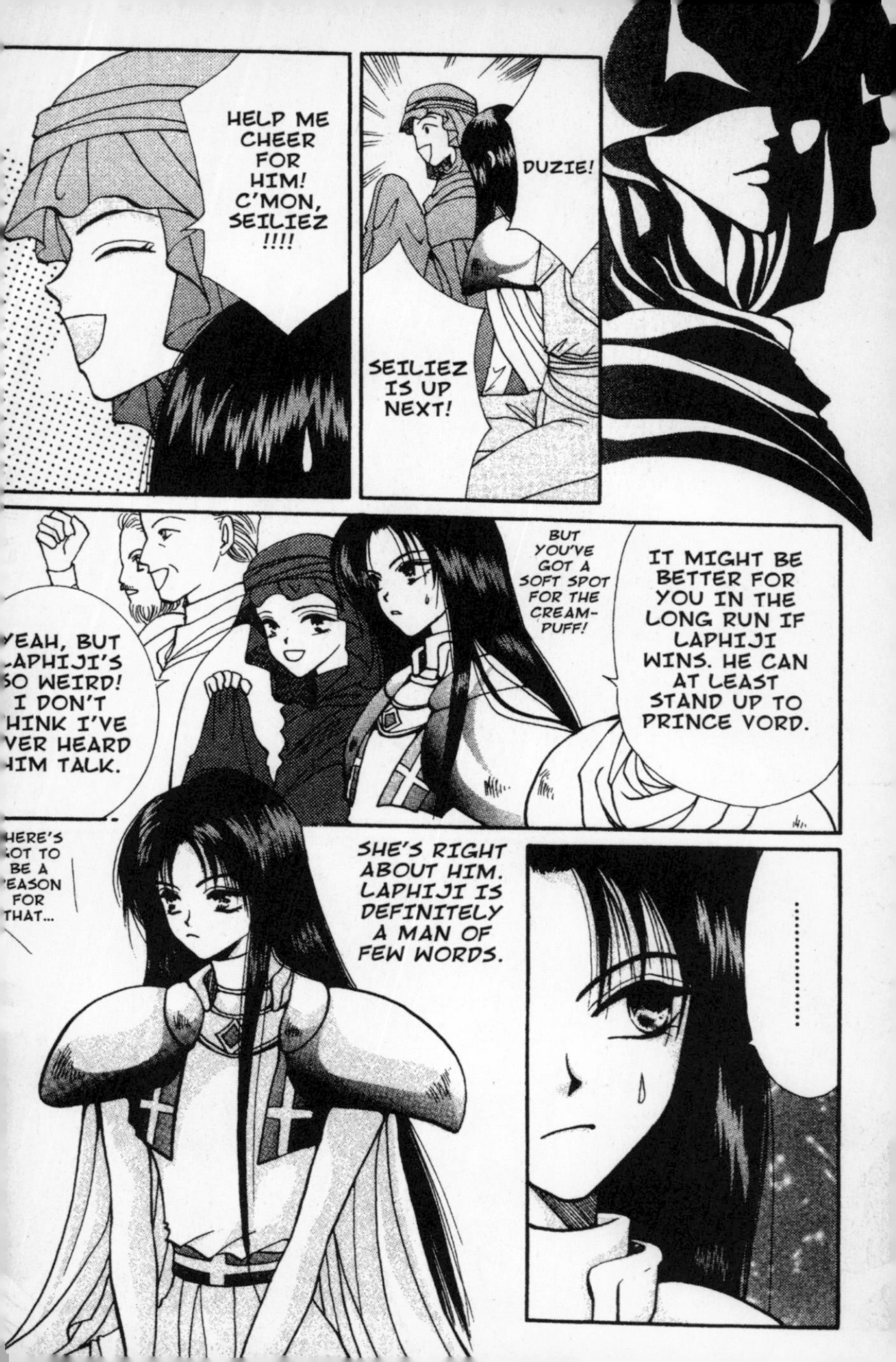
DUZIE!
SEILIEZ IS UP NEXT!
HELP ME CHEER FOR HIM! C'MON, SEILIEZ!!!!
IT MIGHT BE BETTER FOR YOU IN THE LONG RUN IF LAPHIJI WINS. HE CAN AT LEAST STAND UP TO PRINCE VORD.
BUT YOU'VE GOT A SOFT SPOT FOR THE CREAM-PUFF!
YEAH, BUT LAPHIJI'S SO WEIRD! I DON'T HINK I'VE VER HEARD HIM TALK.
......
SHE'S RIGHT ABOUT HIM. LAPHIJI IS DEFINITELY A MAN OF FEW WORDS.
HERE'S GOT TO BE A EASON FOR THAT...

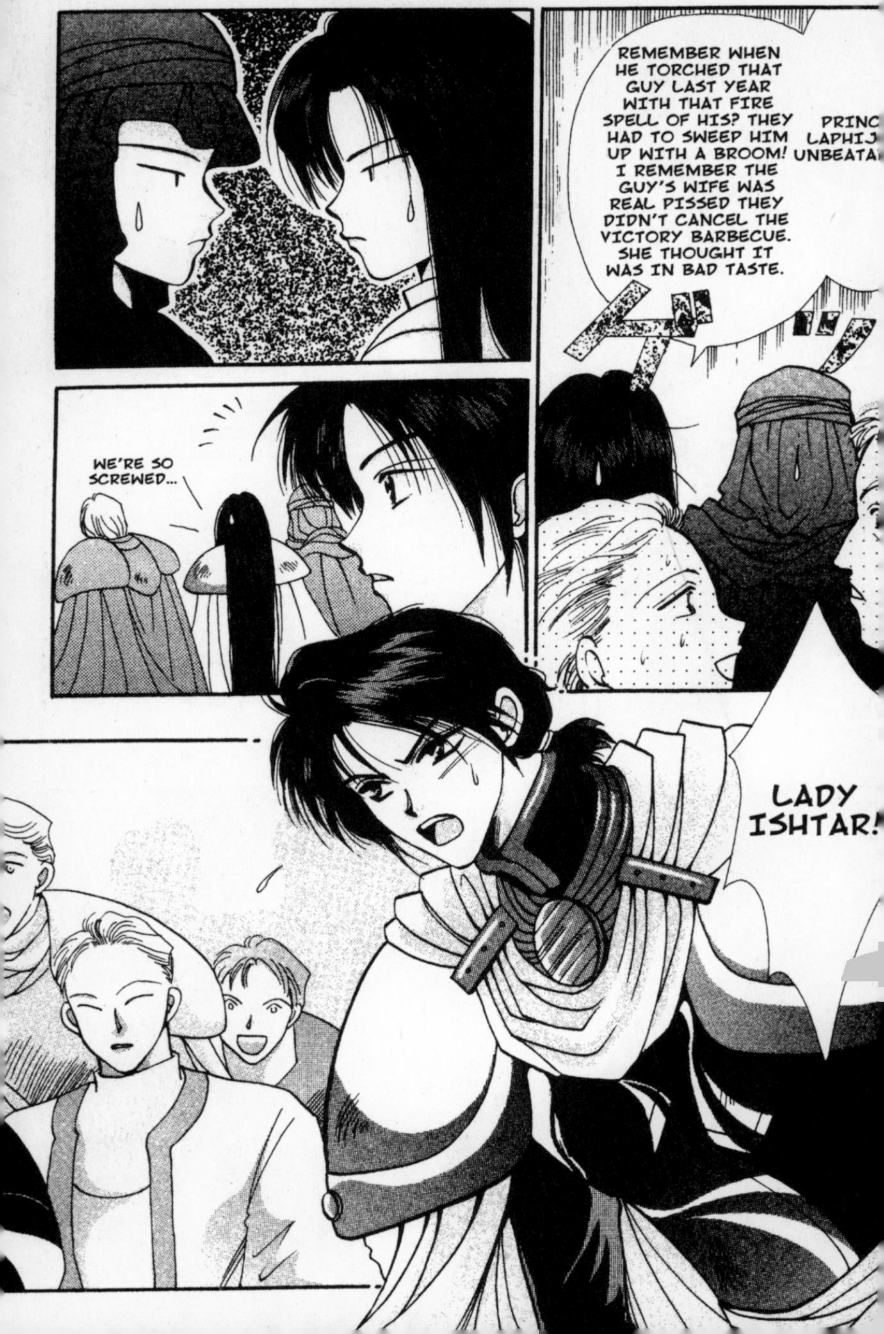
PRINC LAPHIJ UNBEATA
REMEMBER WHEN HE TORCHED THAT GUY LAST YEAR WITH THAT FIRE SPELL OF HIS? THEY HAD TO SWEEP HIM UP WITH A BROOM! I REMEMBER THE GUY'S WIFE WAS REAL PISSED THEY DIDN'T CANCEL THE VICTORY BARBECUE. SHE THOUGHT IT WAS IN BAD TASTE.
WE'RE SO SCREWED...
LADY ISHTAR!

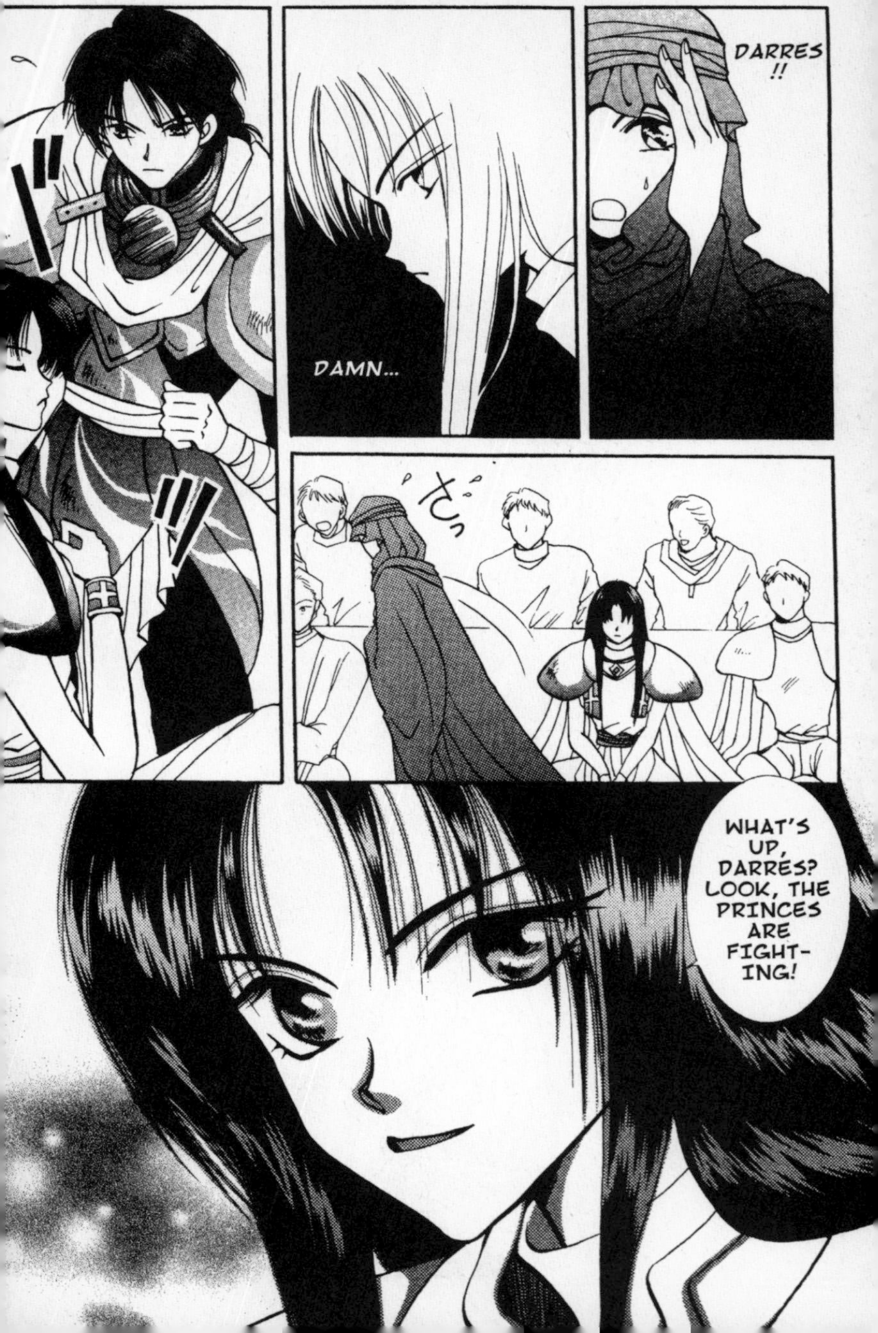
DARRES !!
DAMN...
さっ
WHAT'S UP, DARRES? LOOK, THE PRINCES ARE FIGHT-ING!

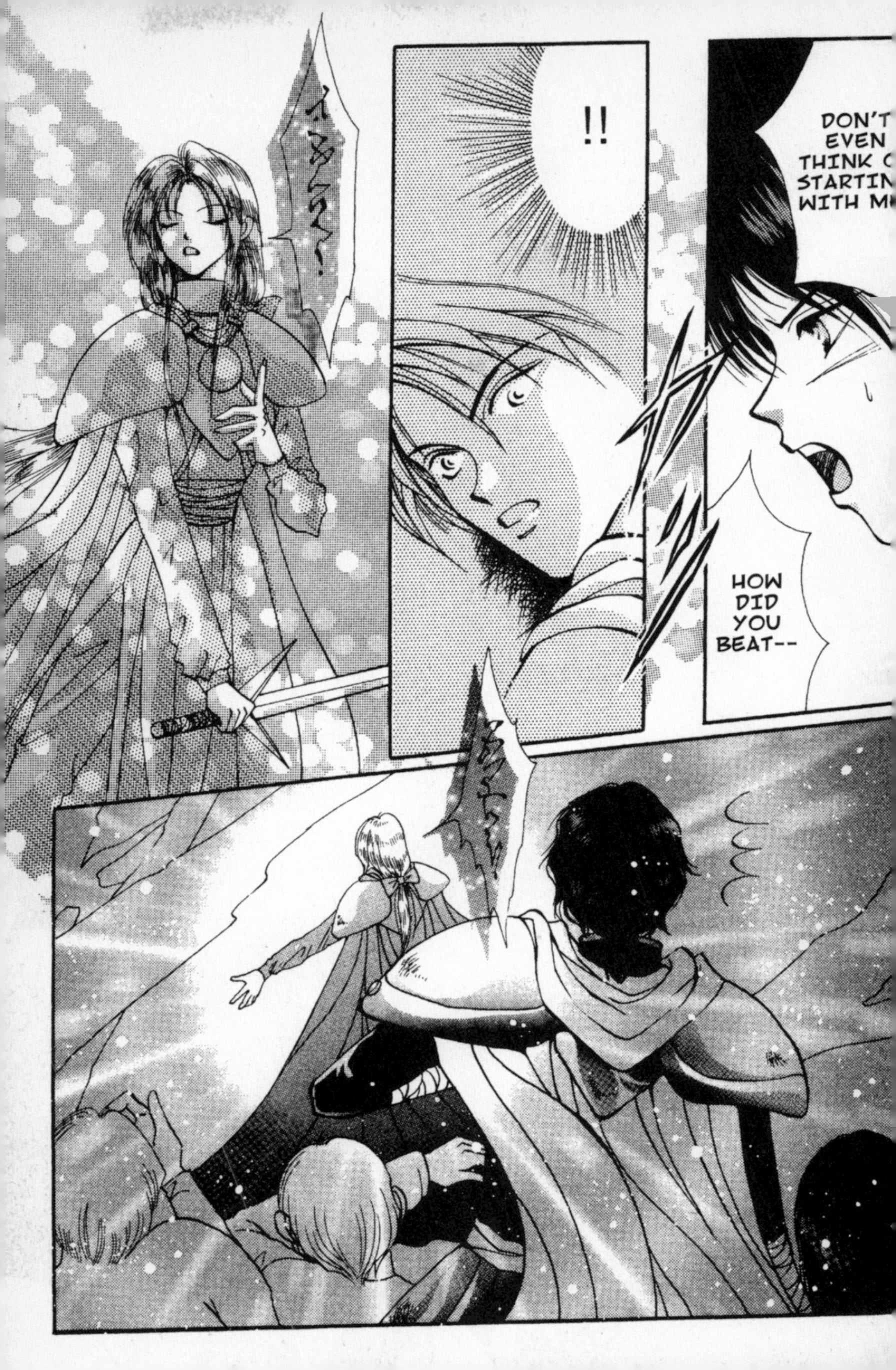

DON'T EVEN THINK O STARTIN WITH M
HOW DID YOU BEAT--
!!

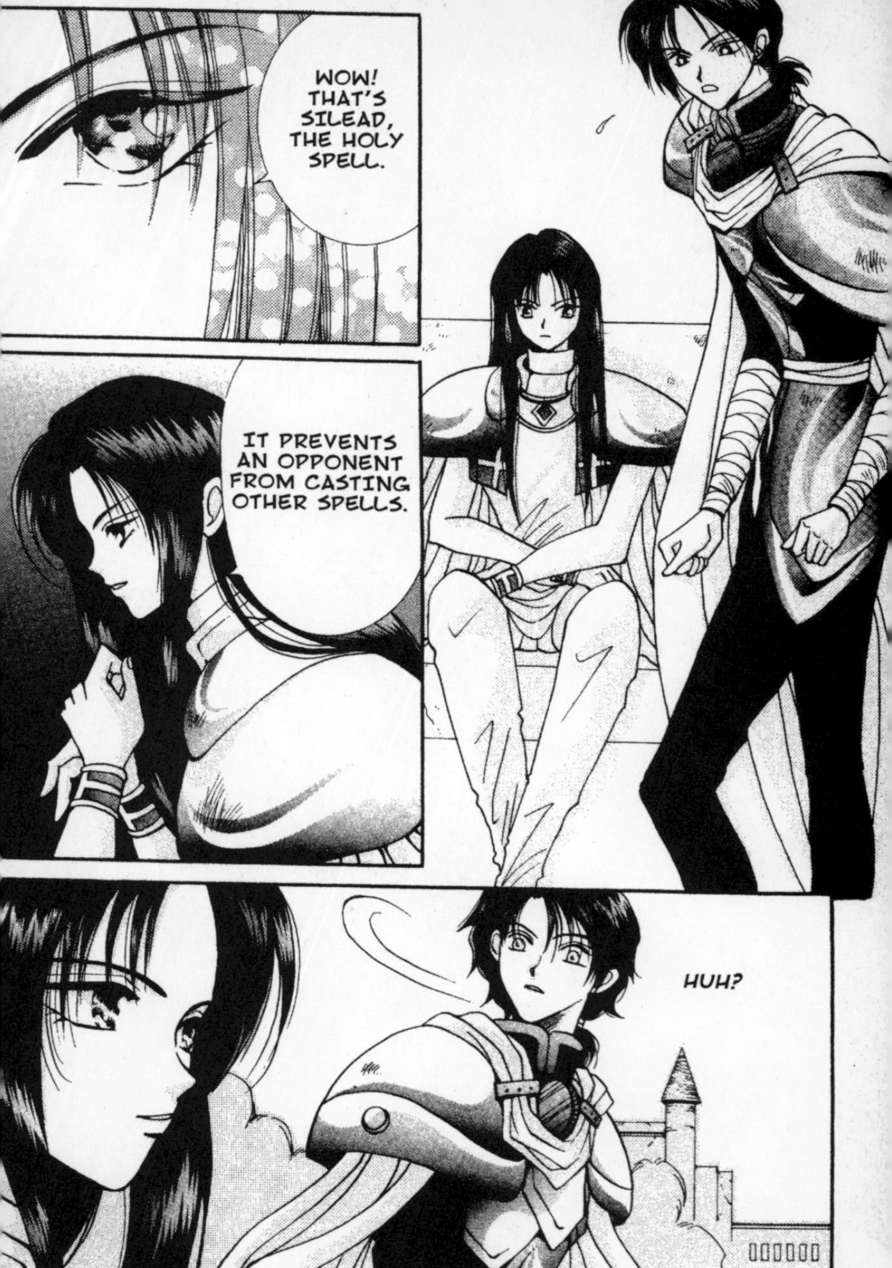
WOW! THAT'S SILEAD, THE HOLY SPELL.
IT PREVENTS AN OPPONENT FROM CASTING OTHER SPELLS.
HUH?

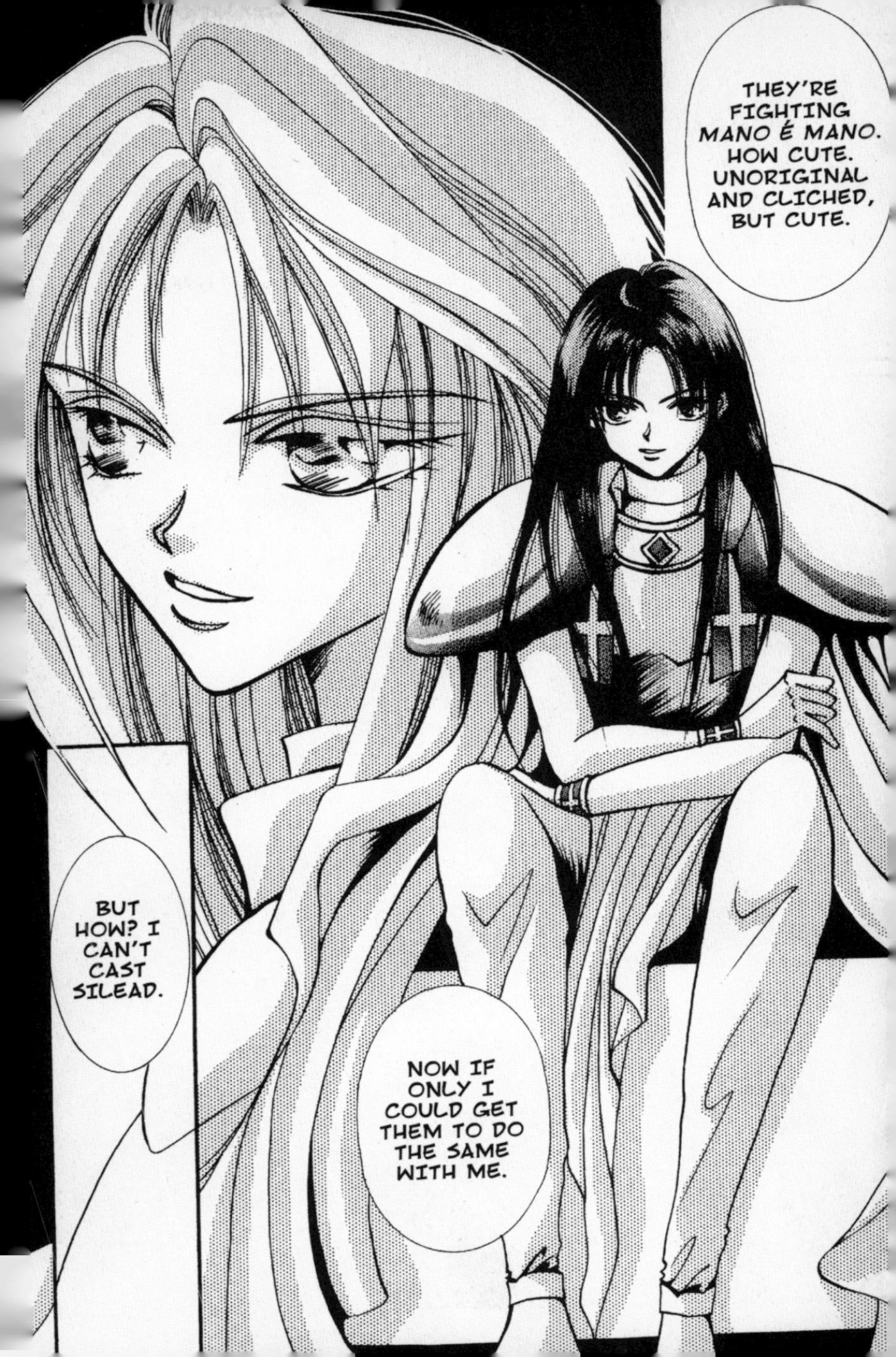
THEY'RE FIGHTING MANO É MANO. HOW CUTE. UNORIGINAL AND CLICHED, BUT CUTE.
NOW IF ONLY I COULD GET THEM TO DO THE SAME WITH ME.
BUT HOW? I CAN'T CAST SILEAD.

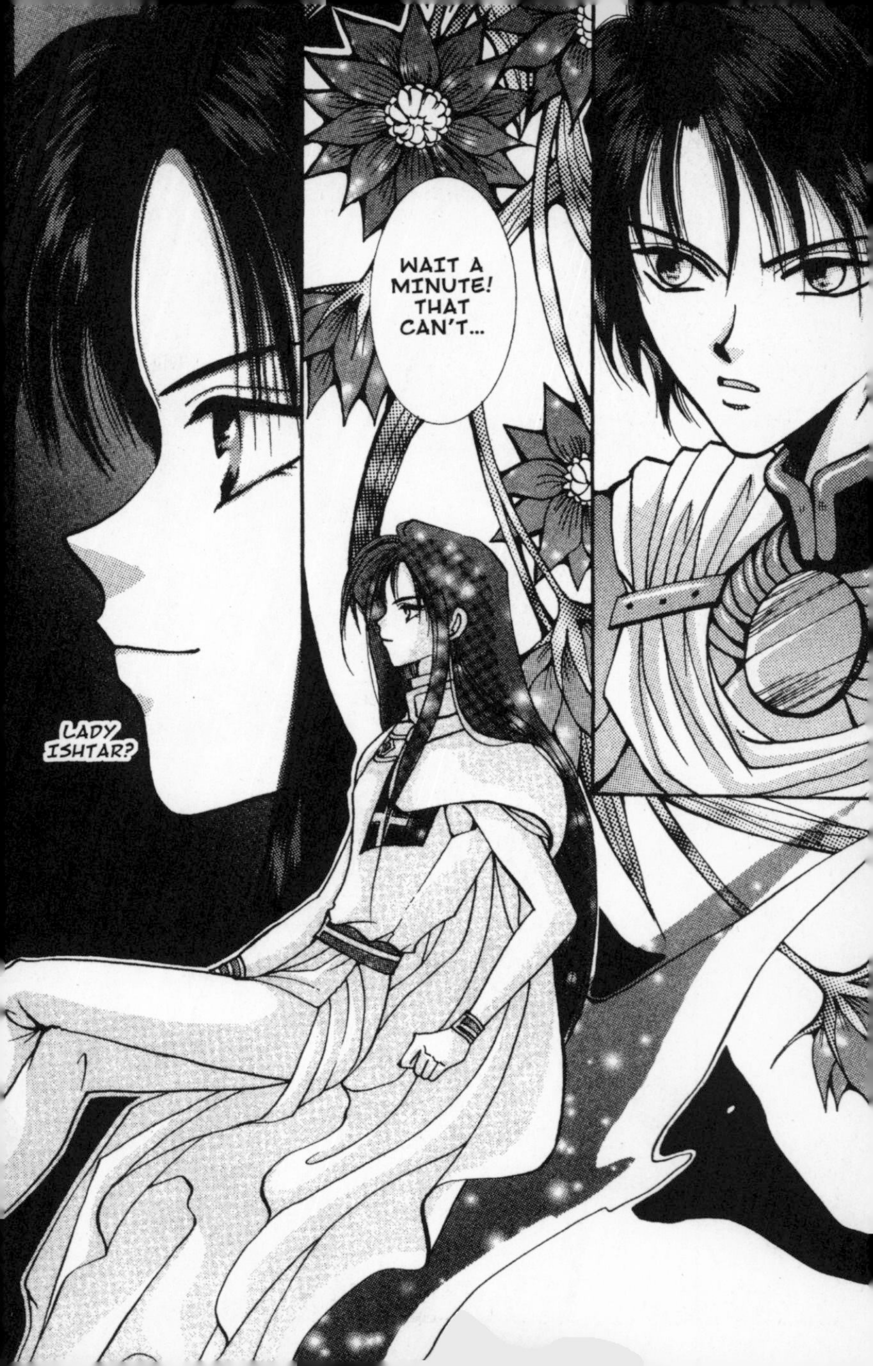
WAIT A MINUTE! THAT CAN'T...
LADY ISHTAR?

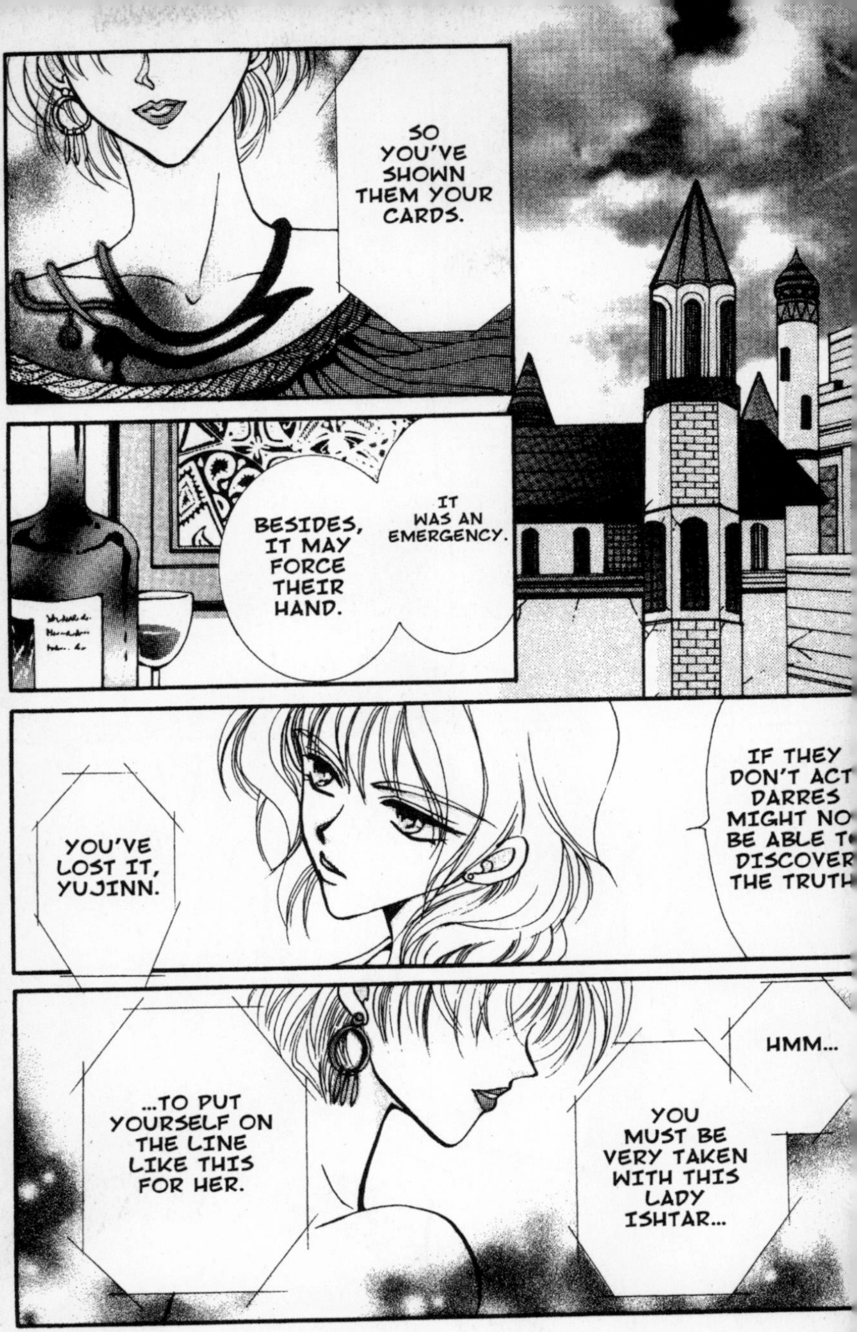
SO YOU'VE SHOWN THEM YOUR CARDS.
IT WAS AN EMERGENCY.
BESIDES, IT MAY FORCE THEIR HAND.
IF THEY DON'T ACT DARRES MIGHT NO BE ABLE T DISCOVER THE TRUTH
YOU'VE LOST IT, YUJINN.
HMM...
YOU MUST BE VERY TAKEN WITH THIS LADY ISHTAR...
...TO PUT YOURSELF ON THE LINE LIKE THIS FOR HER.

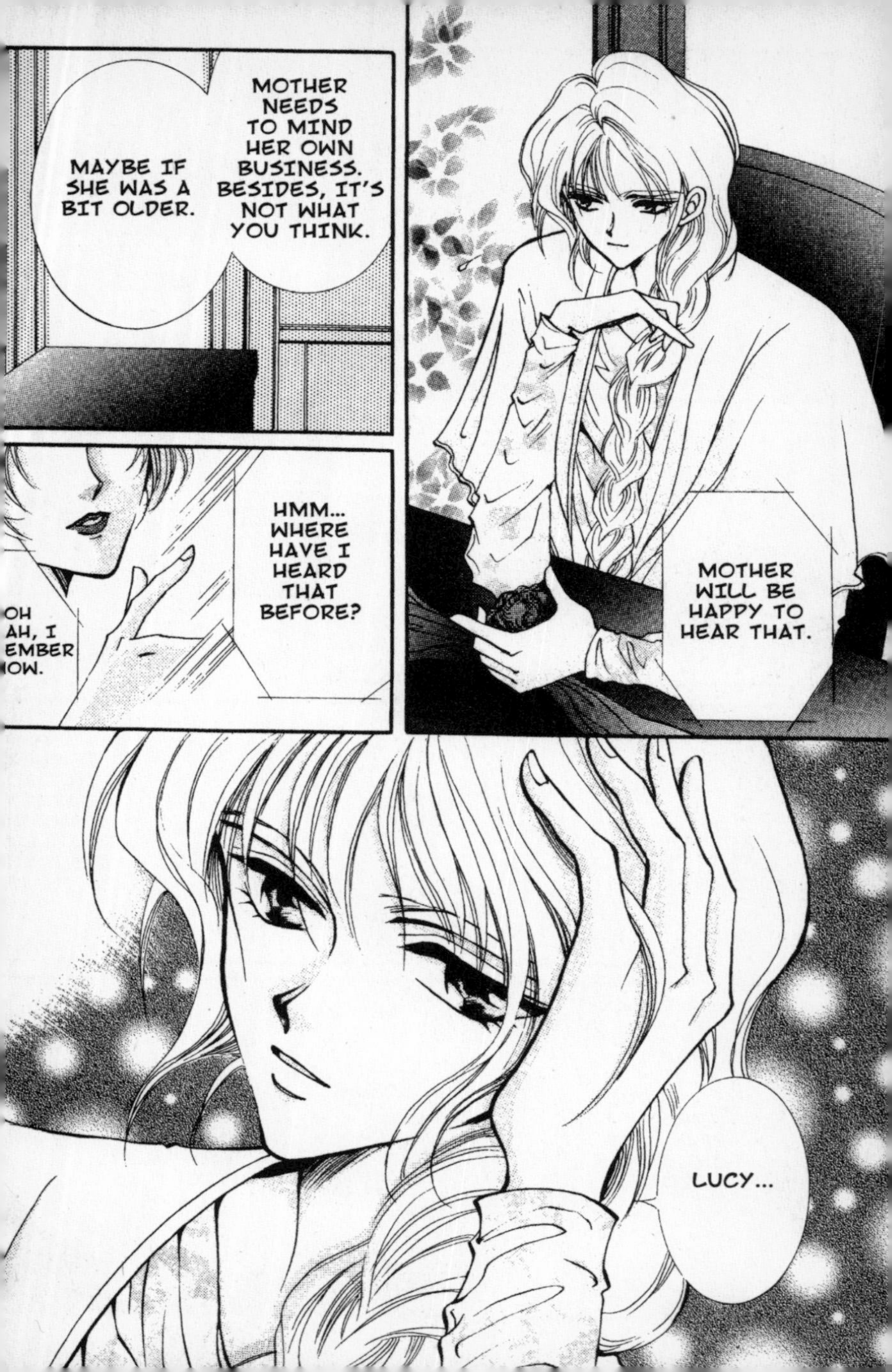
MOTHER WILL BE HAPPY TO HEAR THAT.
MOTHER NEEDS TO MIND HER OWN BUSINESS. BESIDES, IT'S NOT WHAT YOU THINK.
MAYBE IF SHE WAS A BIT OLDER.
HMM... WHERE HAVE I HEARD THAT BEFORE?
OH AH, I EMBER OW.
LUCY...

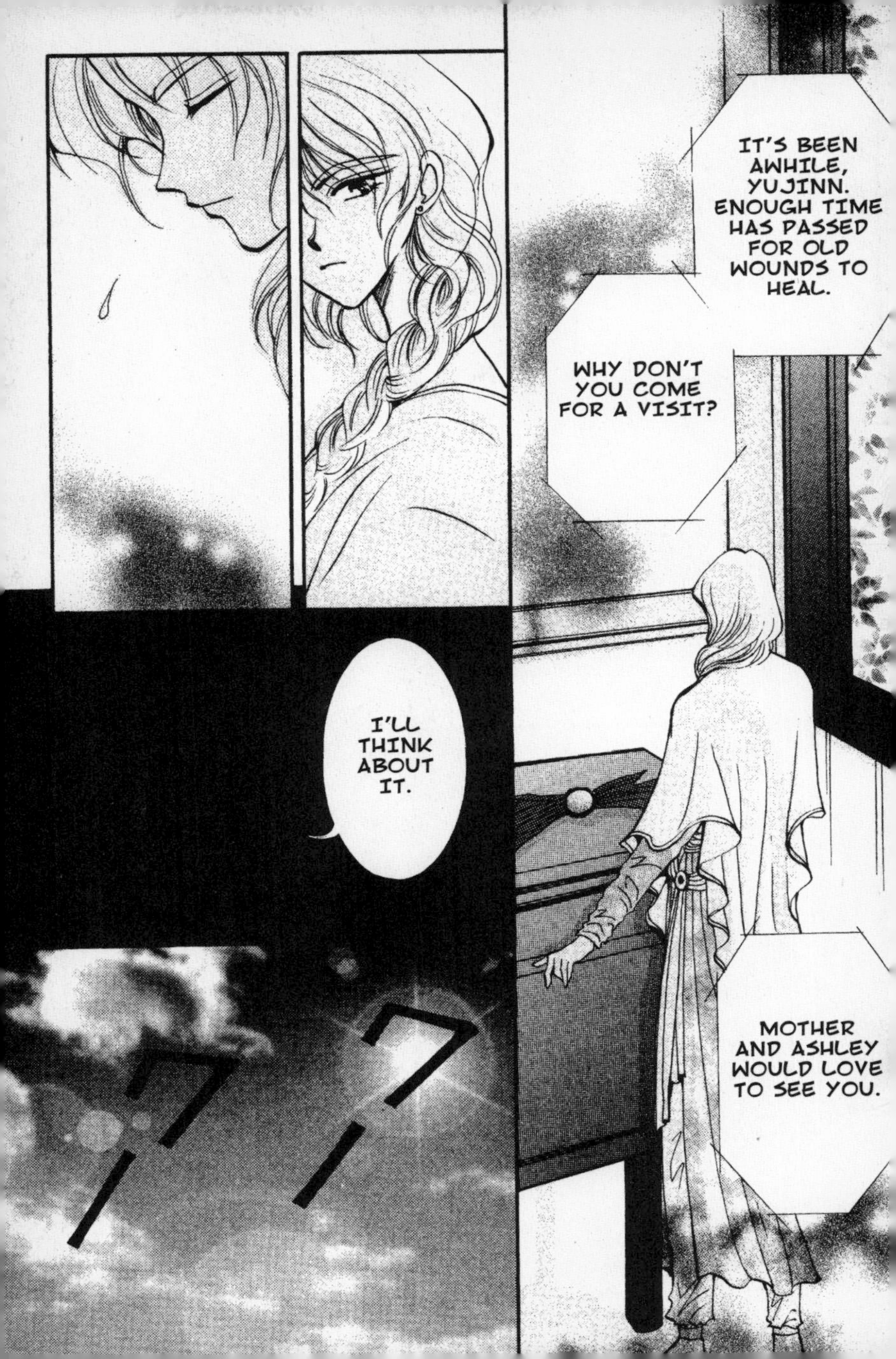
IT'S BEEN AWHILE, YUJINN. ENOUGH TIME HAS PASSED FOR OLD WOUNDS TO HEAL.
WHY DON'T YOU COME FOR A VISIT?
MOTHER AND ASHLEY WOULD LOVE TO SEE YOU.
I'LL THINK ABOUT IT.

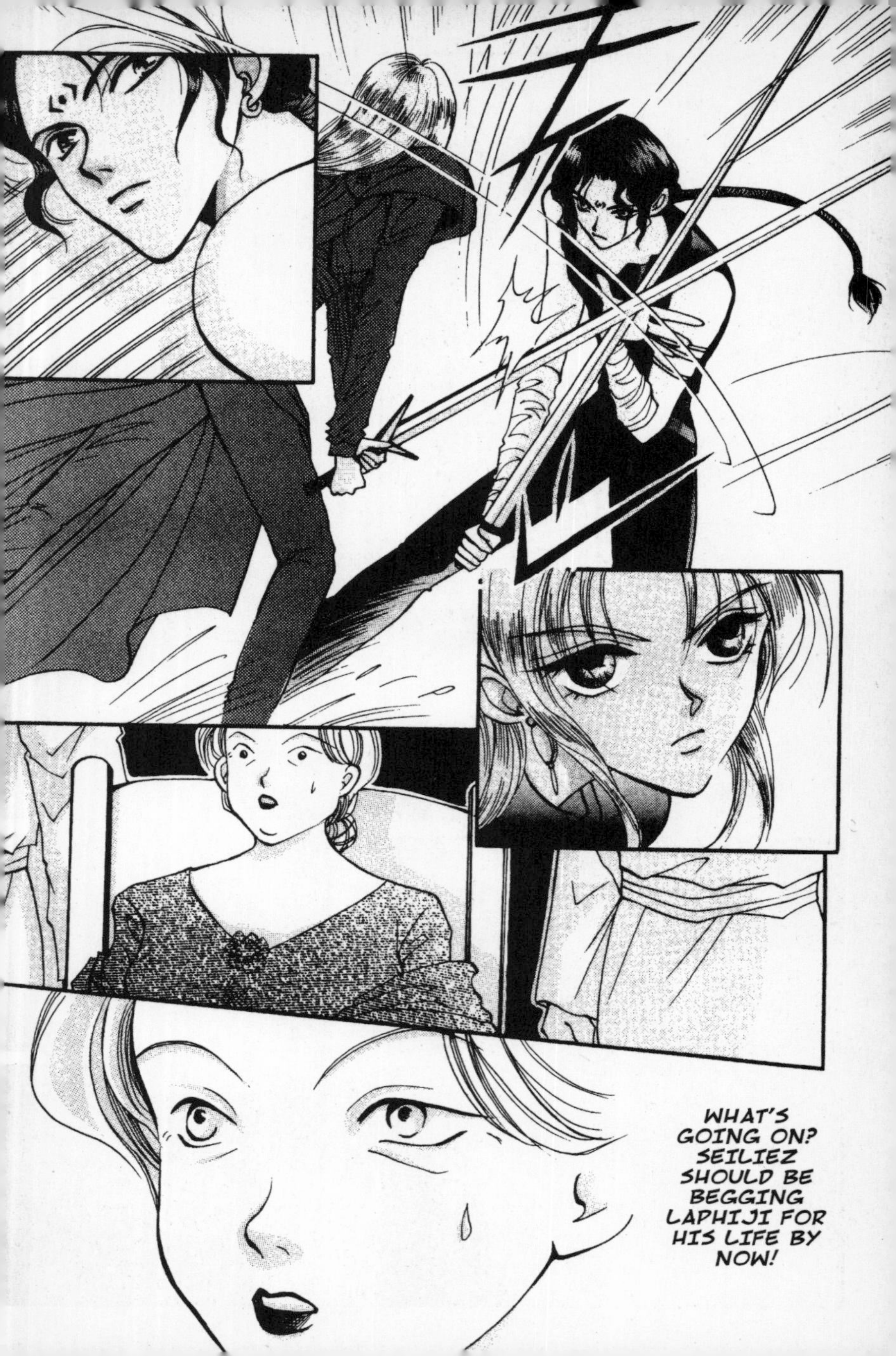
WHAT'S GOING ON? SEILIEZ SHOULD BE BEGGING LAPHIJI FOR HIS LIFE BY NOW!

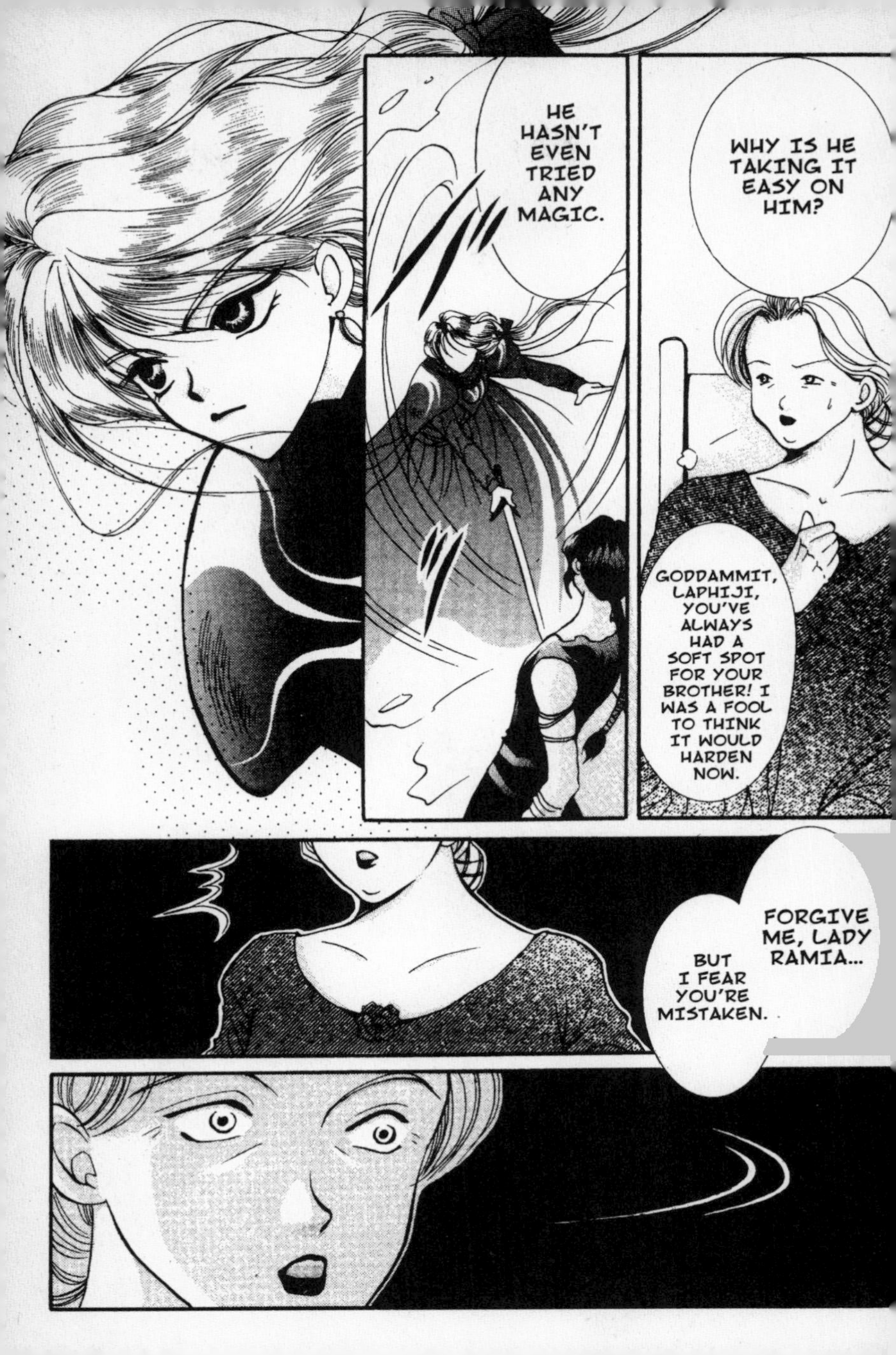
WHY IS HE TAKING IT EASY ON HIM?
GODDAMMIT, LAPHIJI, YOU'VE ALWAYS HAD A SOFT SPOT FOR YOUR BROTHER! I WAS A FOOL TO THINK IT WOULD HARDEN NOW.
HE HASN'T EVEN TRIED ANY MAGIC.
FORGIVE ME, LADY RAMIA...
BUT I FEAR YOU'RE MISTAKEN.

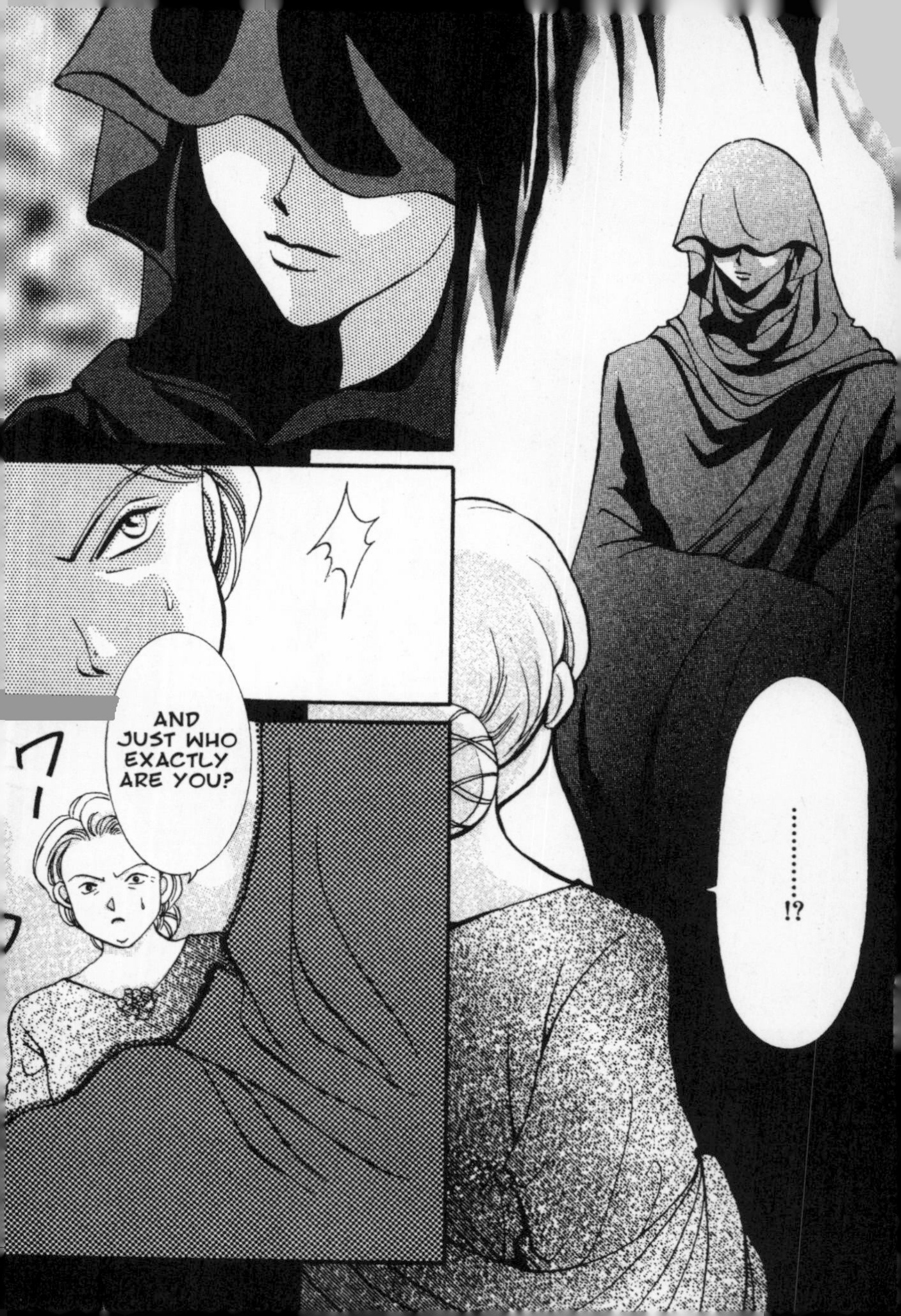
......!?
AND JUST WHO EXACTLY ARE YOU?

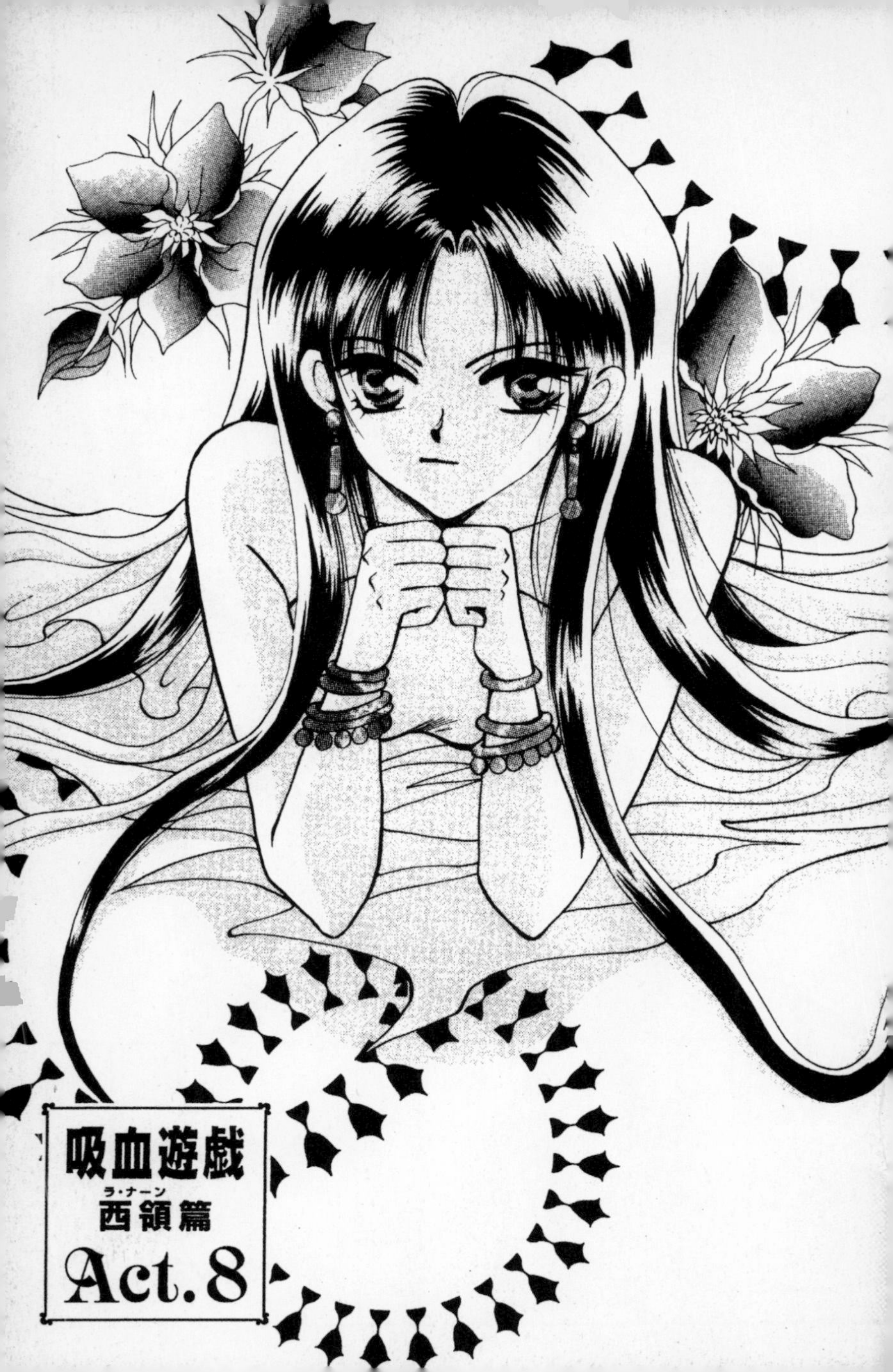
吸血遊戯
ラ・ナーン
西領篇
Act.8

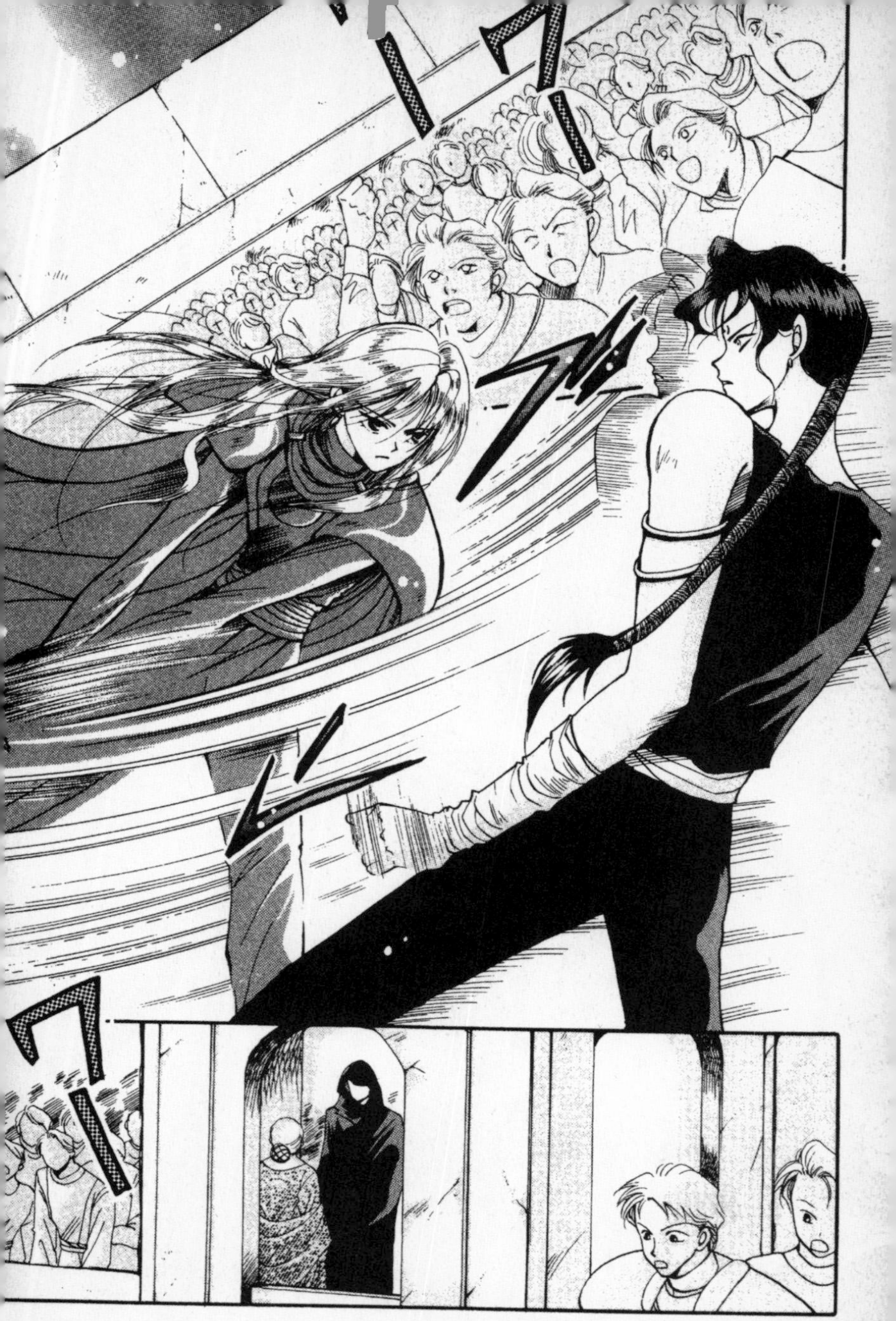

ワー
ブン
ワー

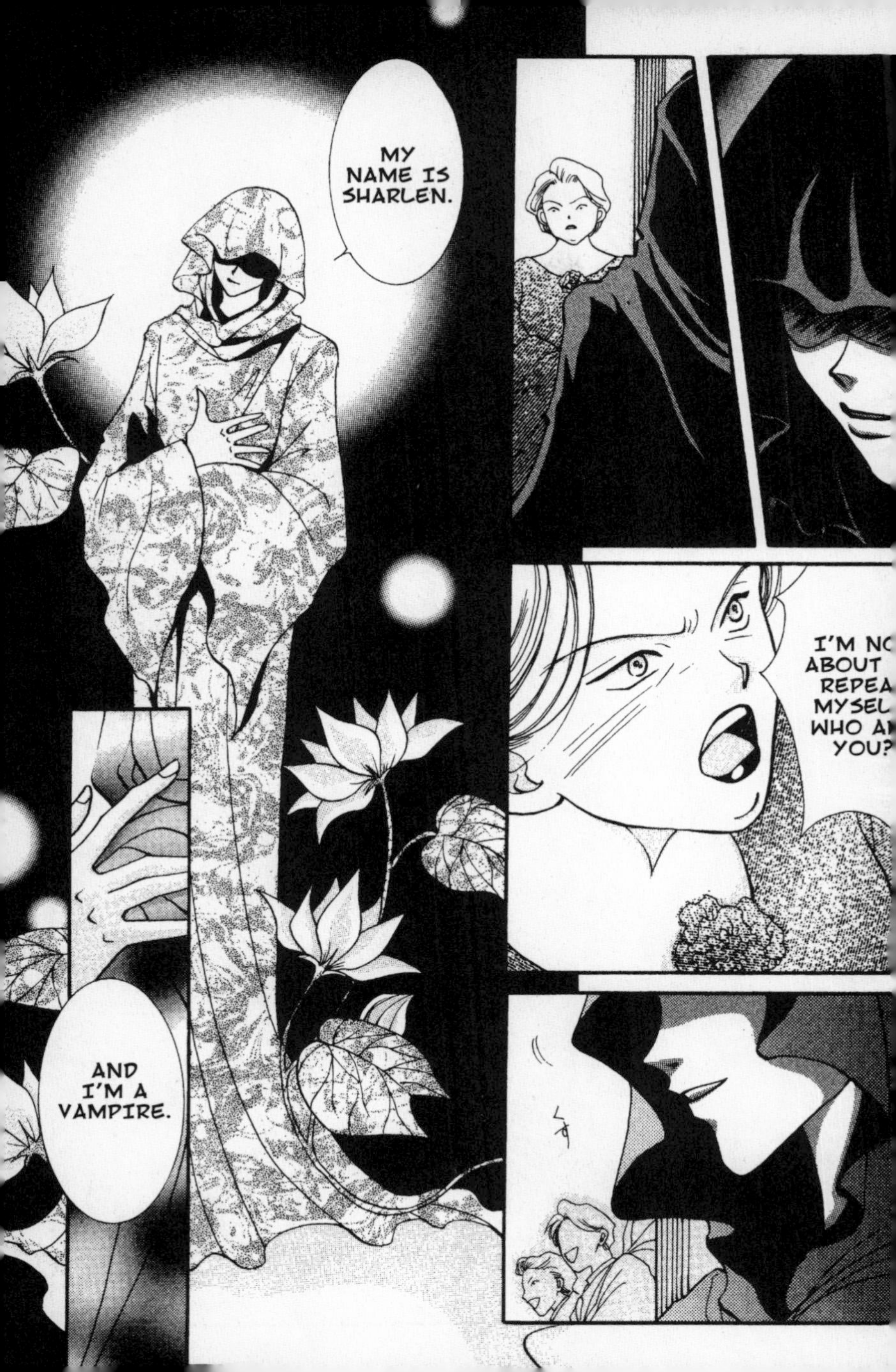
I'M NO ABOUT REPEA MYSEL WHO A YOU?
くす
MY NAME IS SHARLEN.
AND I'M A VAMPIRE.

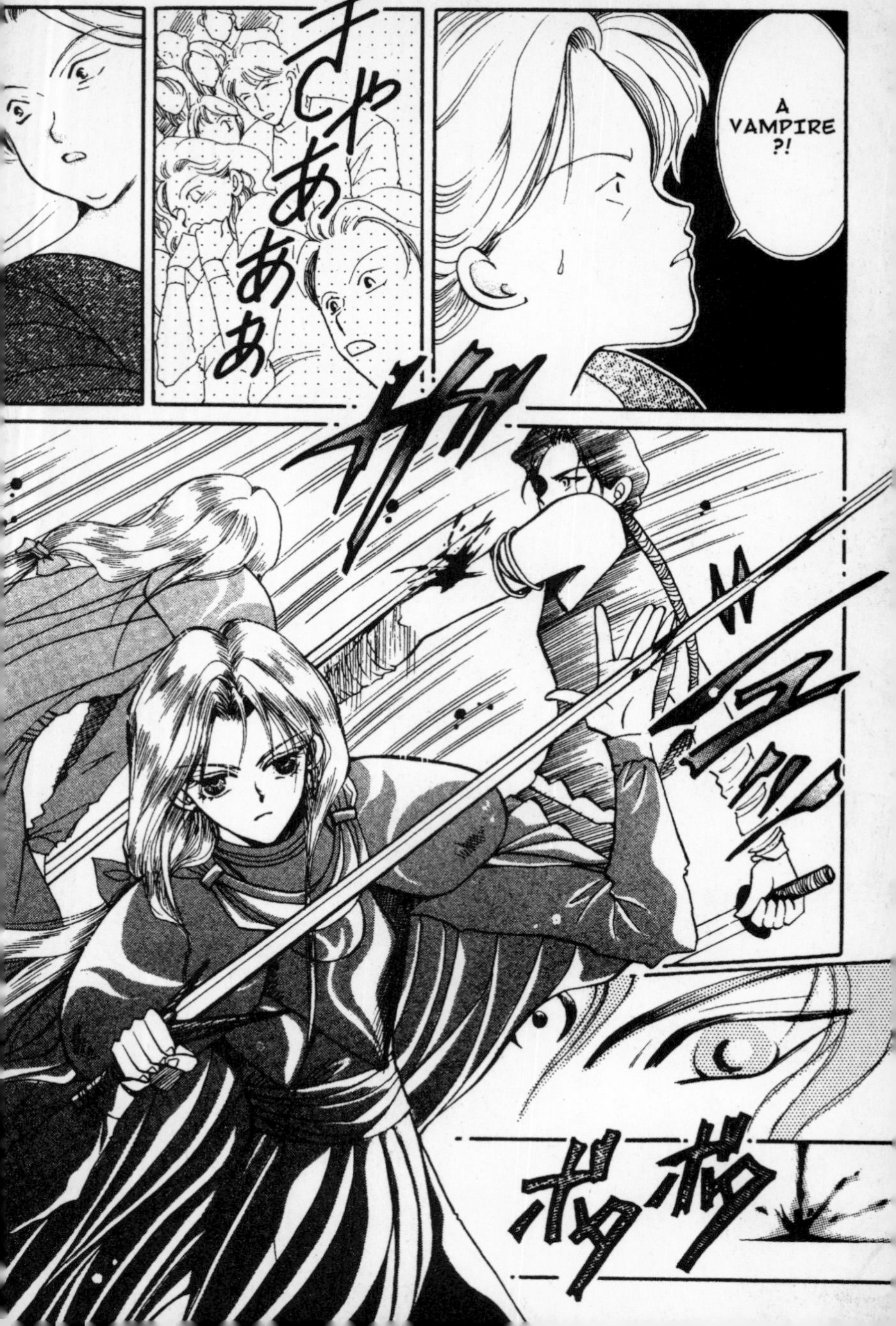
A VAMPIRE ?!
きゃあああ
ボタボタ

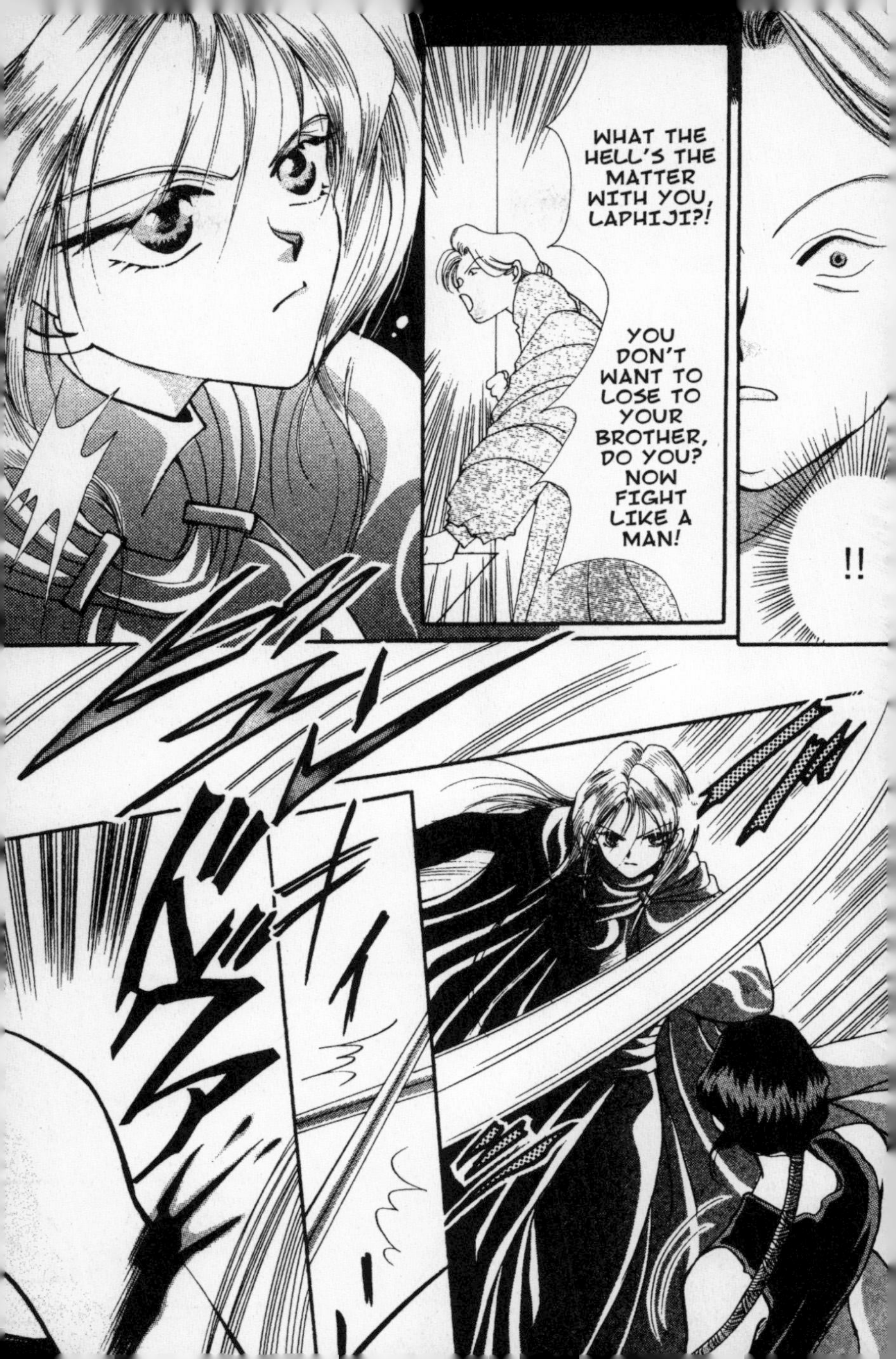
!!
WHAT THE HELL'S THE MATTER WITH YOU, LAPHIJI?!
YOU DON'T WANT TO LOSE TO YOUR BROTHER, DO YOU? NOW FIGHT LIKE A MAN!

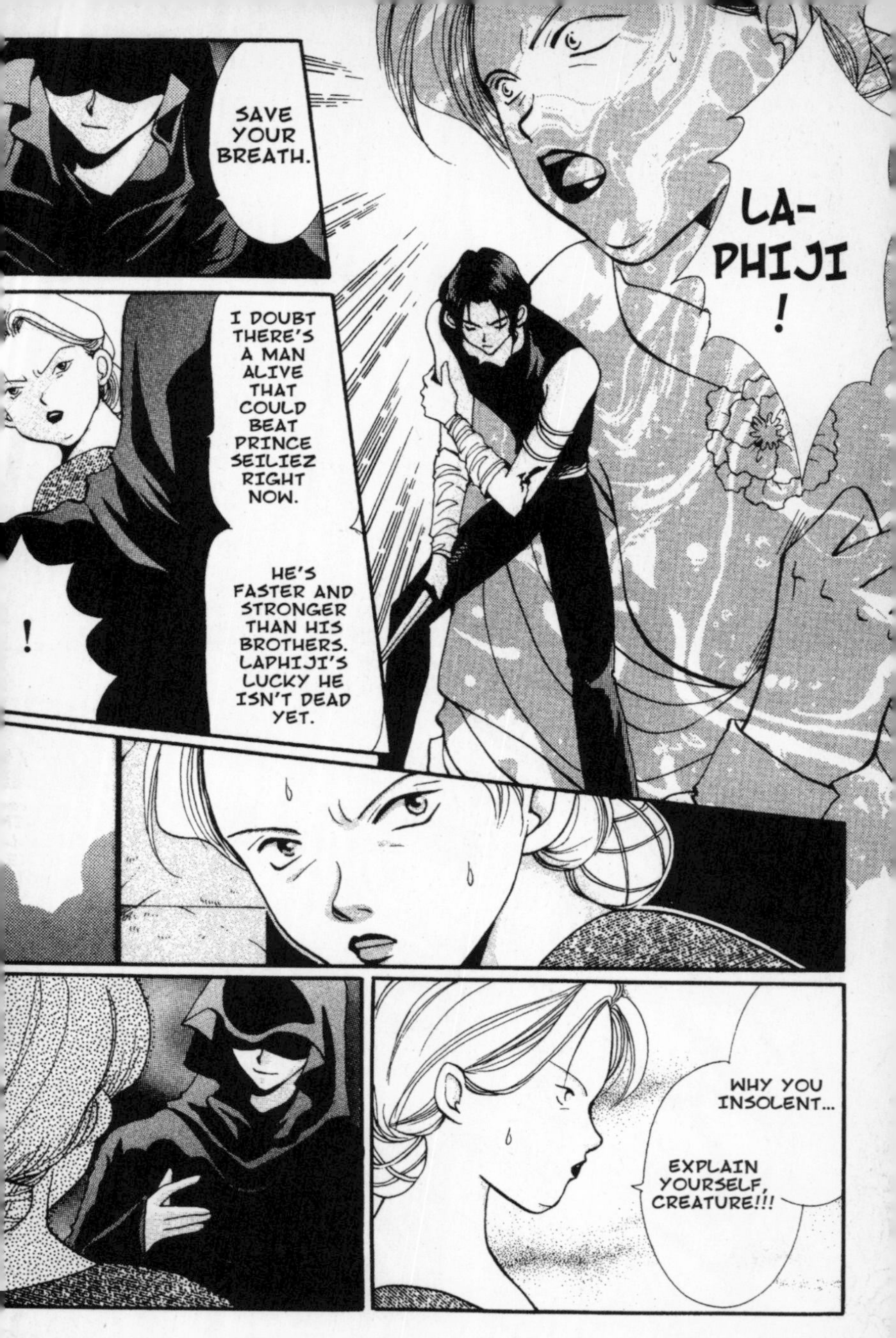
LA-PHIJI!
SAVE YOUR BREATH.
I DOUBT THERE'S A MAN ALIVE THAT COULD BEAT PRINCE SEILIEZ RIGHT NOW.
HE'S FASTER AND STRONGER THAN HIS BROTHERS. LAPHIJI'S LUCKY HE ISN'T DEAD YET.
!
WHY YOU INSOLENT...
EXPLAIN YOURSELF, CREATURE!!!

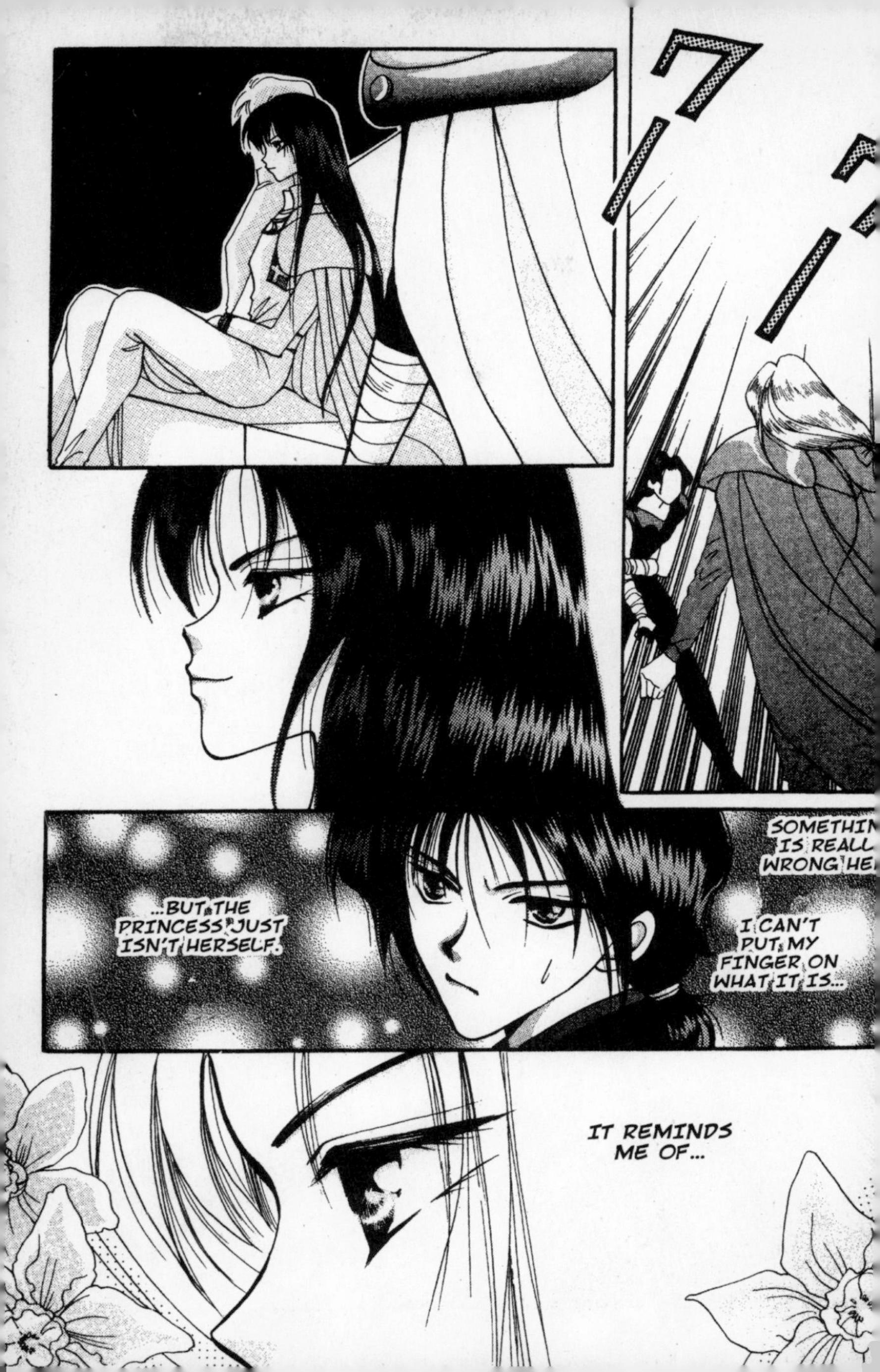
SOMETHIN IS REALL WRONG HE
I CAN'T PUT MY FINGER ON WHAT IT IS...
...BUT THE PRINCESS JUST ISN'T HERSELF.
IT REMINDS ME OF...

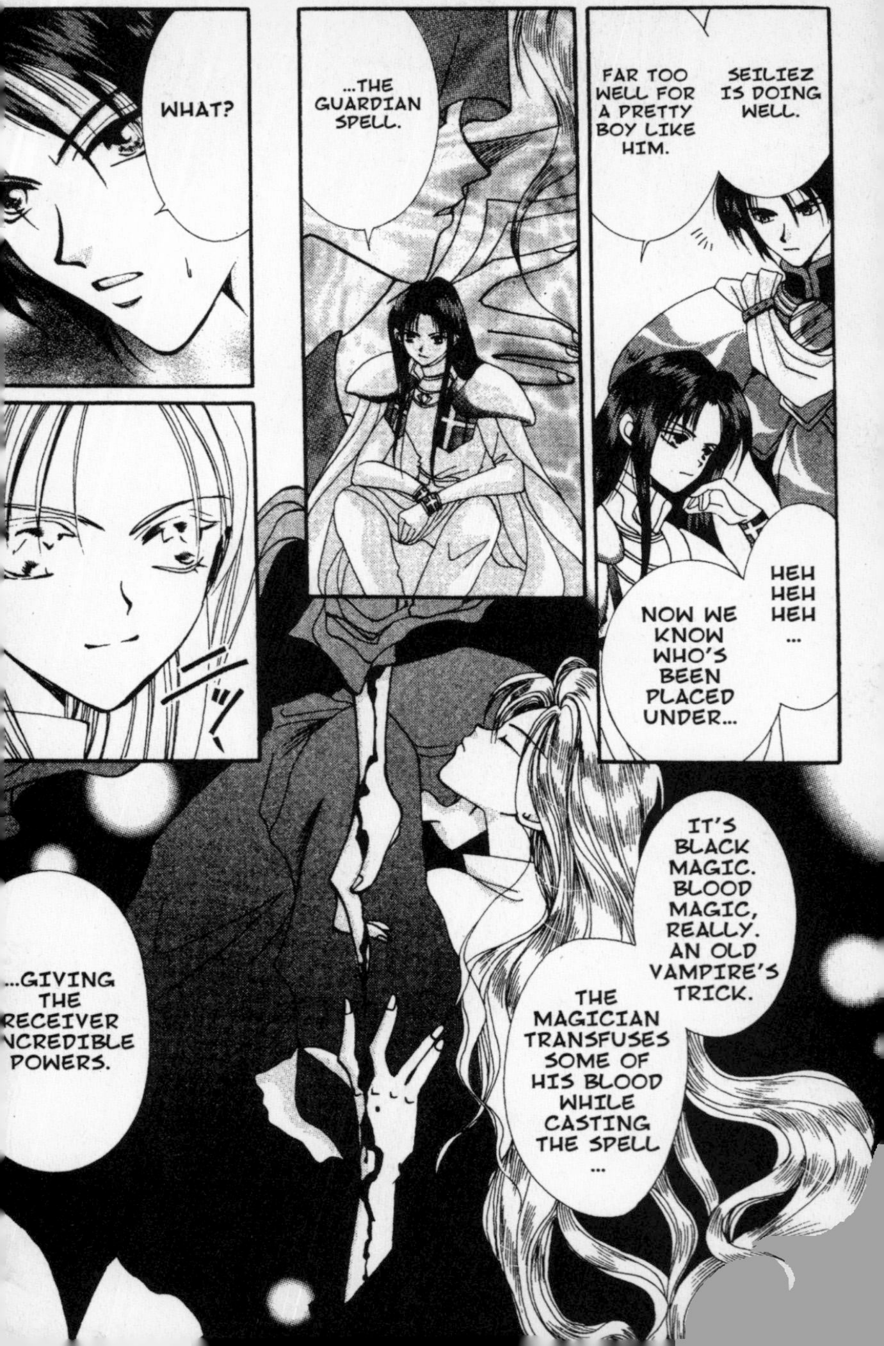
SEILIEZ IS DOING WELL.
FAR TOO WELL FOR A PRETTY BOY LIKE HIM.
HEH HEH HEH...
NOW WE KNOW WHO'S BEEN PLACED UNDER...
...THE GUARDIAN SPELL.
WHAT?
IT'S BLACK MAGIC. BLOOD MAGIC, REALLY. AN OLD VAMPIRE'S TRICK.
THE MAGICIAN TRANSFUSES SOME OF HIS BLOOD WHILE CASTING THE SPELL...
...GIVING THE RECEIVER NCREDIBLE POWERS.

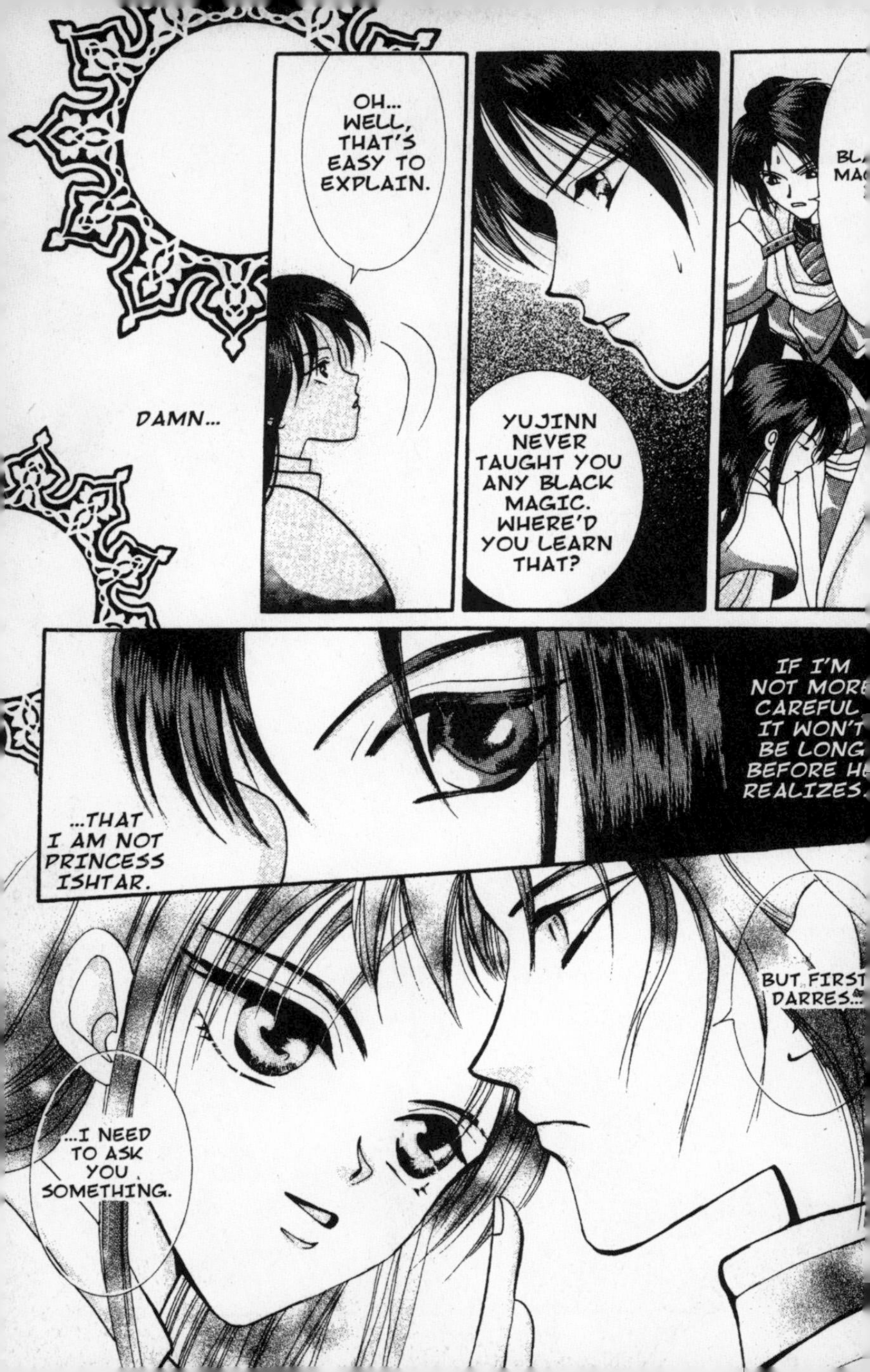
YUJINN NEVER TAUGHT YOU ANY BLACK MAGIC. WHERE'D YOU LEARN THAT?
OH... WELL, THAT'S EASY TO EXPLAIN.
DAMN...
IF I'M NOT MORE CAREFUL IT WON'T BE LONG BEFORE H
REALIZES...
...THAT I AM NOT PRINCESS ISHTAR.
BUT FIRST DARRES...
...I NEED TO ASK YOU SOMETHING.

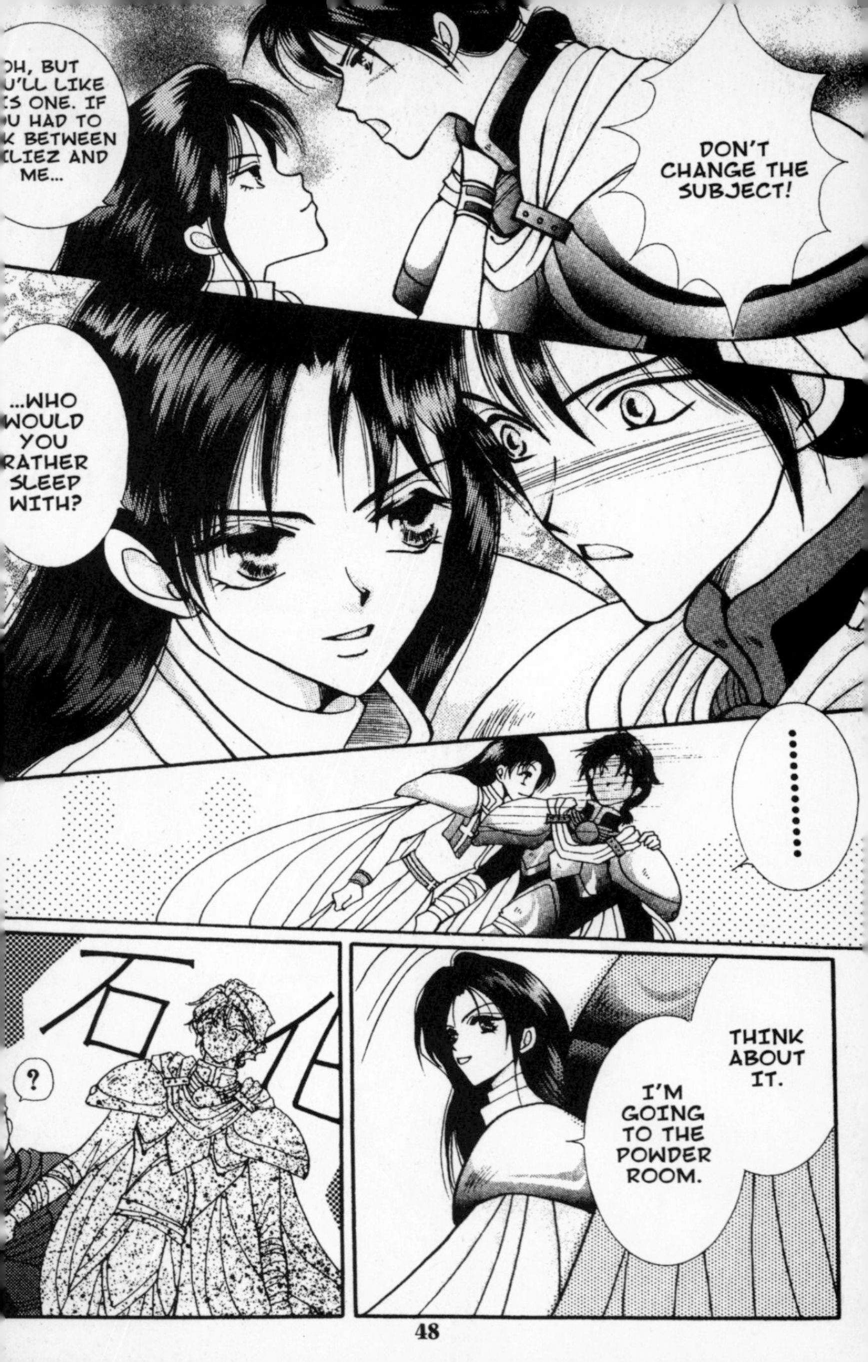
DON'T CHANGE THE SUBJECT!
OH, BUT U'LL LIKE S ONE. IF U HAD TO K BETWEEN LIEZ AND ME...
...WHO WOULD YOU RATHER SLEEP WITH?
....
THINK ABOUT IT.
I'M GOING TO THE POWDER ROOM.
?

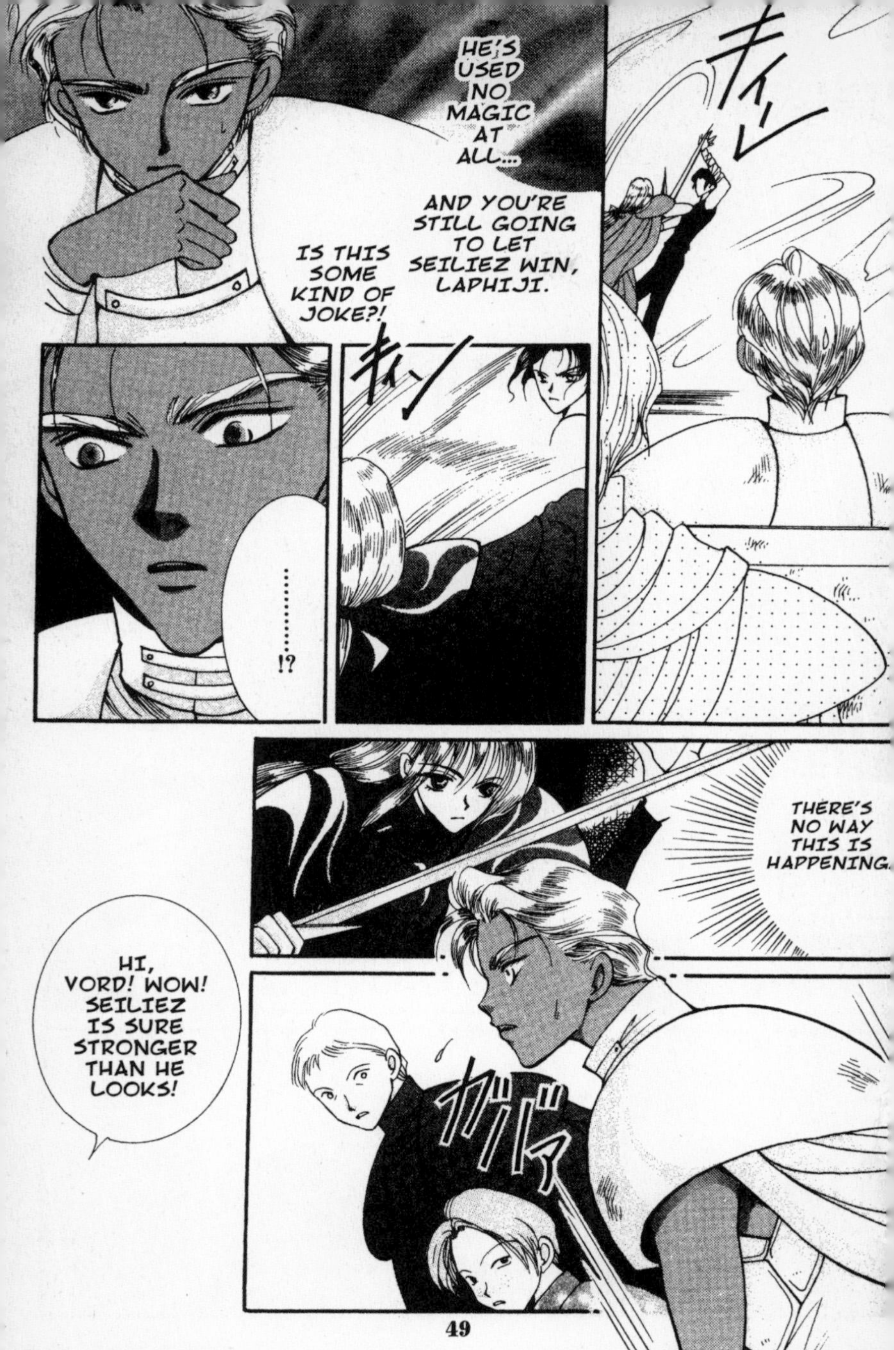

キィン
HE'S USED NO MAGIC AT ALL...
AND YOU'RE STILL GOING TO LET SEILIEZ WIN, LAPHIJI.
IS THIS SOME KIND OF JOKE?!
キィン
......!?
THERE'S NO WAY THIS IS HAPPENING.
ガバァ
HI, VORD! WOW! SEILIEZ IS SURE STRONGER THAN HE LOOKS!

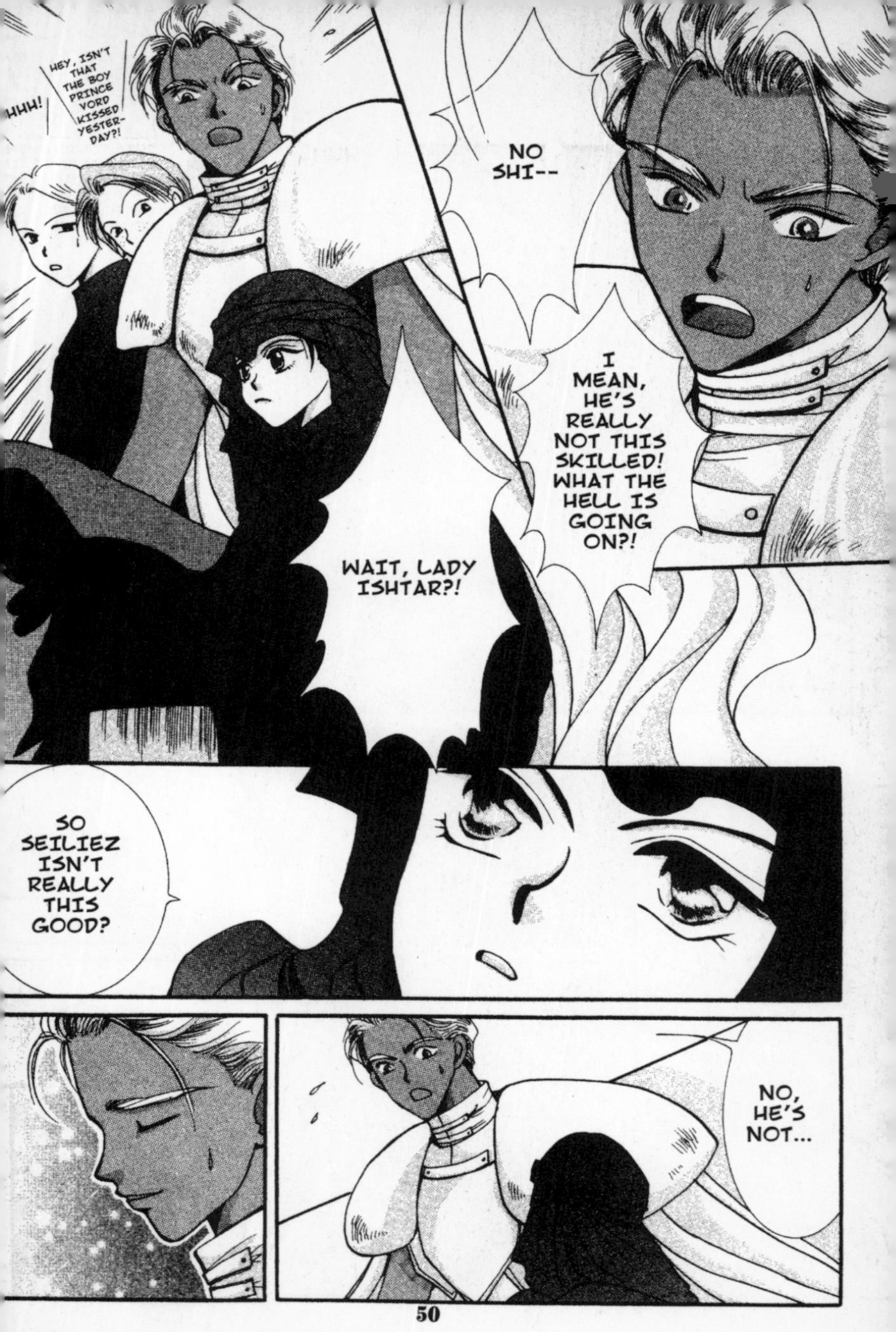
NO SHI--
I MEAN, HE'S REALLY NOT THIS SKILLED! WHAT THE HELL IS GOING ON?!
HEY, ISN'T THAT THE BOY PRINCE VORD KISSED YESTERDAY?!
HHH!
WAIT, LADY ISHTAR?!
SO SEILIEZ ISN'T REALLY THIS GOOD?
NO, HE'S NOT...

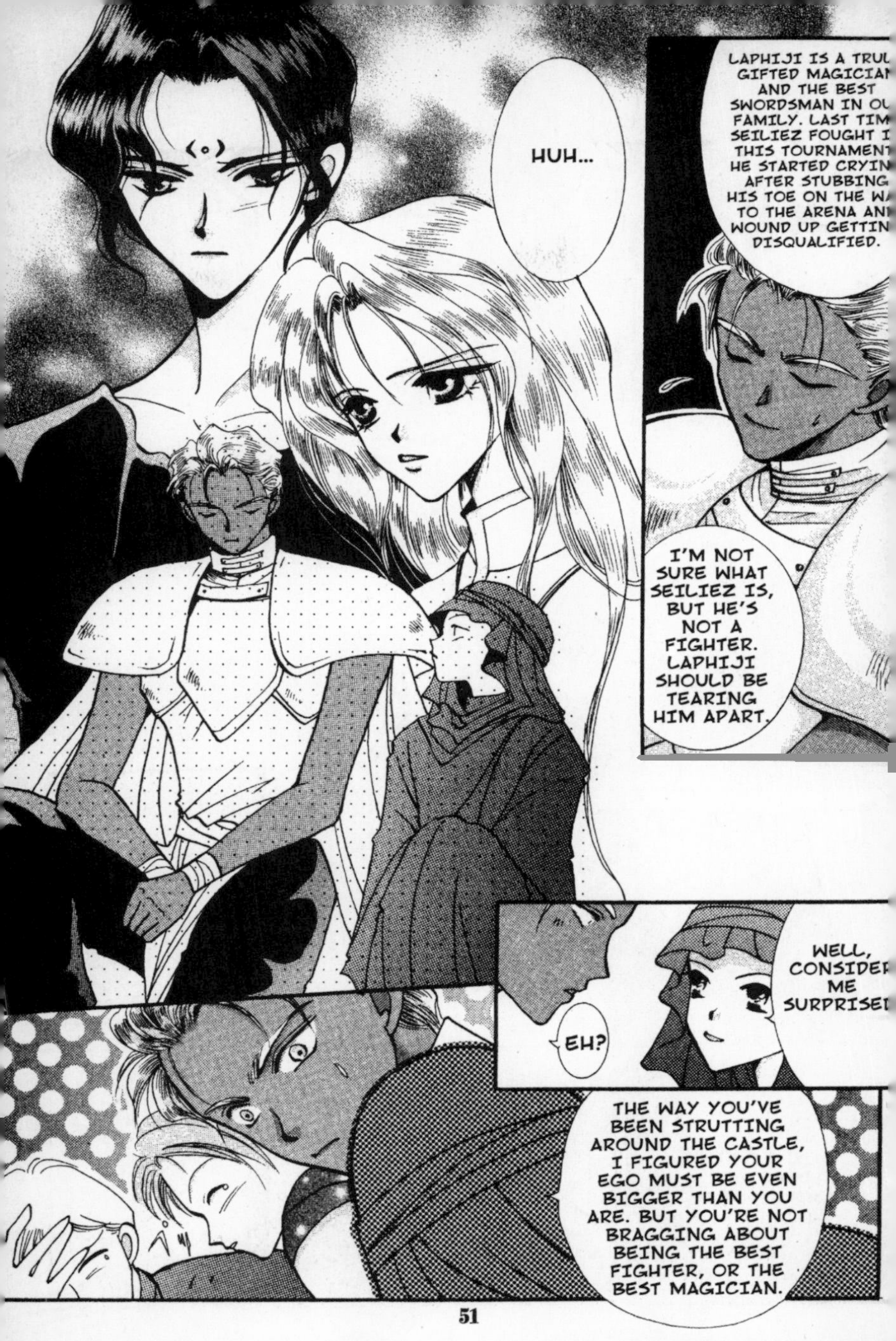
LAPHIJI IS A TRUL GIFTED MAGICIAN AND THE BEST SWORDSMAN IN OU FAMILY. LAST TIM SEILIEZ FOUGHT I THIS TOURNAMENT HE STARTED CRYIN AFTER STUBBING HIS TOE ON THE WA TO THE ARENA AN WOUND UP GETTIN DISQUALIFIED.
I'M NOT SURE WHAT SEILIEZ IS, BUT HE'S NOT A FIGHTER. LAPHIJI SHOULD BE TEARING HIM APART.
HUH...
WELL, CONSIDER ME SURPRISED
EH?
THE WAY YOU'VE BEEN STRUTTING AROUND THE CASTLE, I FIGURED YOUR EGO MUST BE EVEN BIGGER THAN YOU ARE. BUT YOU'RE NOT BRAGGING ABOUT BEING THE BEST FIGHTER, OR THE BEST MAGICIAN.

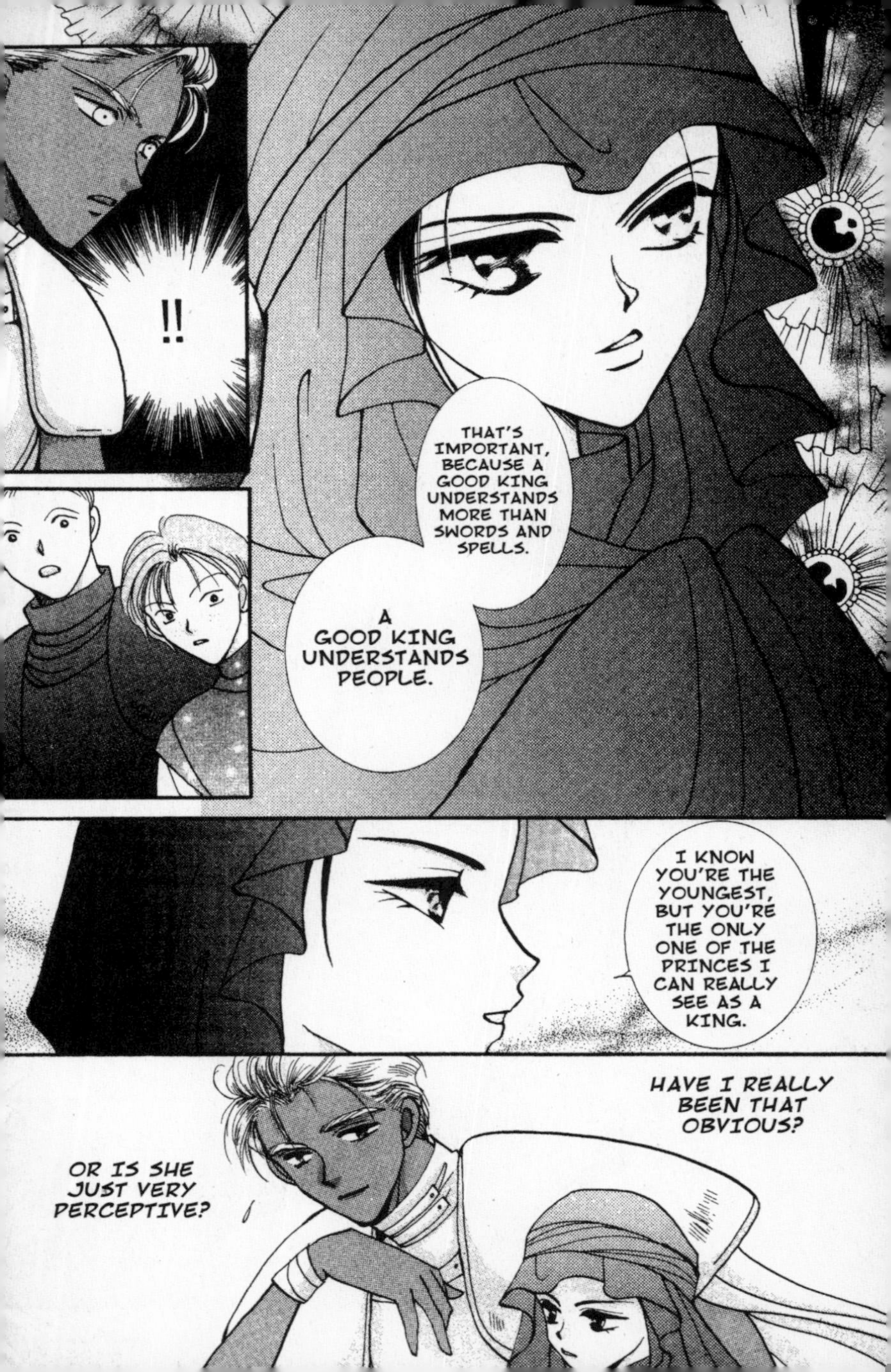
THAT'S IMPORTANT, BECAUSE A GOOD KING UNDERSTANDS MORE THAN SWORDS AND SPELLS.
A GOOD KING UNDERSTANDS PEOPLE.
!!
I KNOW YOU'RE THE YOUNGEST, BUT YOU'RE THE ONLY ONE OF THE PRINCES I CAN REALLY SEE AS A KING.
HAVE I REALLY BEEN THAT OBVIOUS?
OR IS SHE JUST VERY PERCEPTIVE?

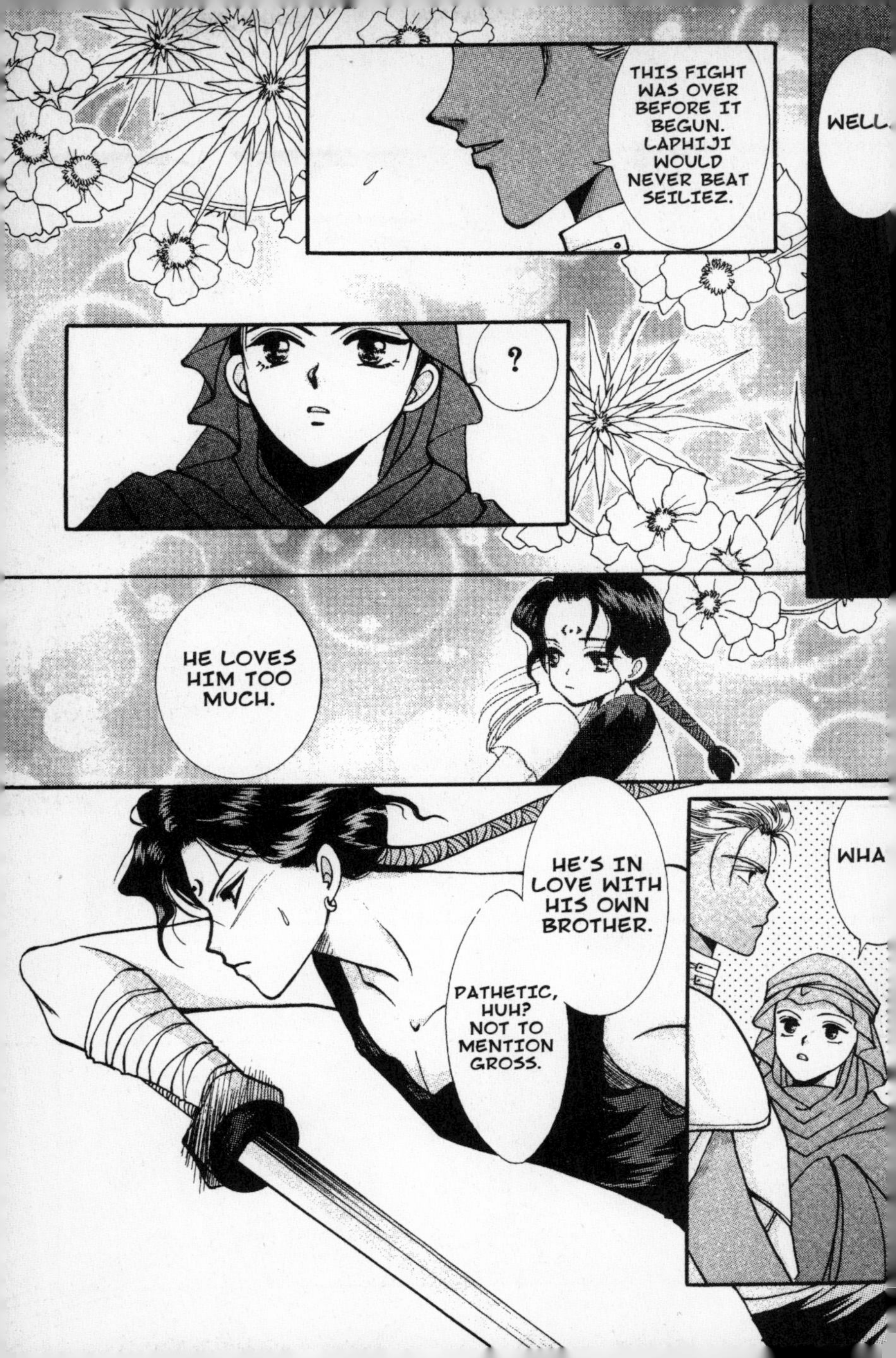

WELL.
THIS FIGHT WAS OVER BEFORE IT BEGUN. LAPHIJI WOULD NEVER BEAT SEILIEZ.
?
HE LOVES HIM TOO MUCH.
WHA
HE'S IN LOVE WITH HIS OWN BROTHER.
PATHETIC, HUH? NOT TO MENTION GROSS.

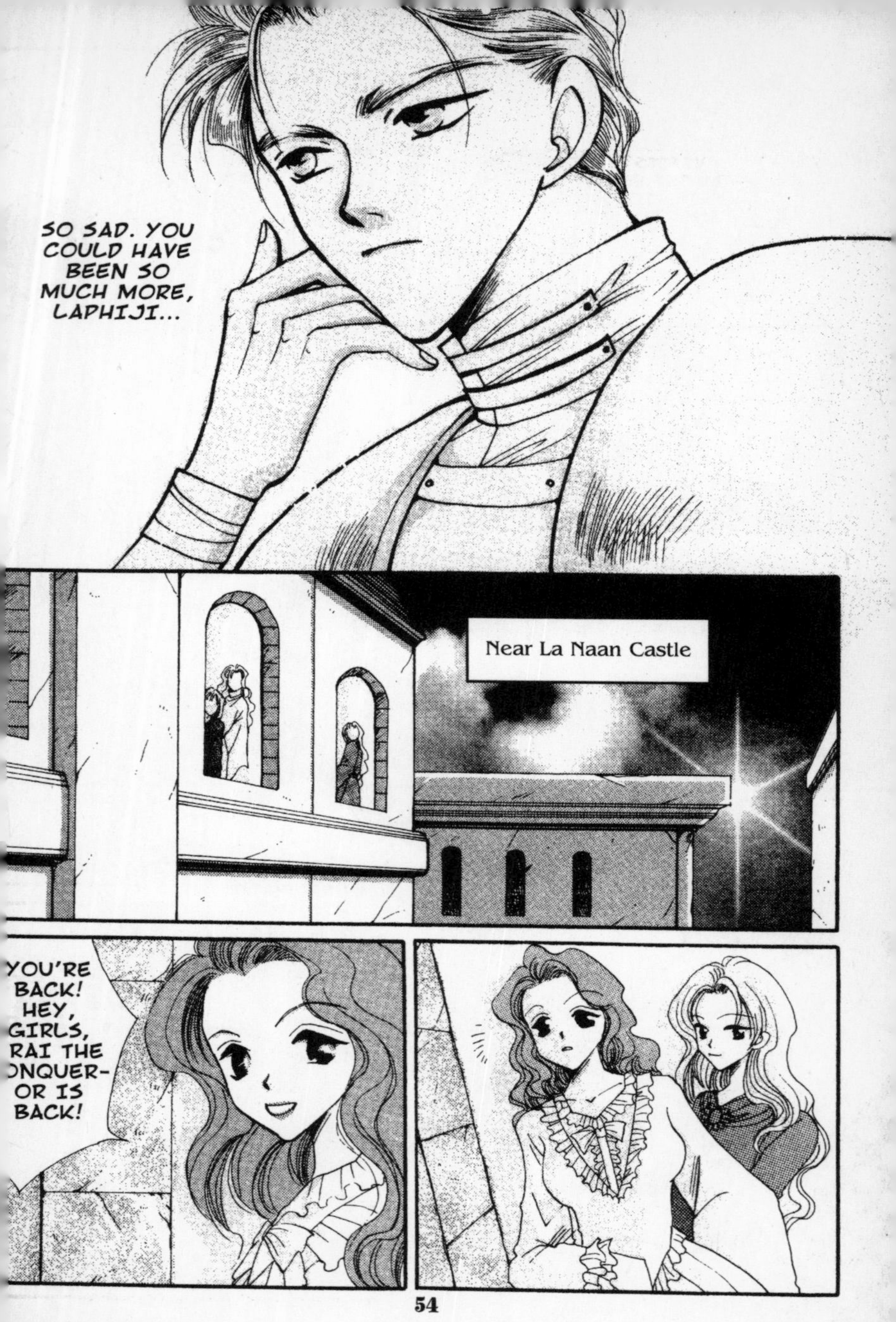
SO SAD. YOU COULD HAVE BEEN SO MUCH MORE, LAPHIJI...
Near La Naan Castle
YOU'RE BACK! HEY, GIRLS, RAI THE ONQUER-OR IS BACK!

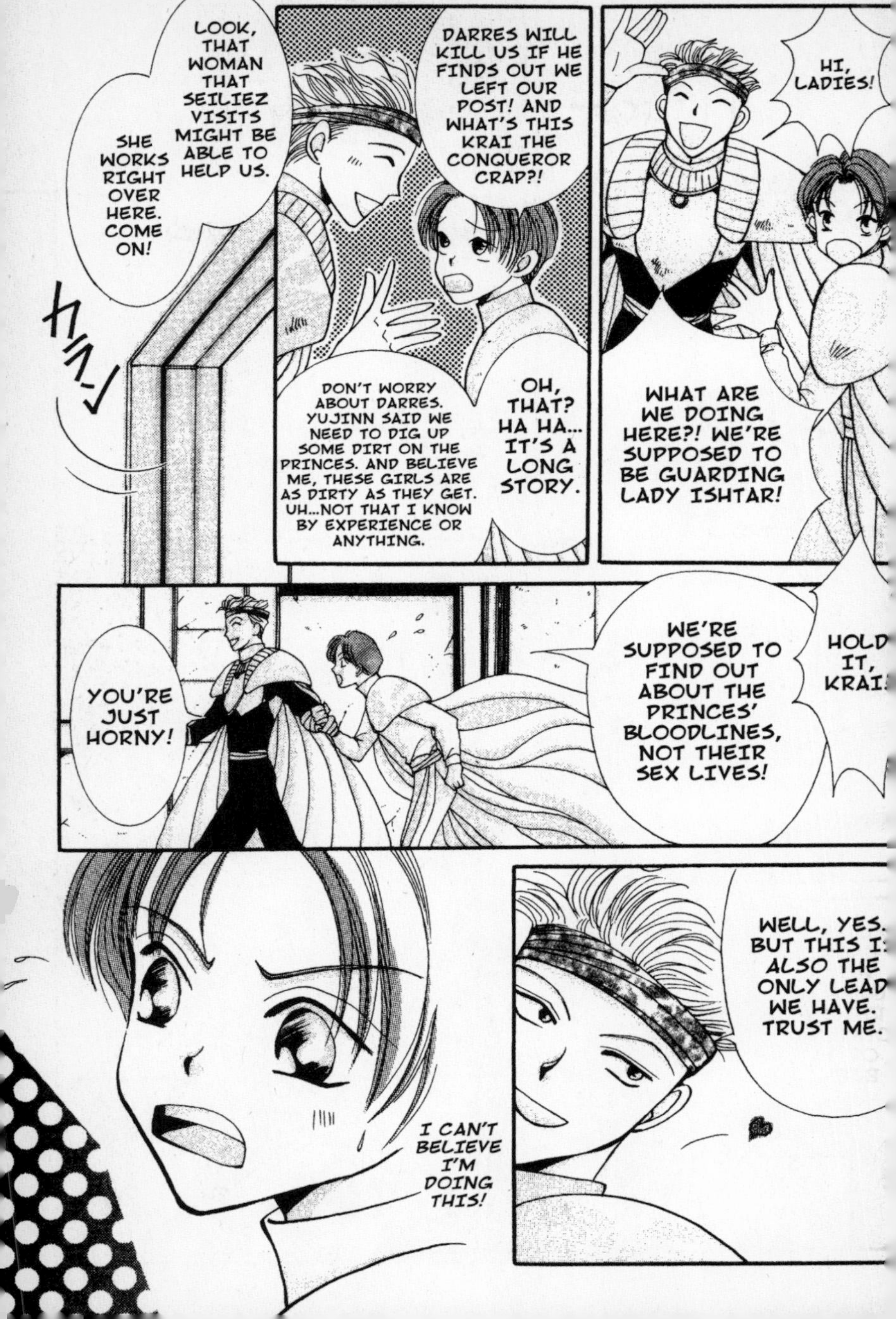
HI, LADIES!
WHAT ARE WE DOING HERE?! WE'RE SUPPOSED TO BE GUARDING LADY ISHTAR!
DARRES WILL KILL US IF HE FINDS OUT WE LEFT OUR POST! AND WHAT'S THIS KRAI THE CONQUEROR CRAP?!
OH, THAT? HA HA... IT'S A LONG STORY.
DON'T WORRY ABOUT DARRES. YUJINN SAID WE NEED TO DIG UP SOME DIRT ON THE PRINCES. AND BELIEVE ME, THESE GIRLS ARE AS DIRTY AS THEY GET. UH...NOT THAT I KNOW BY EXPERIENCE OR ANYTHING.
LOOK, THAT WOMAN THAT SEILIEZ VISITS MIGHT BE ABLE TO HELP US.
SHE WORKS RIGHT OVER HERE. COME ON!
HOLD IT, KRAI!
WE'RE SUPPOSED TO FIND OUT ABOUT THE PRINCES' BLOODLINES, NOT THEIR SEX LIVES!
YOU'RE JUST HORNY!
WELL, YES. BUT THIS I ALSO THE ONLY LEAD WE HAVE. TRUST ME.
I CAN'T BELIEVE I'M DOING THIS!

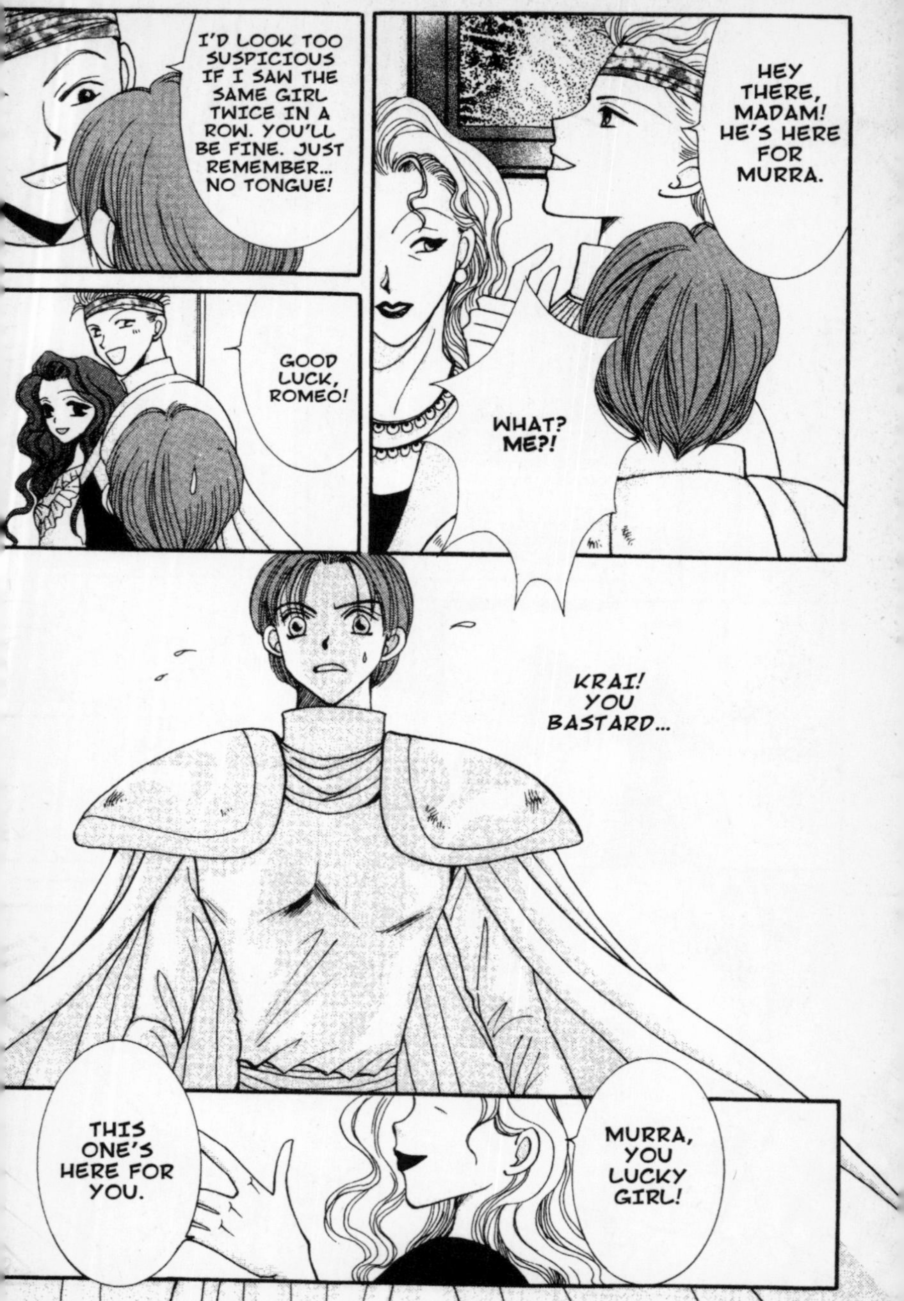
HEY THERE, MADAM! HE'S HERE FOR MURRA.
WHAT? ME?!
I'D LOOK TOO SUSPICIOUS IF I SAW THE SAME GIRL TWICE IN A ROW. YOU'LL BE FINE. JUST REMEMBER... NO TONGUE!
GOOD LUCK, ROMEO!
KRAI! YOU BASTARD...
MURRA, YOU LUCKY GIRL!
THIS ONE'S HERE FOR YOU.

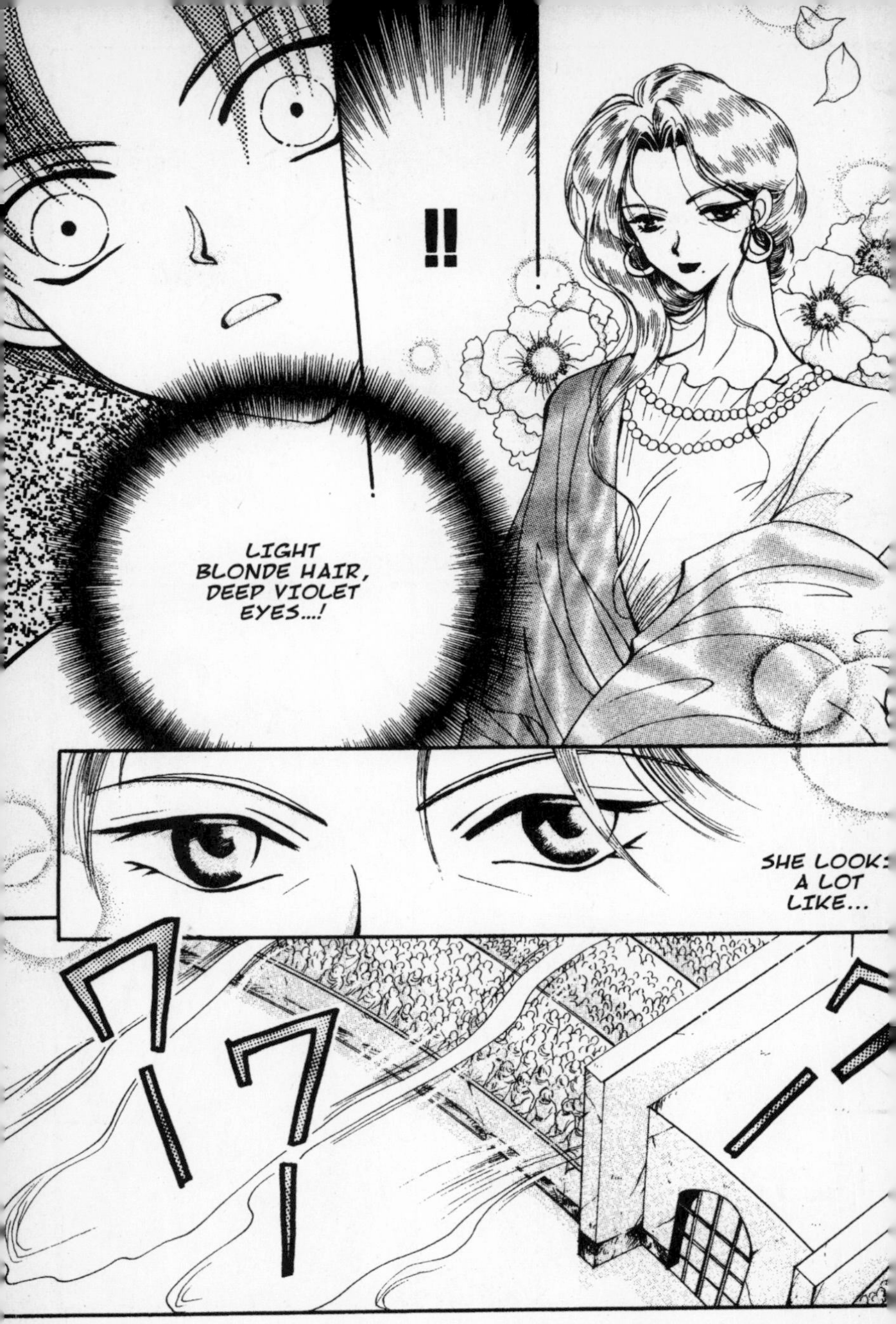
!!
LIGHT BLONDE HAIR, DEEP VIOLET EYES...!
SHE LOOK A LOT LIKE...

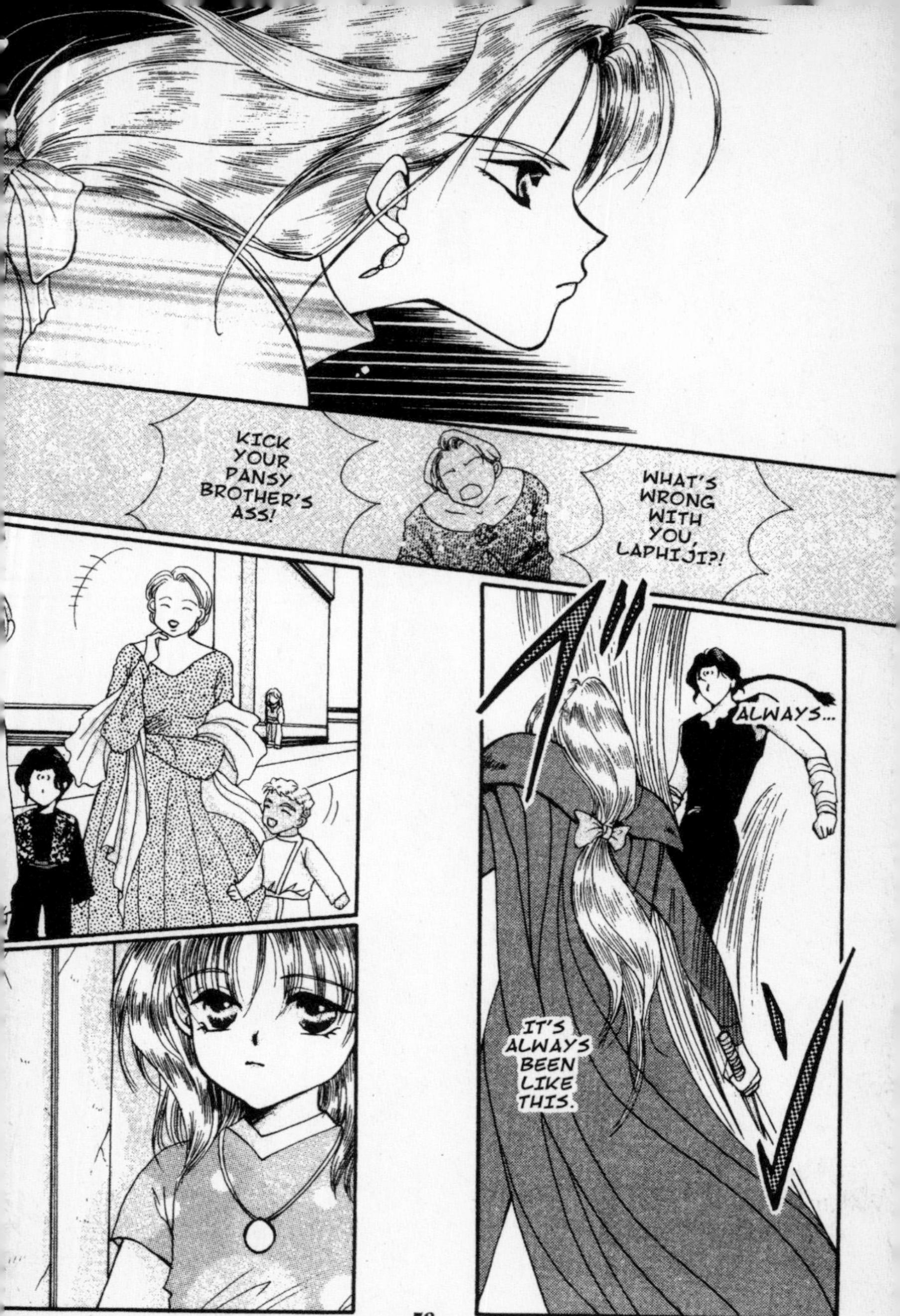
WHAT'S WRONG WITH YOU, LAPHIJI?!
KICK YOUR PANSY BROTHER'S ASS!
ALWAYS...
IT'S ALWAYS BEEN LIKE THIS.

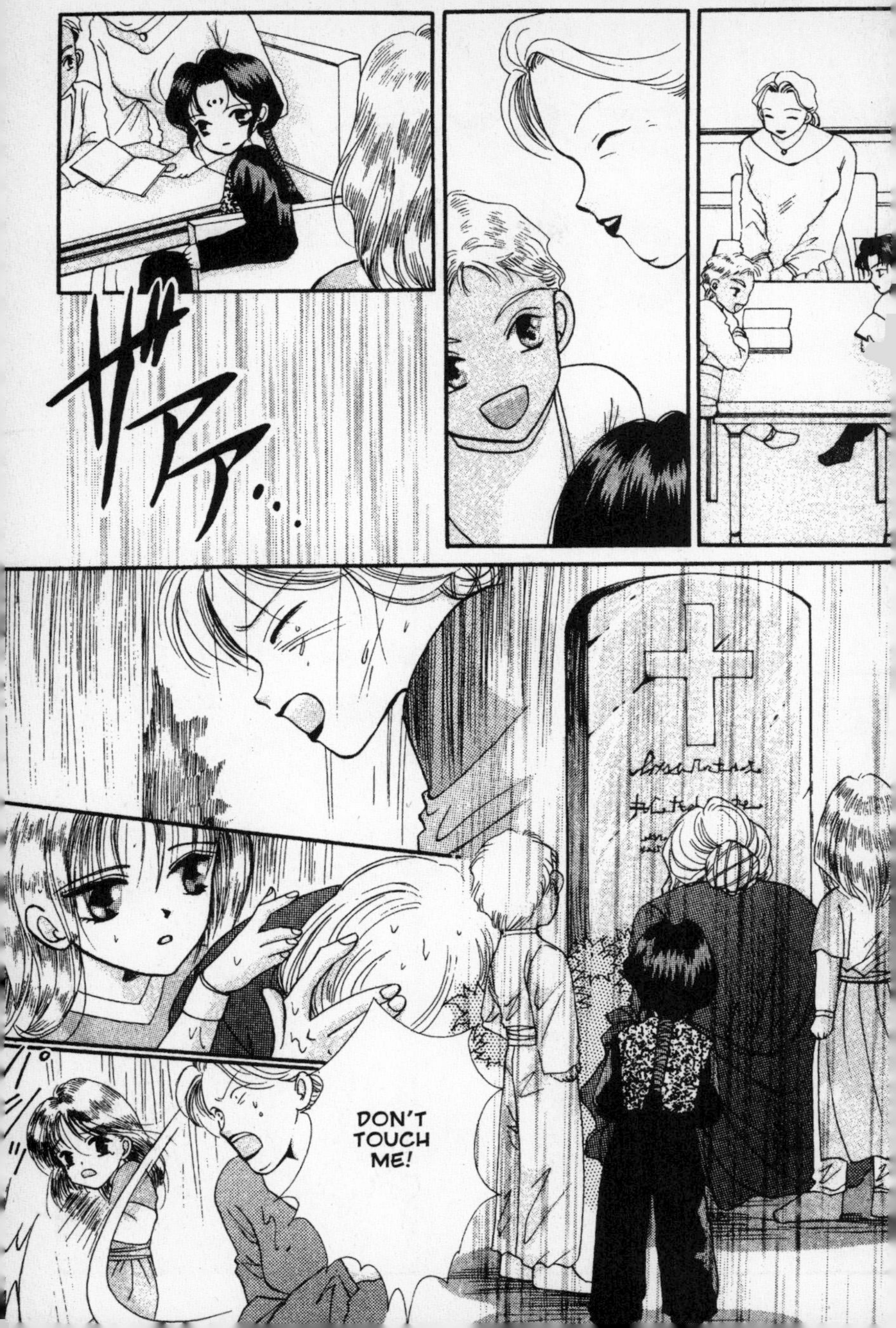

ザァア...
DON'T TOUCH ME!

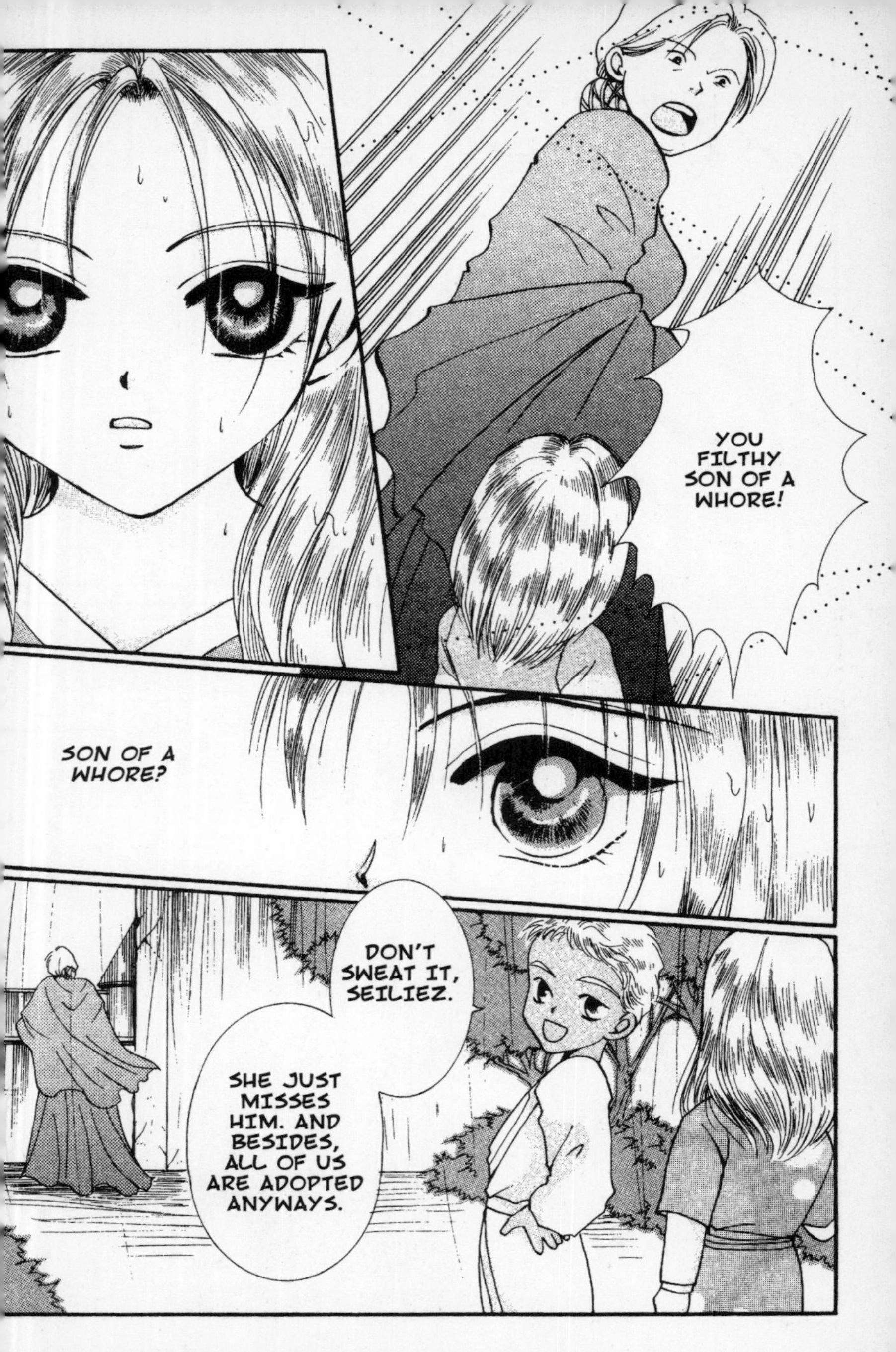
YOU FILTHY SON OF A WHORE!
SON OF A WHORE?
DON'T SWEAT IT, SEILIEZ.
SHE JUST MISSES HIM. AND BESIDES, ALL OF US ARE ADOPTED ANYWAYS.

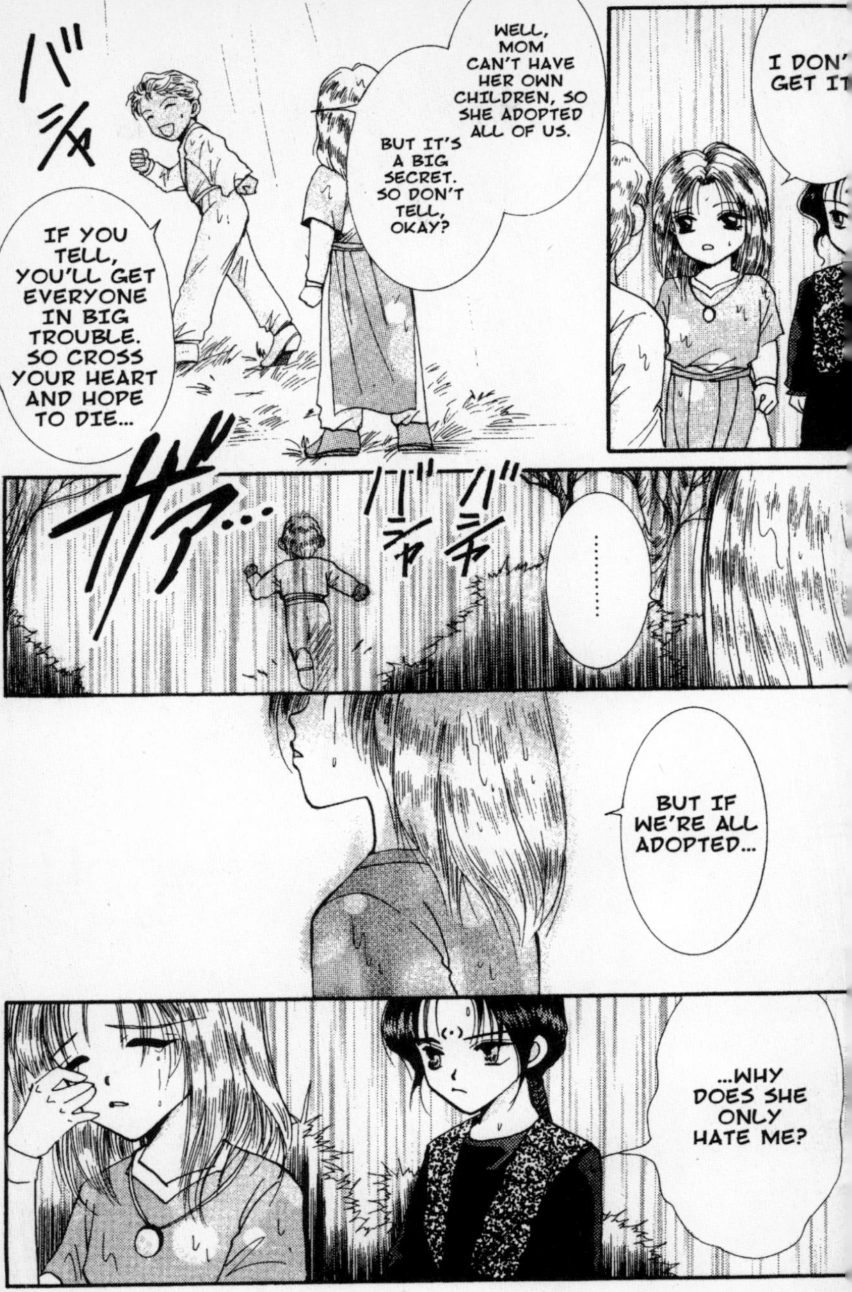
I DON' GET IT
バシャ
WELL, MOM CAN'T HAVE HER OWN CHILDREN, SO SHE ADOPTED ALL OF US.
BUT IT'S A BIG SECRET. SO DON'T TELL, OKAY?
IF YOU TELL, YOU'LL GET EVERYONE IN BIG TROUBLE. SO CROSS YOUR HEART AND HOPE TO DIE...
......
バシャバシャ
ザァ...
BUT IF WE'RE ALL ADOPTED...
...WHY DOES SHE ONLY HATE ME?

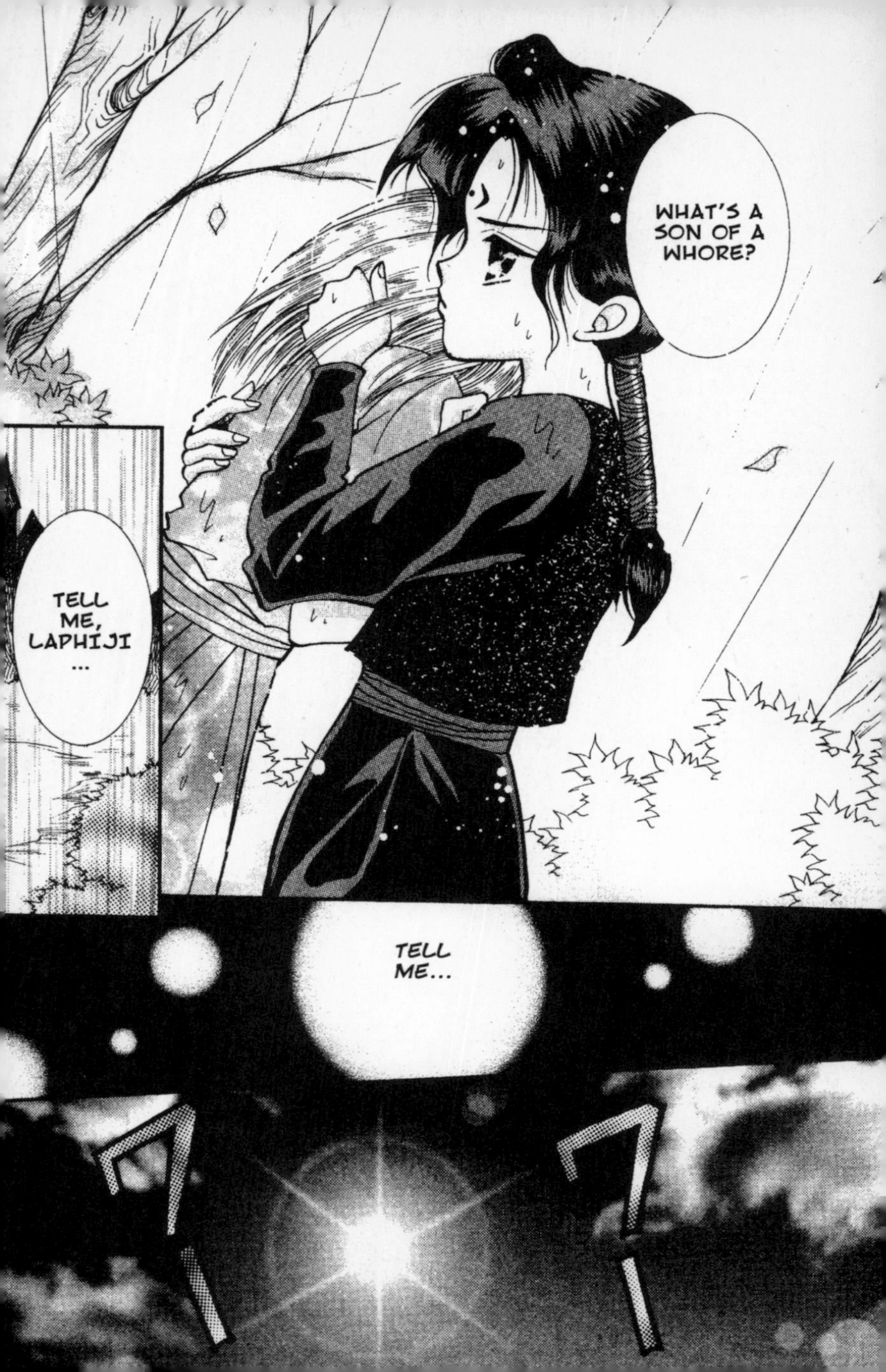
WHAT'S A SON OF A WHORE?
TELL ME, LAPHÍJI ...
TELL ME...

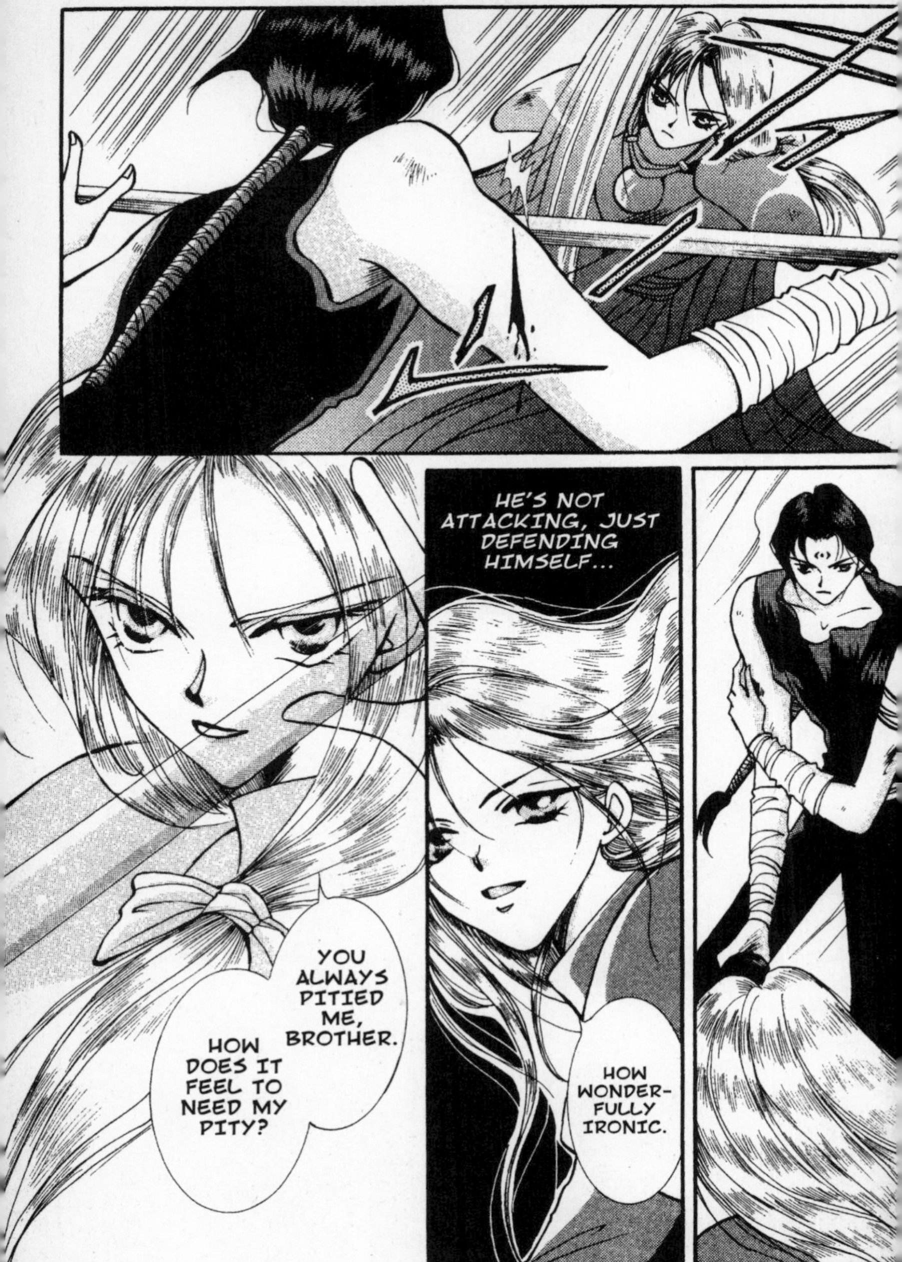
HE'S NOT ATTACKING, JUST DEFENDING HIMSELF...
HOW WONDERFULLY IRONIC.
YOU ALWAYS PITIED ME, BROTHER.
HOW DOES IT FEEL TO NEED MY PITY?

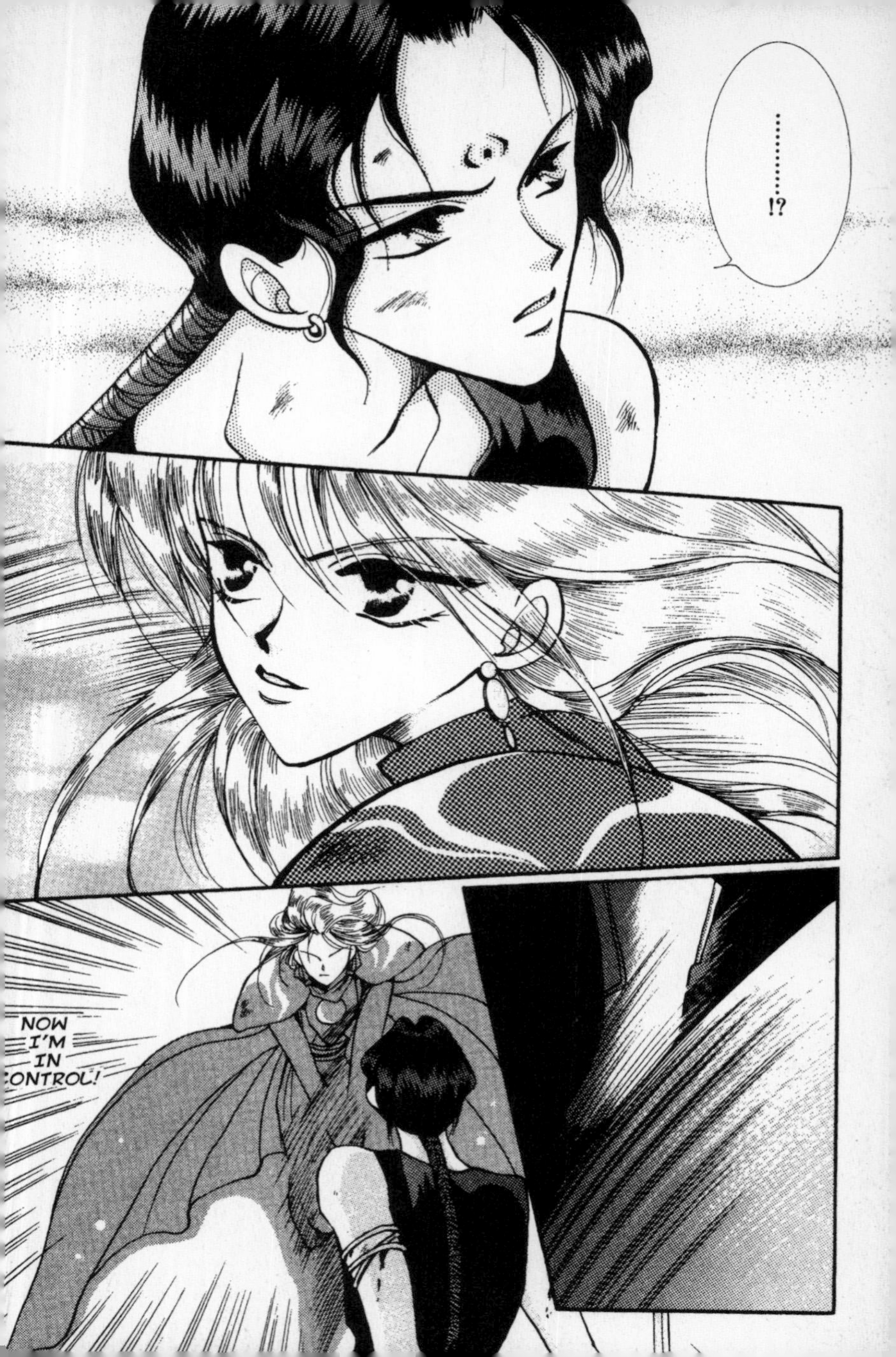
......!?
NOW I'M IN CONTROL!

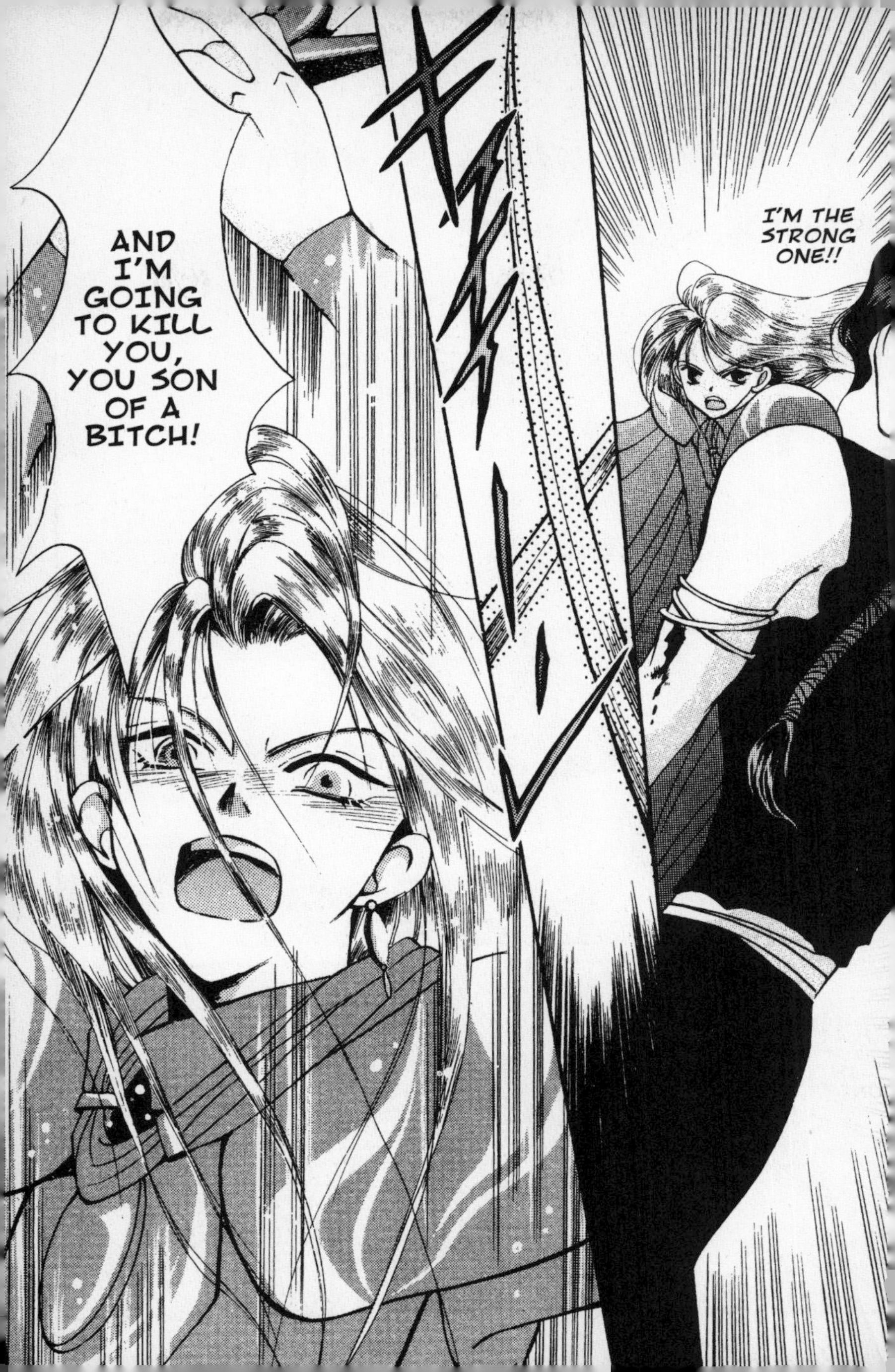
I'M THE STRONG ONE!!
AND I'M GOING TO KILL YOU, YOU SON OF A BITCH!

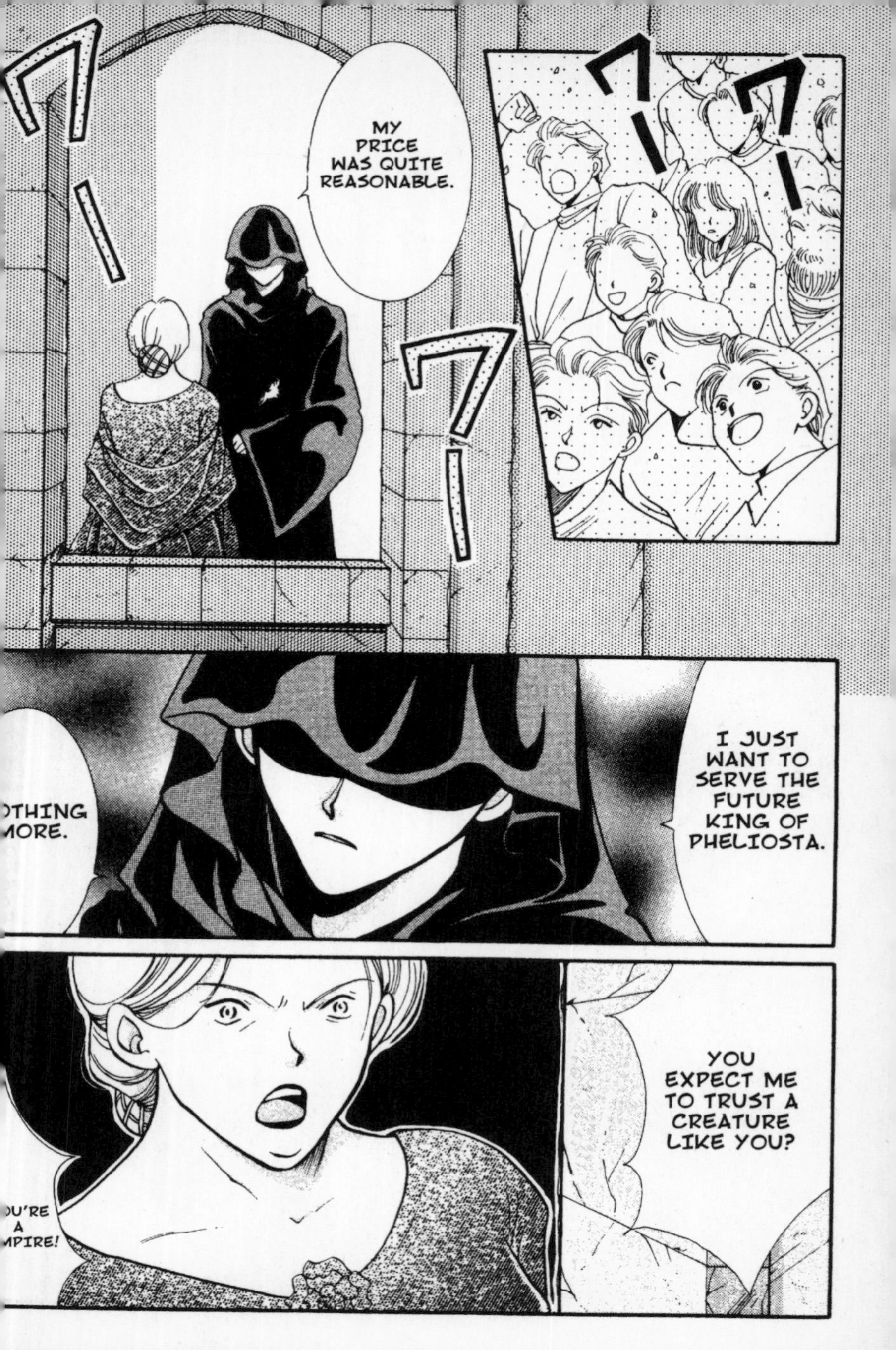
MY PRICE WAS QUITE REASONABLE.
I JUST WANT TO SERVE THE FUTURE KING OF PHELIOSTA.
OTHING MORE.
YOU EXPECT ME TO TRUST A CREATURE LIKE YOU?
U'RE A MPIRE!

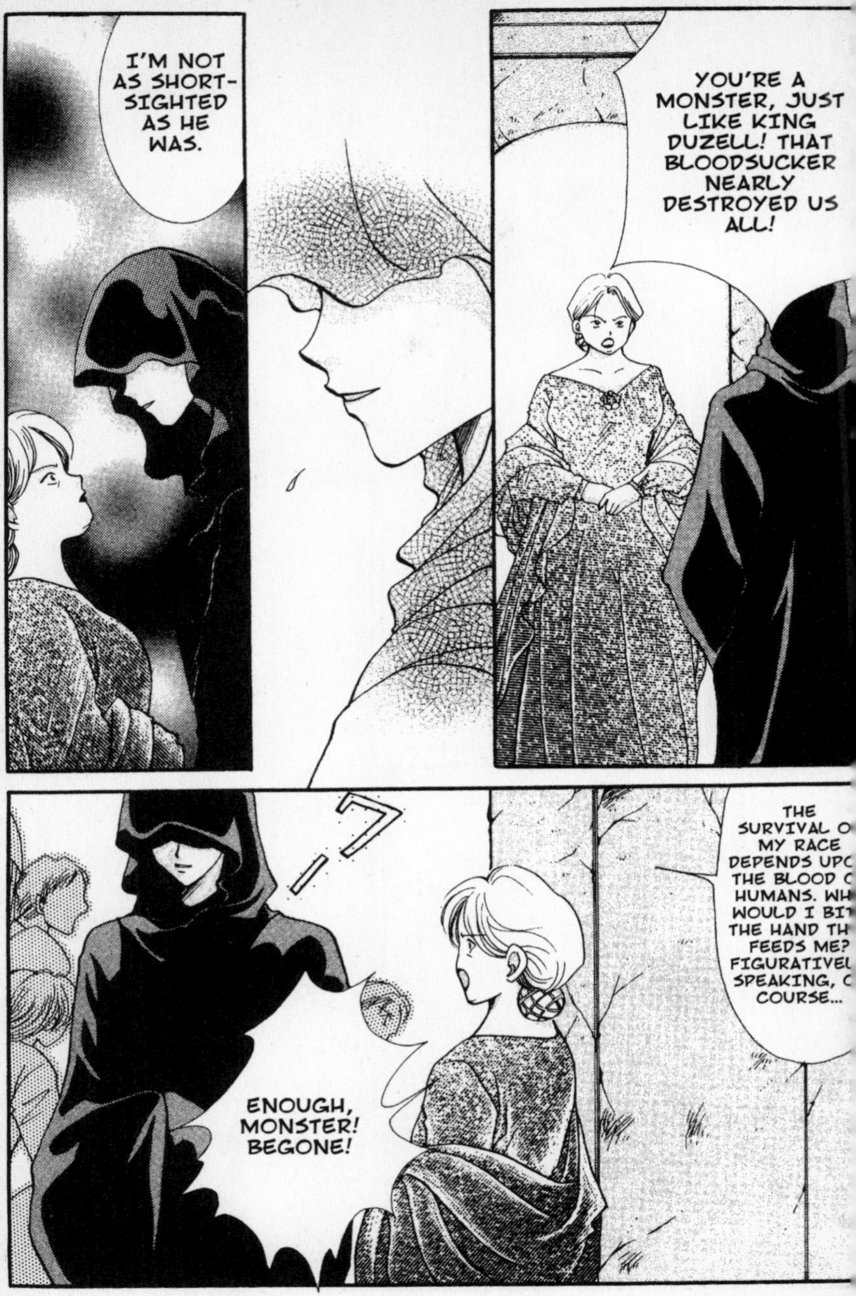
YOU'RE A MONSTER, JUST LIKE KING DUZELL! THAT BLOODSUCKER NEARLY DESTROYED US ALL!
I'M NOT AS SHORT-SIGHTED AS HE WAS.
THE SURVIVAL O MY RACE DEPENDS UPO THE BLOOD O HUMANS. WH WOULD I BIT THE HAND TH FEEDS ME? FIGURATIVEL SPEAKING, O COURSE...
ENOUGH, MONSTER! BEGONE!

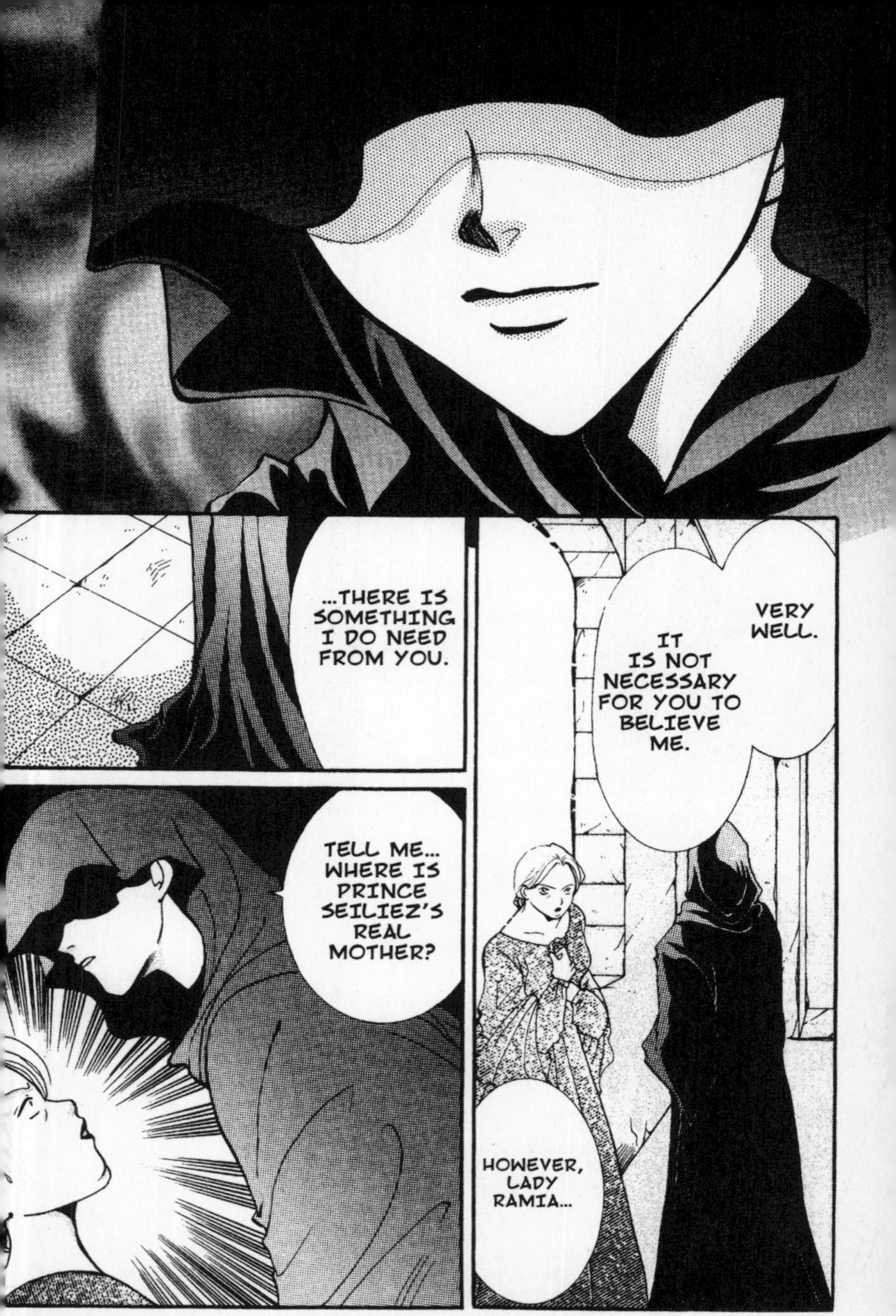
VERY WELL.
IT IS NOT NECESSARY FOR YOU TO BELIEVE ME.
HOWEVER, LADY RAMIA...
...THERE IS SOMETHING I DO NEED FROM YOU.
TELL ME... WHERE IS PRINCE SEILIEZ'S REAL MOTHER?

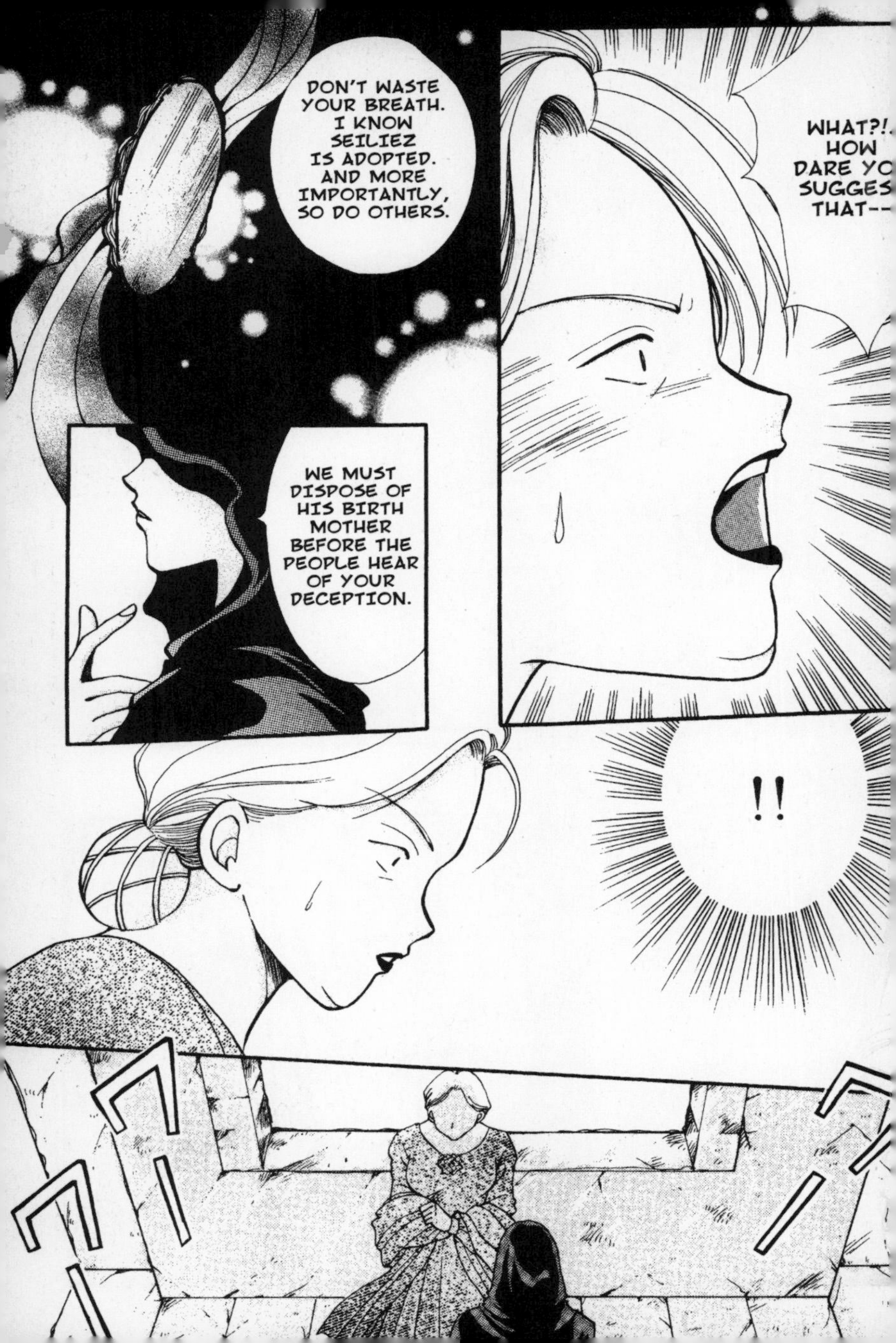
WHAT?!. HOW DARE YO SUGGES THAT--
DON'T WASTE YOUR BREATH. I KNOW SEILIEZ IS ADOPTED. AND MORE IMPORTANTLY, SO DO OTHERS.
WE MUST DISPOSE OF HIS BIRTH MOTHER BEFORE THE PEOPLE HEAR OF YOUR DECEPTION.
!!

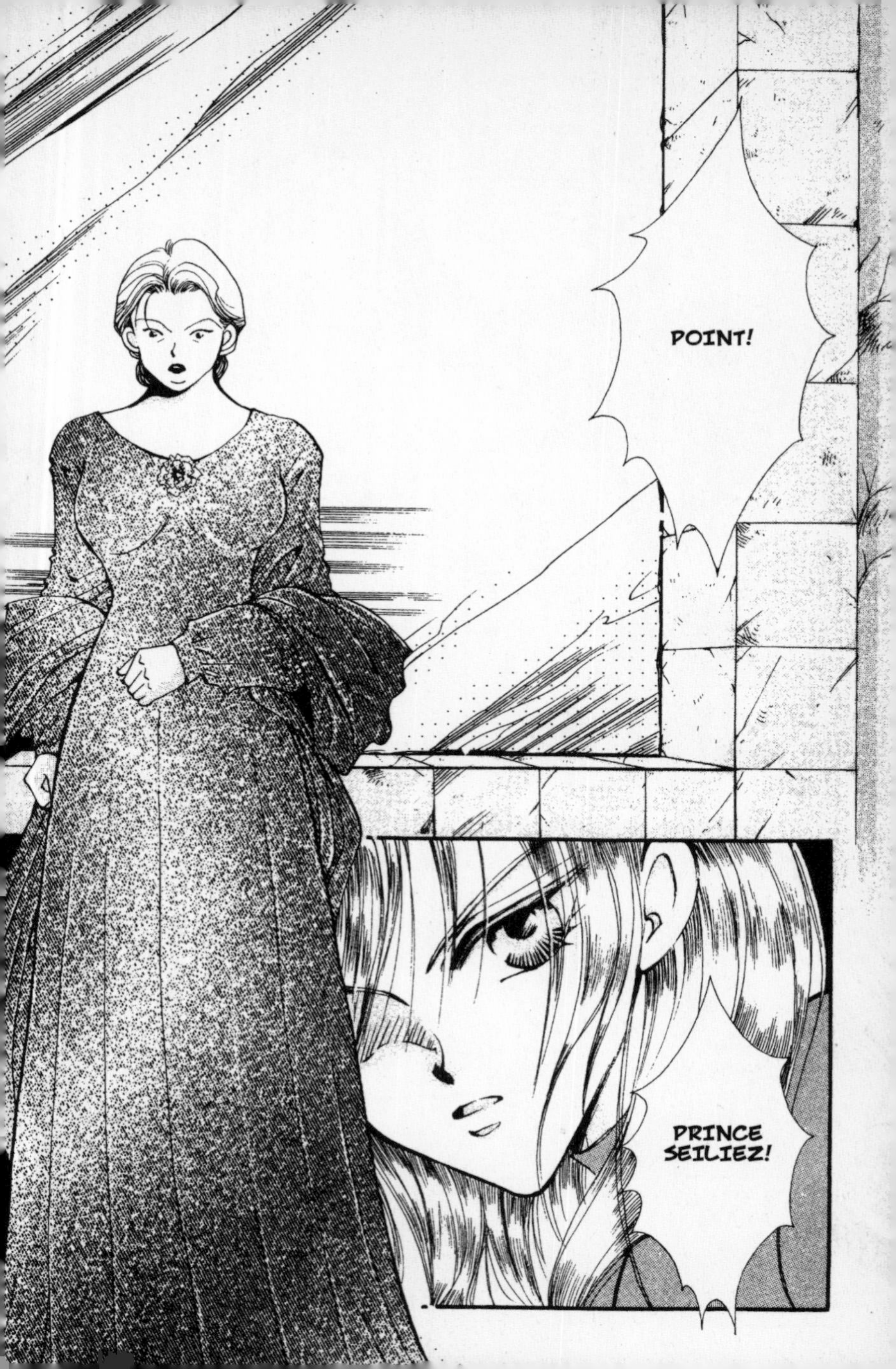
POINT!
PRINCE SEILIEZ!

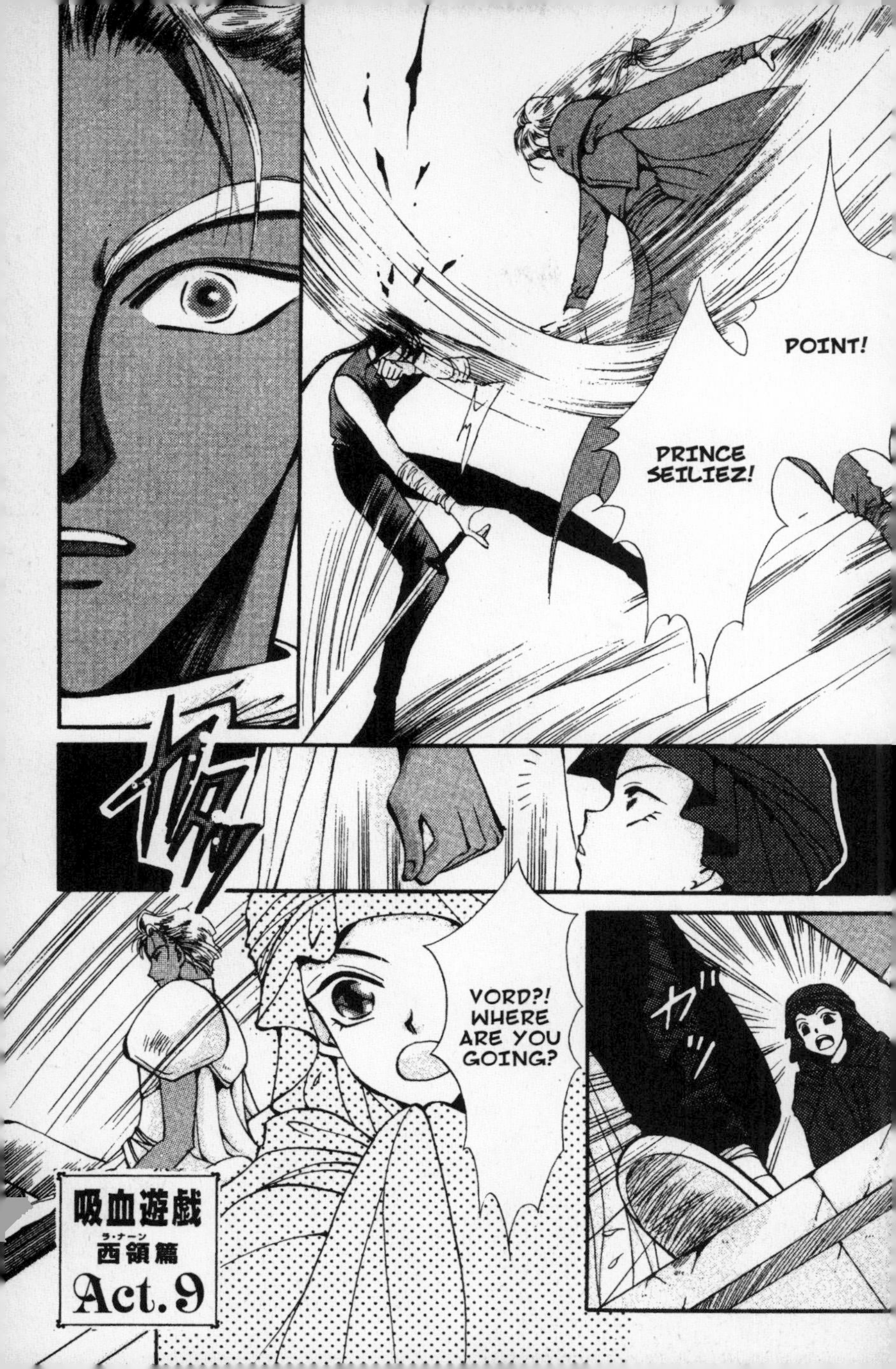
POINT!
PRINCE SEILIEZ!
VORD?! WHERE ARE YOU GOING?
吸血遊戯
ラ・ナーン
西領篇
Act. 9

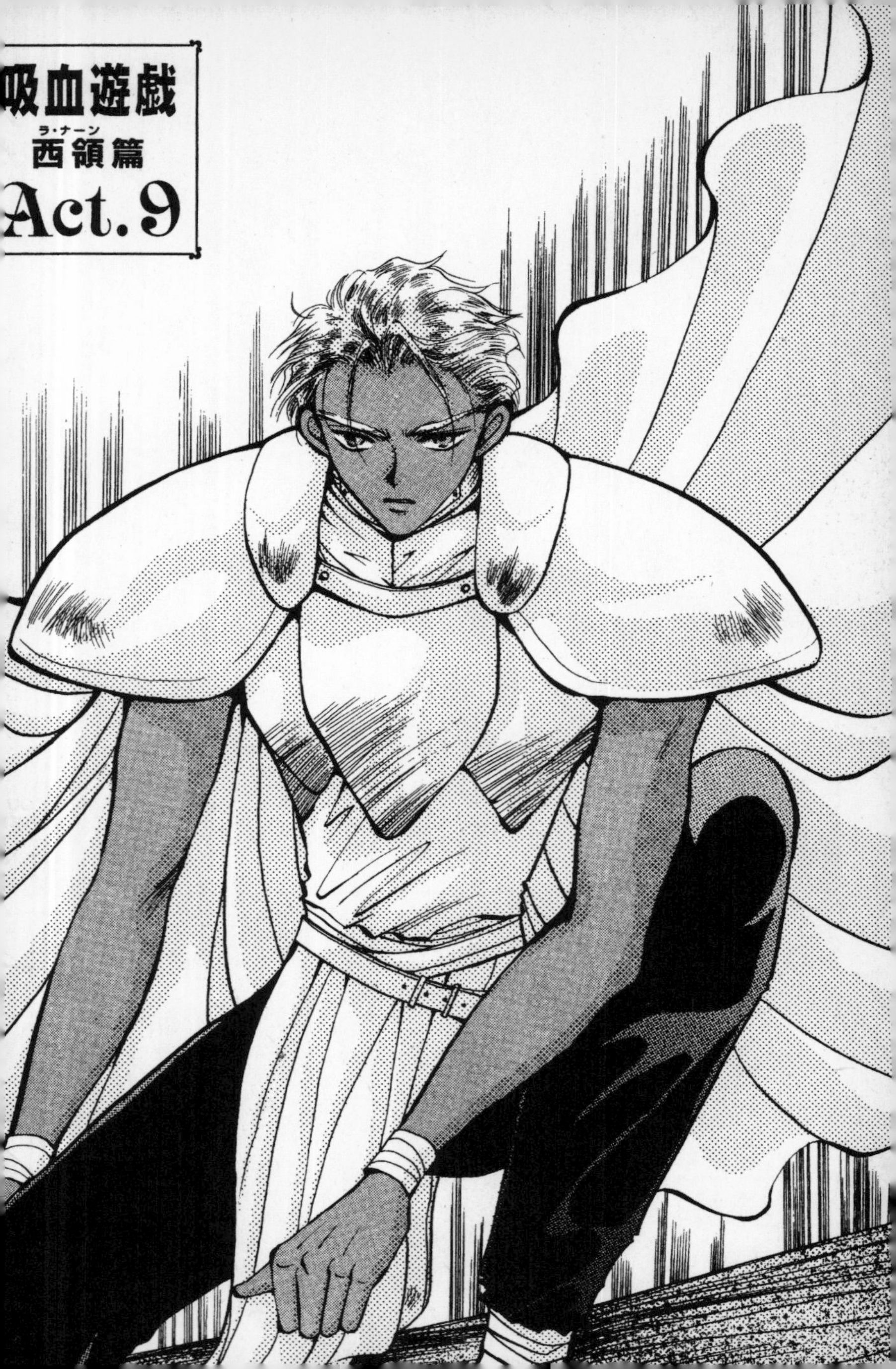
吸血遊戯
西領篇
ラ・ナーン
Act.9

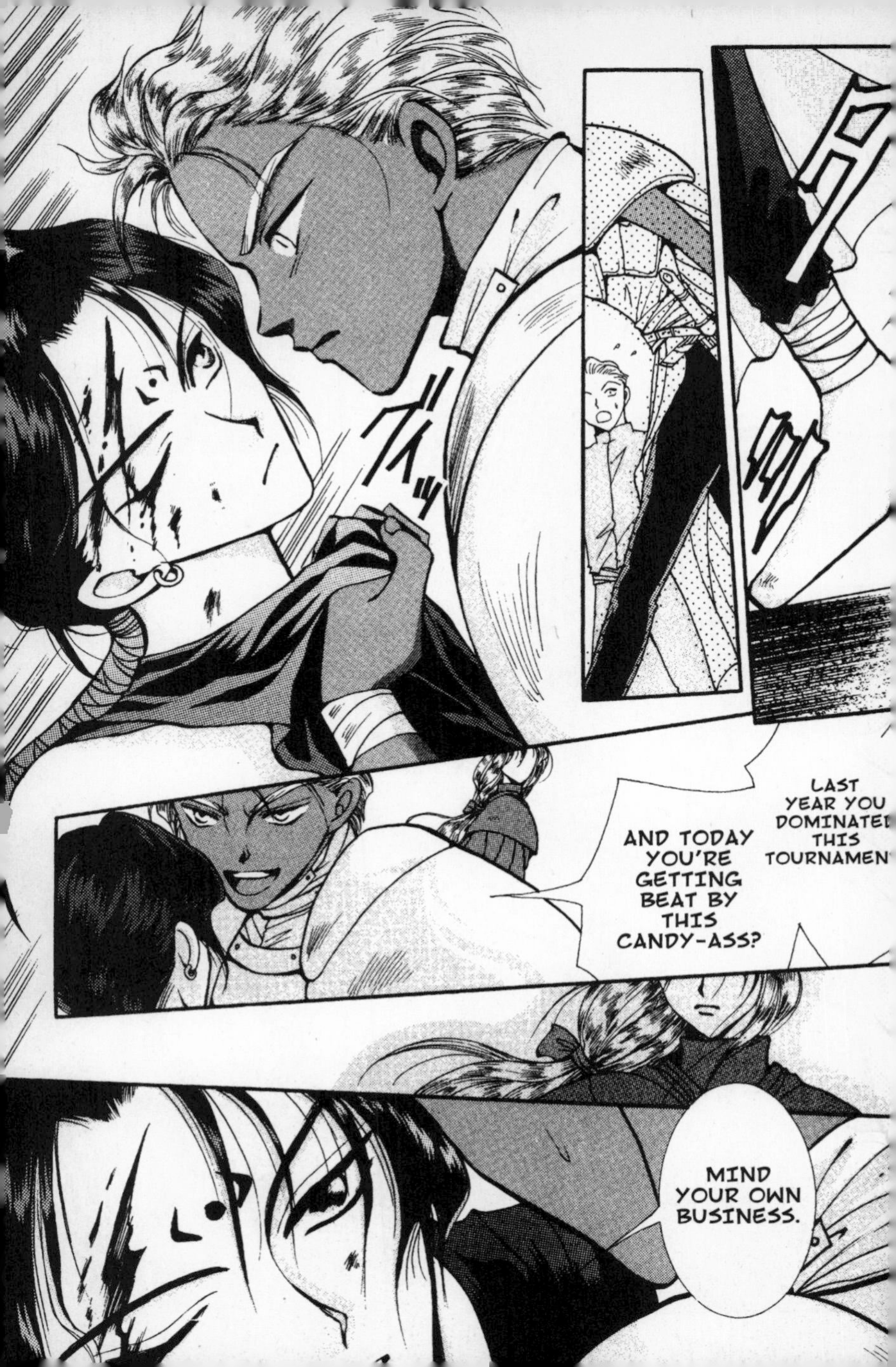
LAST YEAR YOU DOMINATE THIS TOURNAMEN
AND TODAY YOU'RE GETTING BEAT BY THIS CANDY-ASS?
MIND YOUR OWN BUSINESS.

THIS IS MY BUSINESS.

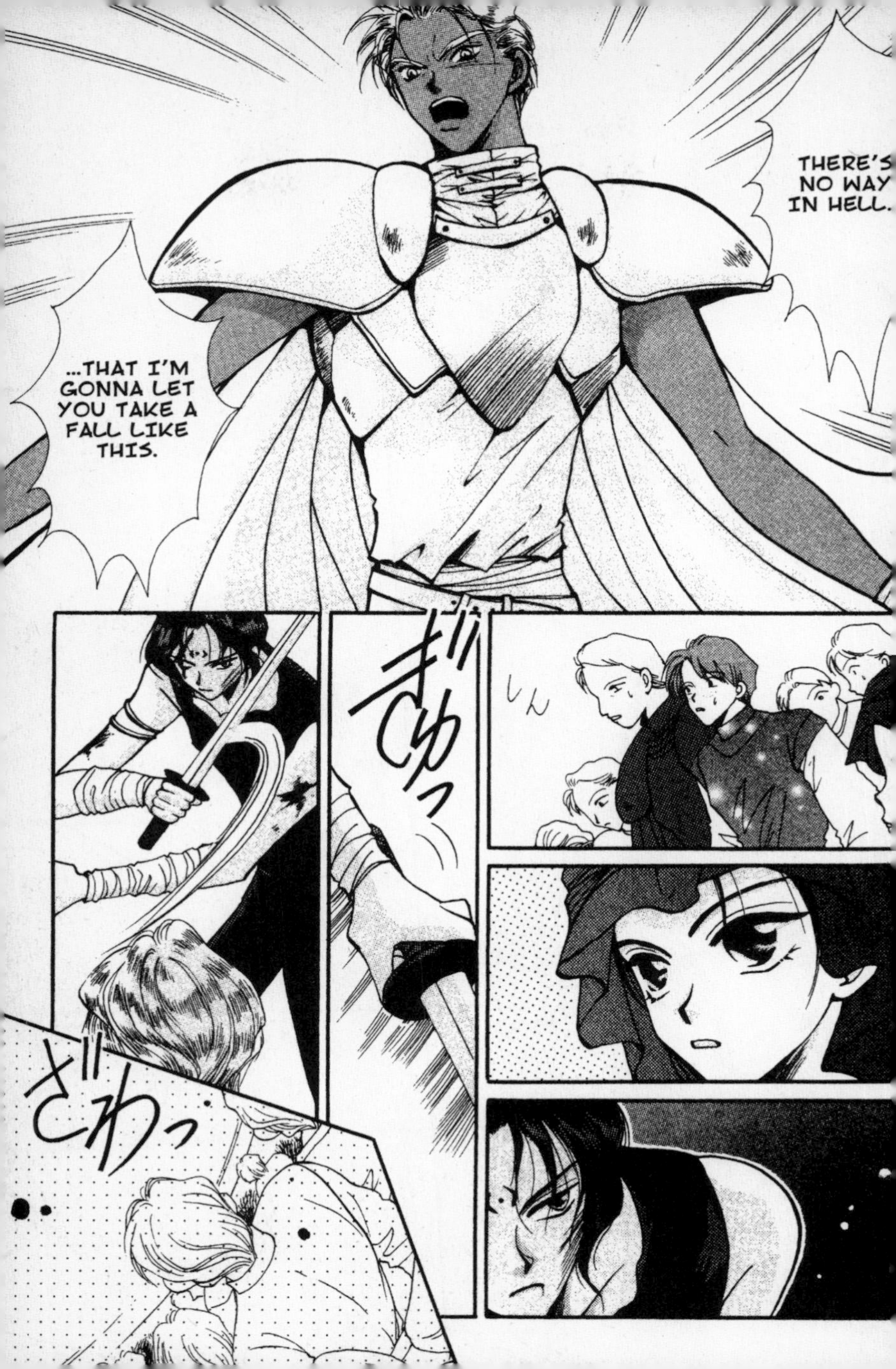
THERE'S NO WAY IN HELL.
...THAT I'M GONNA LET YOU TAKE A FALL LIKE THIS.
しん
ぎゅっ
ざわっ

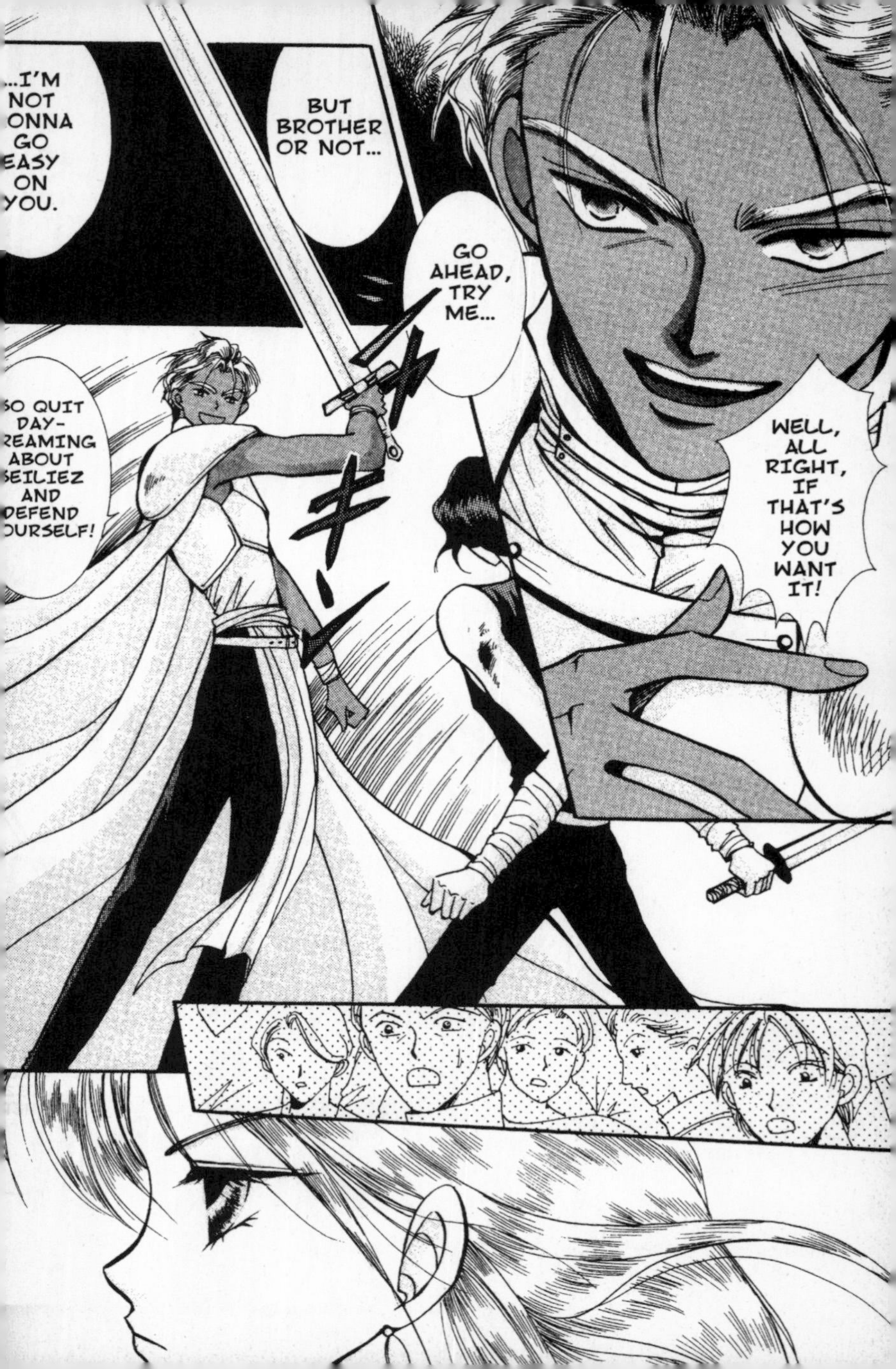
GO AHEAD, TRY ME...
WELL, ALL RIGHT, IF THAT'S HOW YOU WANT IT!
BUT BROTHER OR NOT...
...I'M NOT ONNA GO EASY ON YOU.
SO QUIT DAY-REAMING ABOUT SEILIEZ AND DEFEND OURSELF!

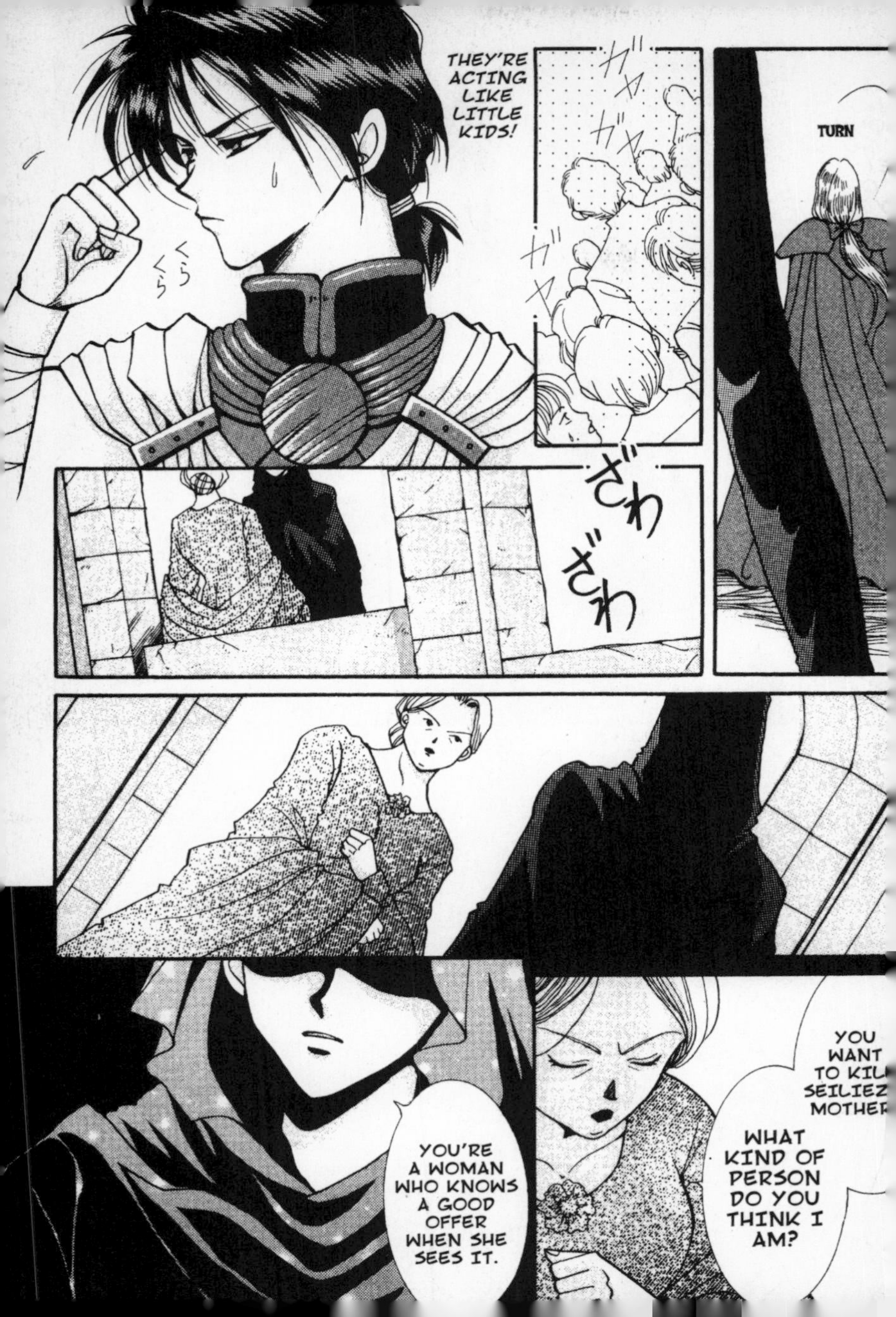
TURN
ガヤガヤ
ガヤ
THEY'RE ACTING LIKE LITTLE KIDS!
くらくら
ざわざわ
YOU WANT TO KIL SEILIEZ MOTHER
WHAT KIND OF PERSON DO YOU THINK I AM?
YOU'RE A WOMAN WHO KNOWS A GOOD OFFER WHEN SHE SEES IT.

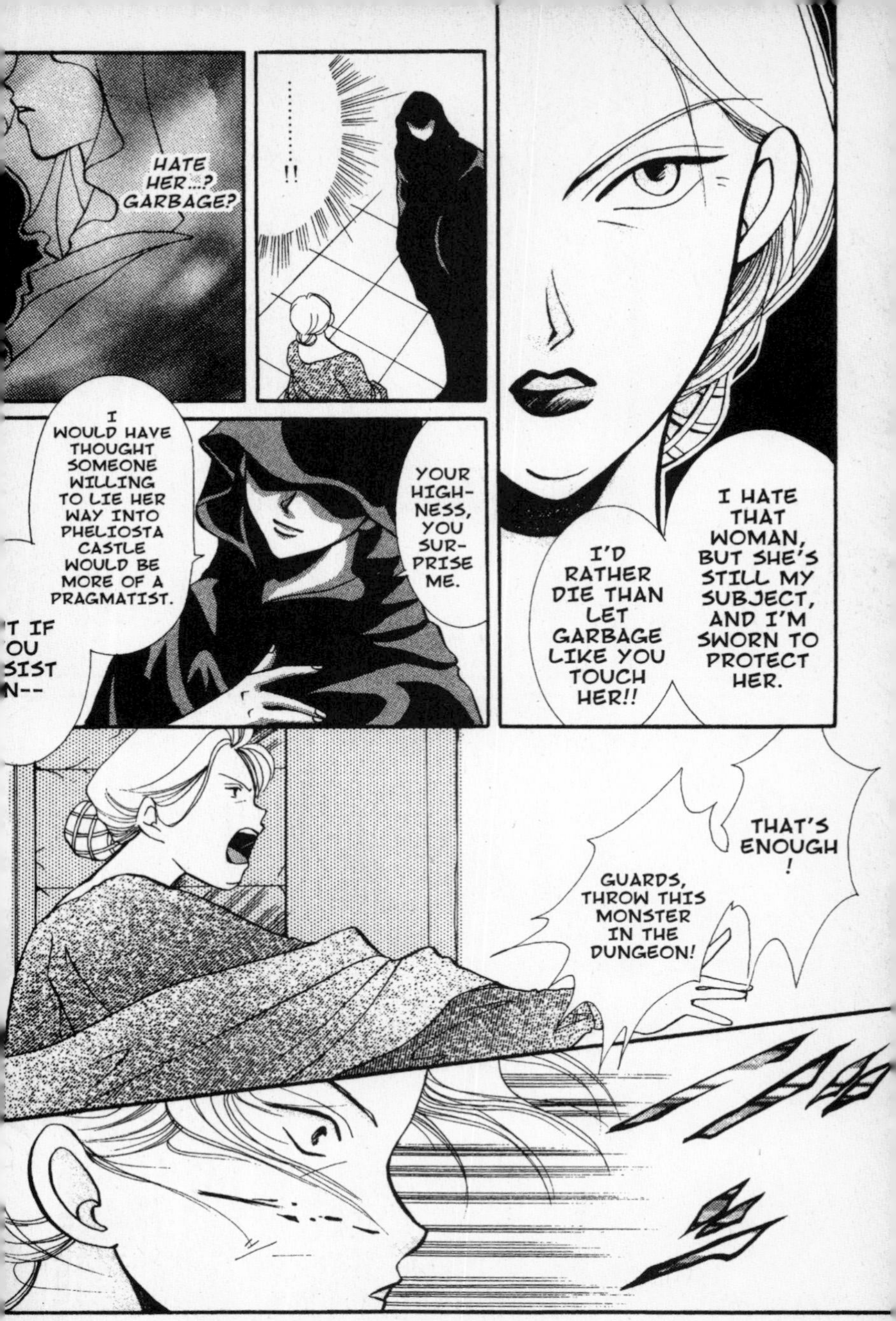

I HATE THAT WOMAN, BUT SHE'S STILL MY SUBJECT, AND I'M SWORN TO PROTECT HER.
I'D RATHER DIE THAN LET GARBAGE LIKE YOU TOUCH HER!!
......!!
HATE HER...? GARBAGE?
YOUR HIGHNESS, YOU SURPRISE ME.
I WOULD HAVE THOUGHT SOMEONE WILLING TO LIE HER WAY INTO PHELIOSTA CASTLE WOULD BE MORE OF A PRAGMATIST.
T IF OU SIST N--
THAT'S ENOUGH!
GUARDS, THROW THIS MONSTER IN THE DUNGEON!

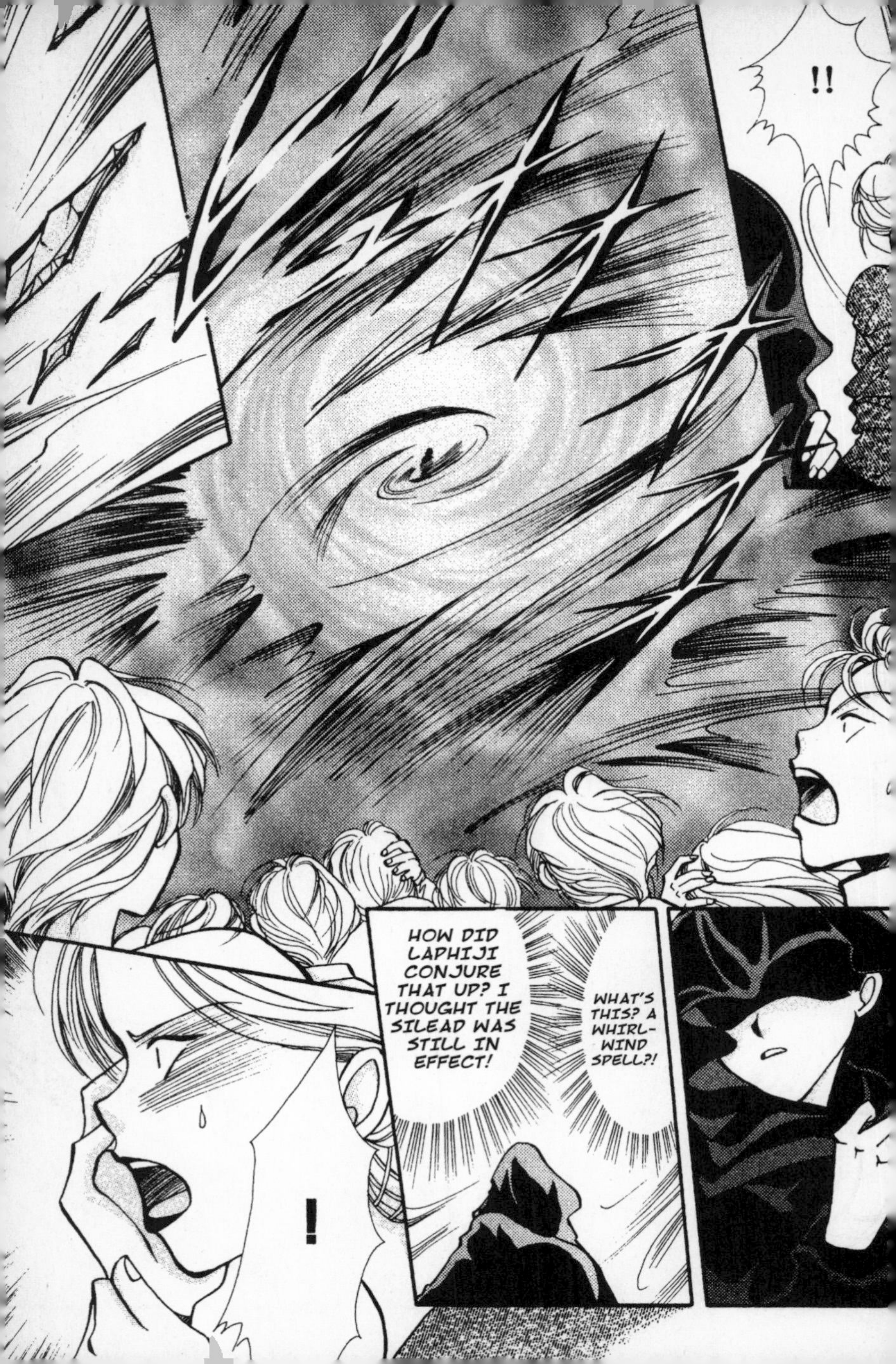
!!
WHAT'S THIS? A WHIRL-WIND SPELL?!
HOW DID LAPHIJI CONJURE THAT UP? I THOUGHT THE SILEAD WAS STILL IN EFFECT!
!

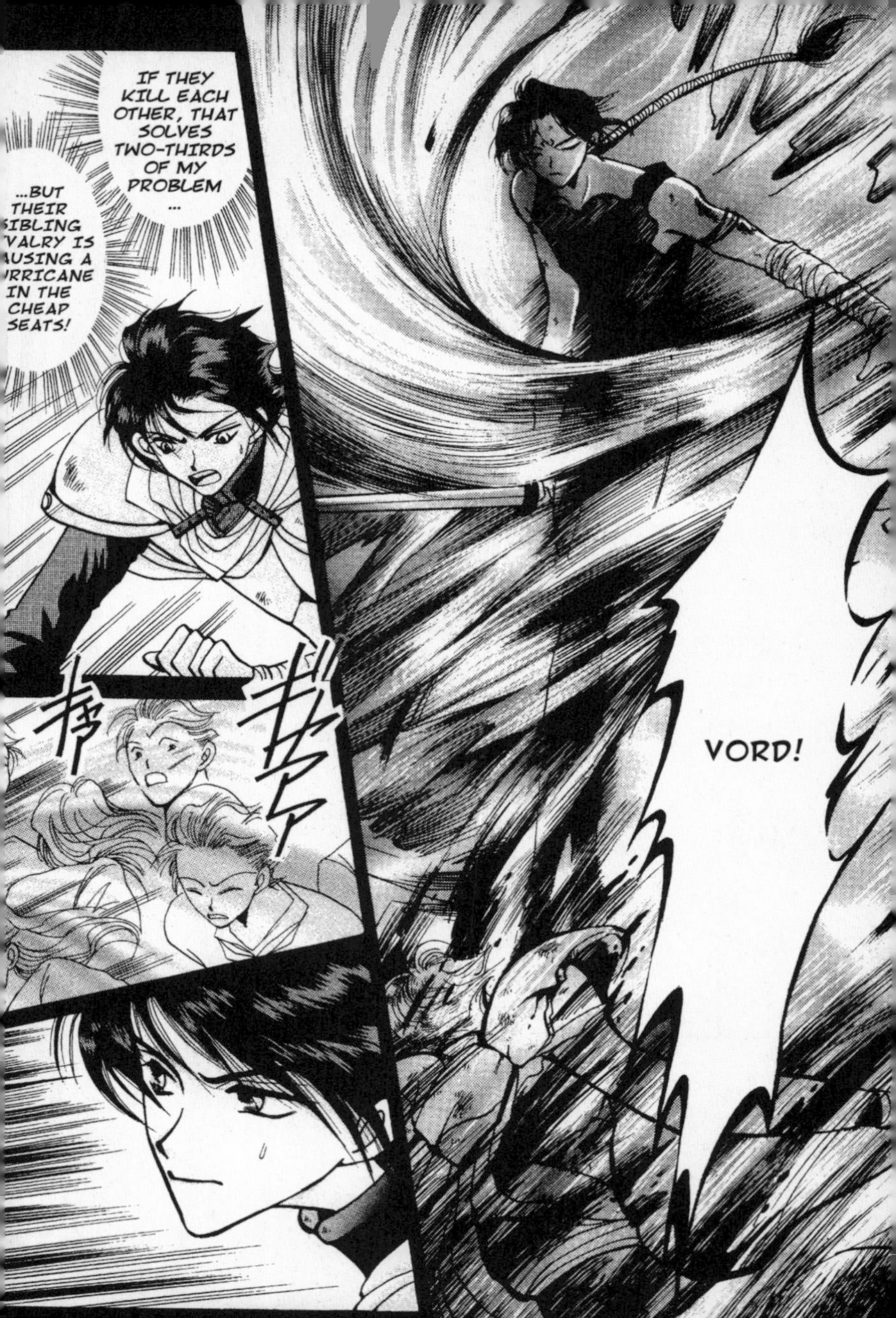
VORD!
IF THEY KILL EACH OTHER, THAT SOLVES TWO-THIRDS OF MY PROBLEM ...
...BUT THEIR SIBLING VALRY IS AUSING A URRICANE IN THE CHEAP SEATS!

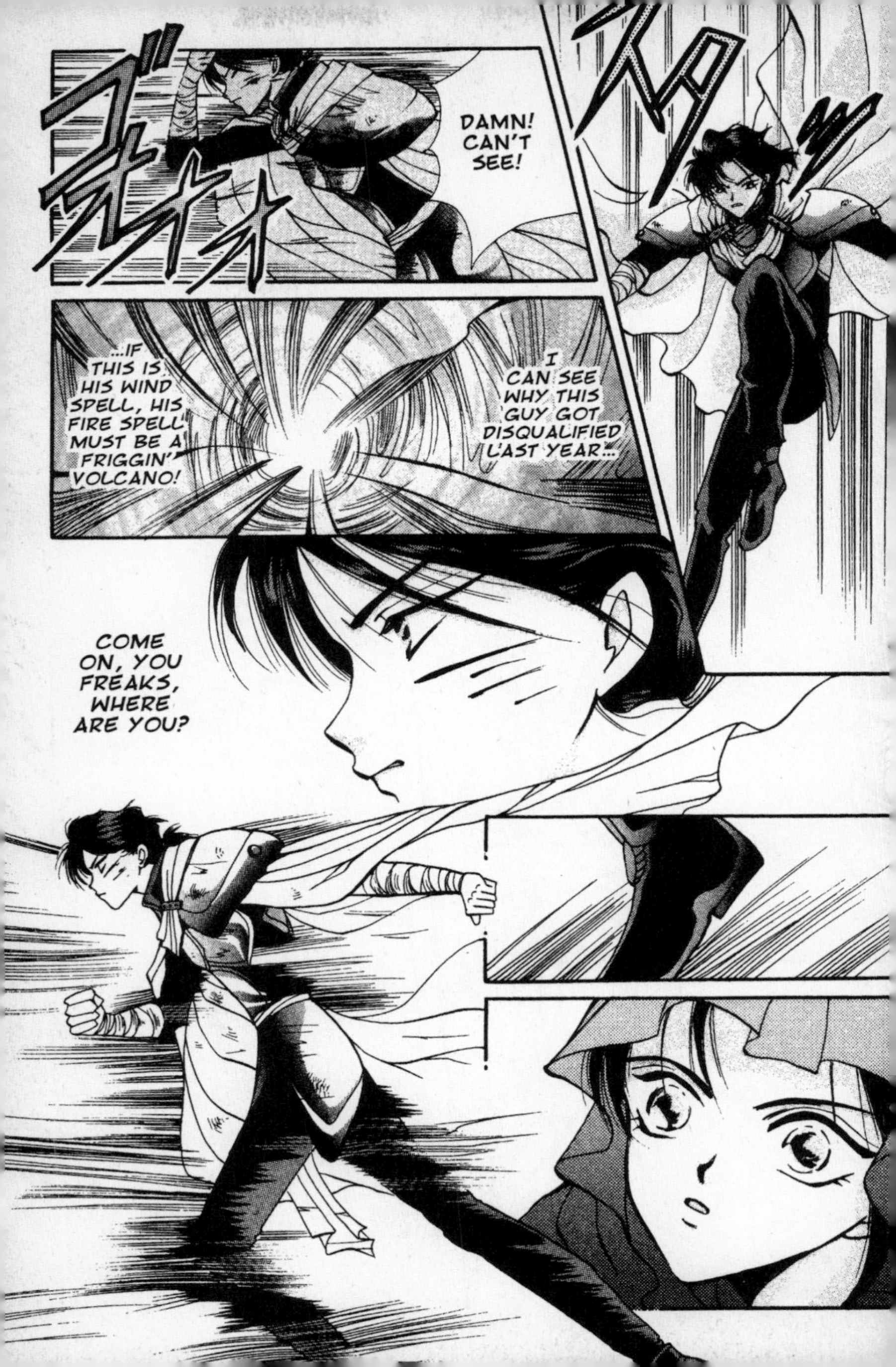
DAMN! CAN'T SEE!
I CAN SEE WHY THIS GUY GOT DISQUALIFIED LAST YEAR...
...IF THIS IS HIS WIND SPELL, HIS FIRE SPELL MUST BE A FRIGGIN' VOLCANO!
COME ON, YOU FREAKS, WHERE ARE YOU?

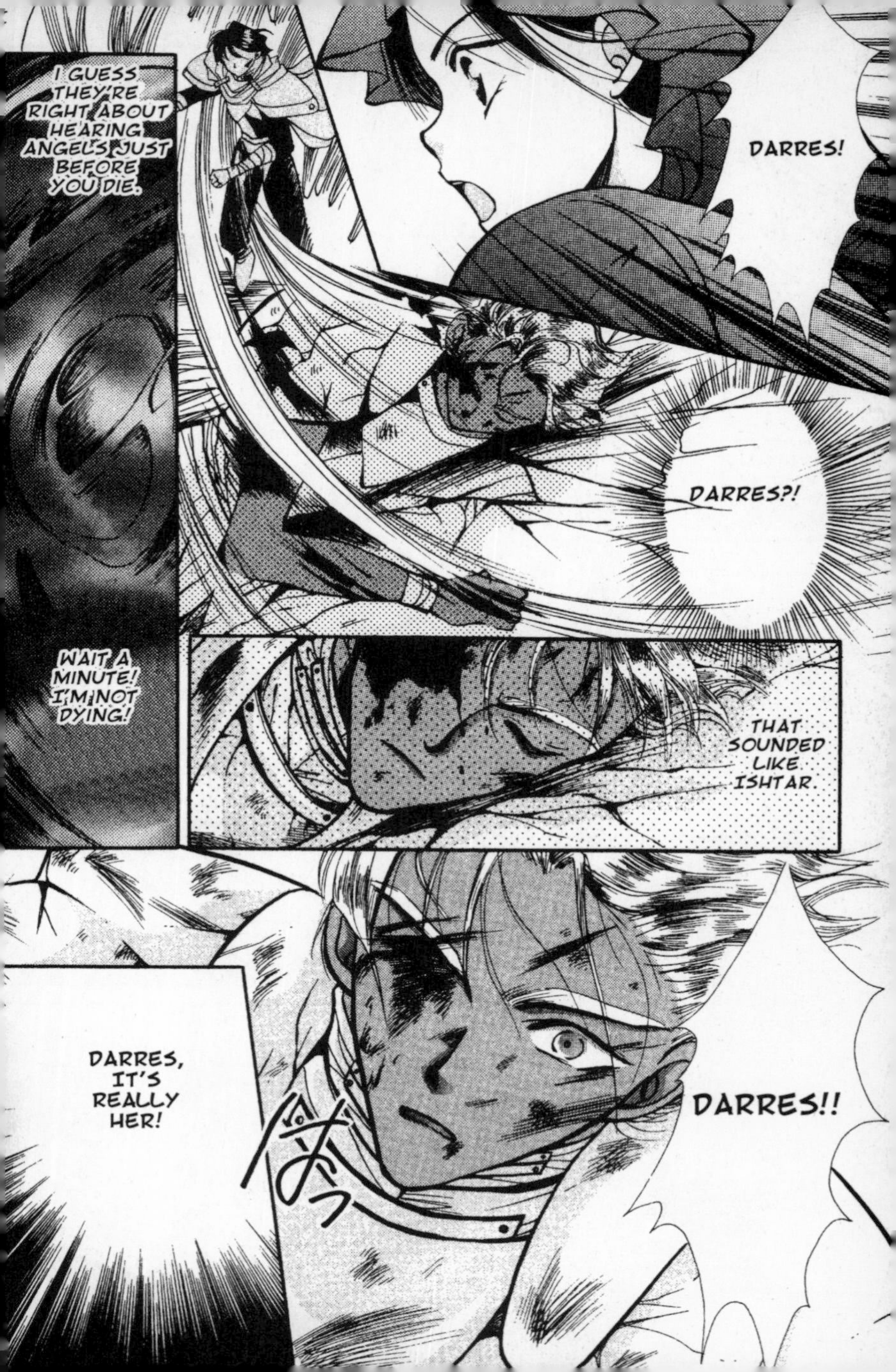
DARRES!
DARRES?!
THAT SOUNDED LIKE ISHTAR.
I GUESS THEY'RE RIGHT ABOUT HEARING ANGELS JUST BEFORE YOU DIE.
WAIT A MINUTE! I'M NOT DYING!
DARRES!!
DARRES, IT'S REALLY HER!

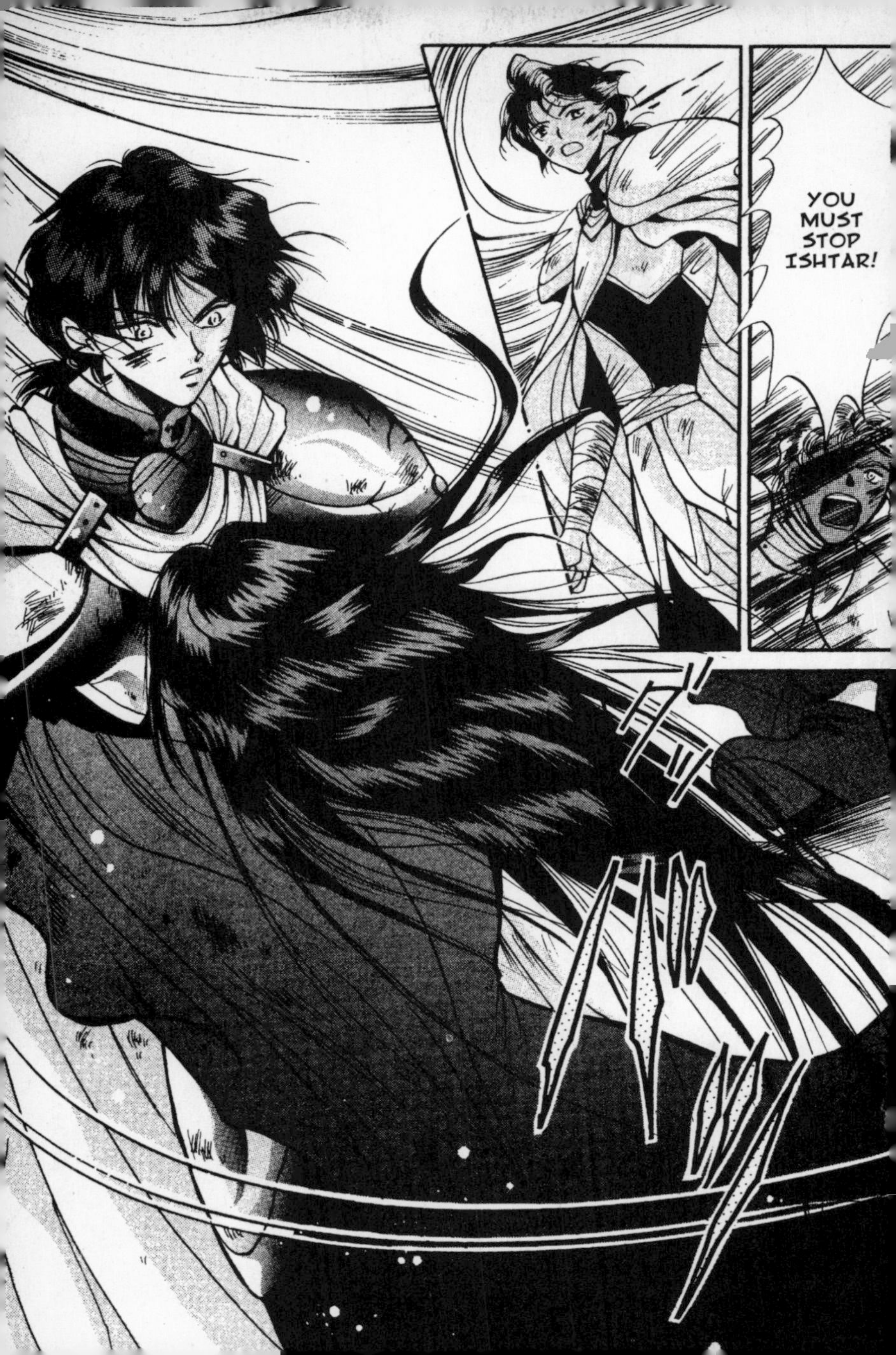
YOU MUST STOP ISHTAR!

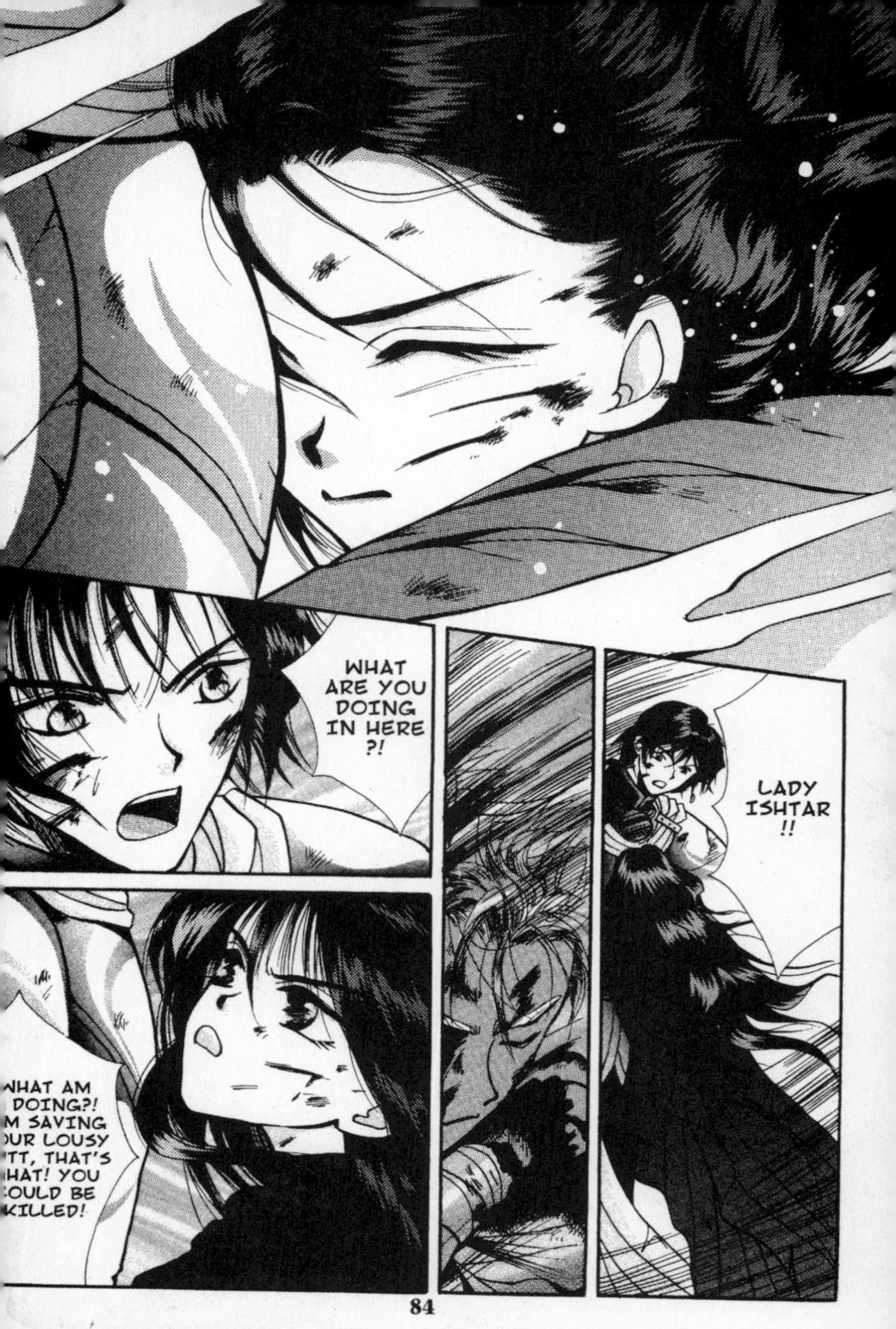
LADY ISHTAR !!
WHAT ARE YOU DOING IN HERE ?!
WHAT AM DOING?! M SAVING OUR LOUSY TT, THAT'S HAT! YOU COULD BE KILLED!

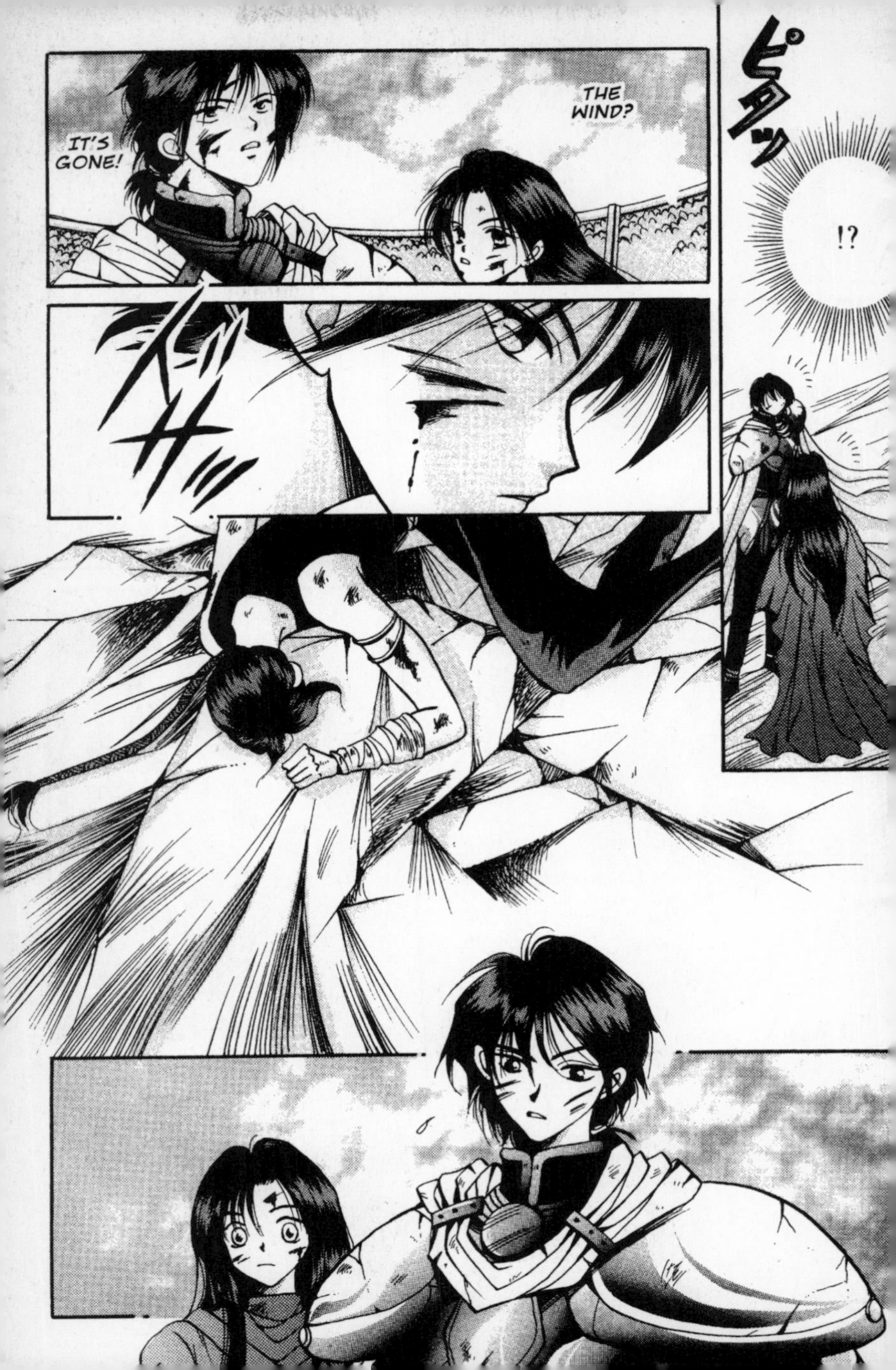
ピタッ
!?
THE WIND?
IT'S GONE!
ズザ

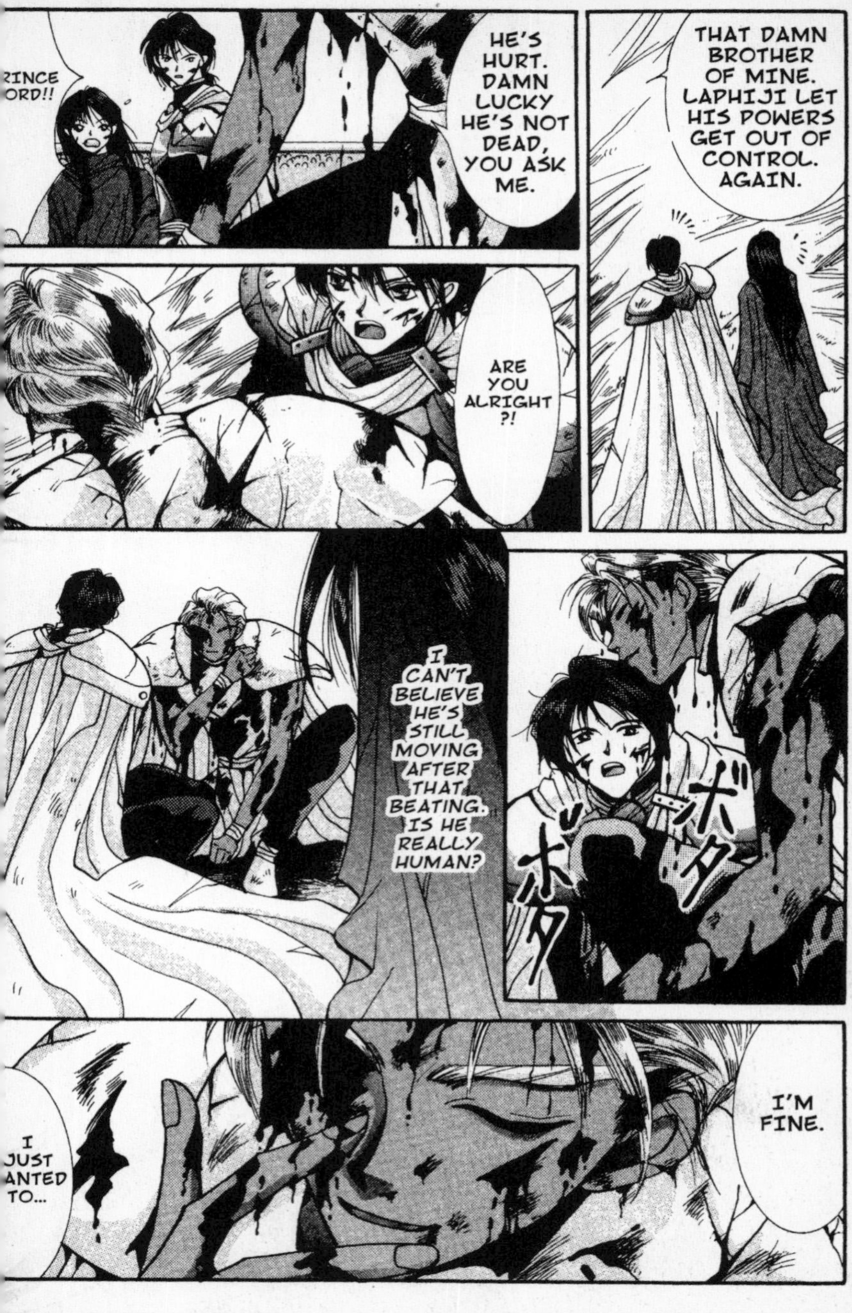
THAT DAMN BROTHER OF MINE. LAPHIJI LET HIS POWERS GET OUT OF CONTROL. AGAIN.
HE'S HURT. DAMN LUCKY HE'S NOT DEAD, YOU ASK ME.
RINCE ORD!!
ARE YOU ALRIGHT ?!
ボタ
ボタ
I CAN'T BELIEVE HE'S STILL MOVING AFTER THAT BEATING. IS HE REALLY HUMAN?
I'M FINE.
I JUST ANTED TO...

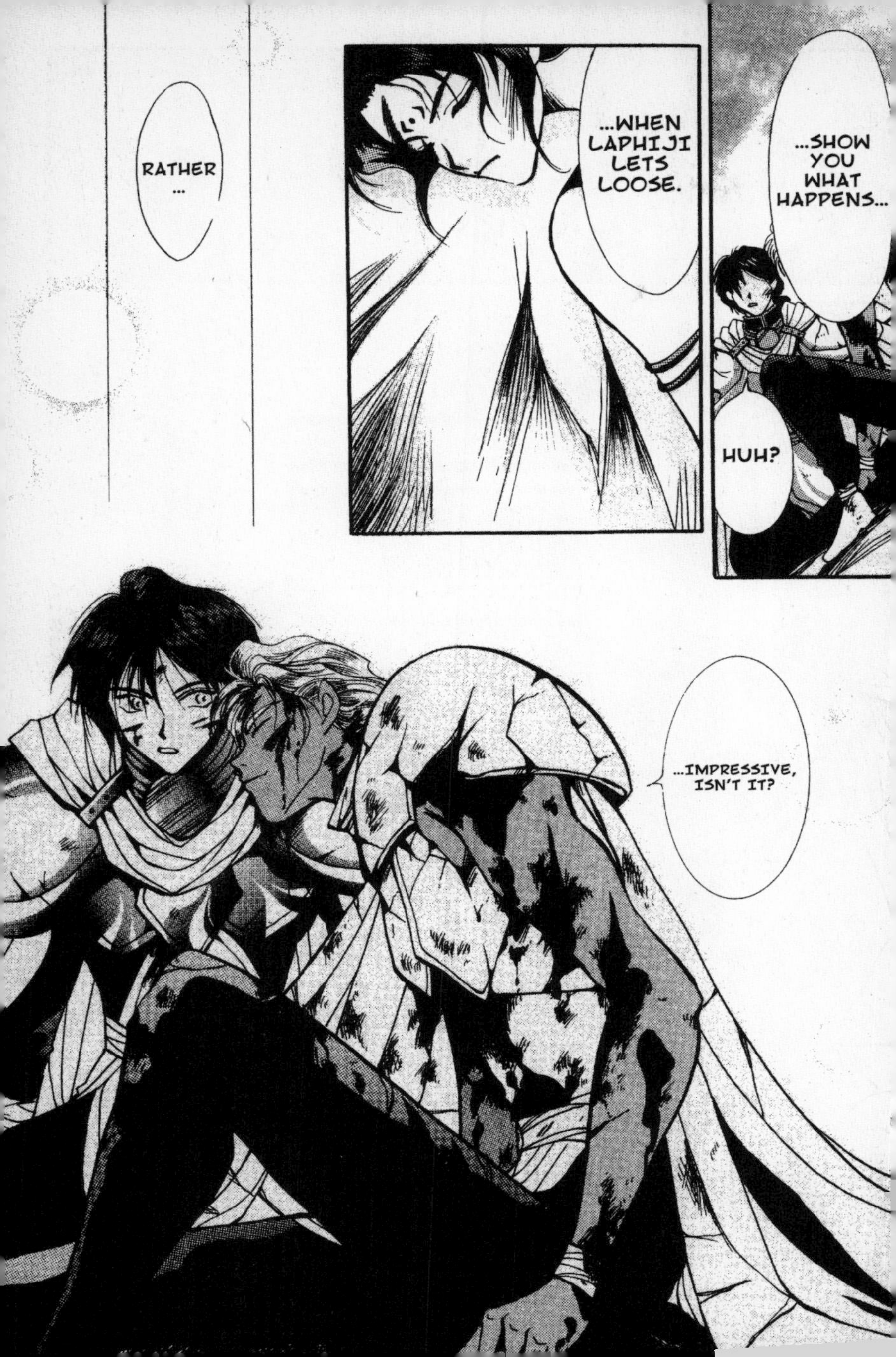
...SHOW YOU WHAT HAPPENS...
HUH?
...WHEN LAPHIJI LETS LOOSE.
RATHER ...
...IMPRESSIVE, ISN'T IT?

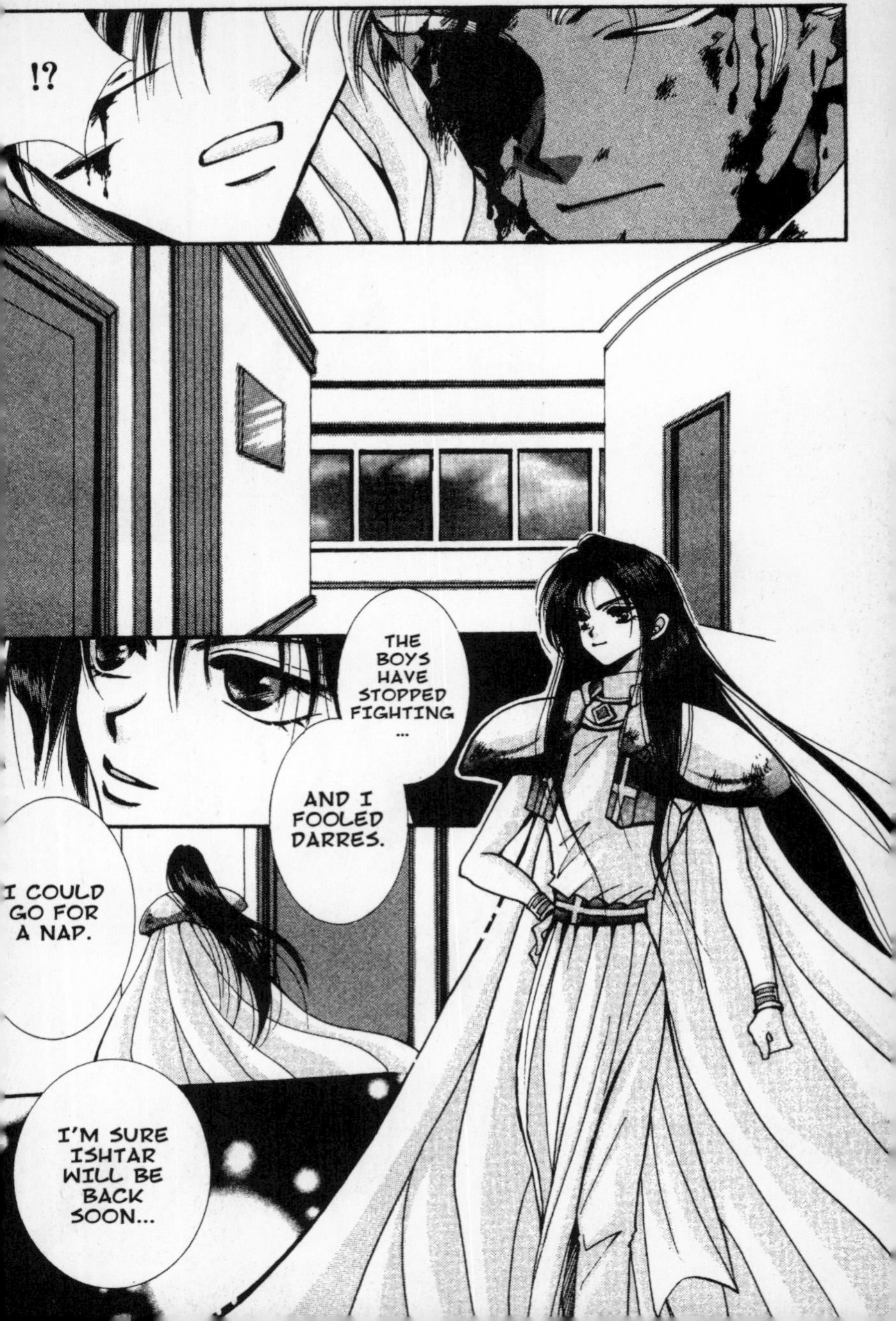
!?
THE BOYS HAVE STOPPED FIGHTING...
AND I FOOLED DARRES.
I COULD GO FOR A NAP.
I'M SURE ISHTAR WILL BE BACK SOON...

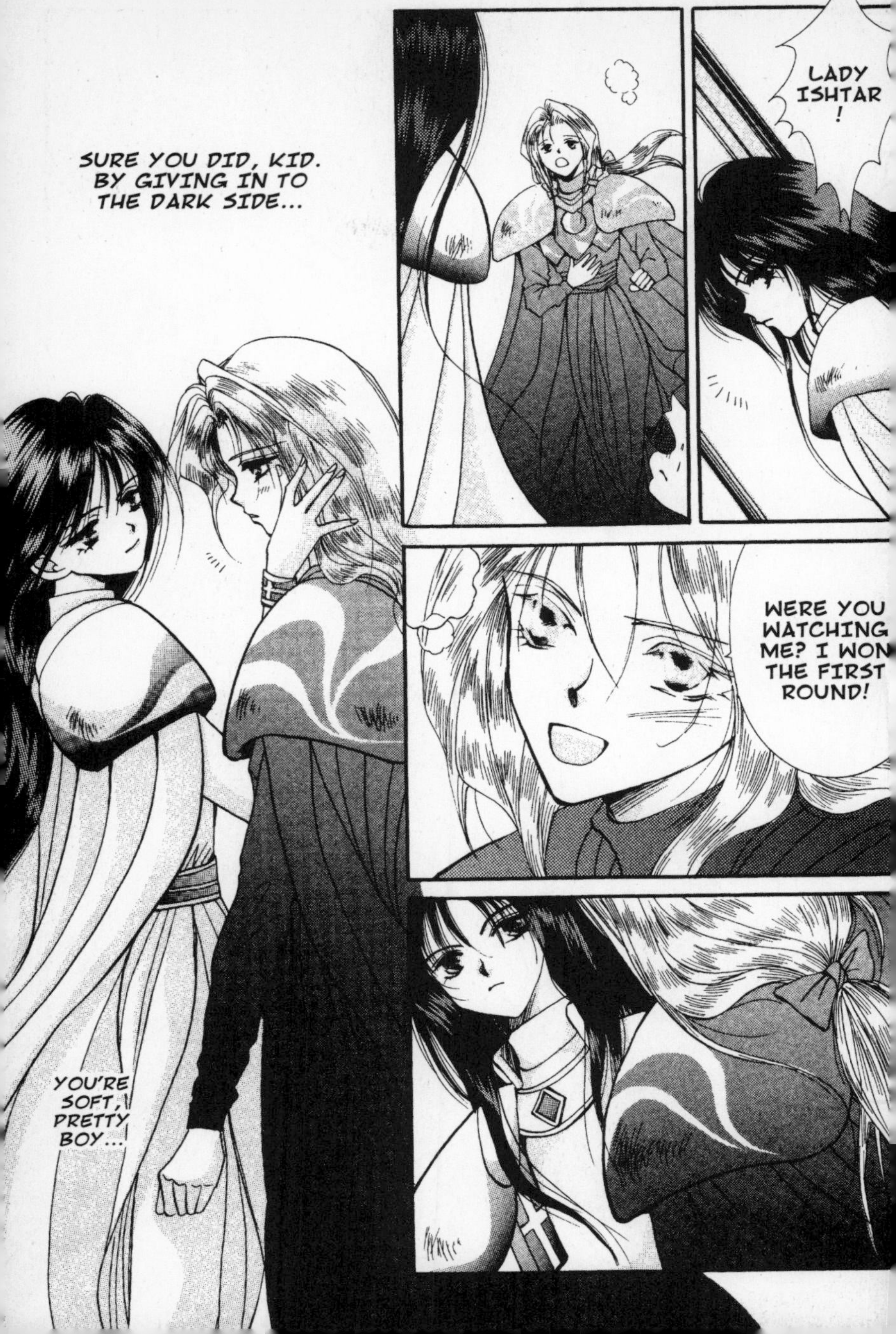
LADY ISHTAR!
WERE YOU WATCHING ME? I WON THE FIRST ROUND!
SURE YOU DID, KID. BY GIVING IN TO THE DARK SIDE...
YOU'RE SOFT, PRETTY BOY...

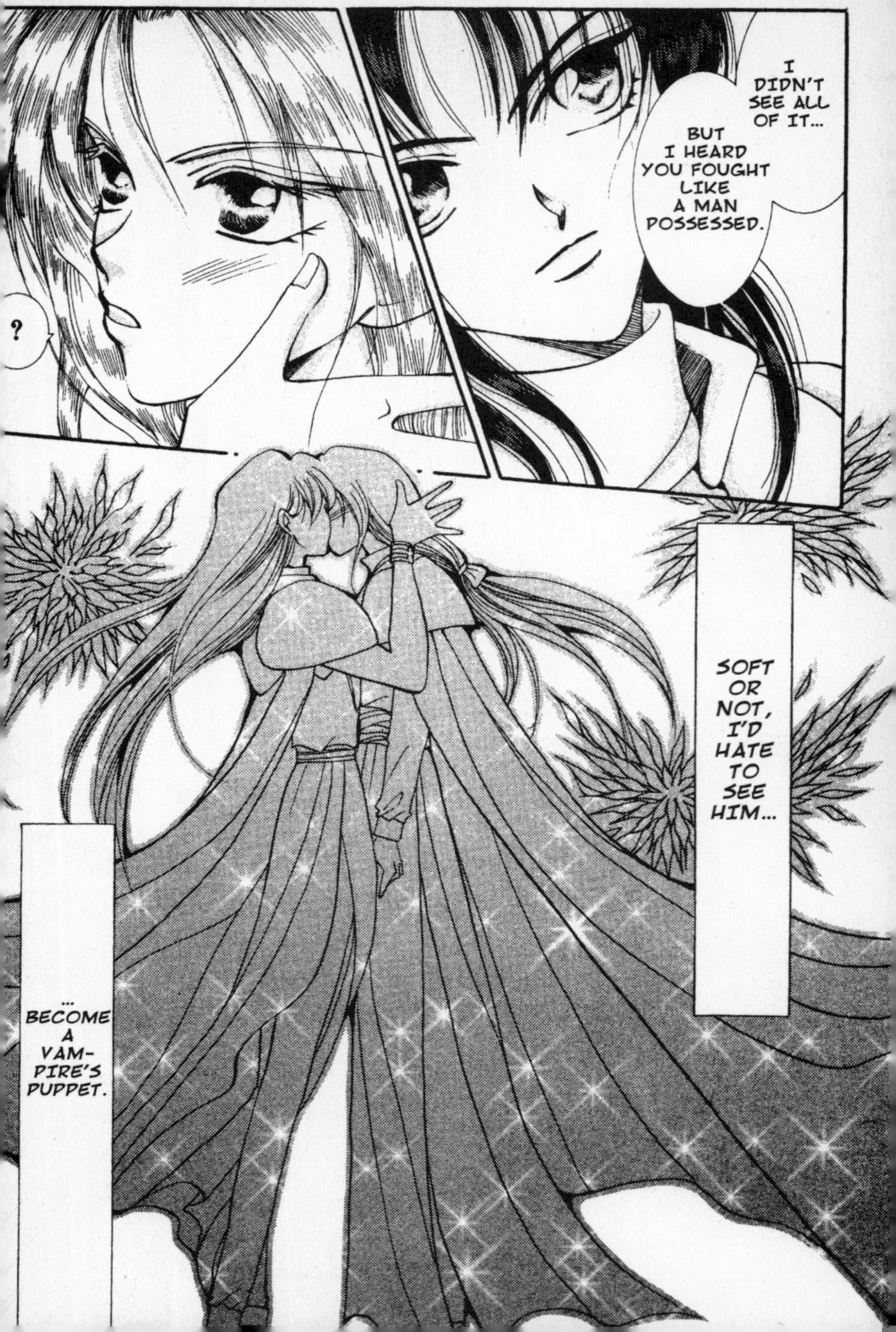
I DIDN'T SEE ALL OF IT...
BUT I HEARD YOU FOUGHT LIKE A MAN POSSESSED.
?
SOFT OR NOT, I'D HATE TO SEE HIM...
... BECOME A VAM-PIRE'S PUPPET.

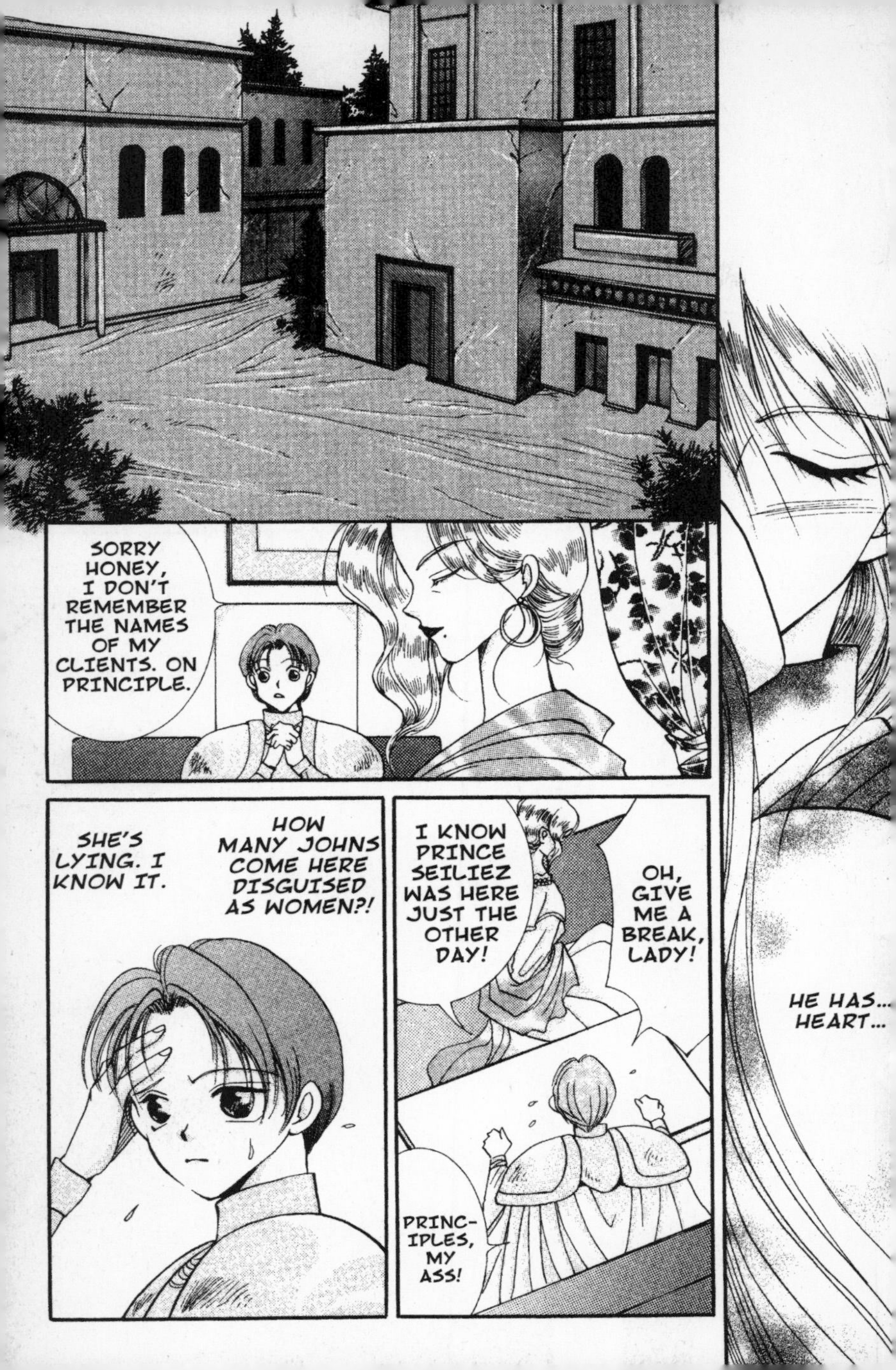
HE HAS... HEART...
SORRY HONEY, I DON'T REMEMBER THE NAMES OF MY CLIENTS. ON PRINCIPLE.
I KNOW PRINCE SEILIEZ WAS HERE JUST THE OTHER DAY!
OH, GIVE ME A BREAK, LADY!
PRINC-IPLES, MY ASS!
HOW MANY JOHNS COME HERE DISGUISED AS WOMEN?!
SHE'S LYING. I KNOW IT.

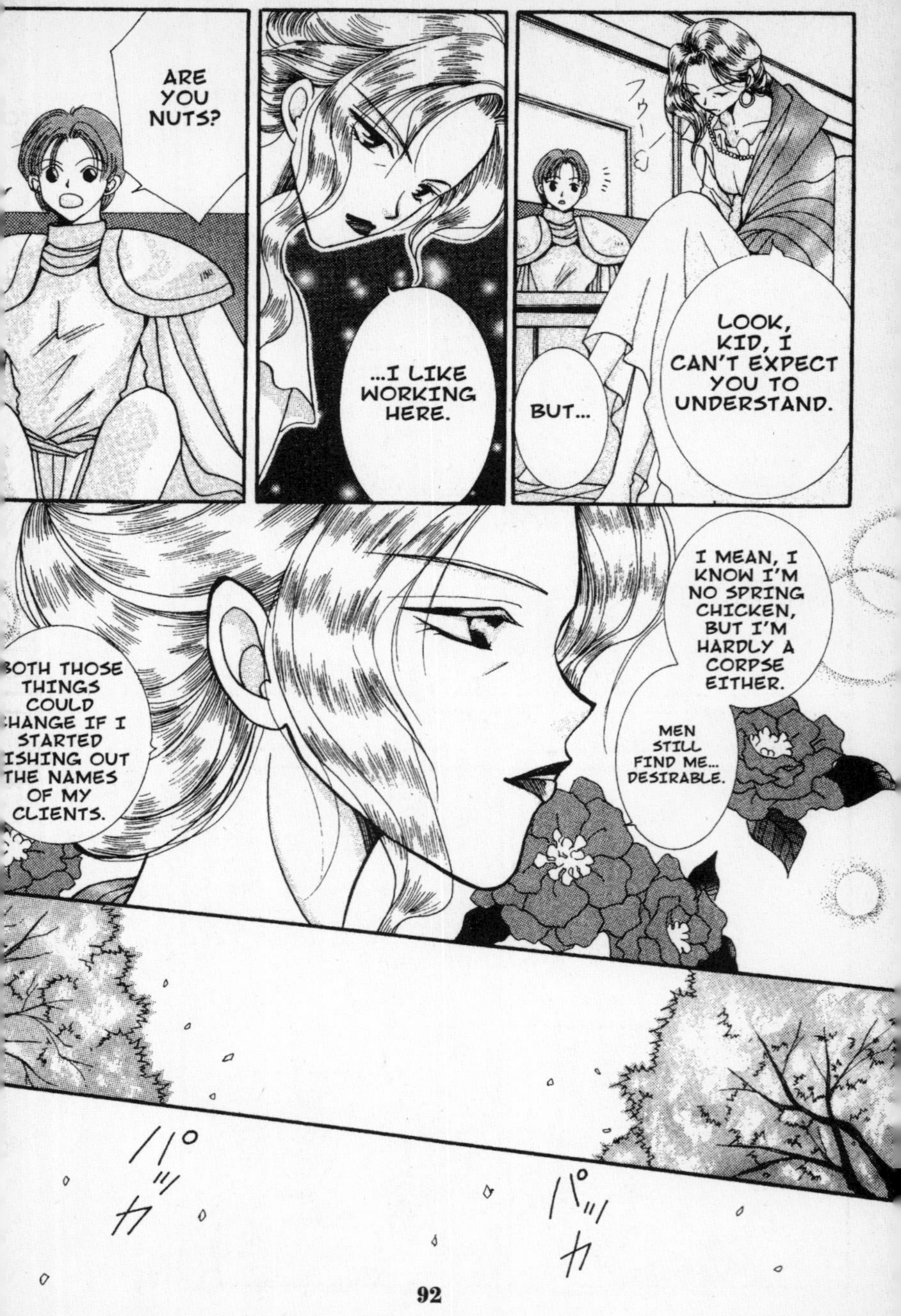
フゥー
LOOK, KID, I CAN'T EXPECT YOU TO UNDERSTAND.
BUT...
...I LIKE WORKING HERE.
ARE YOU NUTS?
I MEAN, I KNOW I'M NO SPRING CHICKEN, BUT I'M HARDLY A CORPSE EITHER.
MEN STILL FIND ME... DESIRABLE.
BOTH THOSE THINGS COULD CHANGE IF I STARTED DISHING OUT THE NAMES OF MY CLIENTS.
パッカ
パッカ

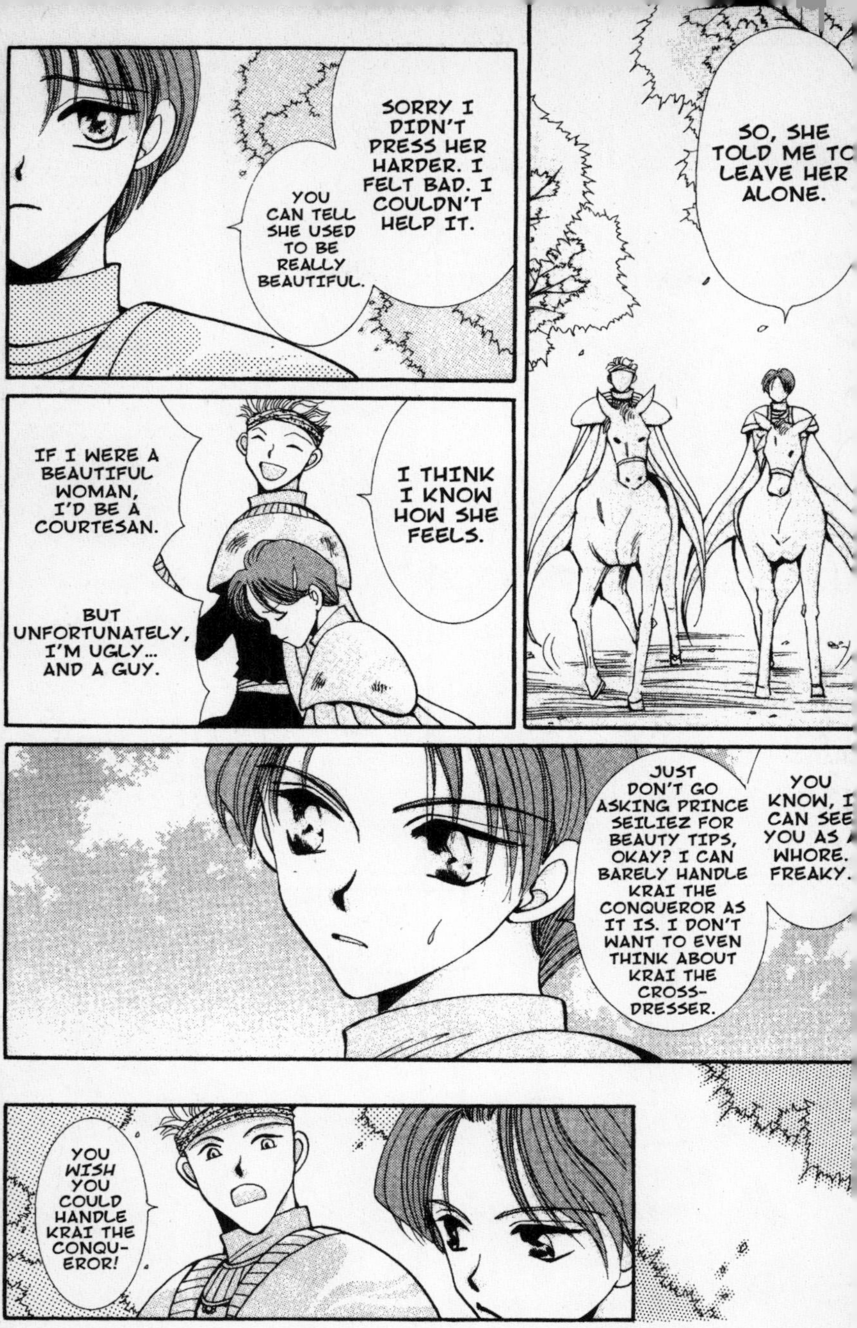
SO, SHE TOLD ME TO LEAVE HER ALONE.
SORRY I DIDN'T PRESS HER HARDER. I FELT BAD. I COULDN'T HELP IT.
YOU CAN TELL SHE USED TO BE REALLY BEAUTIFUL.
I THINK I KNOW HOW SHE FEELS.
IF I WERE A BEAUTIFUL WOMAN, I'D BE A COURTESAN.
BUT UNFORTUNATELY, I'M UGLY... AND A GUY.
YOU KNOW, I CAN SEE YOU AS A WHORE. FREAKY.
JUST DON'T GO ASKING PRINCE SEILIEZ FOR BEAUTY TIPS, OKAY? I CAN BARELY HANDLE KRAI THE CONQUEROR AS IT IS. I DON'T WANT TO EVEN THINK ABOUT KRAI THE CROSS-DRESSER.
YOU WISH YOU COULD HANDLE KRAI THE CONQU-EROR!

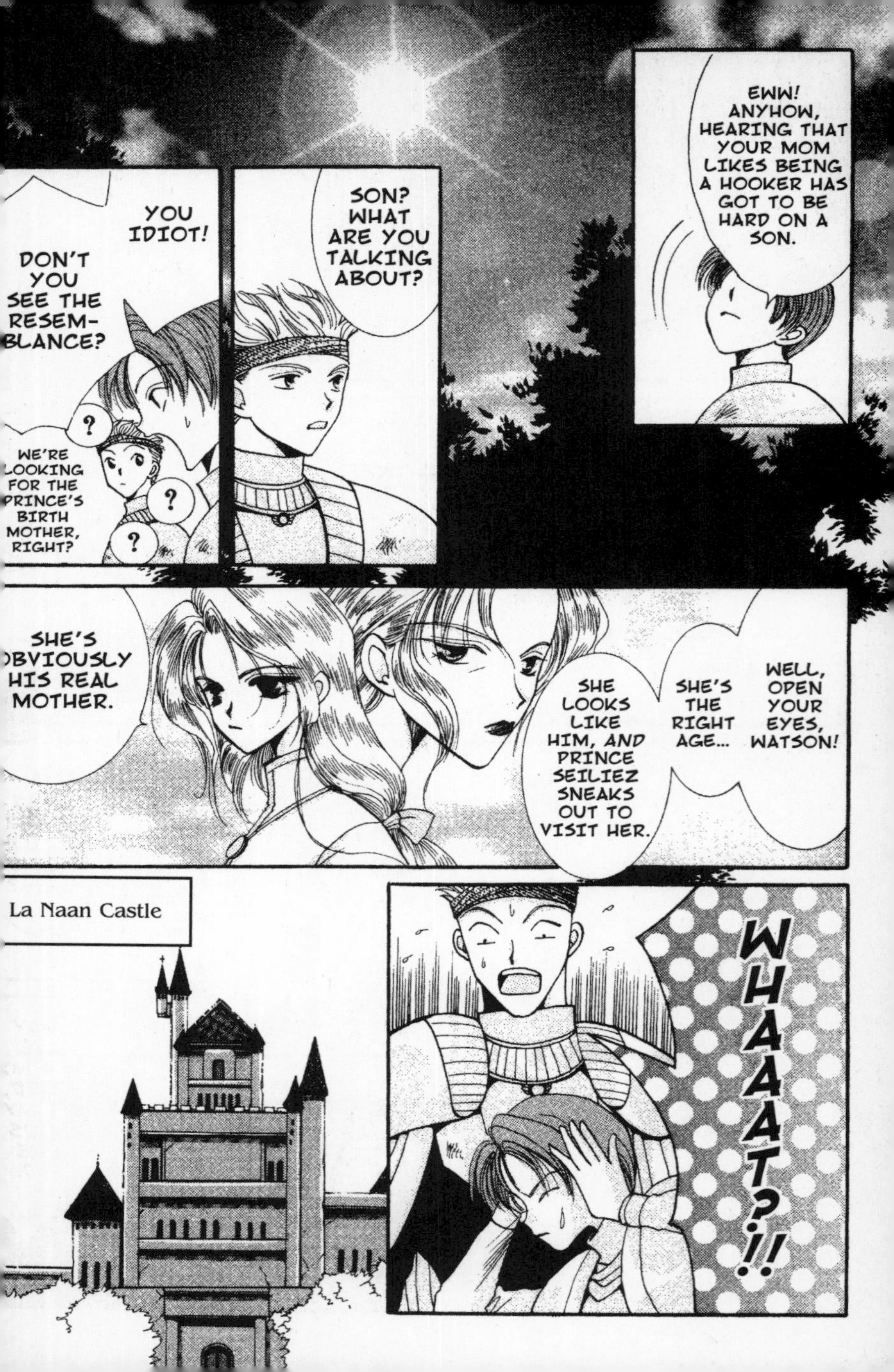
EWW! ANYHOW, HEARING THAT YOUR MOM LIKES BEING A HOOKER HAS GOT TO BE HARD ON A SON.
SON? WHAT ARE YOU TALKING ABOUT?
YOU IDIOT!
DON'T YOU SEE THE RESEM-BLANCE?
?
?
?
WE'RE LOOKING FOR THE PRINCE'S BIRTH MOTHER, RIGHT?
WELL, OPEN YOUR EYES, WATSON!
SHE'S THE RIGHT AGE...
SHE LOOKS LIKE HIM, AND PRINCE SEILIEZ SNEAKS OUT TO VISIT HER.
SHE'S OBVIOUSLY HIS REAL MOTHER.
WHAAAAT?!!
La Naan Castle

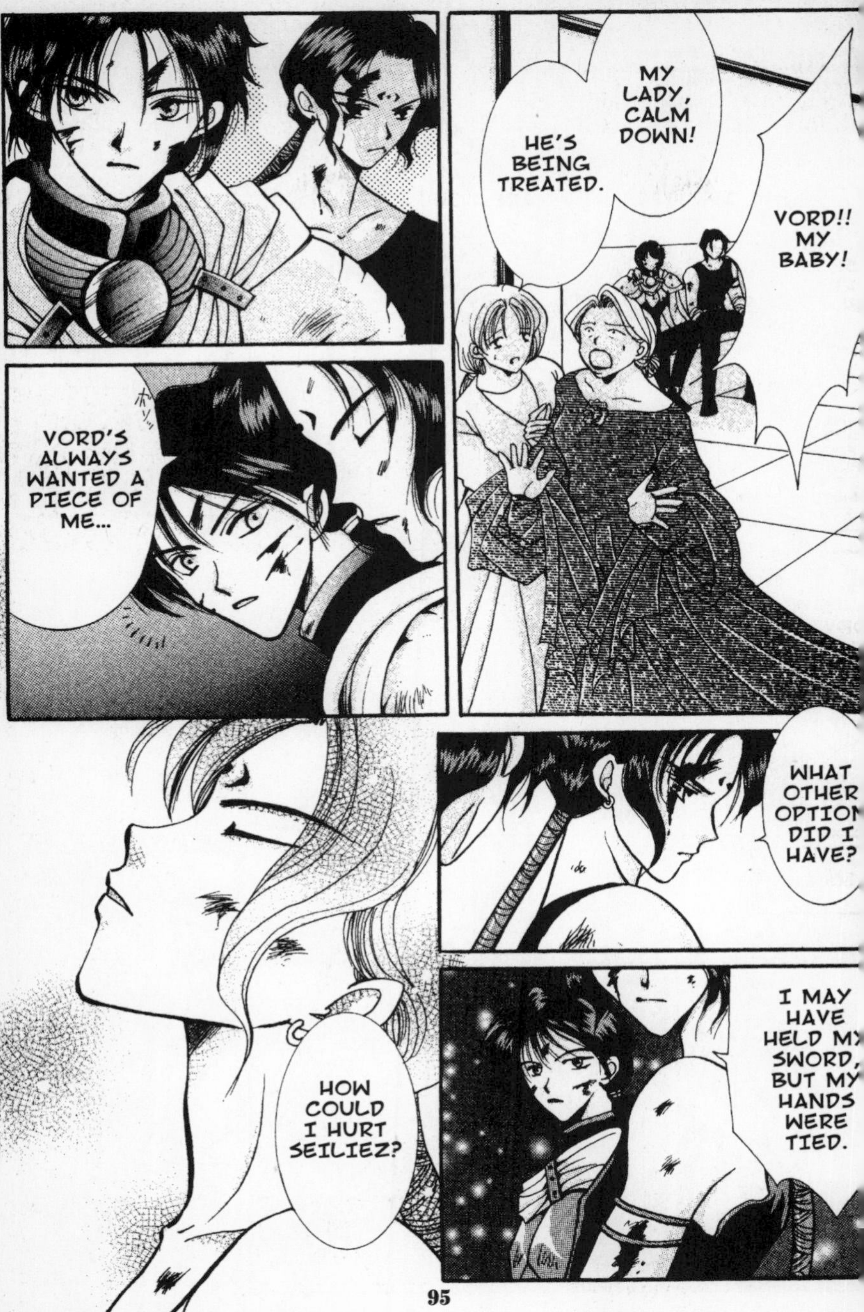
VORD!! MY BABY!
MY LADY, CALM DOWN!
HE'S BEING TREATED.
ボソッ
VORD'S ALWAYS WANTED A PIECE OF ME...
WHAT OTHER OPTION DID I HAVE?
I MAY HAVE HELD MY SWORD, BUT MY HANDS WERE TIED.
HOW COULD I HURT SEILIEZ?

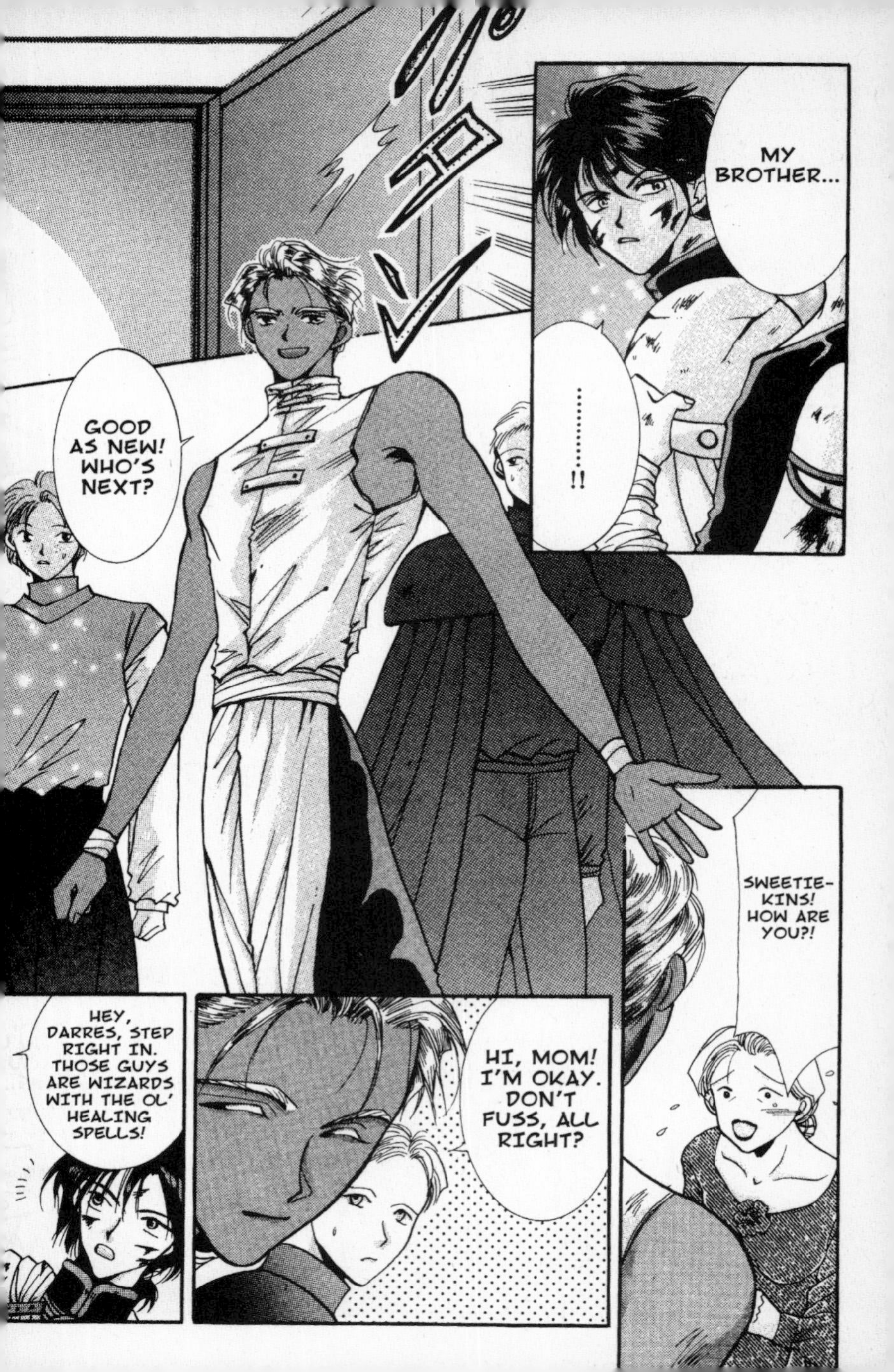
MY BROTHER...
......!!
GOOD AS NEW! WHO'S NEXT?
SWEETIE-KINS! HOW ARE YOU?!
HI, MOM! I'M OKAY. DON'T FUSS, ALL RIGHT?
HEY, DARRES, STEP RIGHT IN. THOSE GUYS ARE WIZARDS WITH THE OL' HEALING SPELLS!

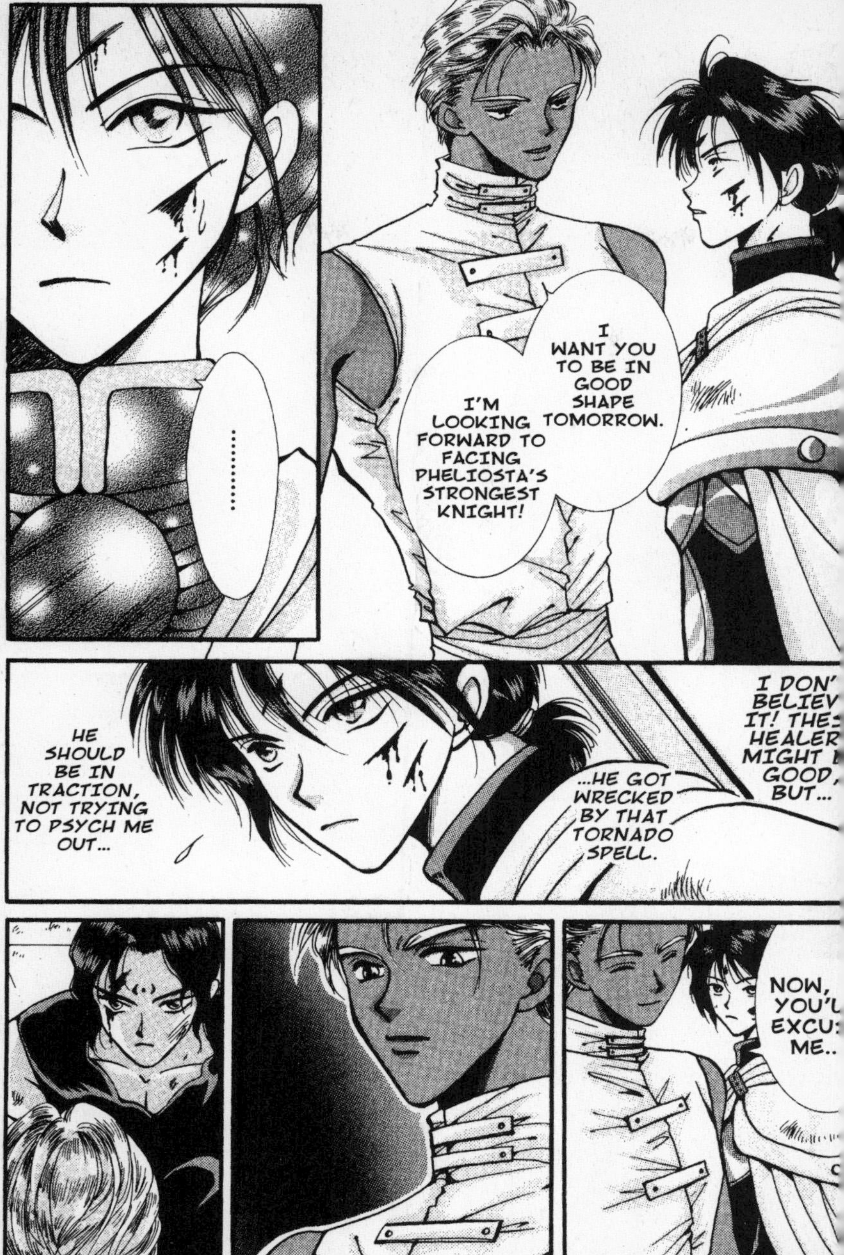
I WANT YOU TO BE IN GOOD SHAPE TOMORROW.
I'M LOOKING FORWARD TO FACING PHELIOSTA'S STRONGEST KNIGHT!
......
I DON' BELIEV IT! THES HEALER MIGHT B GOOD, BUT...
...HE GOT WRECKED BY THAT TORNADO SPELL.
HE SHOULD BE IN TRACTION, NOT TRYING TO PSYCH ME OUT...
NOW, YOU'L EXCU ME..

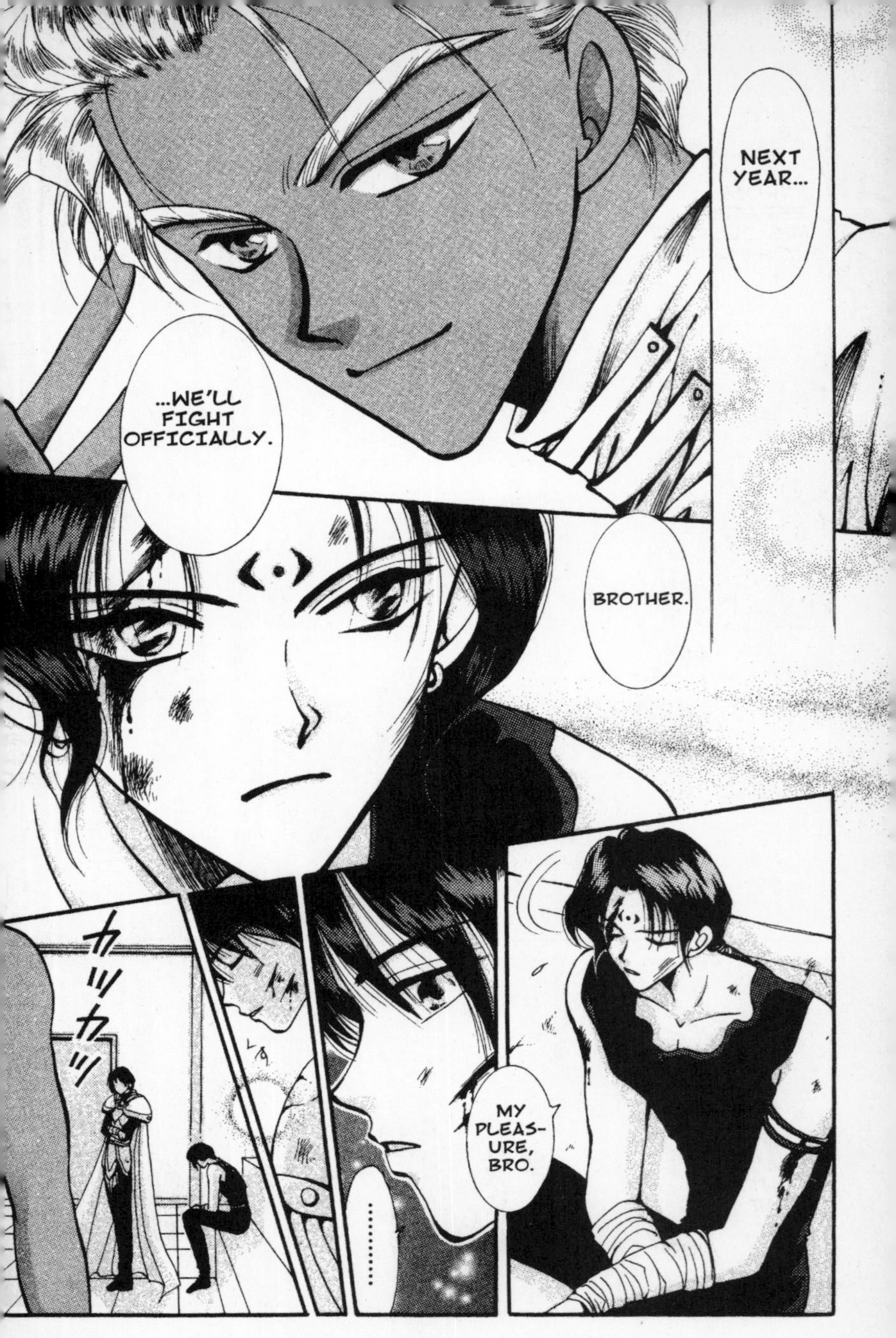
NEXT YEAR...
...WE'LL FIGHT OFFICIALLY.
BROTHER.
MY PLEAS-URE, BRO.
......
カッカッ

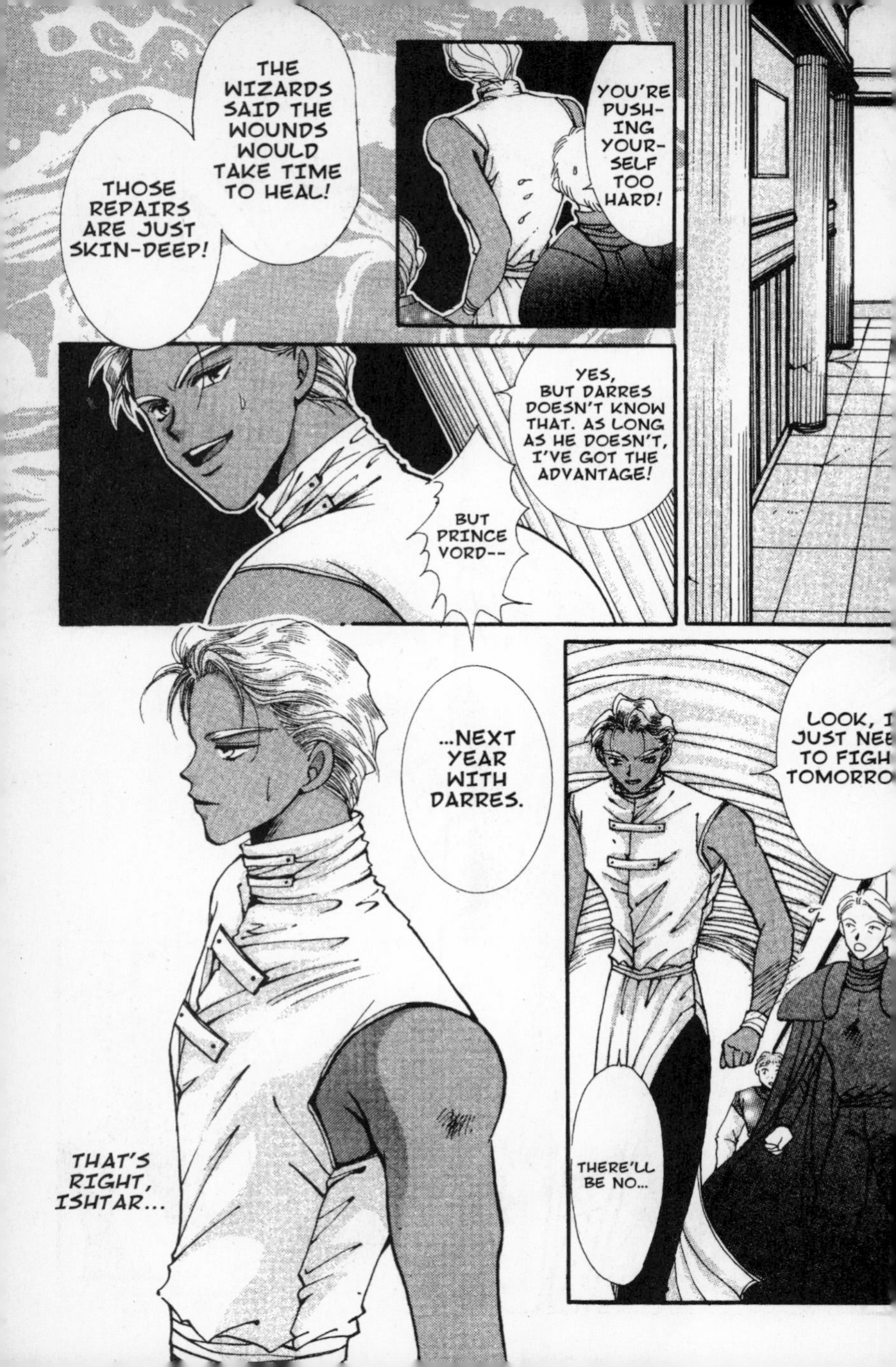
YOU'RE PUSHING YOURSELF TOO HARD!
THE WIZARDS SAID THE WOUNDS WOULD TAKE TIME TO HEAL!
THOSE REPAIRS ARE JUST SKIN-DEEP!
YES, BUT DARRES DOESN'T KNOW THAT. AS LONG AS HE DOESN'T, I'VE GOT THE ADVANTAGE!
BUT PRINCE VORD--
LOOK, I JUST NEE TO FIGH TOMORRO
THERE'LL BE NO...
...NEXT YEAR WITH DARRES.
THAT'S RIGHT, ISHTAR...

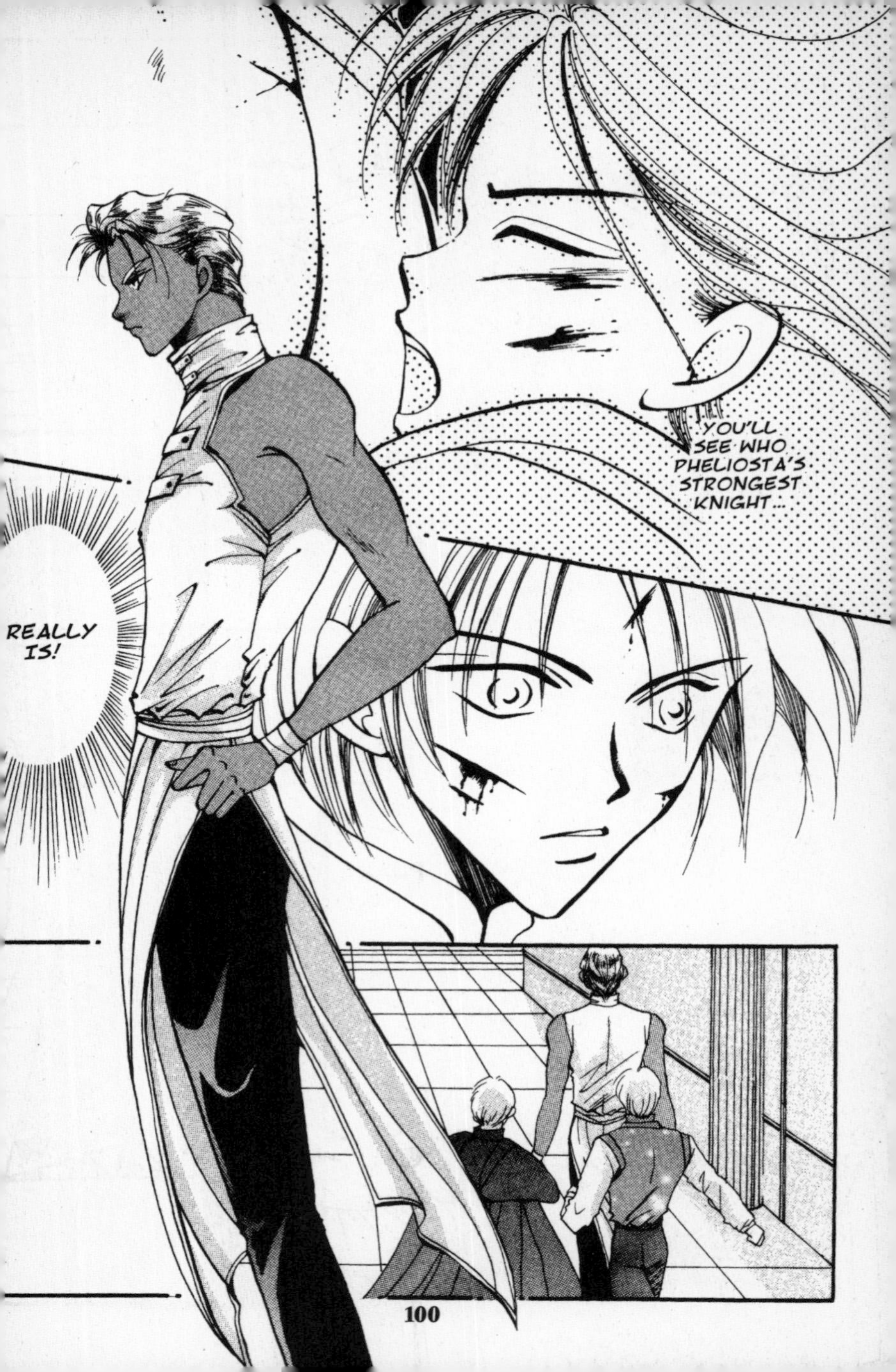
YOU'LL SEE WHO PHELIOSTA'S STRONGEST KNIGHT...
REALLY IS!

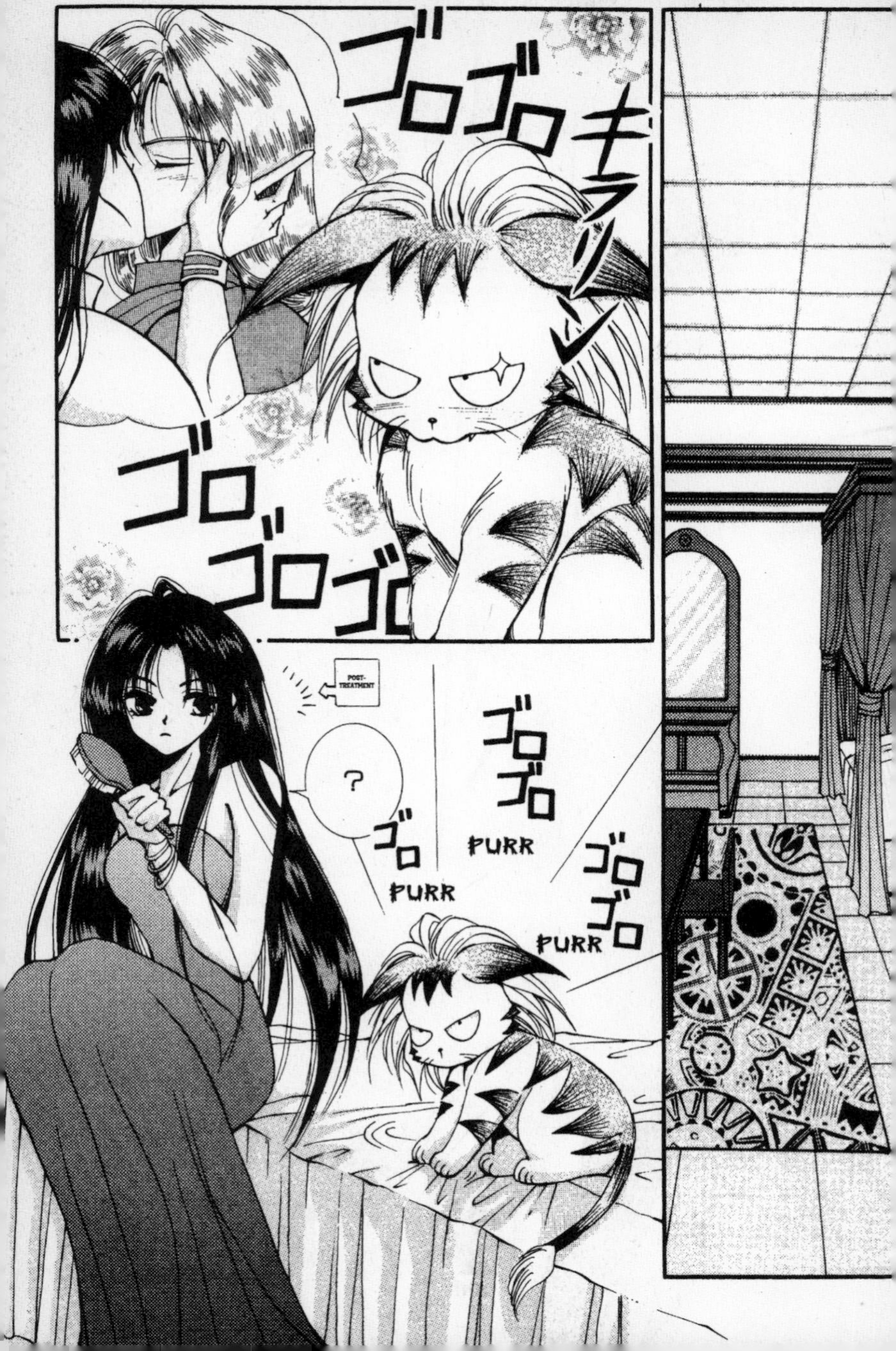
ゴロゴロ
ギラリーン
ゴロゴロゴロ
ゴロゴロ
PURR
ゴロゴロ
PURR
ゴロ
PURR
?
POST-TREATMENT

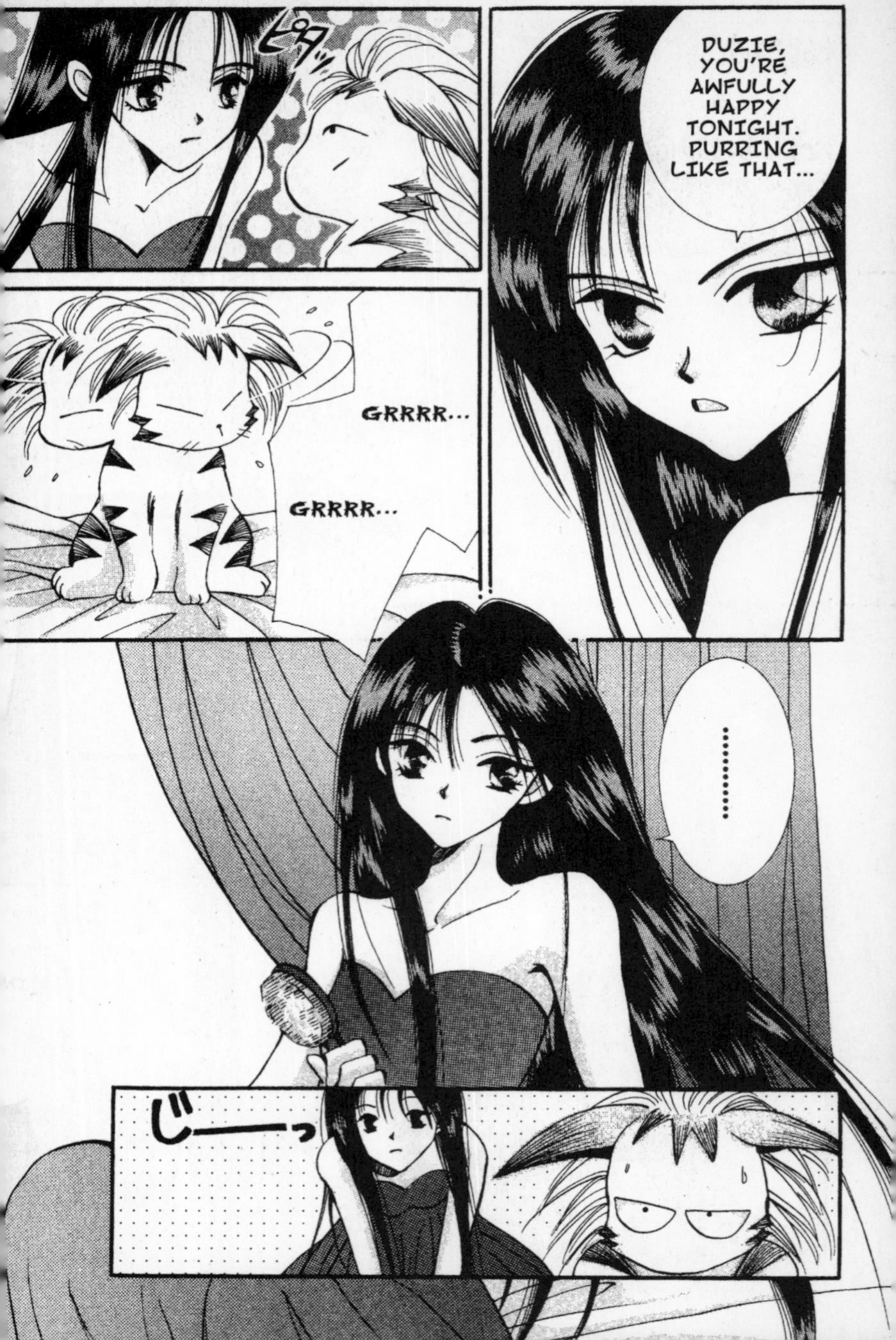
DUZIE, YOU'RE AWFULLY HAPPY TONIGHT. PURRING LIKE THAT...
ピタッ
GRRRR...
GRRRR...
....
じーっ

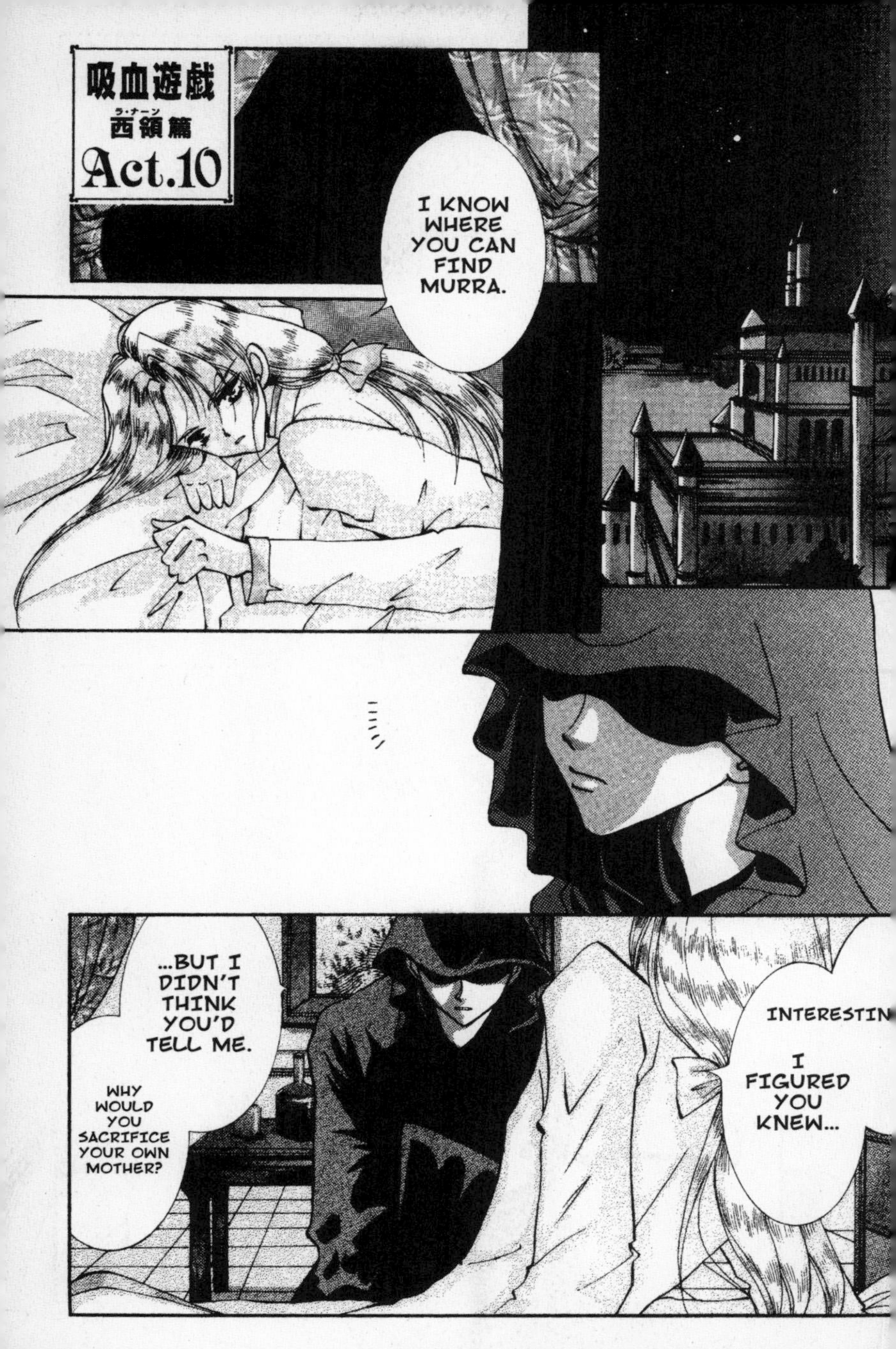
吸血遊戯
ラ・ナーン
西領篇
Act.10
I KNOW WHERE YOU CAN FIND MURRA.
…
INTERESTIN
I FIGURED YOU KNEW...
...BUT I DIDN'T THINK YOU'D TELL ME.
WHY WOULD YOU SACRIFICE YOUR OWN MOTHER?

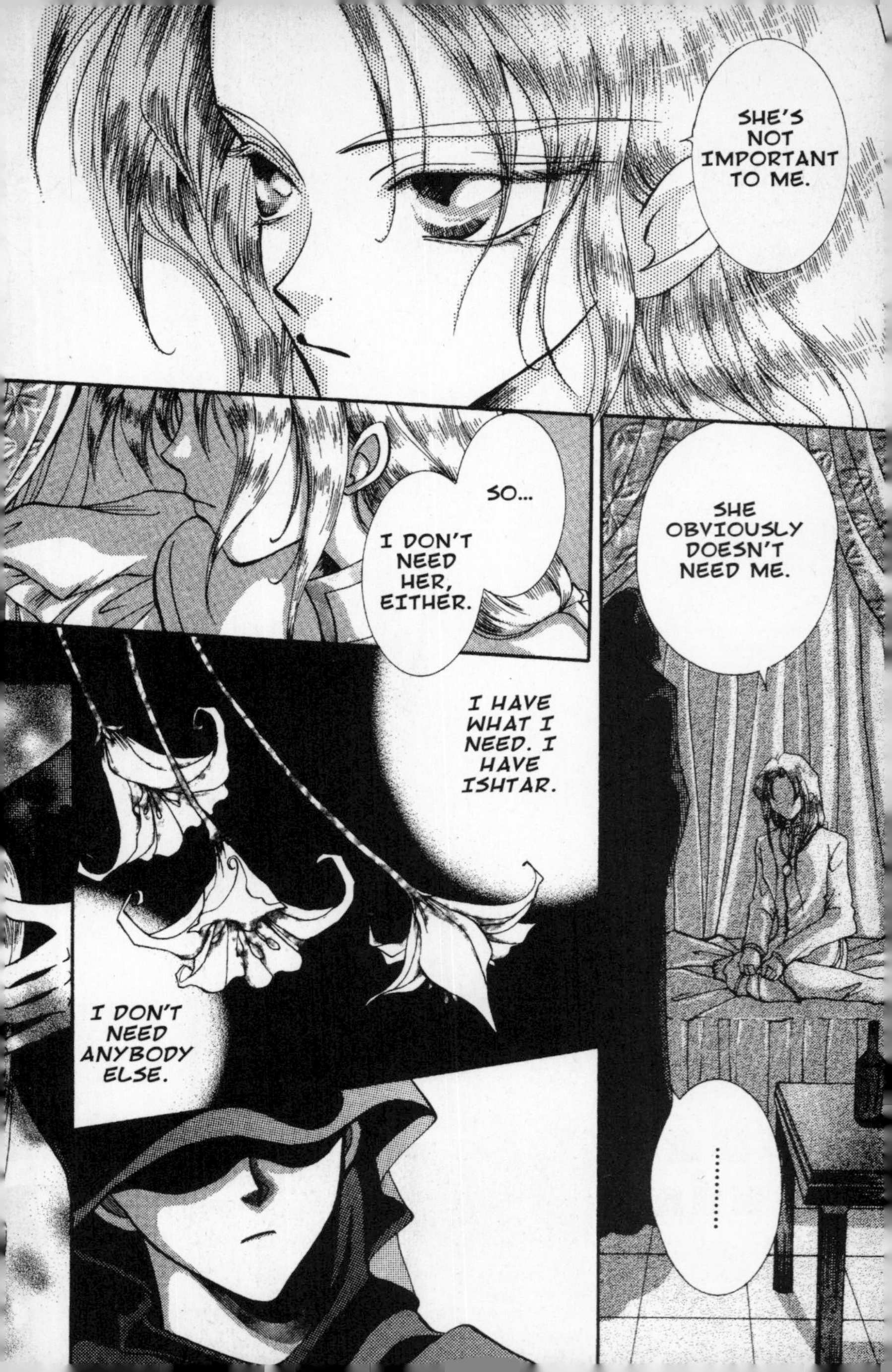
SHE'S NOT IMPORTANT TO ME.
SHE OBVIOUSLY DOESN'T NEED ME.
......
SO...
I DON'T NEED HER, EITHER.
I HAVE WHAT I NEED. I HAVE ISHTAR.
I DON'T NEED ANYBODY ELSE.

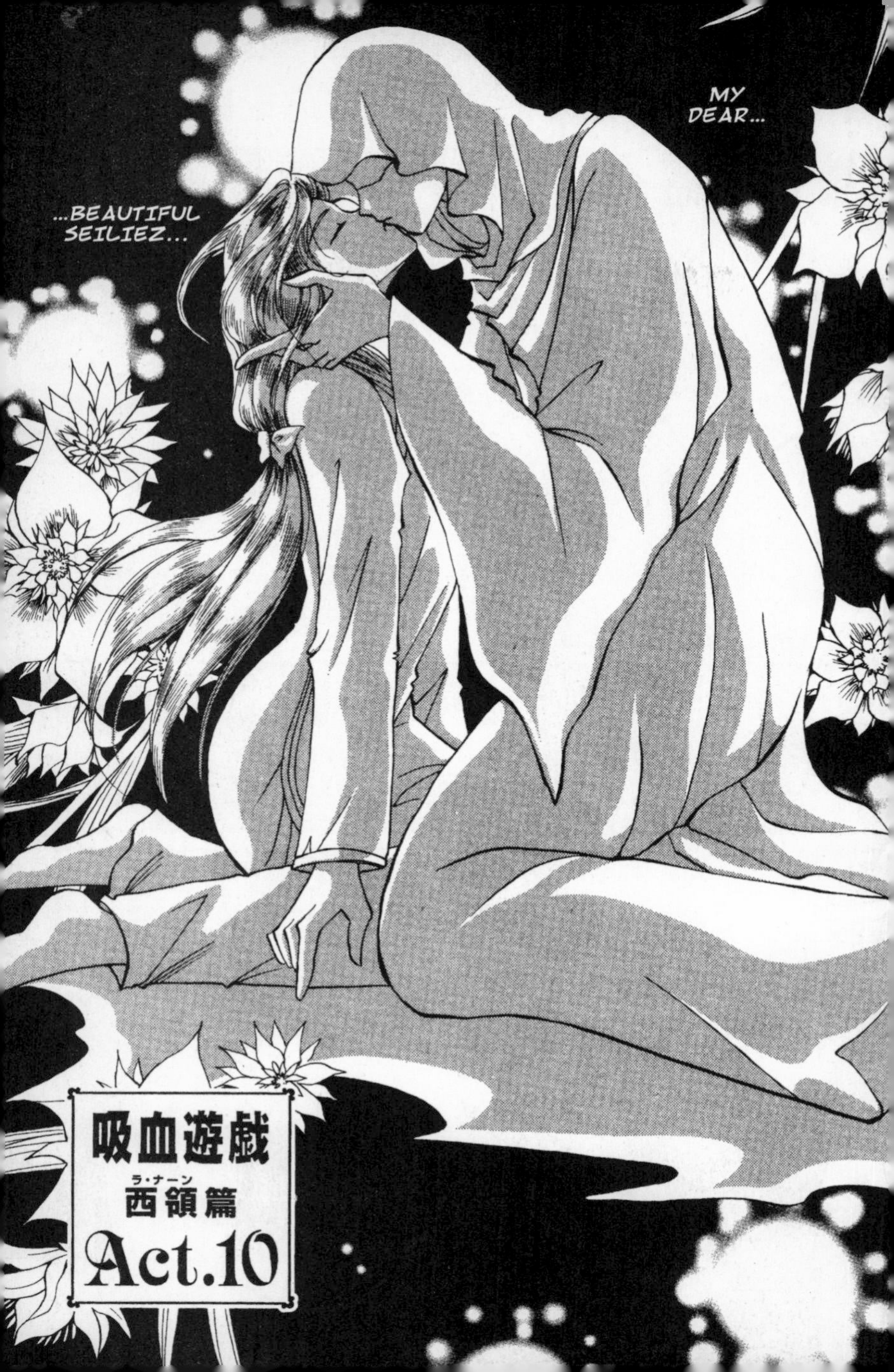
MY DEAR...
...BEAUTIFUL SEILIEZ...
吸血遊戯
ラ・ナーン
西領篇
Act.10

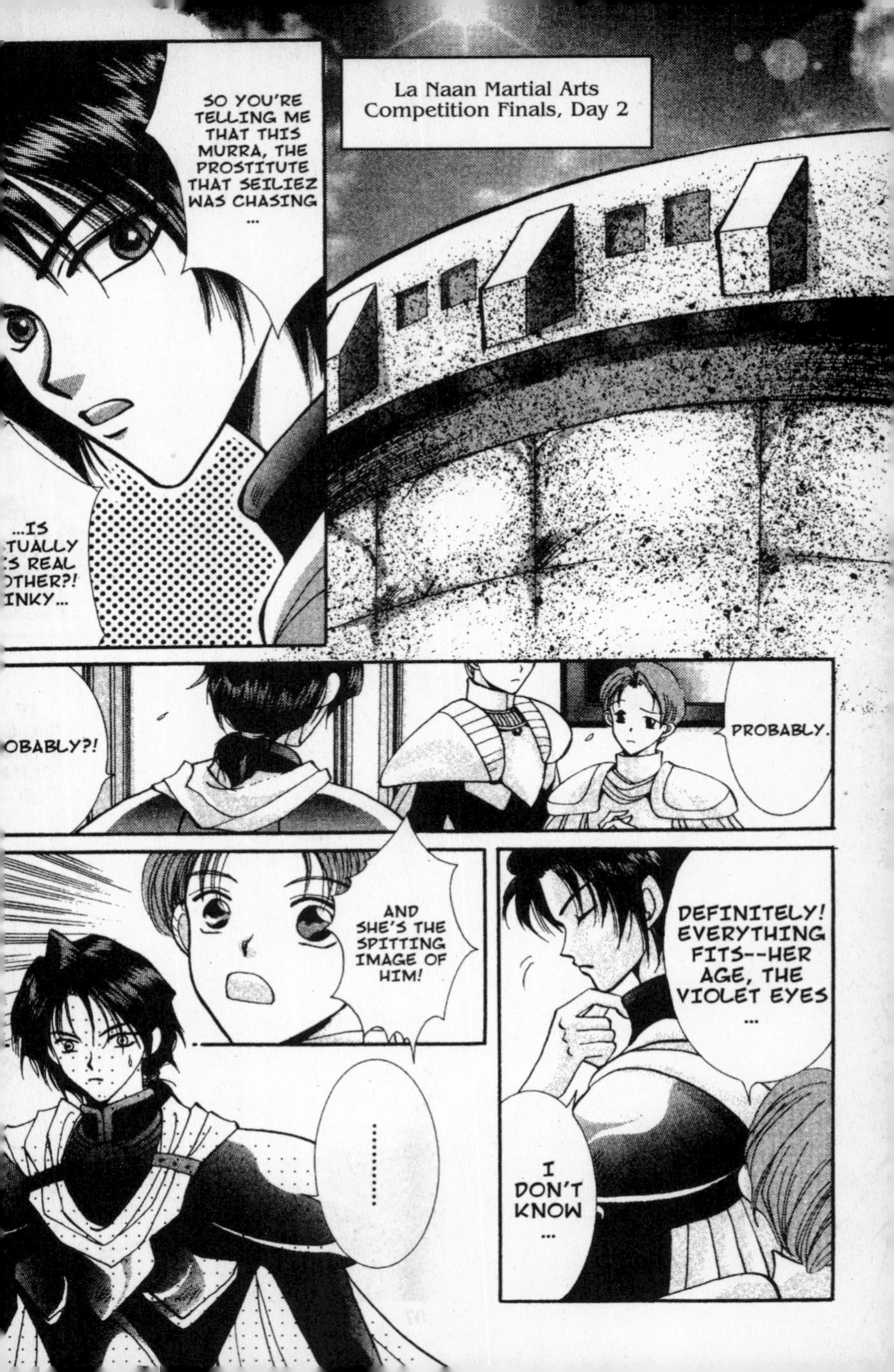

La Naan Martial Arts Competition Finals, Day 2
SO YOU'RE TELLING ME THAT THIS MURRA, THE PROSTITUTE THAT SEILIEZ WAS CHASING ...
...IS TUALLY S REAL OTHER?! INKY...
PROBABLY.
OBABLY?!
DEFINITELY! EVERYTHING FITS--HER AGE, THE VIOLET EYES ...
I DON'T KNOW ...
AND SHE'S THE SPITTING IMAGE OF HIM!
....

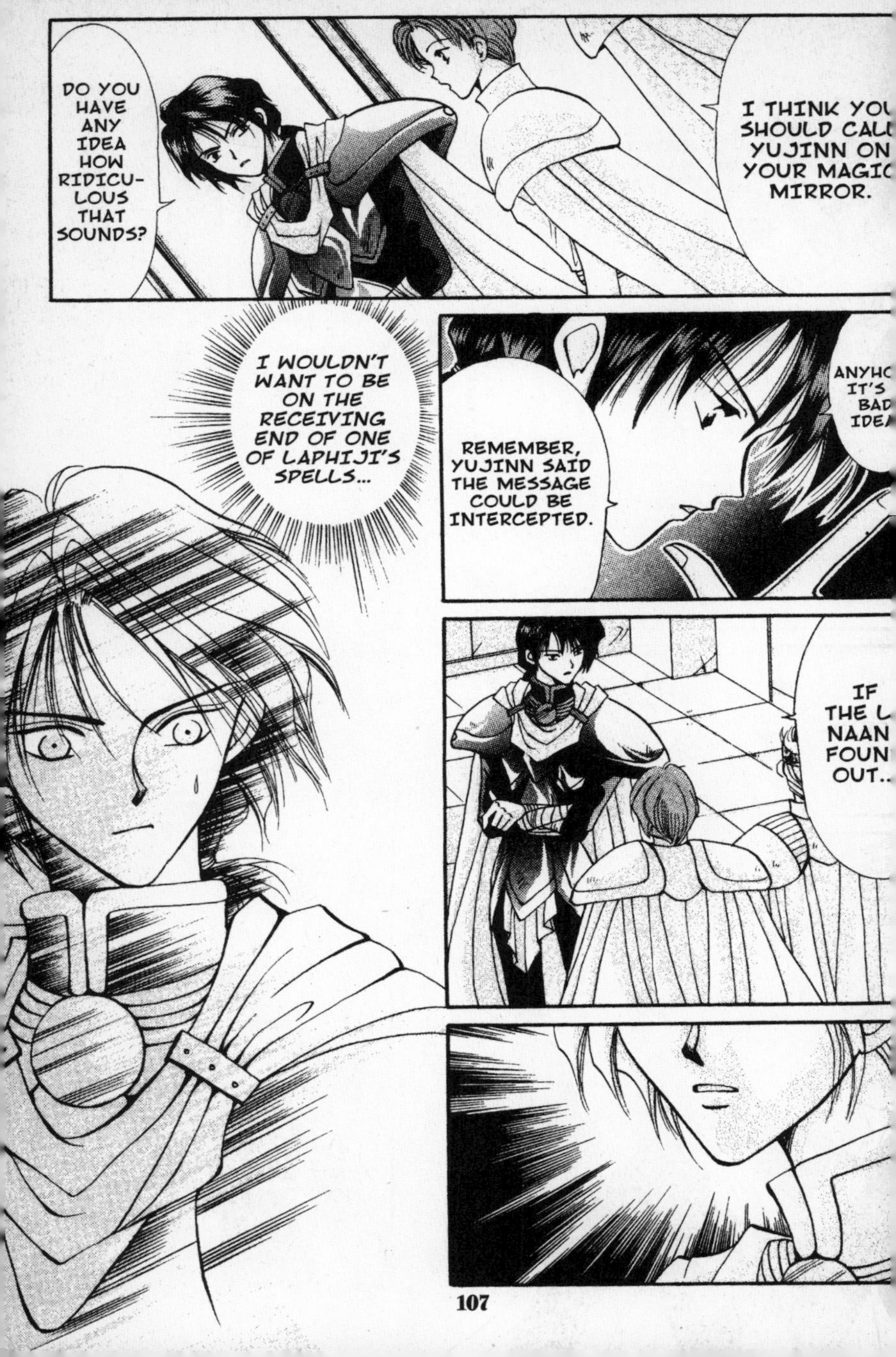
I THINK YOU SHOULD CALL YUJINN ON YOUR MAGIC MIRROR.
DO YOU HAVE ANY IDEA HOW RIDICU-LOUS THAT SOUNDS?
ANYHO IT'S BAD IDEA
REMEMBER, YUJINN SAID THE MESSAGE COULD BE INTERCEPTED.
IF THE NAAN FOUN OUT...
I WOULDN'T WANT TO BE ON THE RECEIVING END OF ONE OF LAPHIJI'S SPELLS...

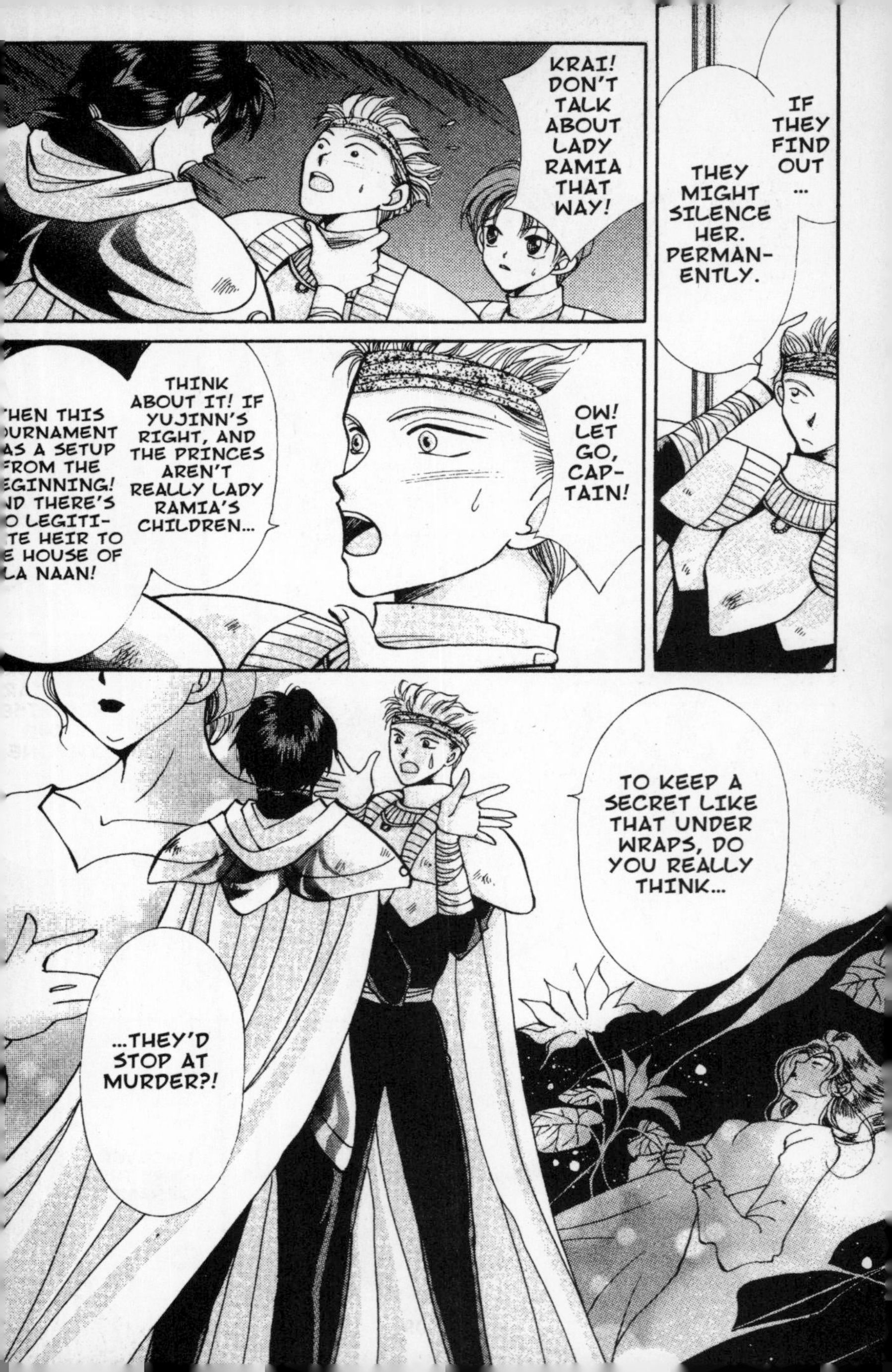

IF THEY FIND OUT ...
THEY MIGHT SILENCE HER. PERMANENTLY.
KRAI! DON'T TALK ABOUT LADY RAMIA THAT WAY!
OW! LET GO, CAP-TAIN!
THINK ABOUT IT! IF YUJINN'S RIGHT, AND THE PRINCES AREN'T REALLY LADY RAMIA'S CHILDREN...
HEN THIS OURNAMENT AS A SETUP FROM THE EGINNING! ND THERE'S O LEGITI-TE HEIR TO E HOUSE OF LA NAAN!
TO KEEP A SECRET LIKE THAT UNDER WRAPS, DO YOU REALLY THINK...
...THEY'D STOP AT MURDER?!

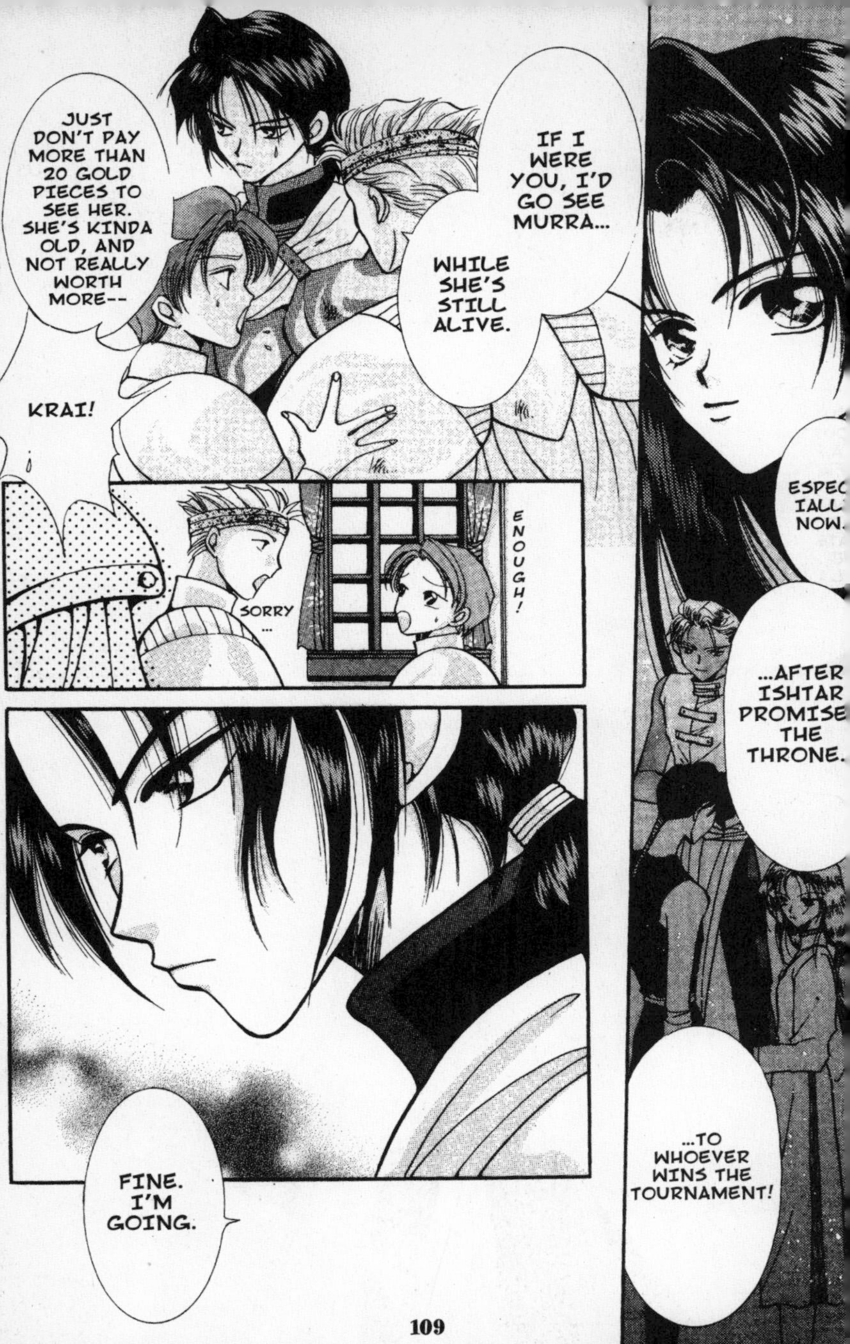
ESPEC IALL NOW.
...AFTER ISHTAR PROMISE THE THRONE.
...TO WHOEVER WINS THE TOURNAMENT!
IF I WERE YOU, I'D GO SEE MURRA...
WHILE SHE'S STILL ALIVE.
JUST DON'T PAY MORE THAN 20 GOLD PIECES TO SEE HER. SHE'S KINDA OLD, AND NOT REALLY WORTH MORE--
KRAI!
ENOUGH!
SORRY ...
FINE. I'M GOING.

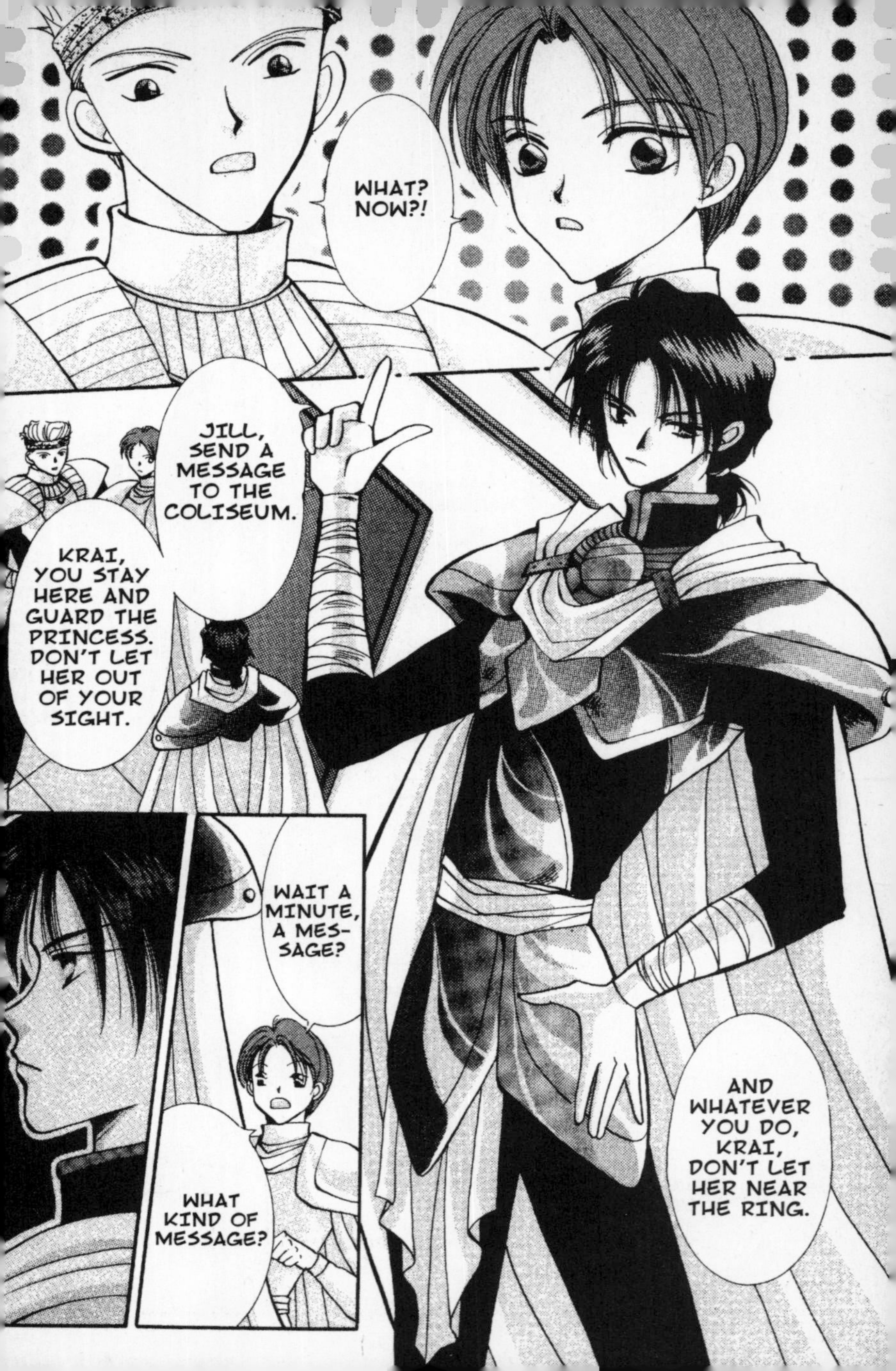
WHAT? NOW?!
JILL, SEND A MESSAGE TO THE COLISEUM.
KRAI, YOU STAY HERE AND GUARD THE PRINCESS. DON'T LET HER OUT OF YOUR SIGHT.
AND WHATEVER YOU DO, KRAI, DON'T LET HER NEAR THE RING.
WAIT A MINUTE, A MES-SAGE?
WHAT KIND OF MESSAGE?

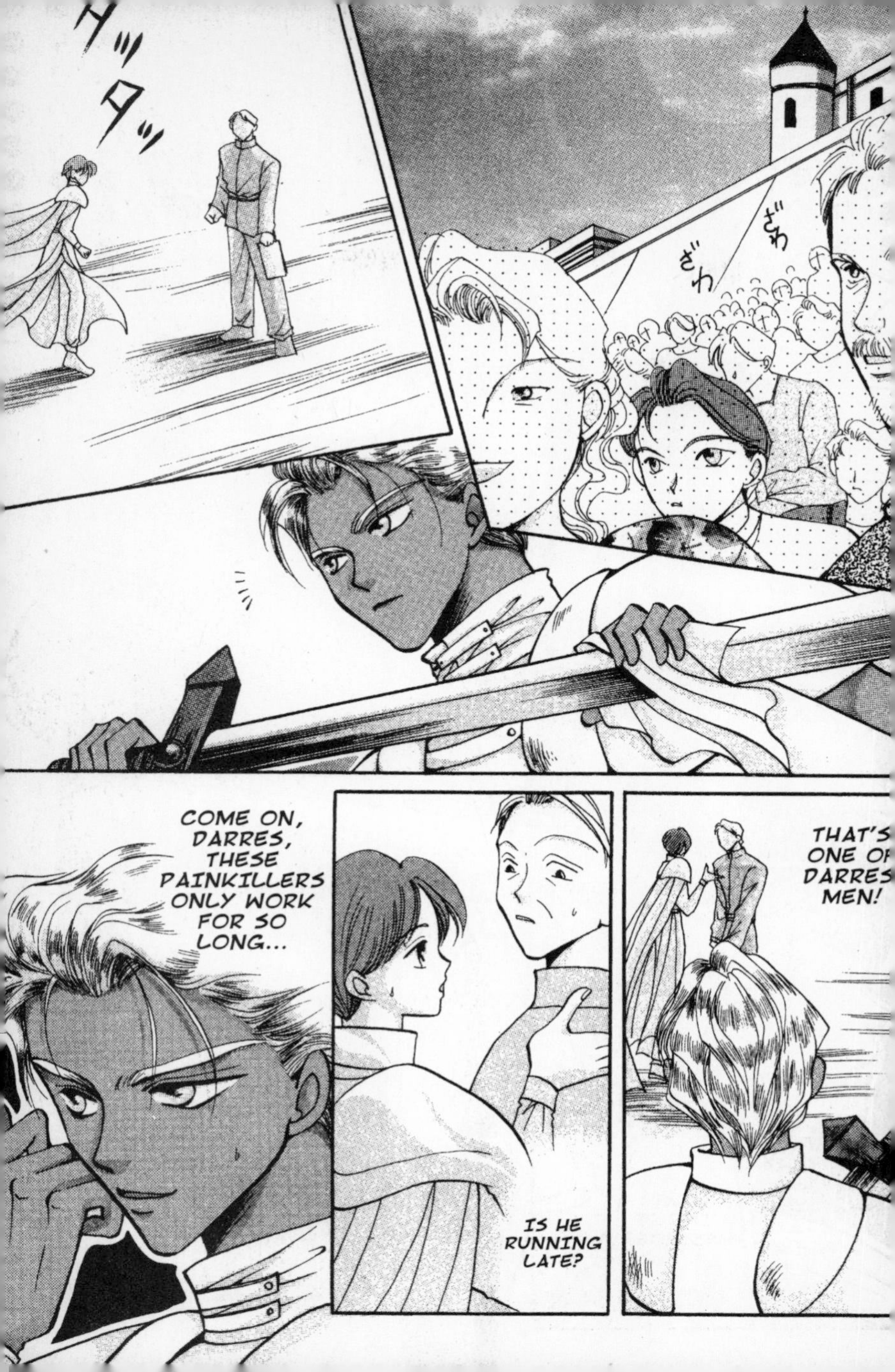
ざわ ざわ
ダッタッ
THAT'S ONE OF DARRES' MEN!
IS HE RUNNING LATE?
COME ON, DARRES, THESE PAINKILLERS ONLY WORK FOR SO LONG...

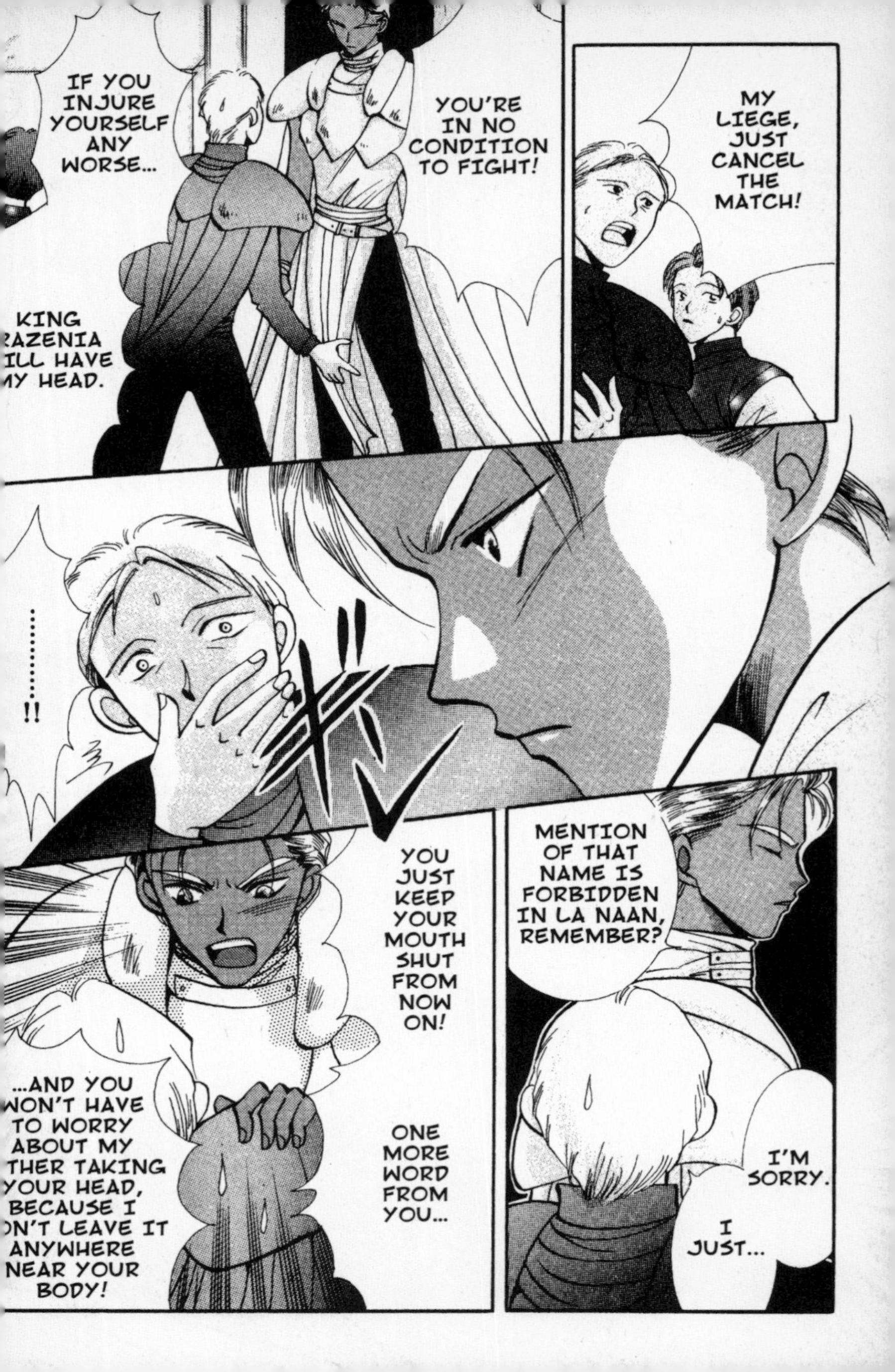
MY LIEGE, JUST CANCEL THE MATCH!
YOU'RE IN NO CONDITION TO FIGHT!
IF YOU INJURE YOURSELF ANY WORSE...
KING RAZENIA ILL HAVE MY HEAD.
......!!
MENTION OF THAT NAME IS FORBIDDEN IN LA NAAN, REMEMBER?
I'M SORRY.
I JUST...
YOU JUST KEEP YOUR MOUTH SHUT FROM NOW ON!
ONE MORE WORD FROM YOU...
...AND YOU ON'T HAVE TO WORRY ABOUT MY THER TAKING YOUR HEAD, BECAUSE I N'T LEAVE IT ANYWHERE NEAR YOUR BODY!

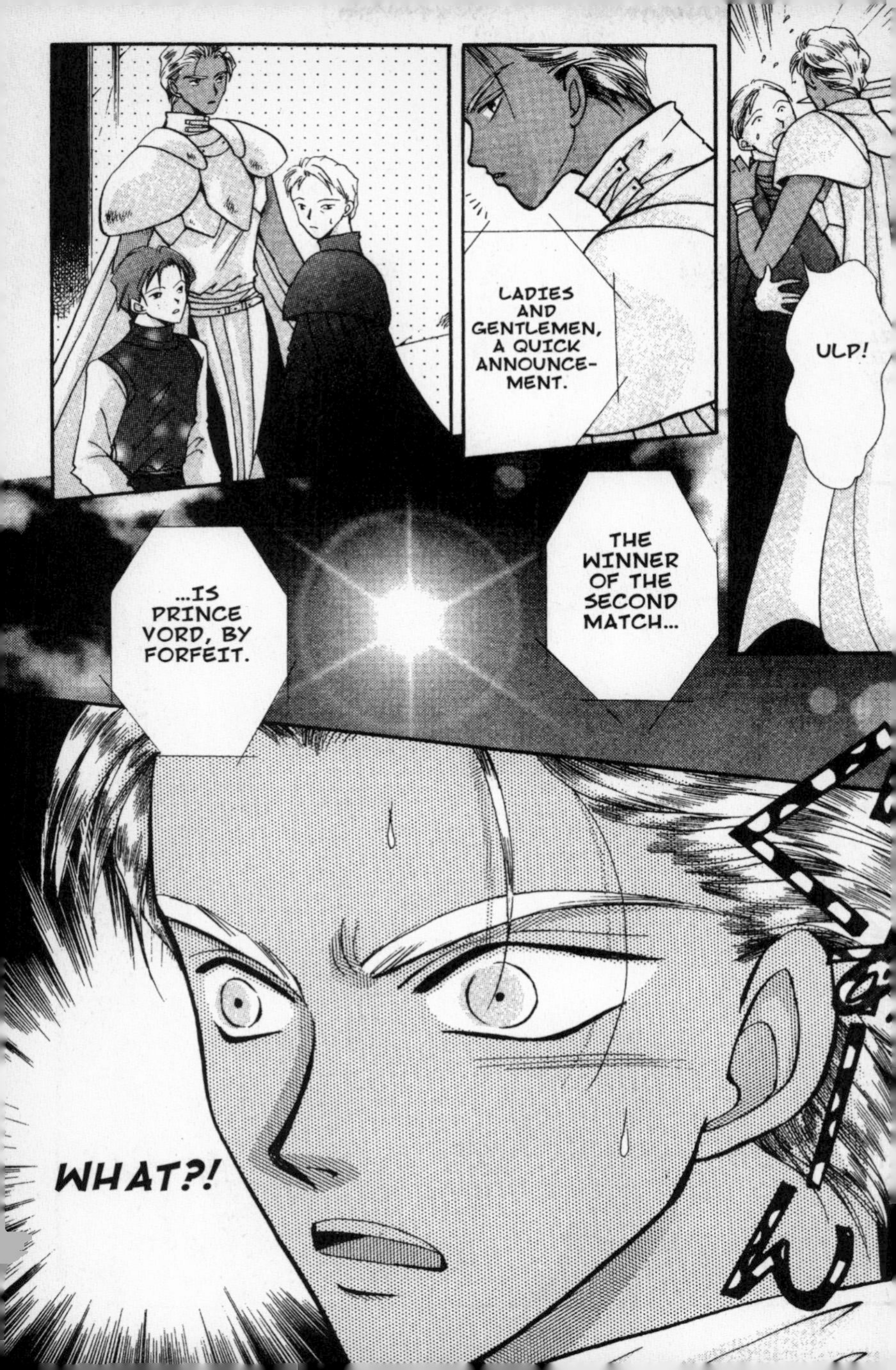
ULP!
LADIES AND GENTLEMEN, A QUICK ANNOUNCEMENT.
THE WINNER OF THE SECOND MATCH...
...IS PRINCE VORD, BY FORFEIT.
WHAT?!

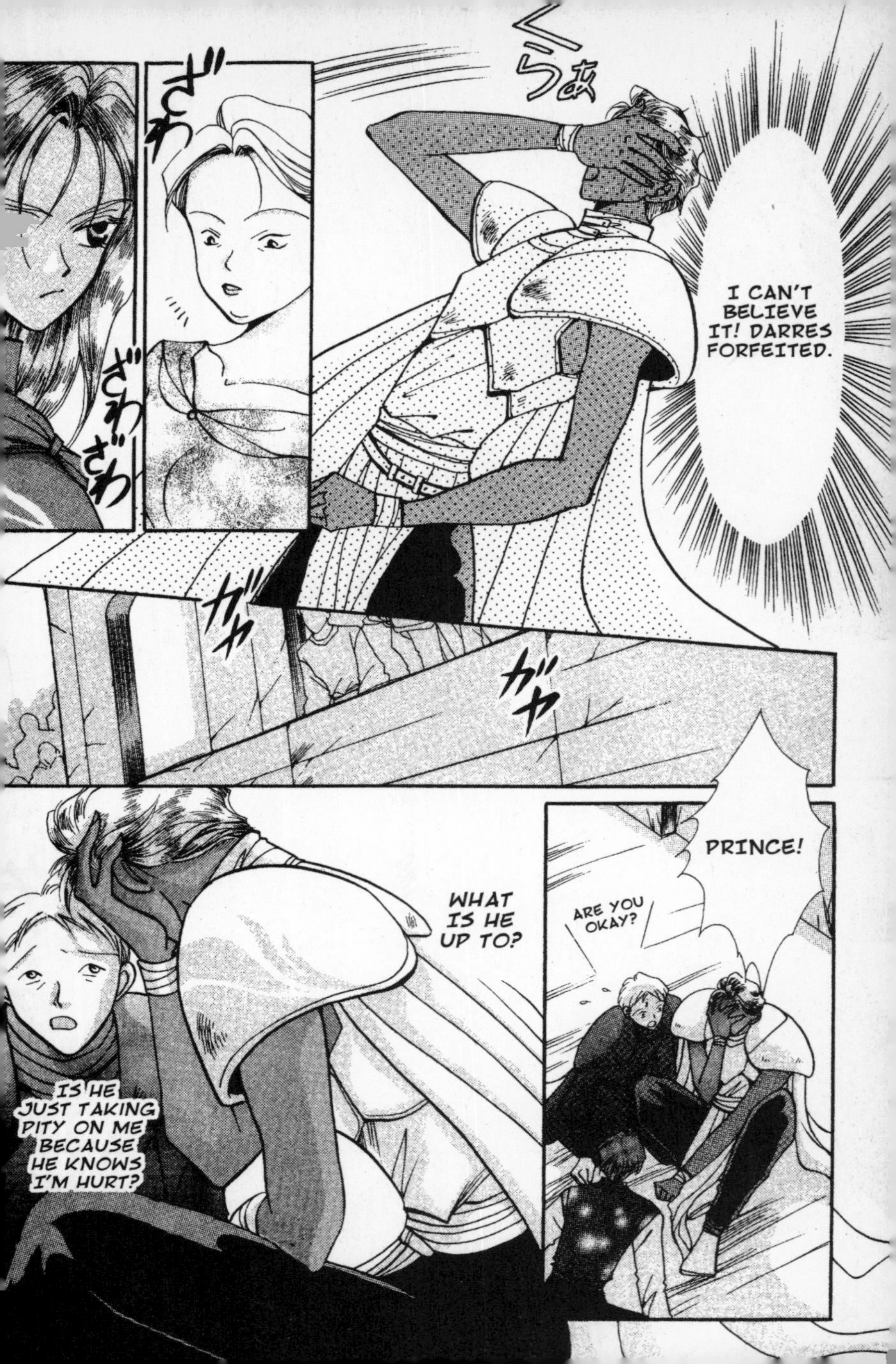
くらぁ
I CAN'T BELIEVE IT! DARRES FORFEITED.
ざわ
ざわざわ
ガヤ
ガヤ
PRINCE!
ARE YOU OKAY?
WHAT IS HE UP TO?
IS HE JUST TAKING PITY ON ME BECAUSE HE KNOWS I'M HURT?

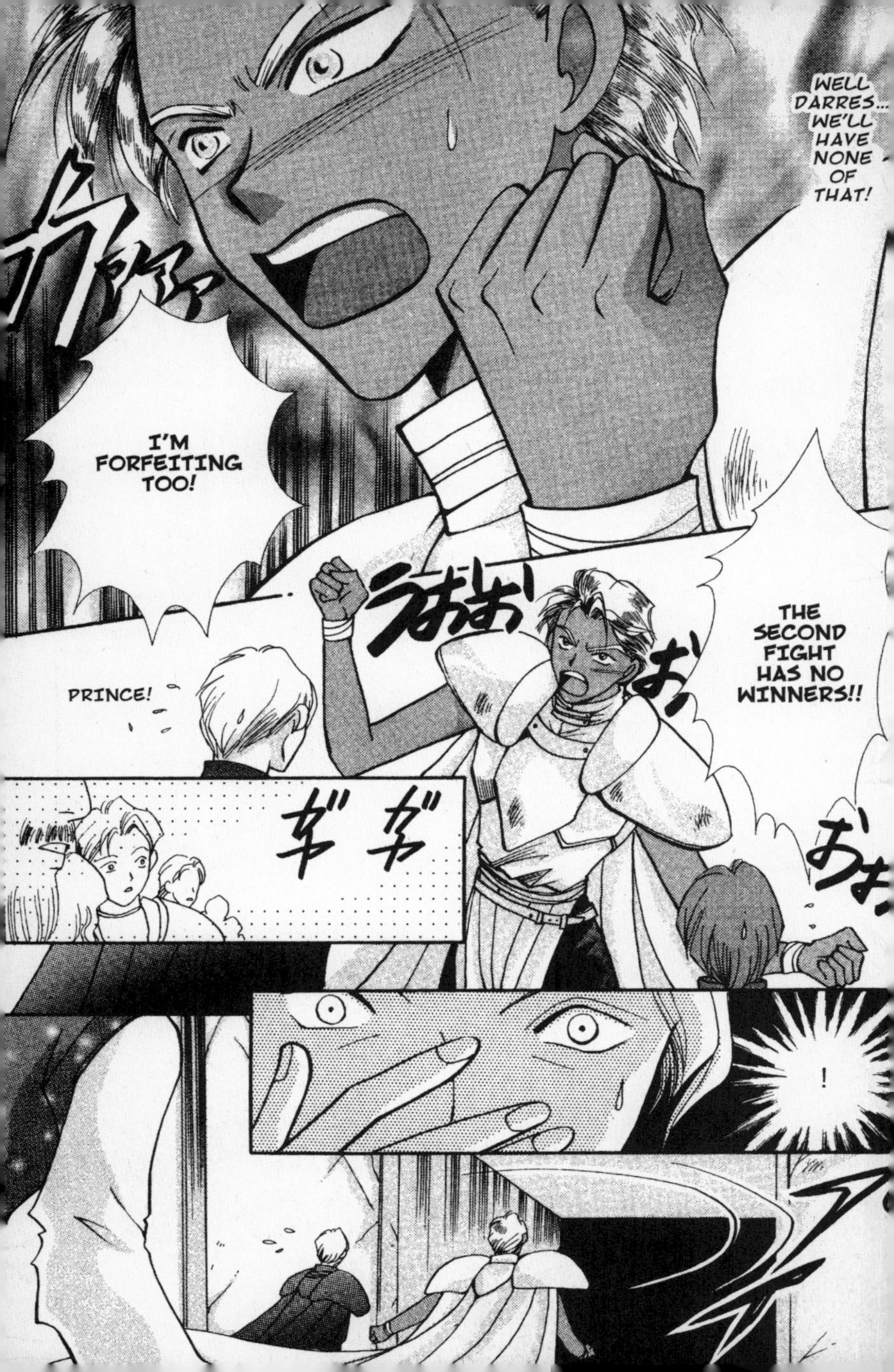
WELL DARRES... WE'LL HAVE NONE OF THAT!
I'M FORFEITING TOO!
THE SECOND FIGHT HAS NO WINNERS!!
PRINCE!
!

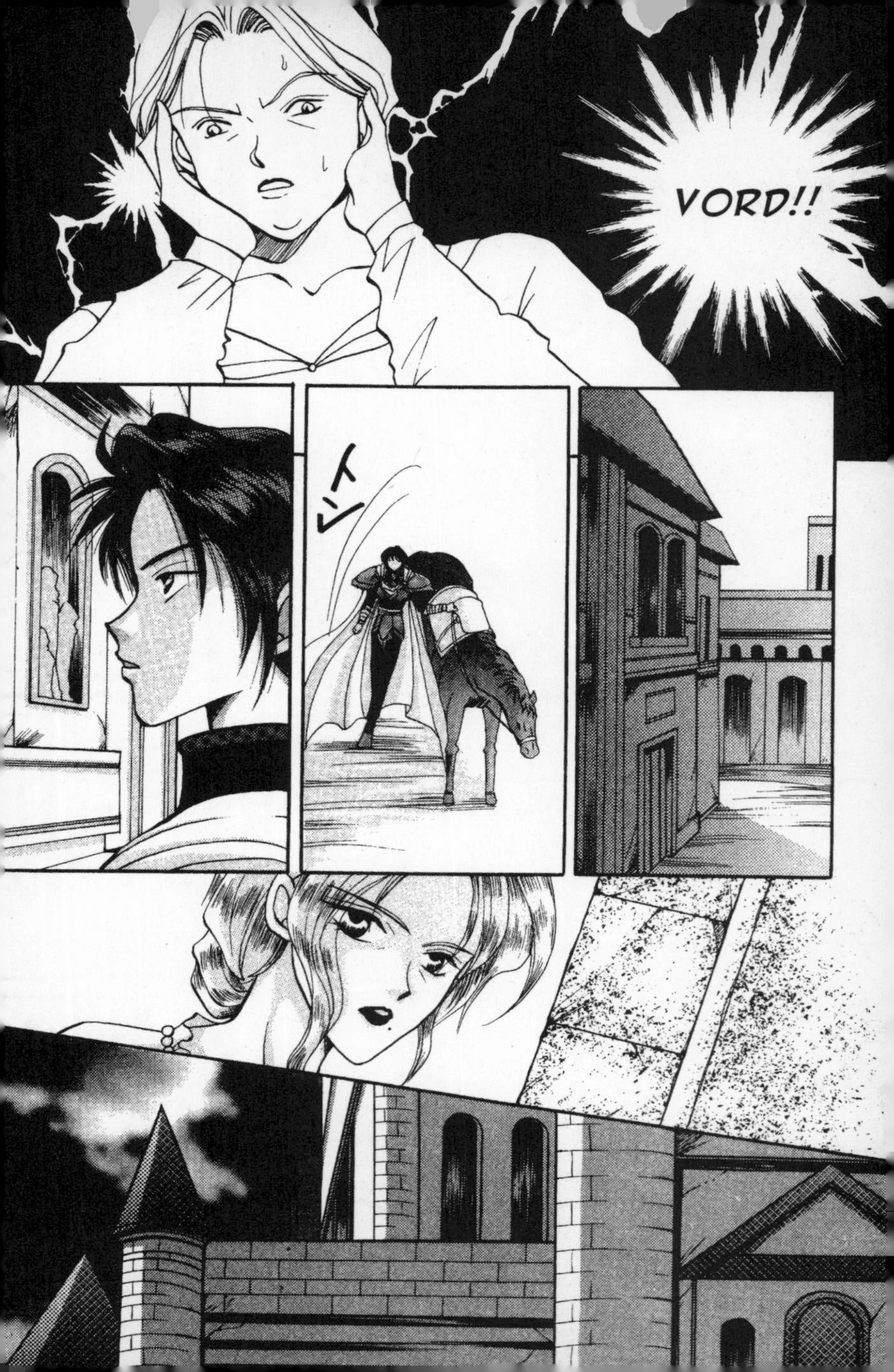
VORD!!
トン

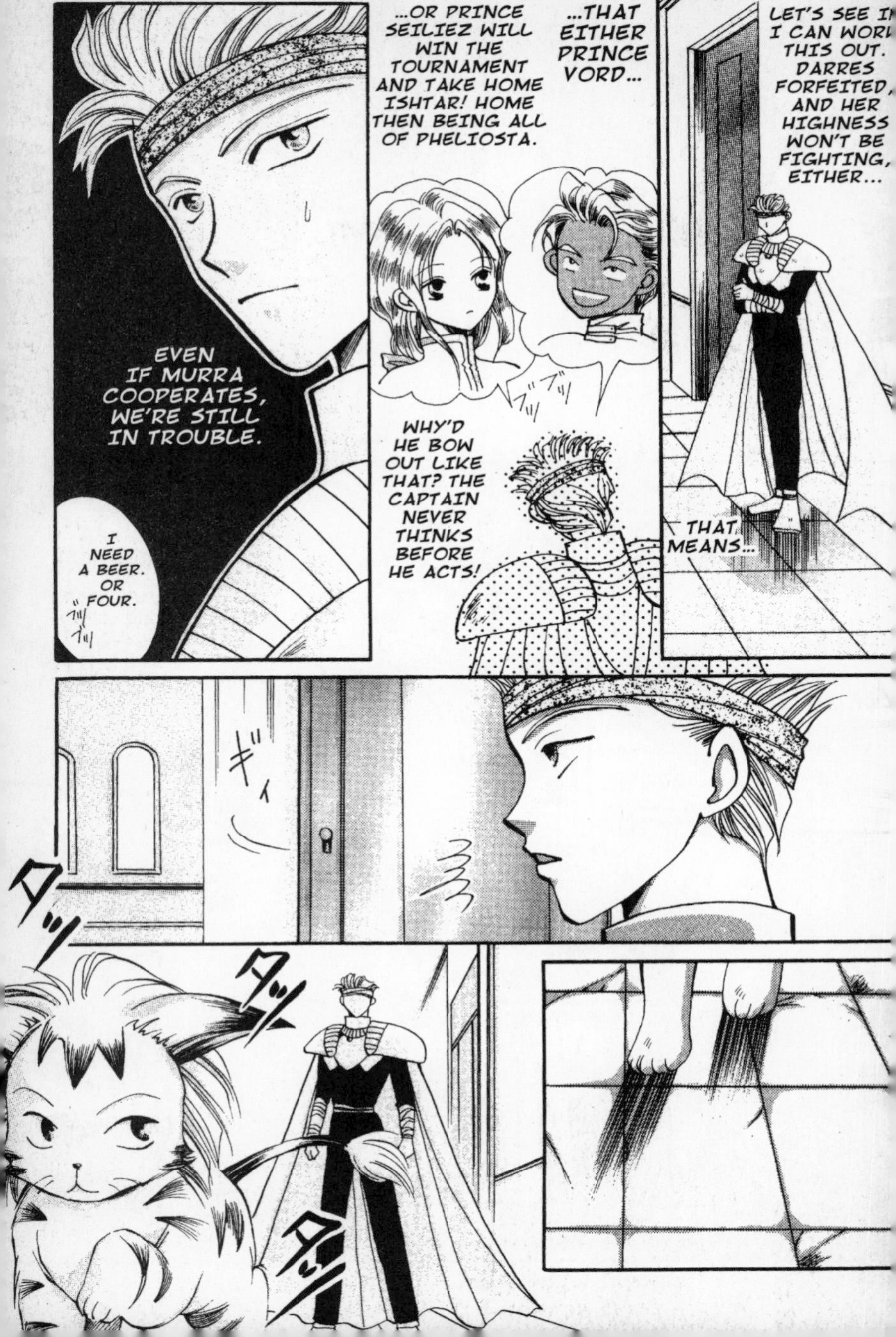
LET'S SEE I
I CAN WOR
THIS OUT.
DARRES
FORFEITED,
AND HER
HIGHNESS
WON'T BE
FIGHTING,
EITHER...
THAT MEANS...
...THAT EITHER PRINCE VORD...
...OR PRINCE SEILIEZ WILL WIN THE TOURNAMENT AND TAKE HOME ISHTAR! HOME THEN BEING ALL OF PHELIOSTA.
WHY'D HE BOW OUT LIKE THAT? THE CAPTAIN NEVER THINKS BEFORE HE ACTS!
EVEN IF MURRA COOPERATES, WE'RE STILL IN TROUBLE.
I NEED A BEER. OR FOUR.
ギィ
タッ
タッ
タッ

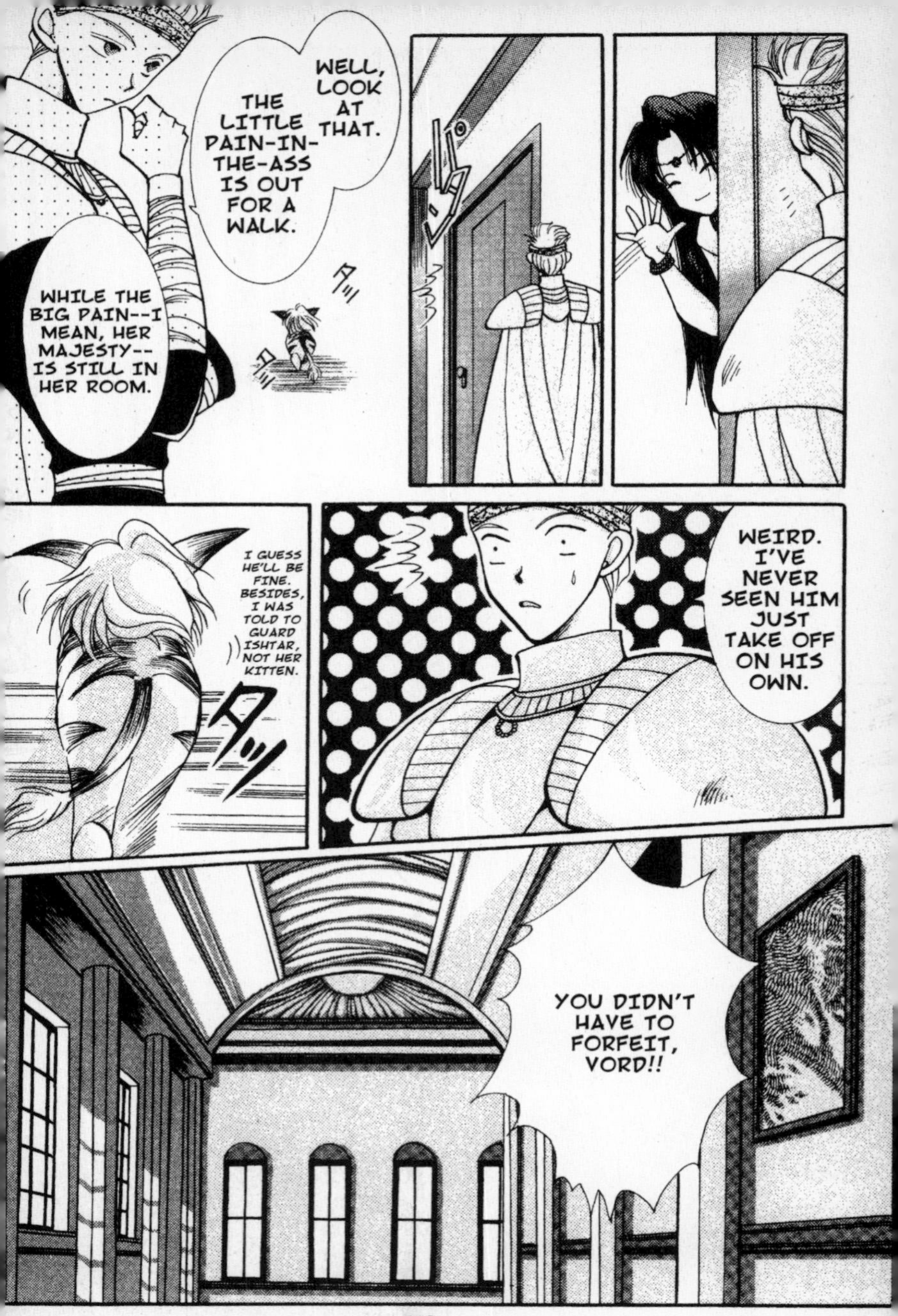
WELL, LOOK AT THAT.
THE LITTLE PAIN-IN-THE-ASS IS OUT FOR A WALK.
WHILE THE BIG PAIN--I MEAN, HER MAJESTY--IS STILL IN HER ROOM.
WEIRD. I'VE NEVER SEEN HIM JUST TAKE OFF ON HIS OWN.
I GUESS HE'LL BE FINE. BESIDES, I WAS TOLD TO GUARD ISHTAR, NOT HER KITTEN.
YOU DIDN'T HAVE TO FORFEIT, VORD!!

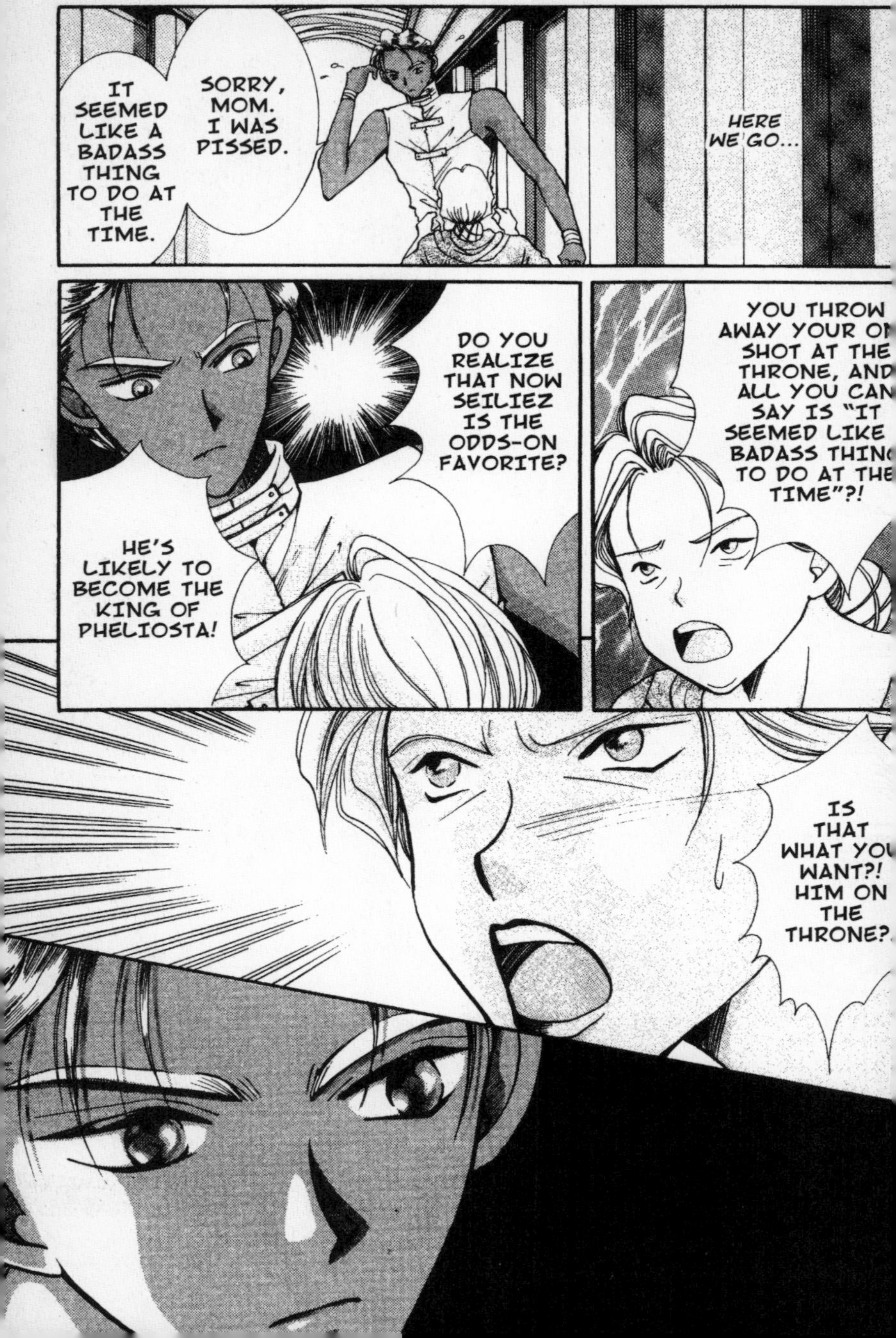
HERE WE GO...
SORRY, MOM. I WAS PISSED.
IT SEEMED LIKE A BADASS THING TO DO AT THE TIME.
YOU THROW AWAY YOUR ON SHOT AT THE THRONE, AND ALL YOU CAN SAY IS "IT SEEMED LIKE BADASS THIN TO DO AT THE TIME"?!
DO YOU REALIZE THAT NOW SEILIEZ IS THE ODDS-ON FAVORITE?
HE'S LIKELY TO BECOME THE KING OF PHELIOSTA!
IS THAT WHAT YOU WANT?! HIM ON THE THRONE?

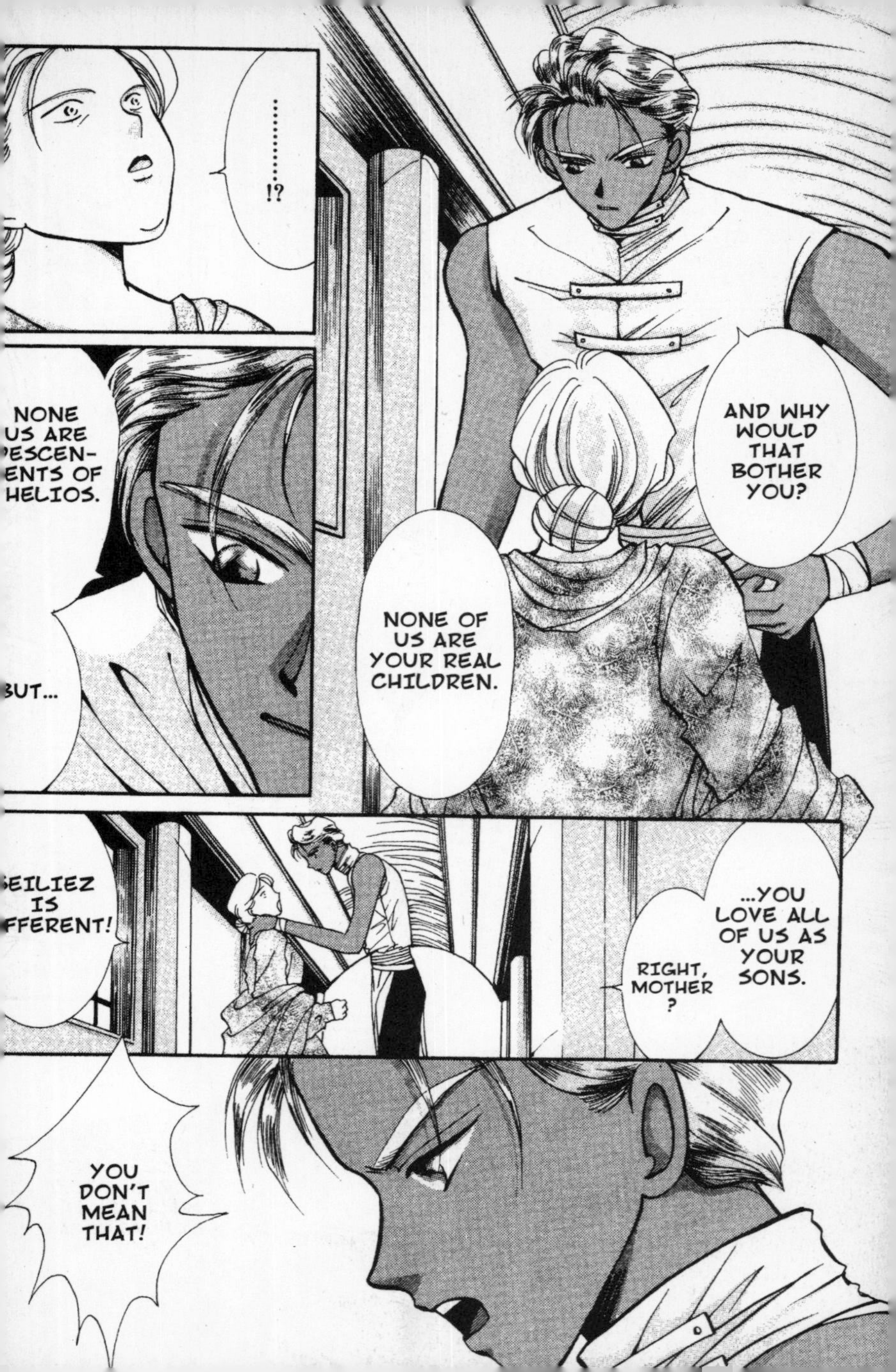
AND WHY WOULD THAT BOTHER YOU?
NONE OF US ARE YOUR REAL CHILDREN.
......!?
NONE US ARE ESCEN- ENTS OF HELIOS.
BUT...
...YOU LOVE ALL OF US AS YOUR SONS.
RIGHT, MOTHER?
EILIEZ IS FFERENT!
YOU DON'T MEAN THAT!

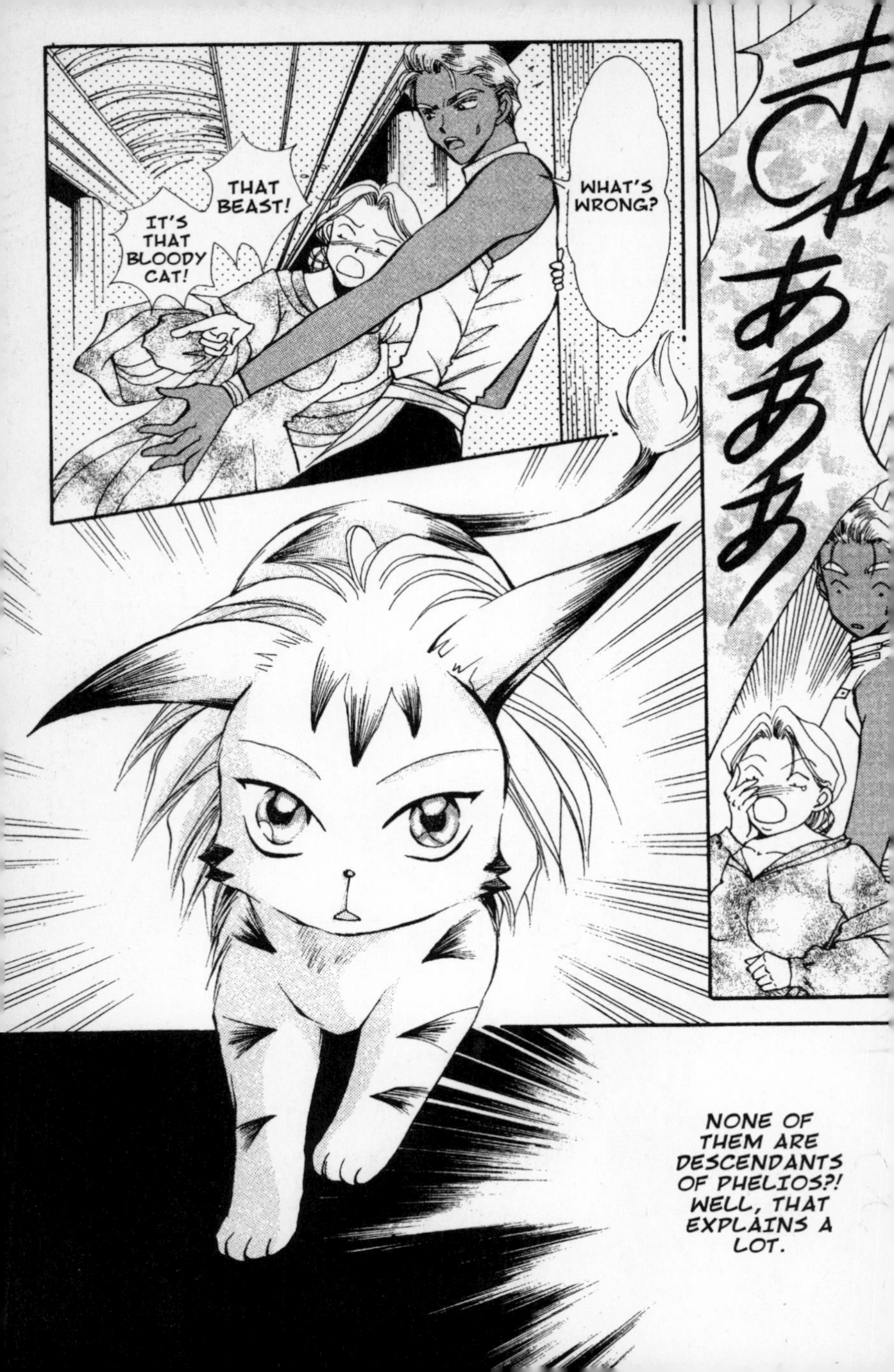
WHAT'S WRONG?
THAT BEAST!
IT'S THAT BLOODY CAT!
NONE OF THEM ARE DESCENDANTS OF PHELIOS?! WELL, THAT EXPLAINS A LOT.

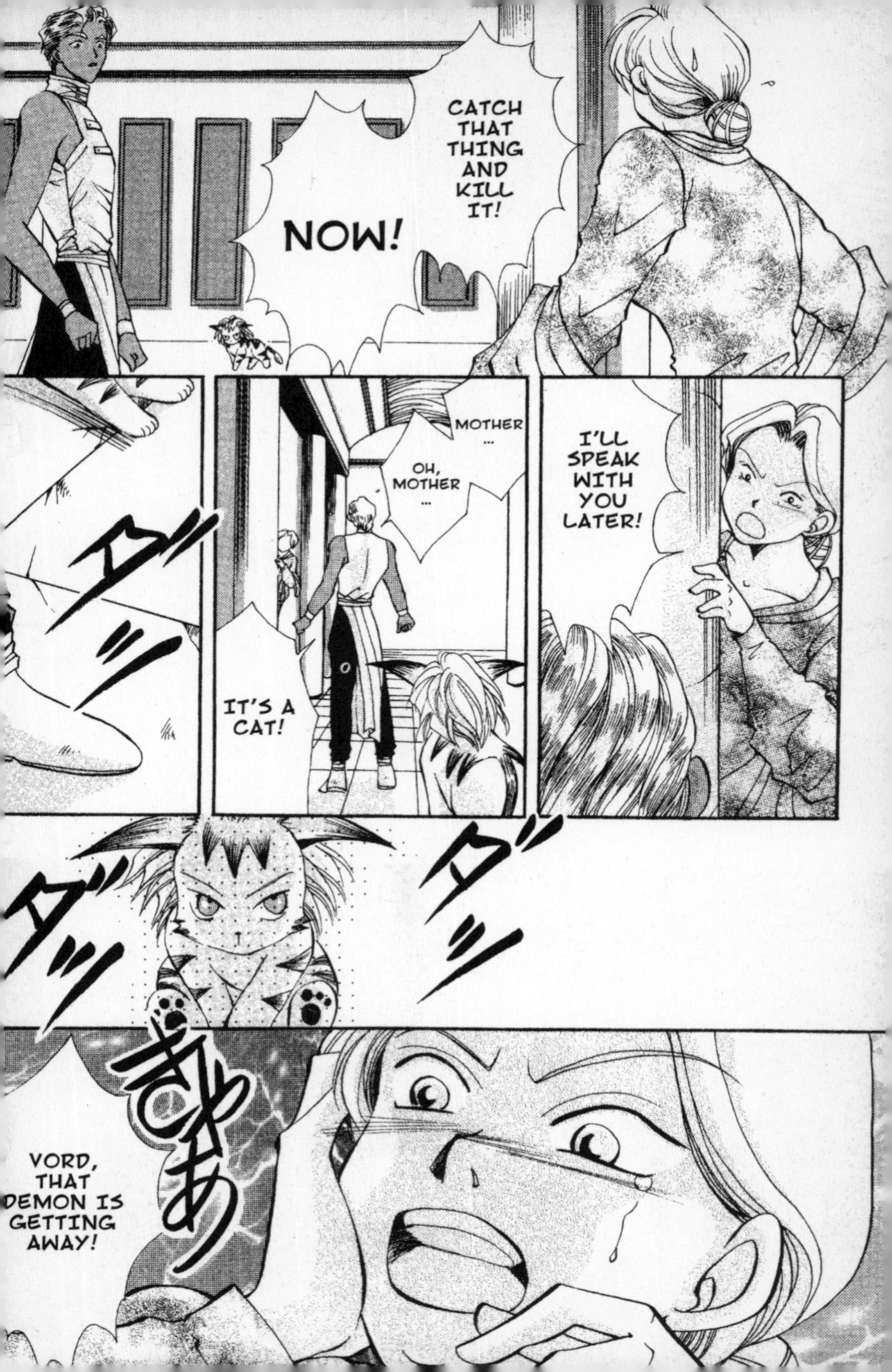
CATCH THAT THING AND KILL IT!
NOW!
I'LL SPEAK WITH YOU LATER!
MOTHER ...
OH, MOTHER ...
IT'S A CAT!
ダッ
ダッ
ダッ
きゃあ
VORD, THAT DEMON IS GETTING AWAY!

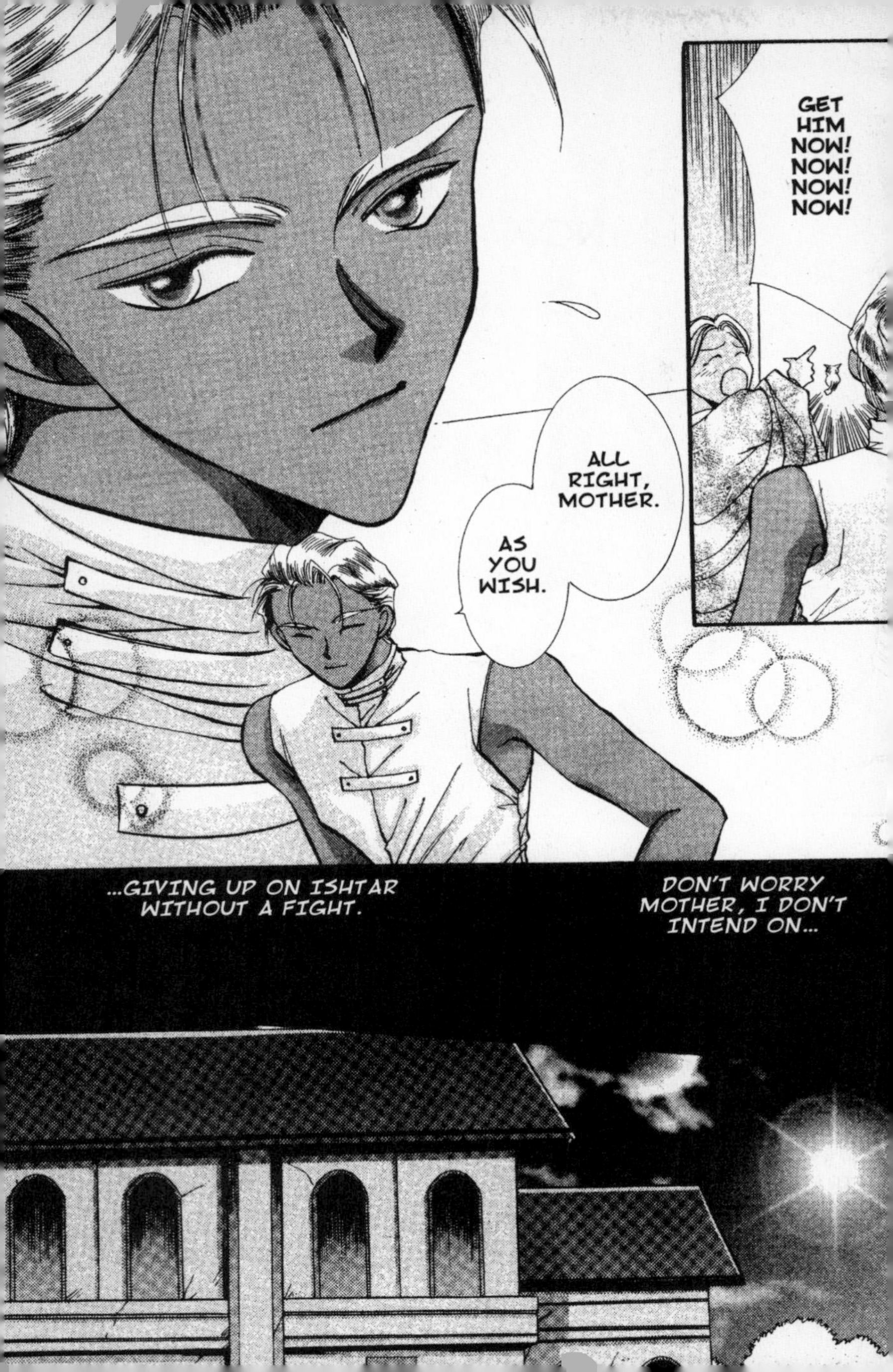
GET HIM NOW! NOW! NOW! NOW!
ALL RIGHT, MOTHER.
AS YOU WISH.
DON'T WORRY MOTHER, I DON'T INTEND ON...
...GIVING UP ON ISHTAR WITHOUT A FIGHT.

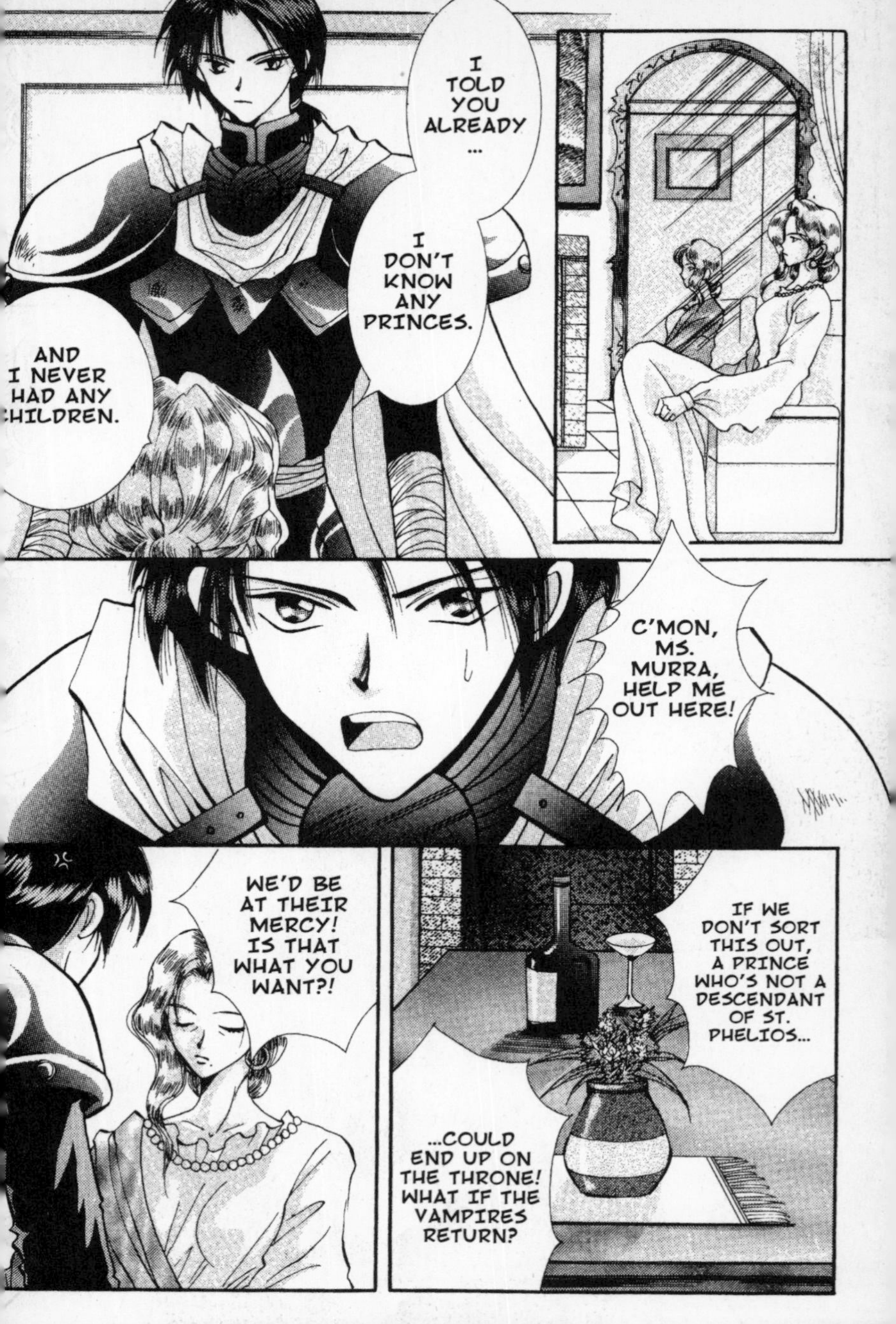
I TOLD YOU ALREADY ...
I DON'T KNOW ANY PRINCES.
AND I NEVER HAD ANY CHILDREN.
C'MON, MS. MURRA, HELP ME OUT HERE!
IF WE DON'T SORT THIS OUT, A PRINCE WHO'S NOT A DESCENDANT OF ST. PHELIOS...
...COULD END UP ON THE THRONE! WHAT IF THE VAMPIRES RETURN?
WE'D BE AT THEIR MERCY! IS THAT WHAT YOU WANT?!

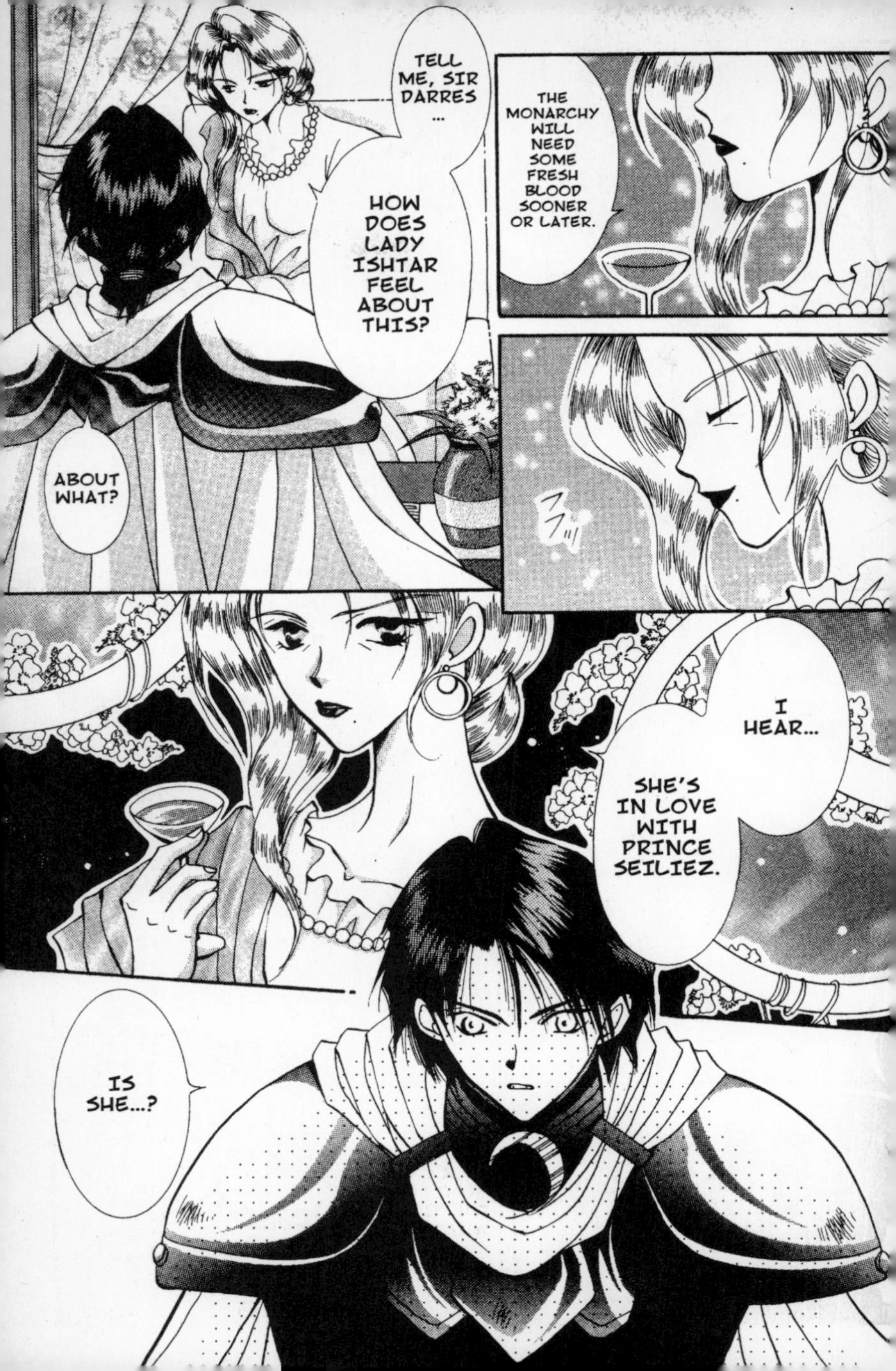
THE MONARCHY WILL NEED SOME FRESH BLOOD SOONER OR LATER.
フフッ
TELL ME, SIR DARRES ...
HOW DOES LADY ISHTAR FEEL ABOUT THIS?
ABOUT WHAT?
I HEAR...
SHE'S IN LOVE WITH PRINCE SEILIEZ.
IS SHE...?

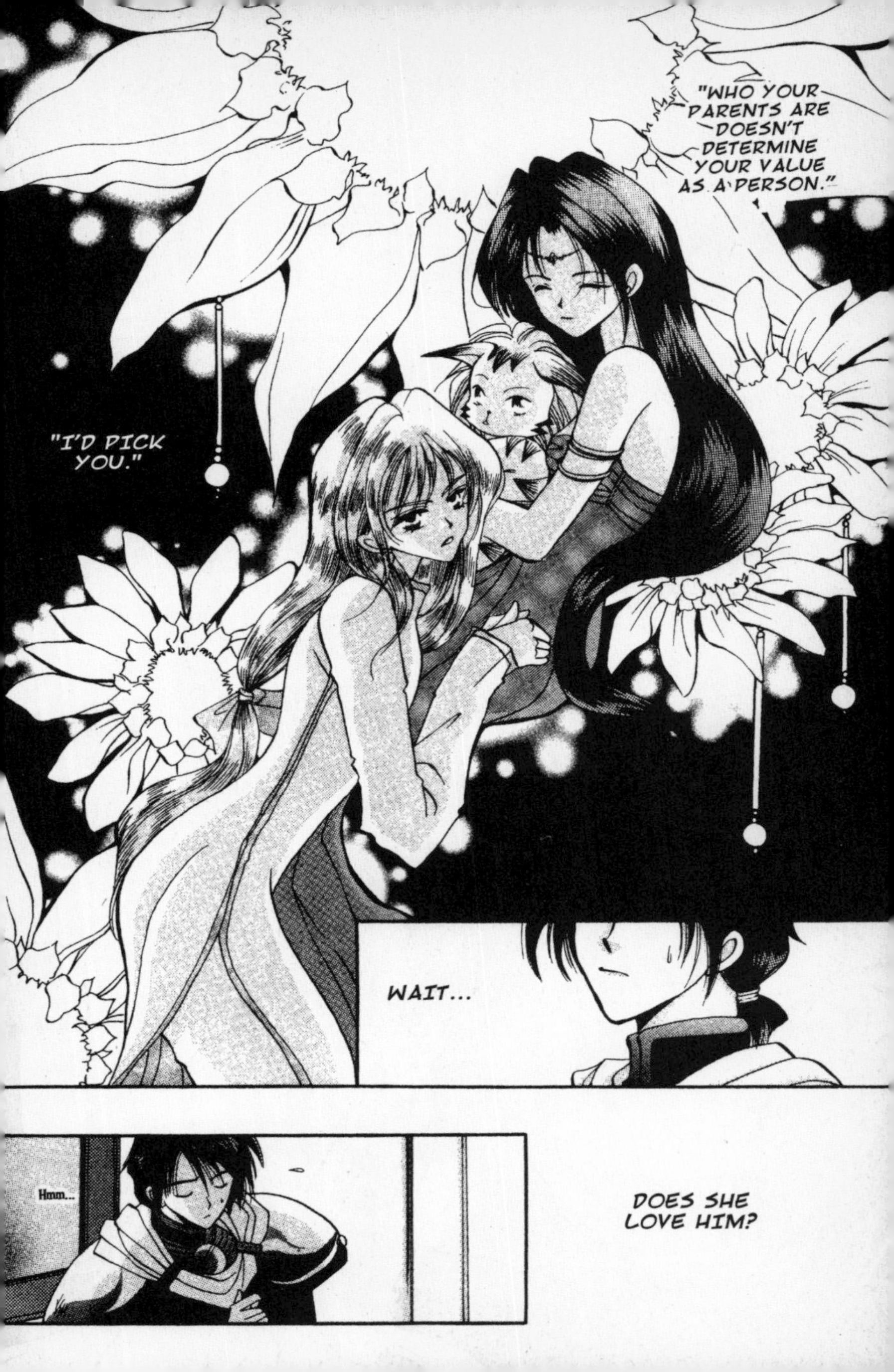
"WHO YOUR PARENTS ARE DOESN'T DETERMINE YOUR VALUE AS A PERSON."
"I'D PICK YOU."
WAIT...
DOES SHE LOVE HIM?
Hmm...

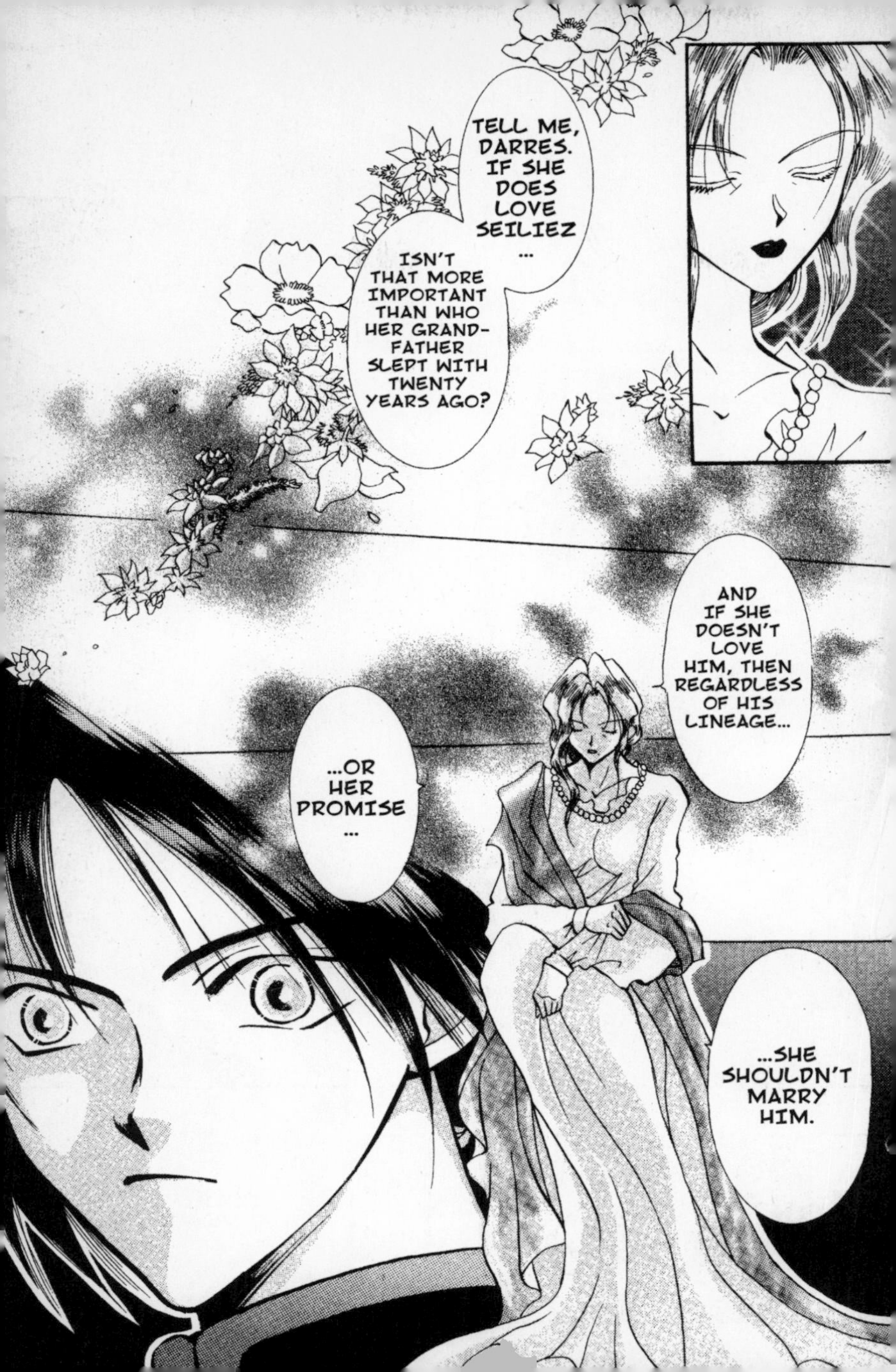
TELL ME, DARRES. IF SHE DOES LOVE SEILIEZ ...
ISN'T THAT MORE IMPORTANT THAN WHO HER GRAND-FATHER SLEPT WITH TWENTY YEARS AGO?
AND IF SHE DOESN'T LOVE HIM, THEN REGARDLESS OF HIS LINEAGE...
...OR HER PROMISE ...
...SHE SHOULDN'T MARRY HIM.

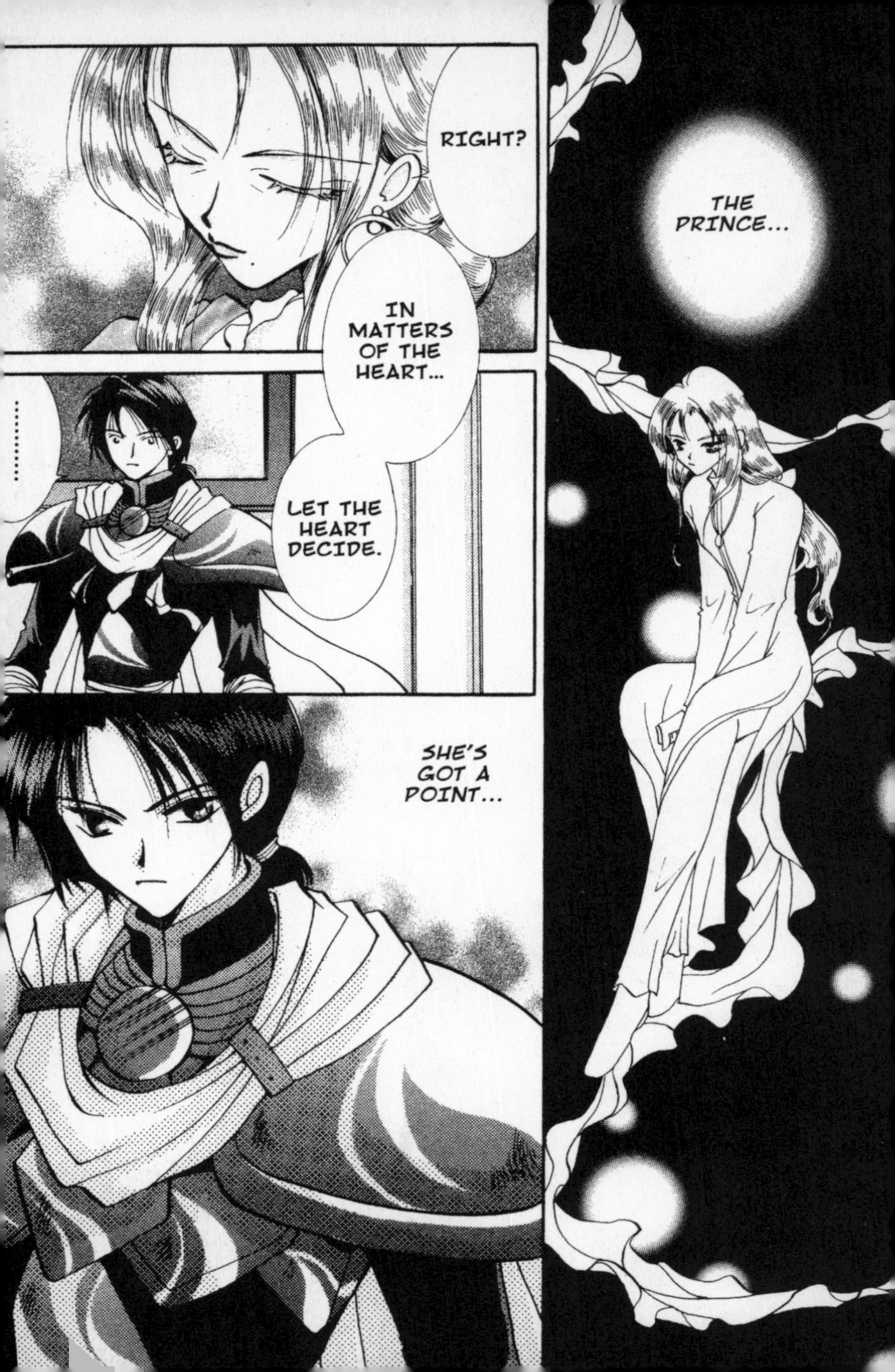
THE PRINCE...
RIGHT?
IN MATTERS OF THE HEART...
LET THE HEART DECIDE.
......
SHE'S GOT A POINT...

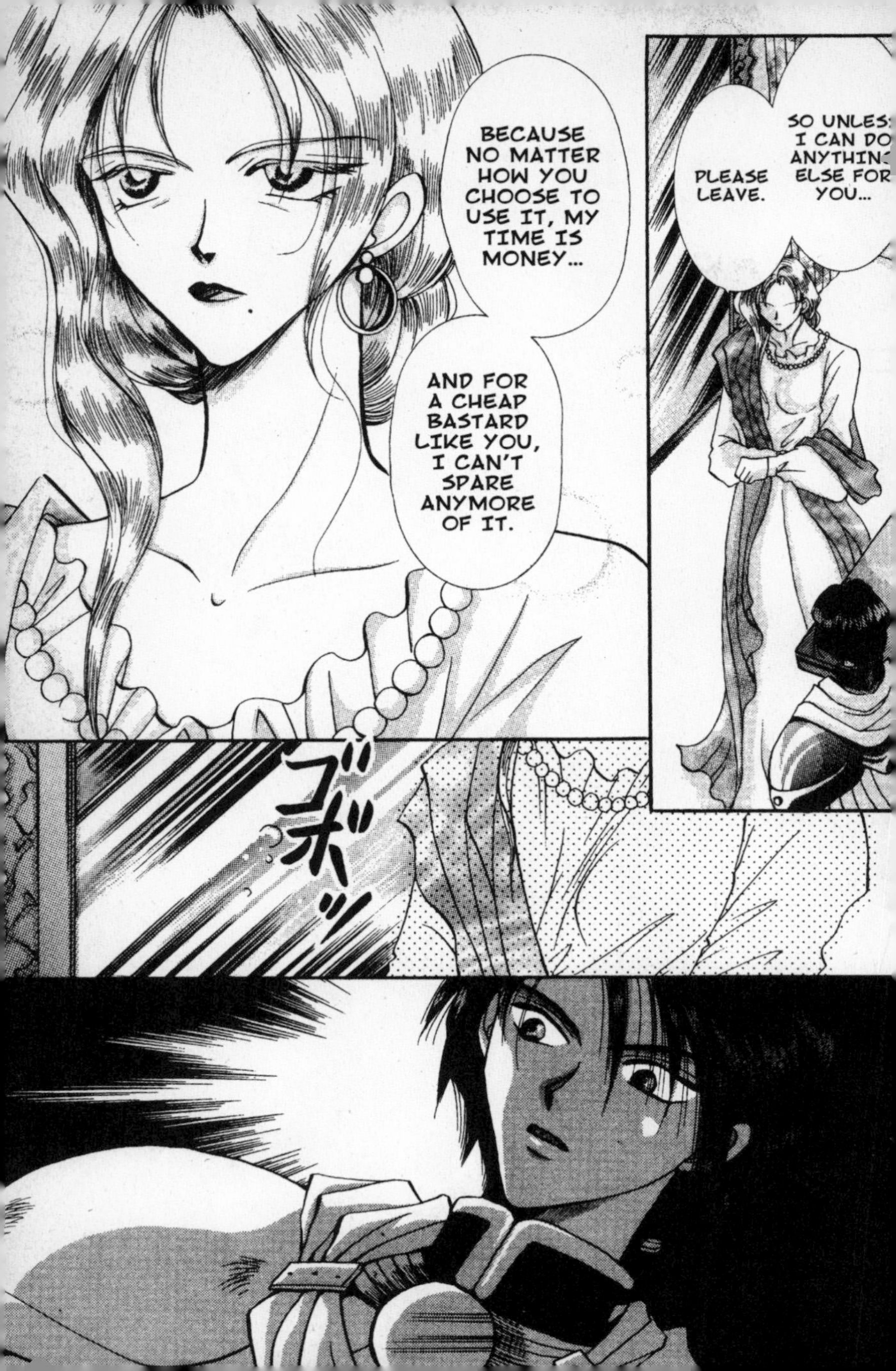
SO UNLES I CAN DO ANYTHIN ELSE FOR YOU...
PLEASE LEAVE.
BECAUSE NO MATTER HOW YOU CHOOSE TO USE IT, MY TIME IS MONEY...
AND FOR A CHEAP BASTARD LIKE YOU, I CAN'T SPARE ANYMORE OF IT.
ゴボッ

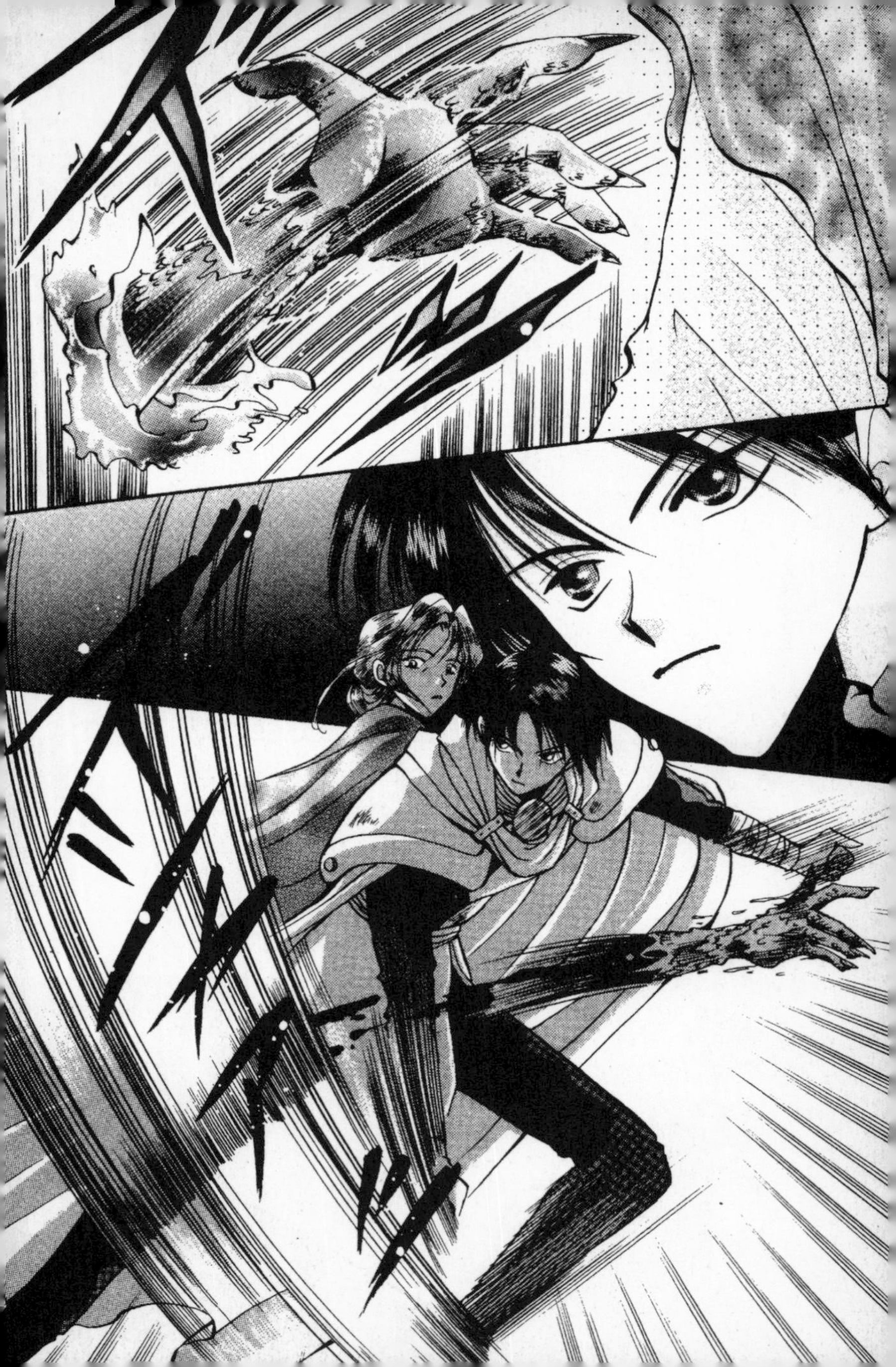

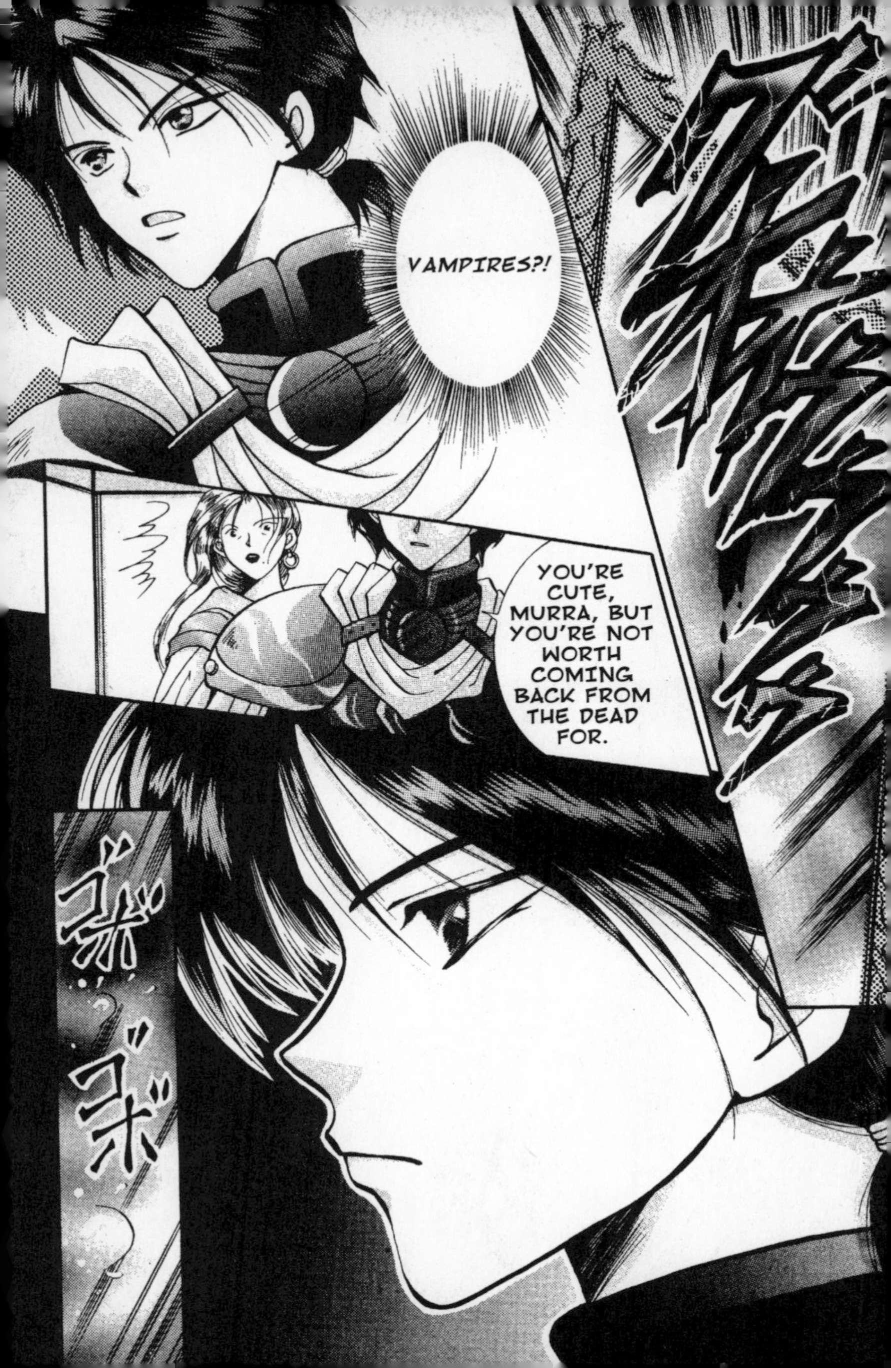
VAMPIRES?!
YOU'RE CUTE, MURRA, BUT YOU'RE NOT WORTH COMING BACK FROM THE DEAD FOR.
ゴボ ゴボ

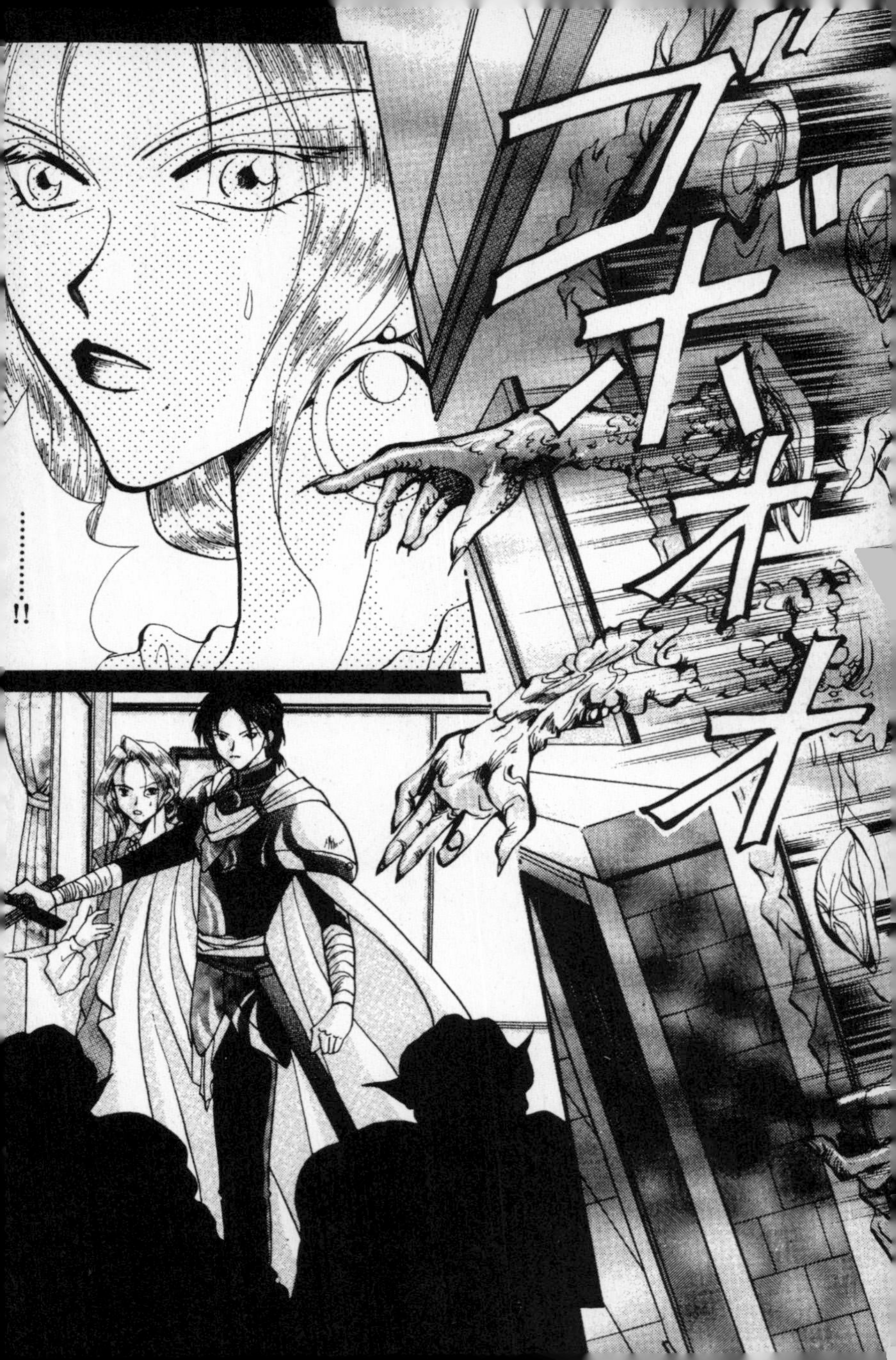
ブオオオ
……!!

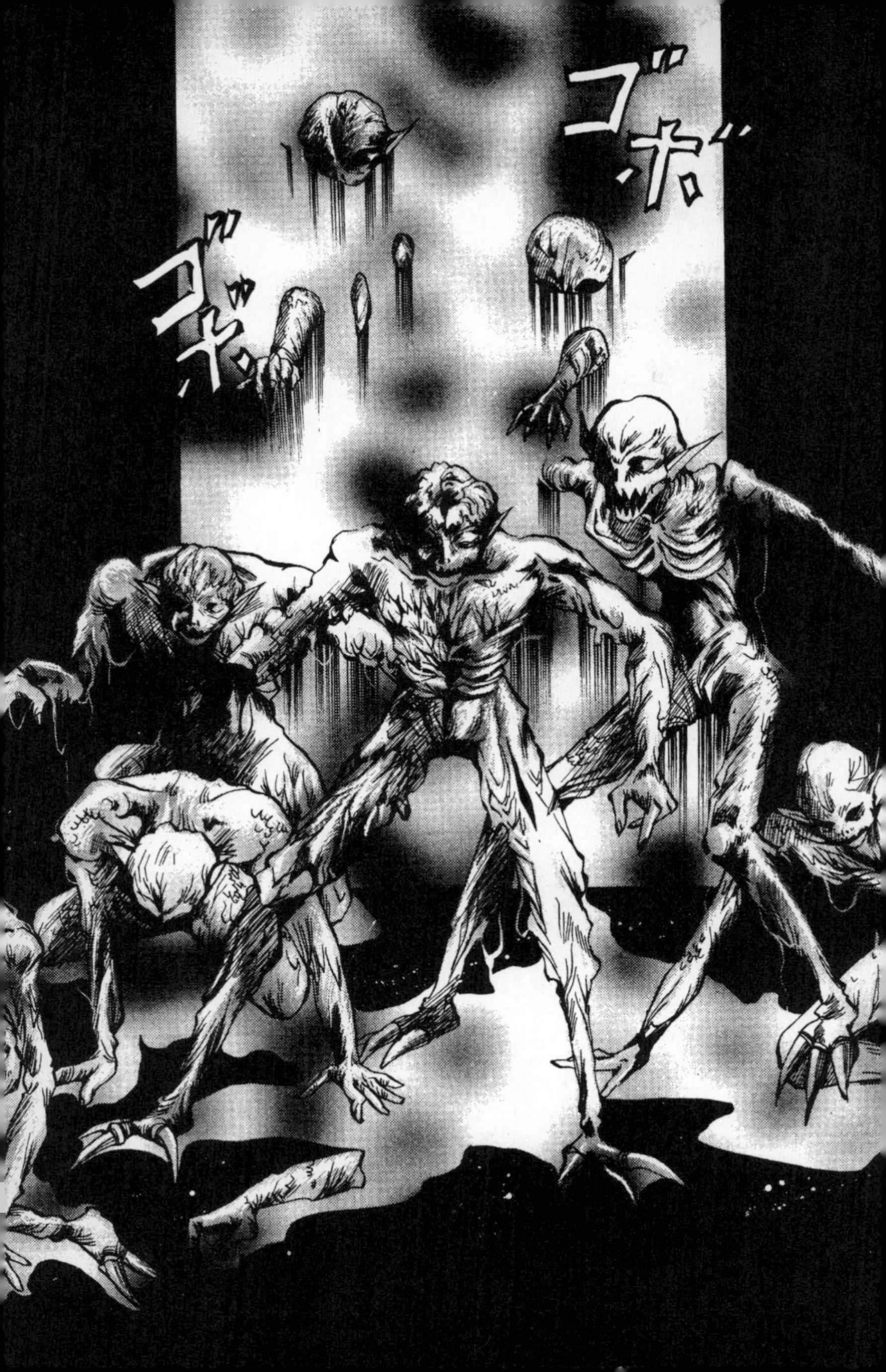
ゴポ
ゴポッ

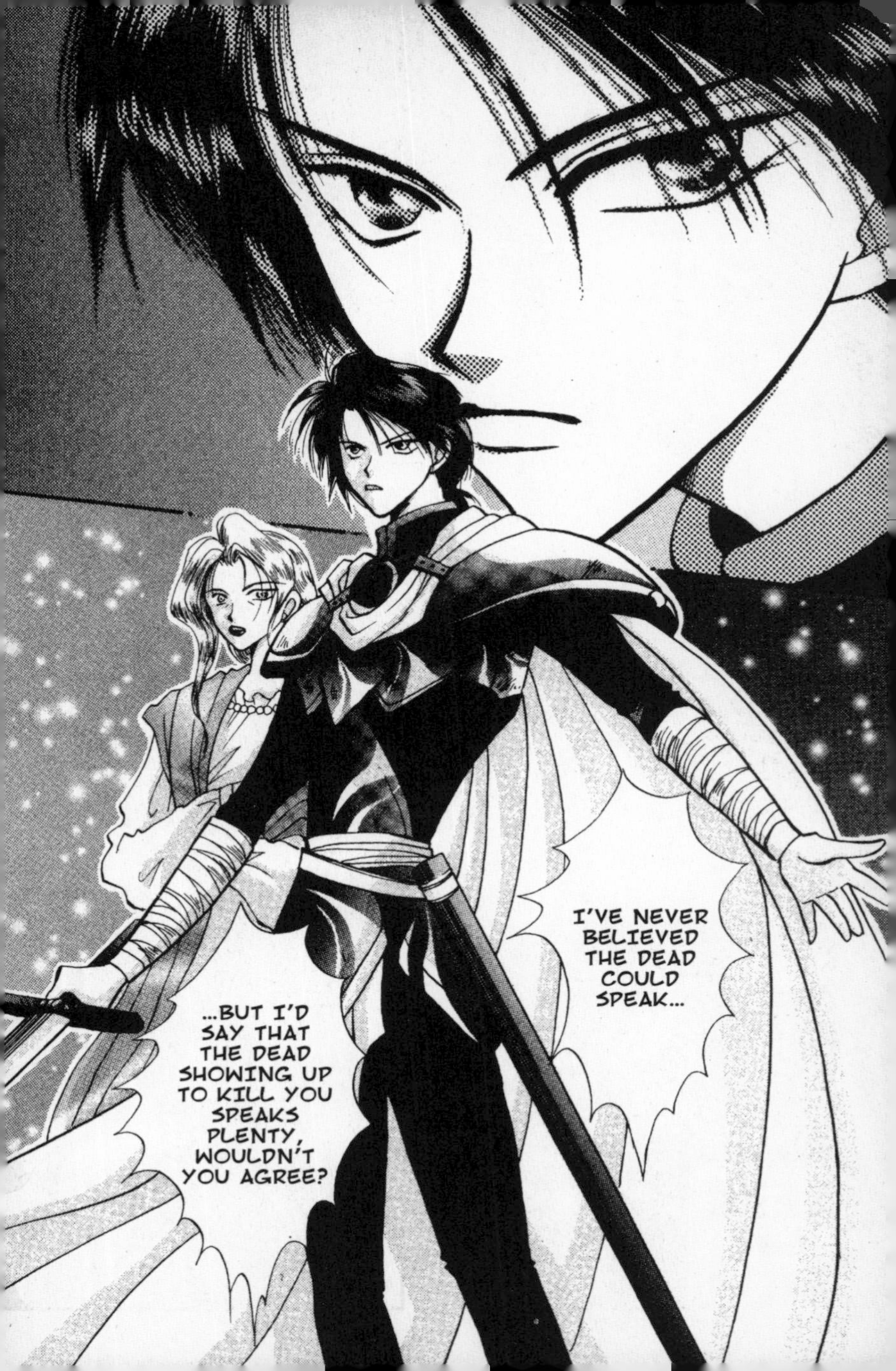
I'VE NEVER BELIEVED THE DEAD COULD SPEAK...
...BUT I'D SAY THAT THE DEAD SHOWING UP TO KILL YOU SPEAKS PLENTY, WOULDN'T YOU AGREE?

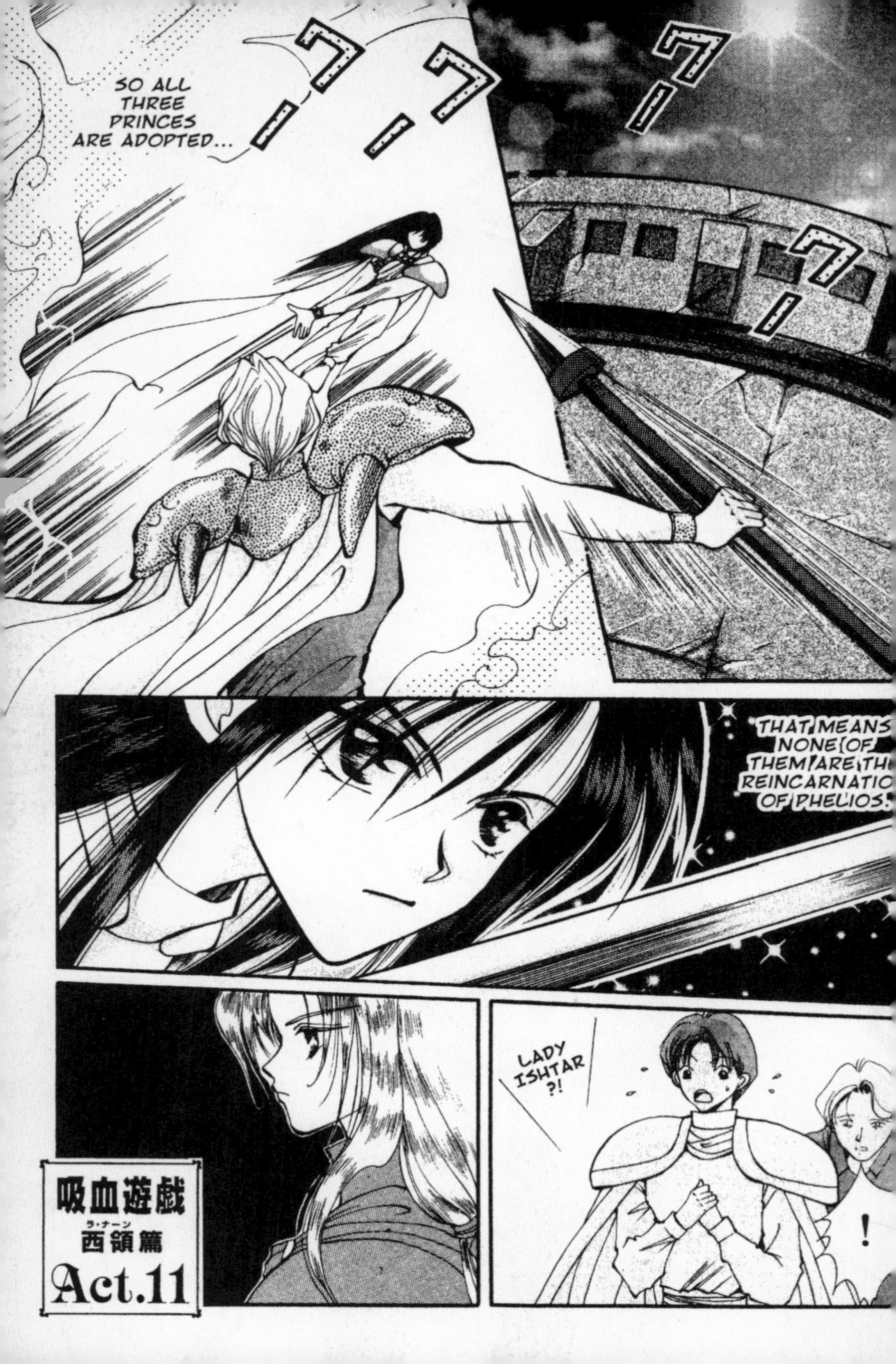
SO ALL THREE PRINCES ARE ADOPTED...
THAT MEANS NONE OF THEM ARE TH REINCARNATIO OF PHELIOS.
LADY ISHTAR ?!
!
吸血遊戯
ラ・ナーン
西領篇
Act.11

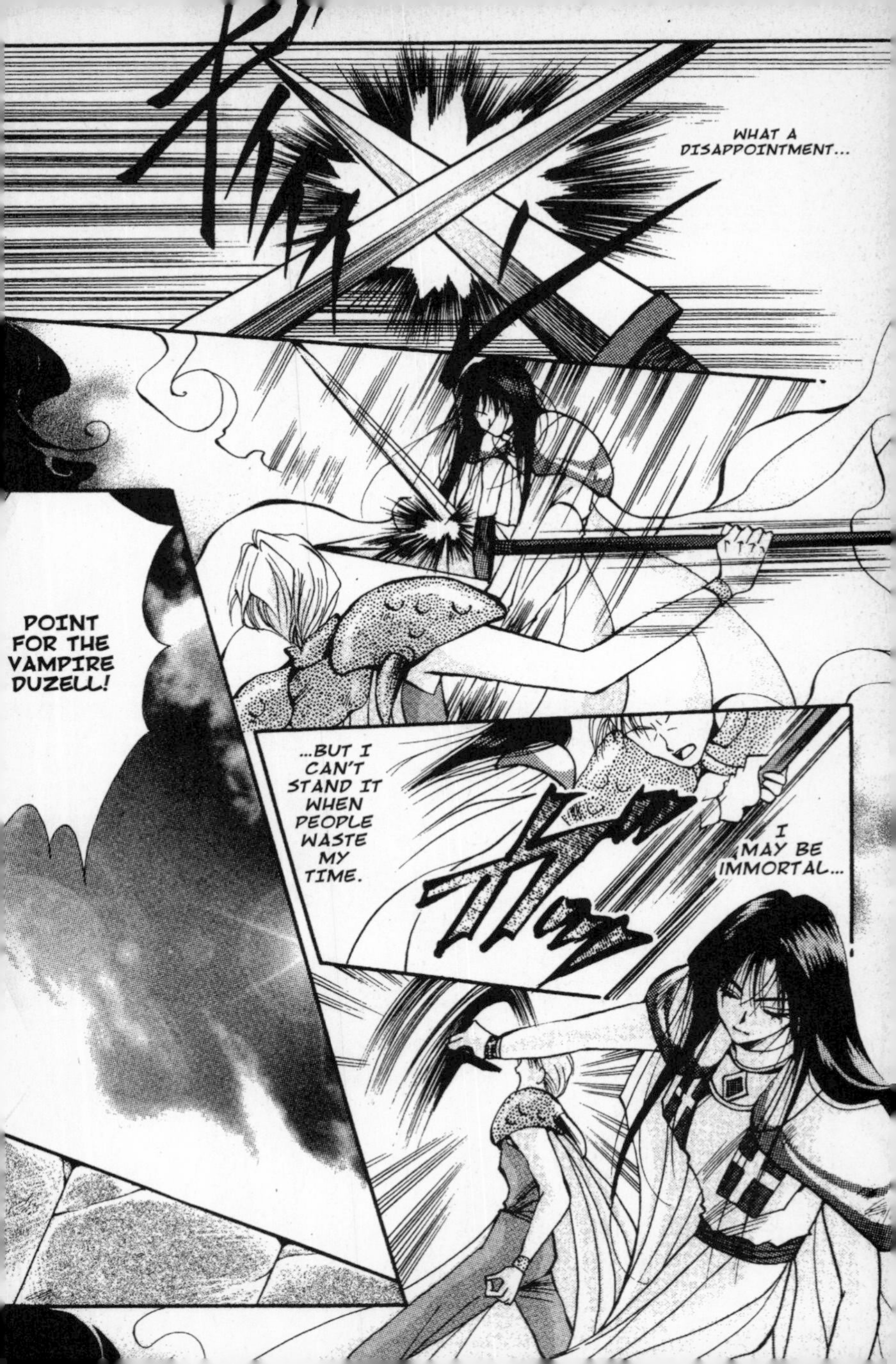
WHAT A DISAPPOINTMENT...
I MAY BE IMMORTAL...
...BUT I CAN'T STAND IT WHEN PEOPLE WASTE MY TIME.
POINT FOR THE VAMPIRE DUZELL!

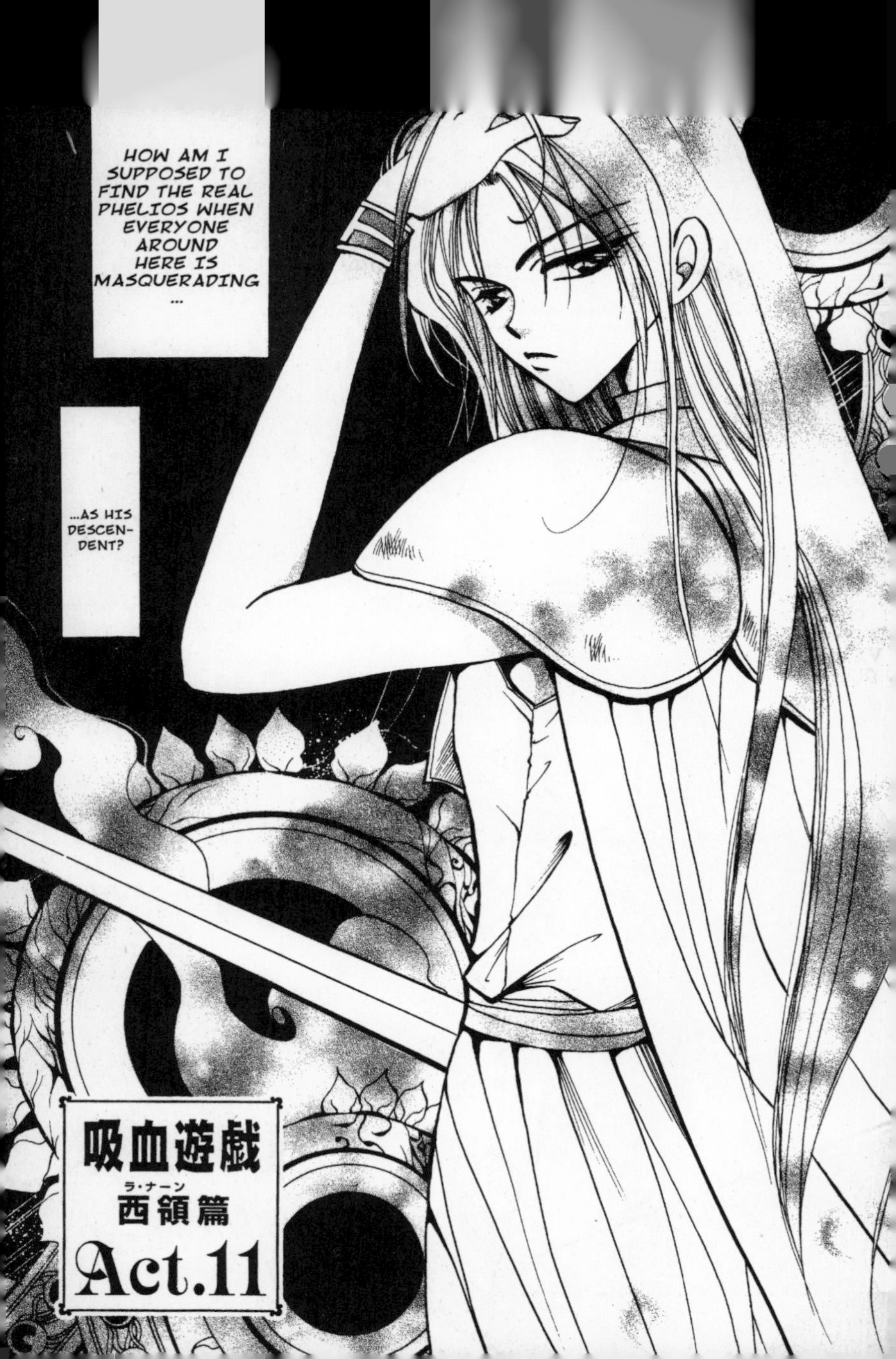
HOW AM I SUPPOSED TO FIND THE REAL PHELIOS WHEN EVERYONE AROUND HERE IS MASQUERADING...
...AS HIS DESCENDENT?
吸血遊戯
ラ・ナーン
西領篇
Act.11

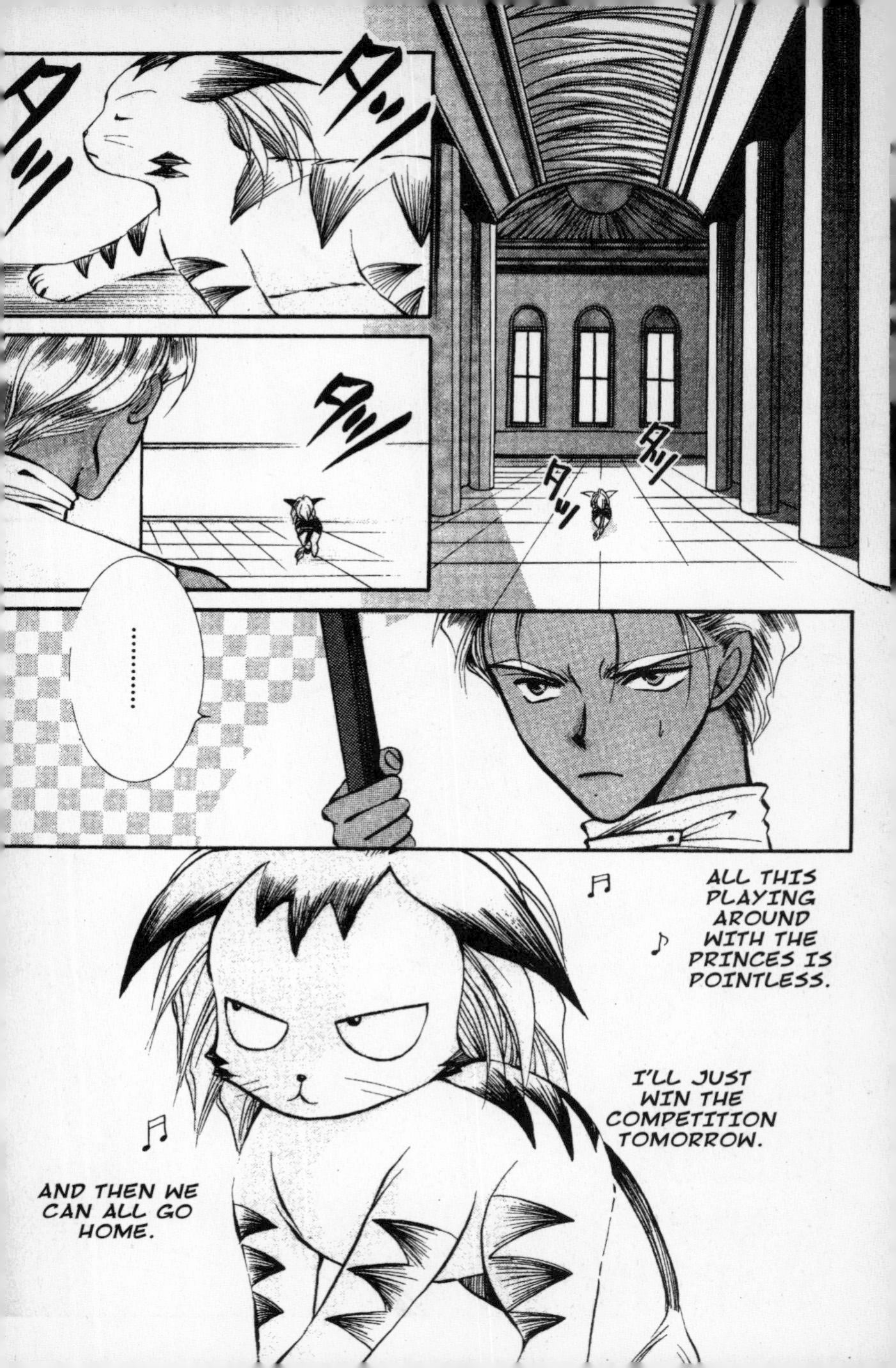

タッ
タッ
タッ
タッ
タッ
……
ALL THIS PLAYING AROUND WITH THE PRINCES IS POINTLESS.
I'LL JUST WIN THE COMPETITION TOMORROW.
AND THEN WE CAN ALL GO HOME.

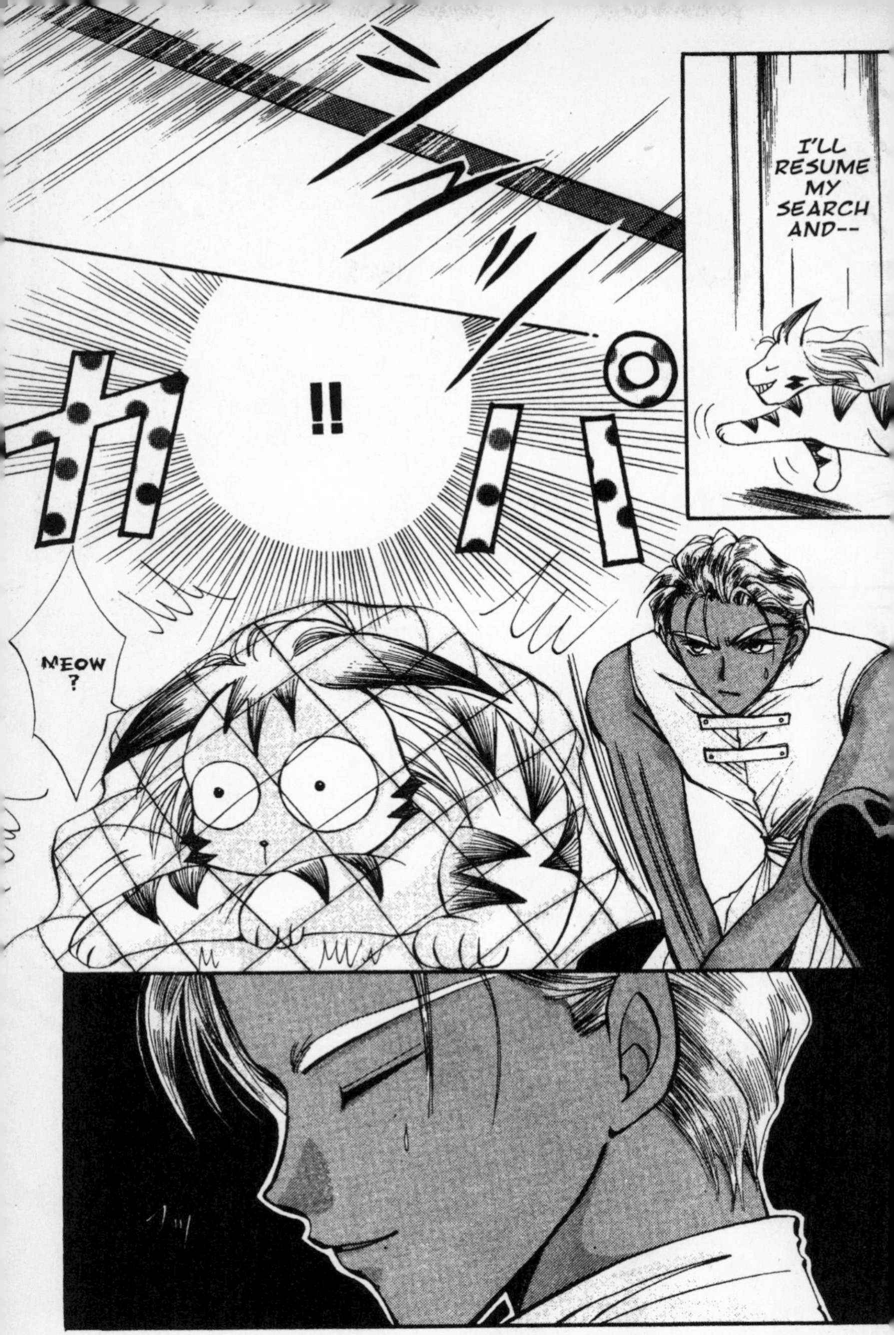
I'LL RESUME MY SEARCH AND--
!!
MEOW ?

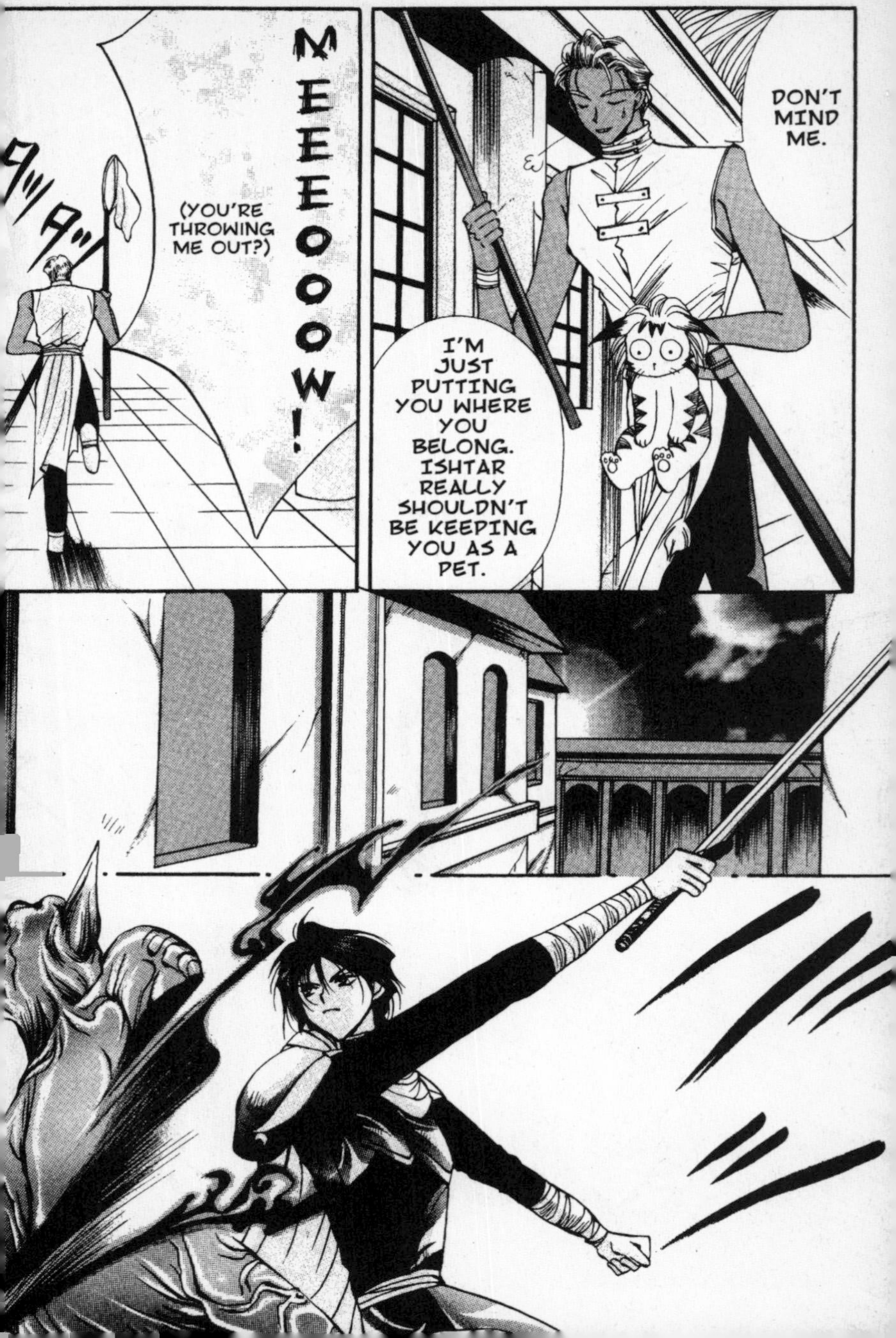
DON'T MIND ME.
I'M JUST PUTTING YOU WHERE YOU BELONG. ISHTAR REALLY SHOULDN'T BE KEEPING YOU AS A PET.
MEEEOOOW!
(YOU'RE THROWING ME OUT?)
タッタッ

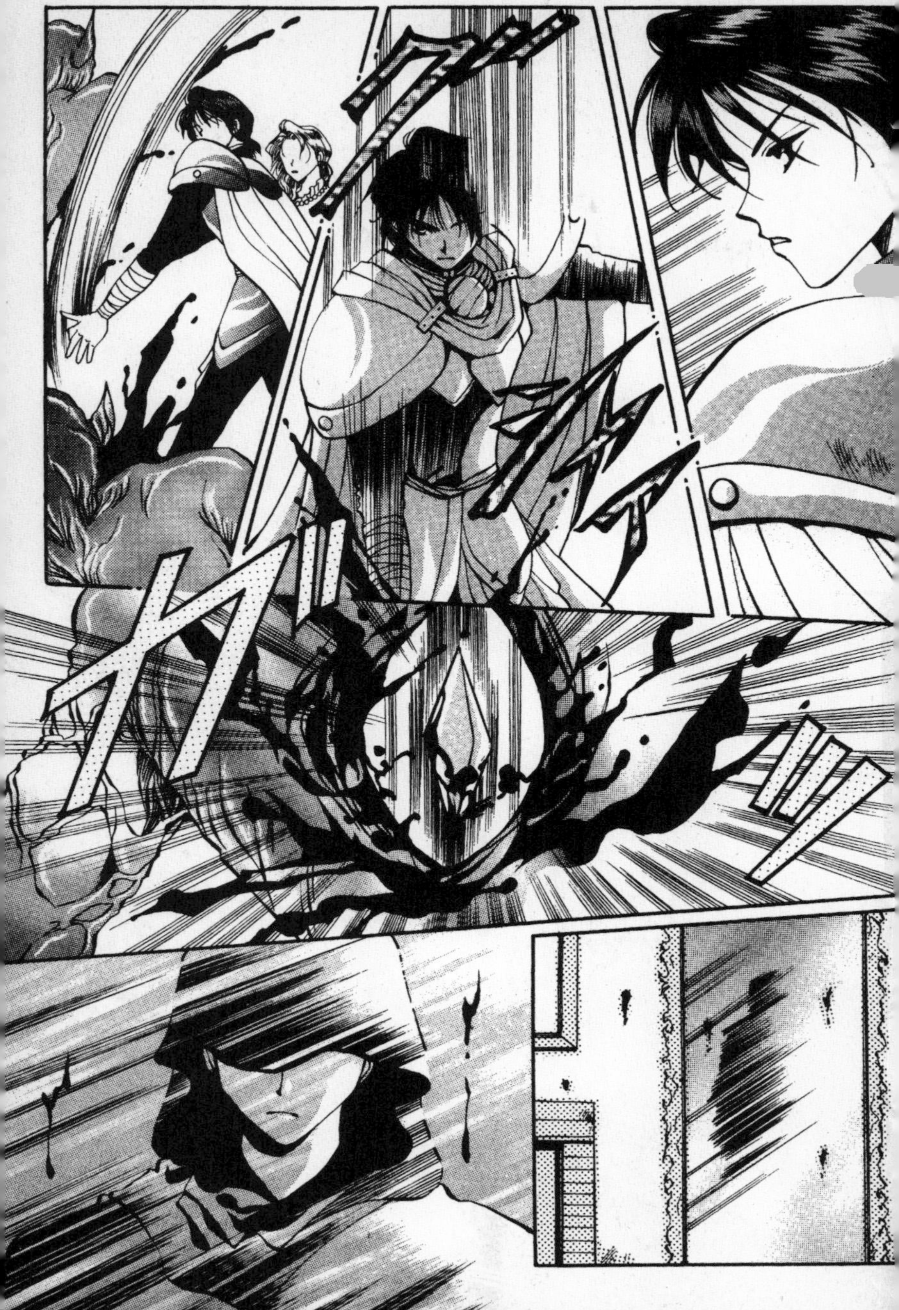

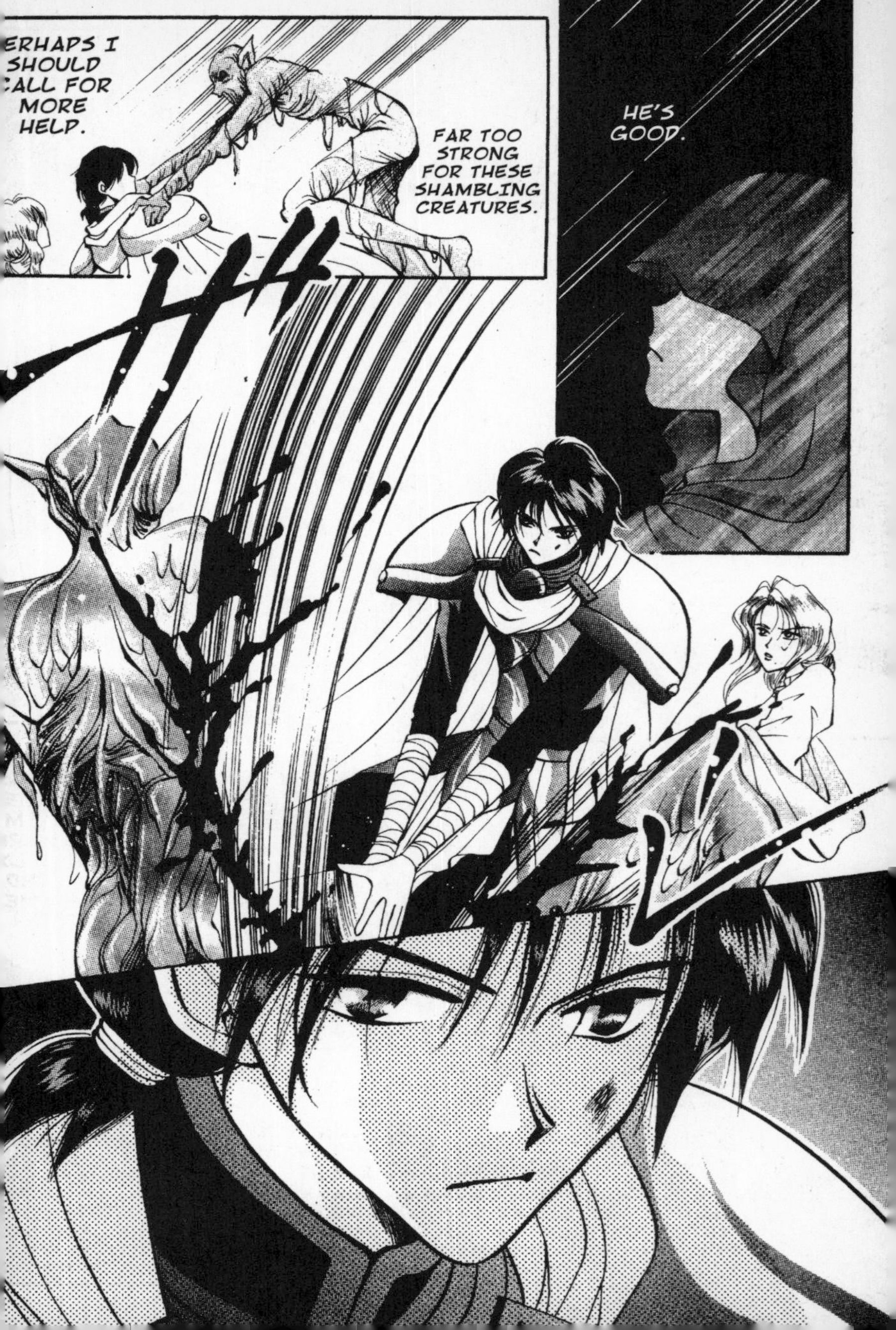
HE'S GOOD.
FAR TOO STRONG FOR THESE SHAMBLING CREATURES.
ERHAPS I SHOULD CALL FOR MORE HELP.

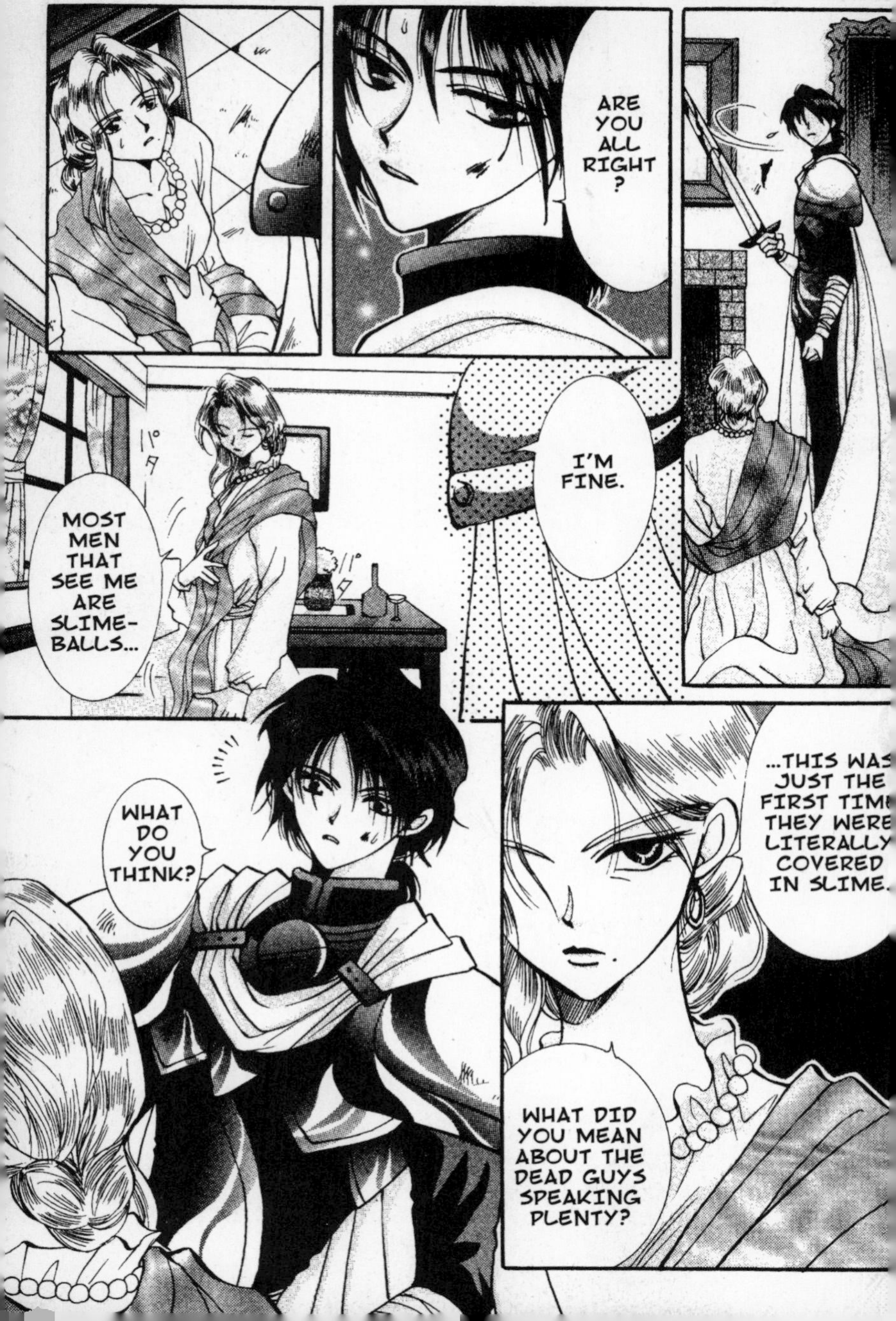

ARE YOU ALL RIGHT?
I'M FINE.
MOST MEN THAT SEE ME ARE SLIME-BALLS...
パタ
パ
...THIS WAS JUST THE FIRST TIME THEY WERE LITERALLY COVERED IN SLIME.
WHAT DID YOU MEAN ABOUT THE DEAD GUYS SPEAKING PLENTY?
WHAT DO YOU THINK?

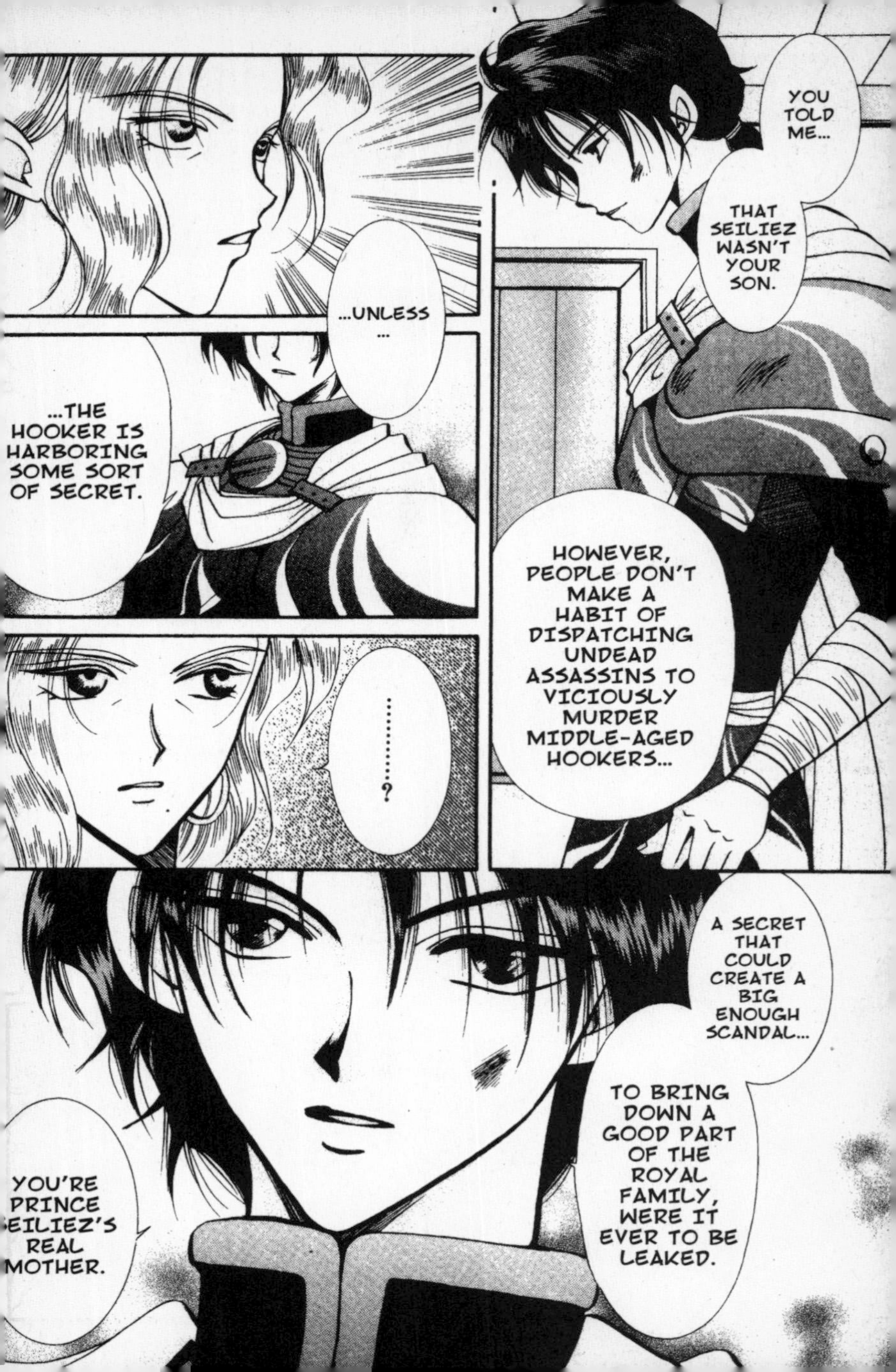
YOU TOLD ME...
THAT SEILIEZ WASN'T YOUR SON.
HOWEVER, PEOPLE DON'T MAKE A HABIT OF DISPATCHING UNDEAD ASSASSINS TO VICIOUSLY MURDER MIDDLE-AGED HOOKERS...
...UNLESS ...
...THE HOOKER IS HARBORING SOME SORT OF SECRET.
.........?
A SECRET THAT COULD CREATE A BIG ENOUGH SCANDAL...
TO BRING DOWN A GOOD PART OF THE ROYAL FAMILY, WERE IT EVER TO BE LEAKED.
YOU'RE PRINCE EILIEZ'S REAL MOTHER.

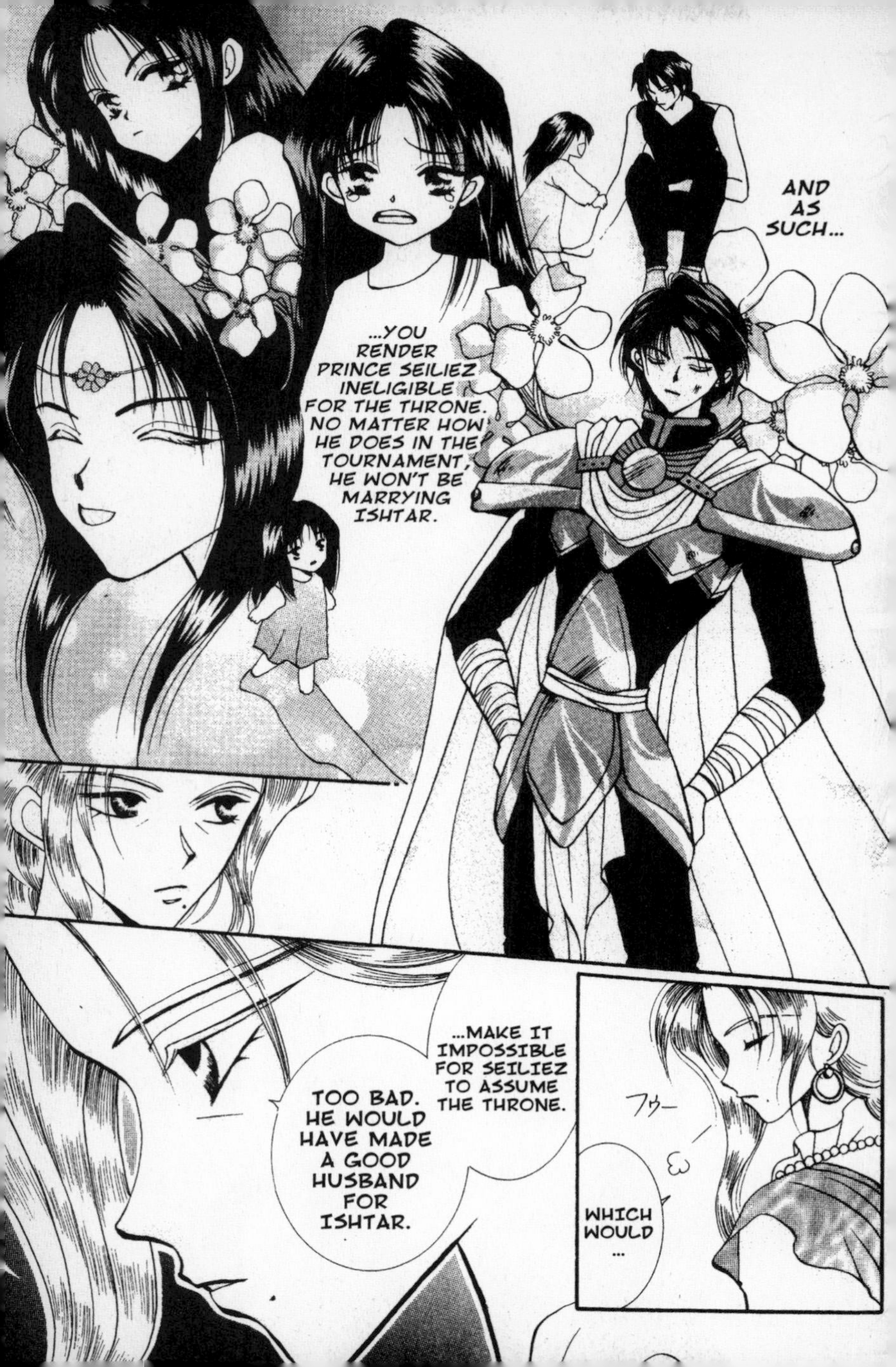
AND AS SUCH...
...YOU RENDER PRINCE SEILIEZ INELIGIBLE FOR THE THRONE. NO MATTER HOW HE DOES IN THE TOURNAMENT, HE WON'T BE MARRYING ISHTAR.
フゥー
WHICH WOULD ...
...MAKE IT IMPOSSIBLE FOR SEILIEZ TO ASSUME THE THRONE.
TOO BAD. HE WOULD HAVE MADE A GOOD HUSBAND FOR ISHTAR.

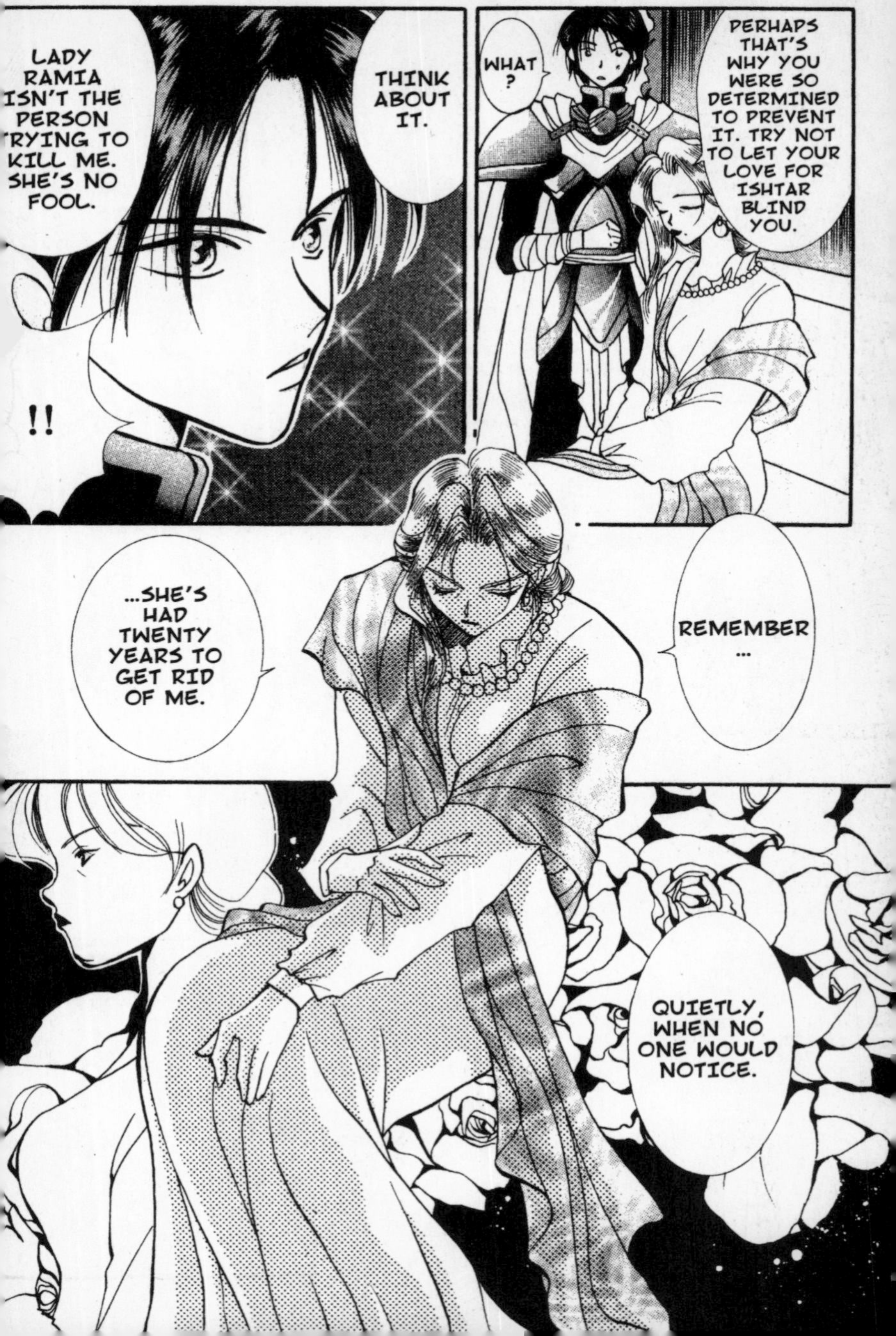
PERHAPS THAT'S WHY YOU WERE SO DETERMINED TO PREVENT IT. TRY NOT TO LET YOUR LOVE FOR ISHTAR BLIND YOU.
WHAT?
THINK ABOUT IT.
LADY RAMIA ISN'T THE PERSON TRYING TO KILL ME. SHE'S NO FOOL.
!!
REMEMBER...
...SHE'S HAD TWENTY YEARS TO GET RID OF ME.
QUIETLY, WHEN NO ONE WOULD NOTICE.

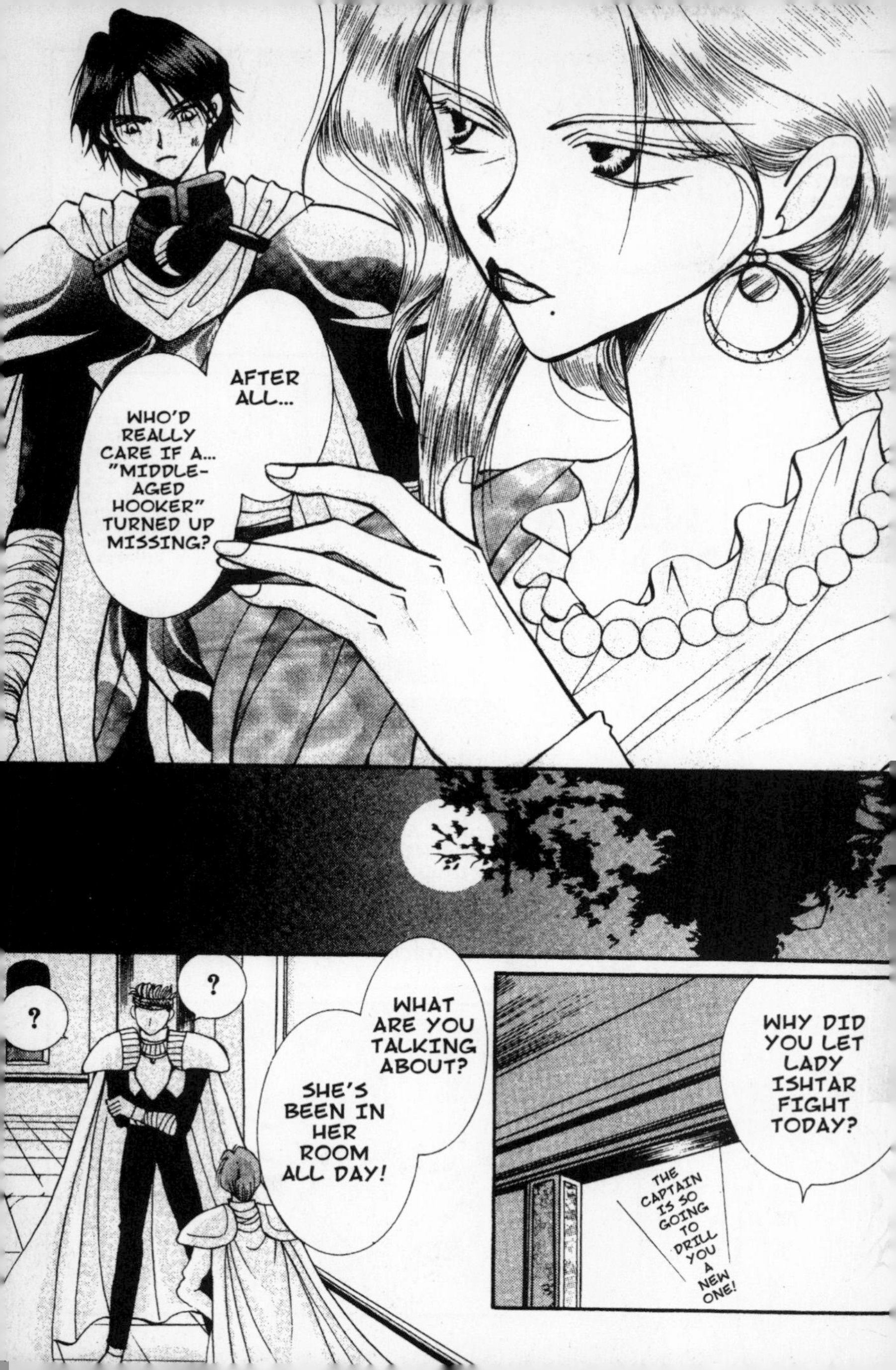
AFTER ALL...
WHO'D REALLY CARE IF A... "MIDDLE-AGED HOOKER" TURNED UP MISSING?
WHY DID YOU LET LADY ISHTAR FIGHT TODAY?
THE CAPTAIN IS SO GOING TO DRILL YOU A NEW ONE!
WHAT ARE YOU TALKING ABOUT?
SHE'S BEEN IN HER ROOM ALL DAY!
?
?

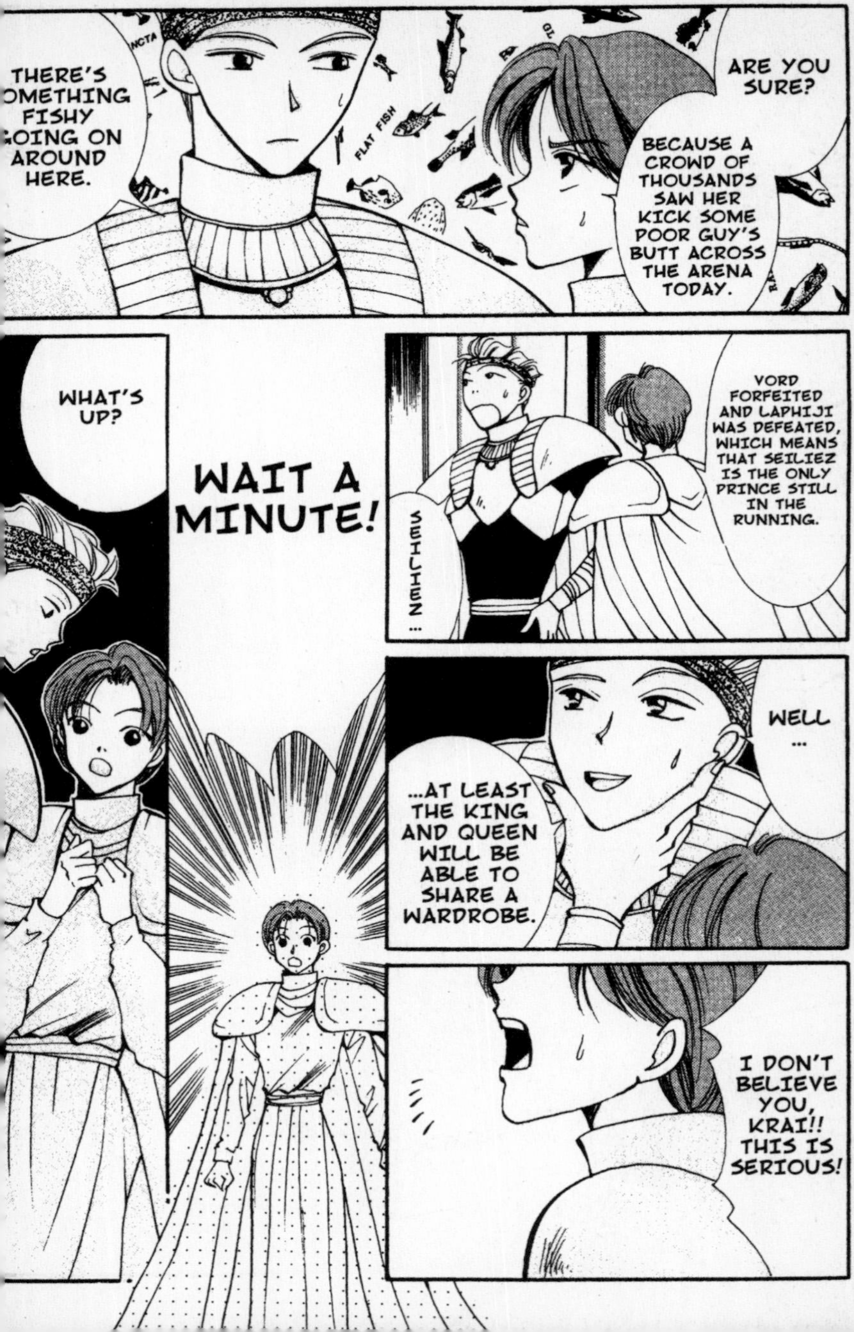
ARE YOU SURE?
BECAUSE A CROWD OF THOUSANDS SAW HER KICK SOME POOR GUY'S BUTT ACROSS THE ARENA TODAY.
THERE'S OMETHING FISHY GOING ON AROUND HERE.
FLAT FISH
VORD FORFEITED AND LAPHIJI WAS DEFEATED, WHICH MEANS THAT SEILIEZ IS THE ONLY PRINCE STILL IN THE RUNNING.
SEILIEZ...
WELL...
...AT LEAST THE KING AND QUEEN WILL BE ABLE TO SHARE A WARDROBE.
I DON'T BELIEVE YOU, KRAI!! THIS IS SERIOUS!
WAIT A MINUTE!
WHAT'S UP?

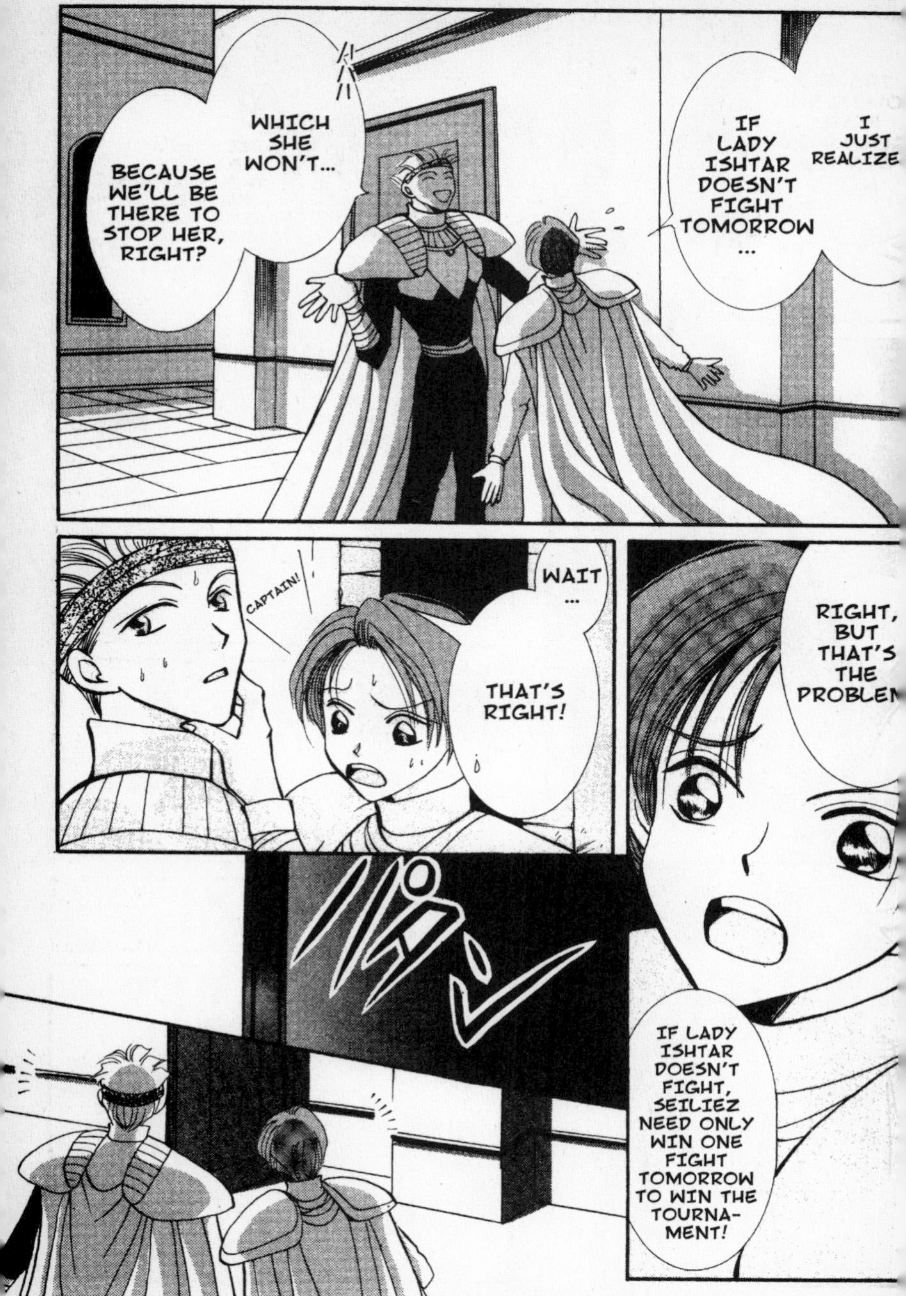
I JUST REALIZE
IF LADY ISHTAR DOESN'T FIGHT TOMORROW ...
WHICH SHE WON'T...
BECAUSE WE'LL BE THERE TO STOP HER, RIGHT?
RIGHT, BUT THAT'S THE PROBLE
WAIT ...
THAT'S RIGHT!
CAPTAIN!
IF LADY ISHTAR DOESN'T FIGHT, SEILIEZ NEED ONLY WIN ONE FIGHT TOMORROW TO WIN THE TOURNA-MENT!
パッ

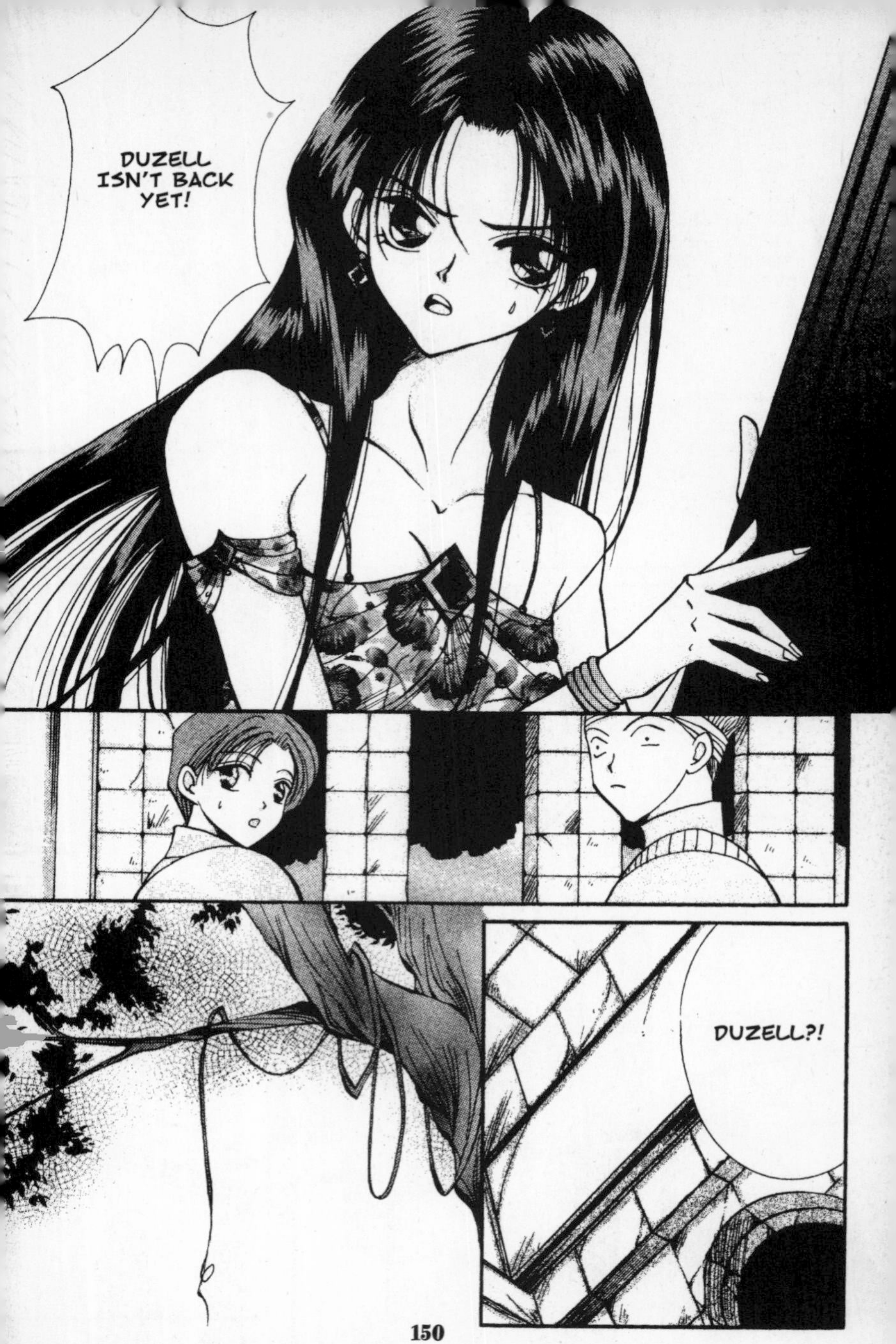
DUZELL ISN'T BACK YET!
DUZELL?!

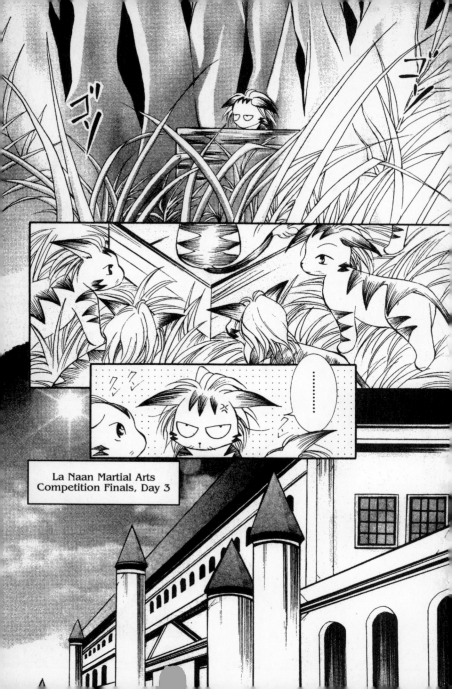

La Naan Martial Arts
Competition Finals, Day 3

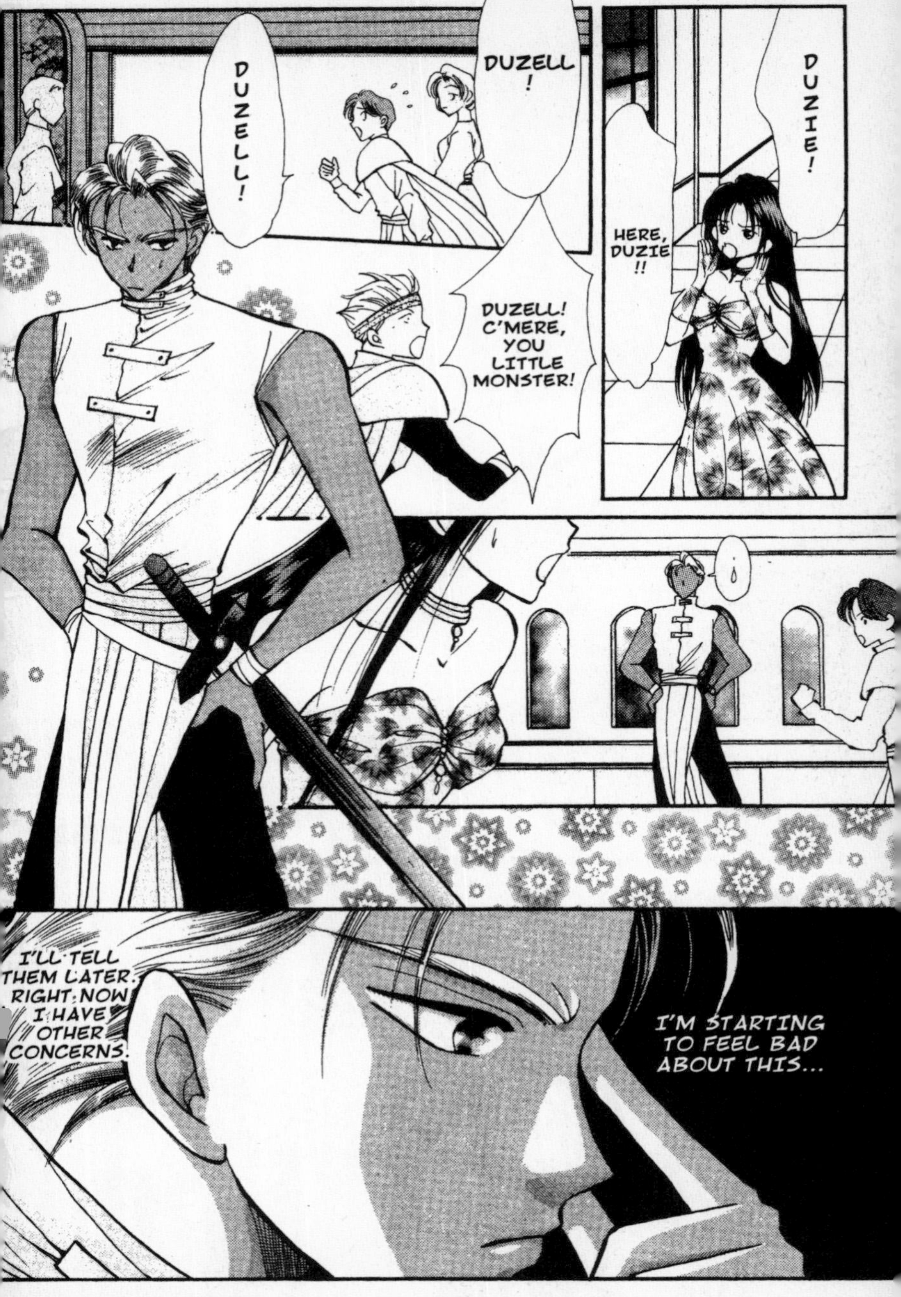
DUZIE!
HERE, DUZIE!!
DUZELL!
DUZELL!
DUZELL! C'MERE, YOU LITTLE MONSTER!
I'M STARTING TO FEEL BAD ABOUT THIS...
I'LL TELL THEM LATER. RIGHT NOW I HAVE OTHER CONCERNS.

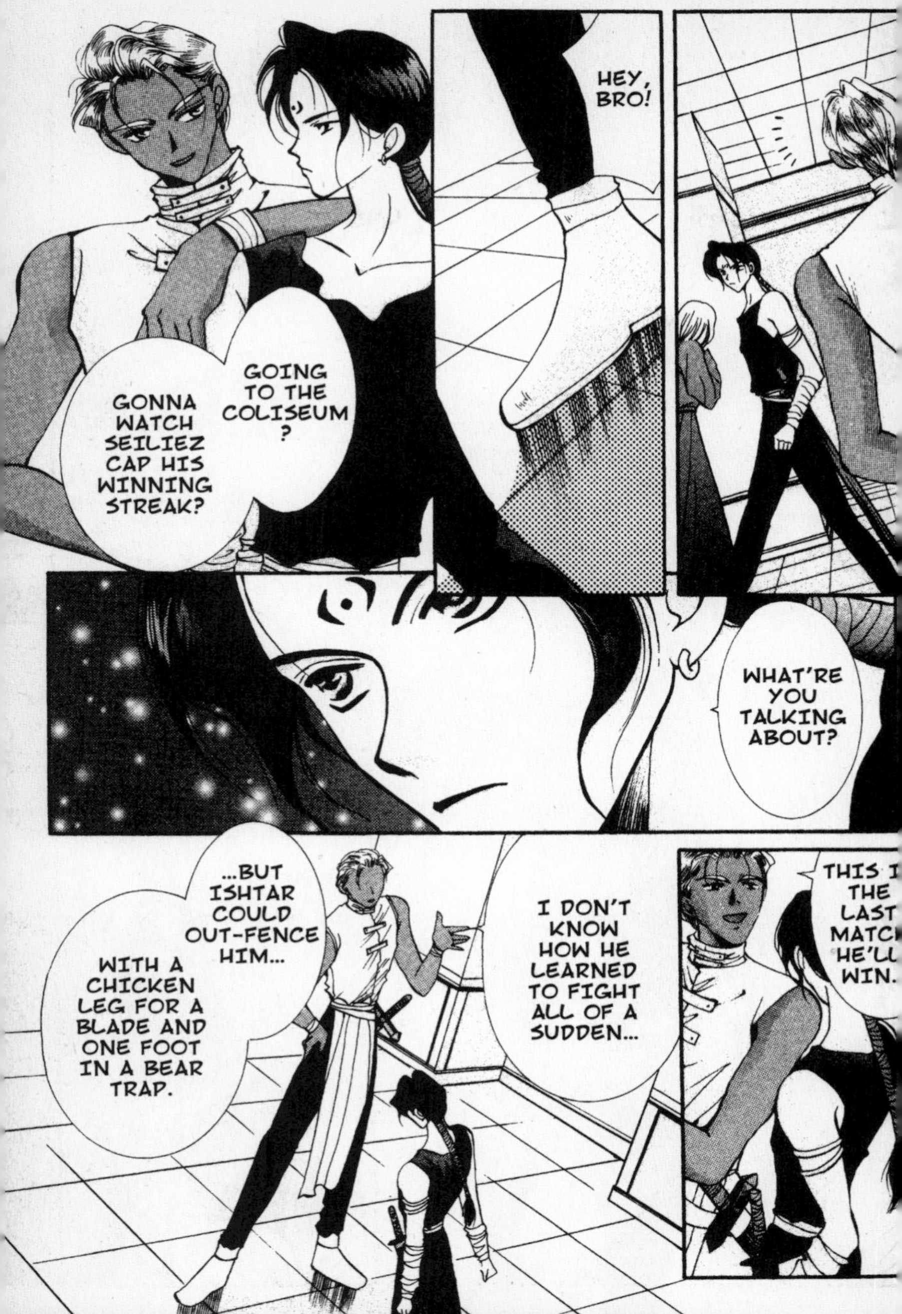
HEY, BRO!
GOING TO THE COLISEUM?
GONNA WATCH SEILIEZ CAP HIS WINNING STREAK?
WHAT'RE YOU TALKING ABOUT?
THIS I THE LAST MATC HE'LL WIN.
I DON'T KNOW HOW HE LEARNED TO FIGHT ALL OF A SUDDEN...
...BUT ISHTAR COULD OUT-FENCE HIM...
WITH A CHICKEN LEG FOR A BLADE AND ONE FOOT IN A BEAR TRAP.

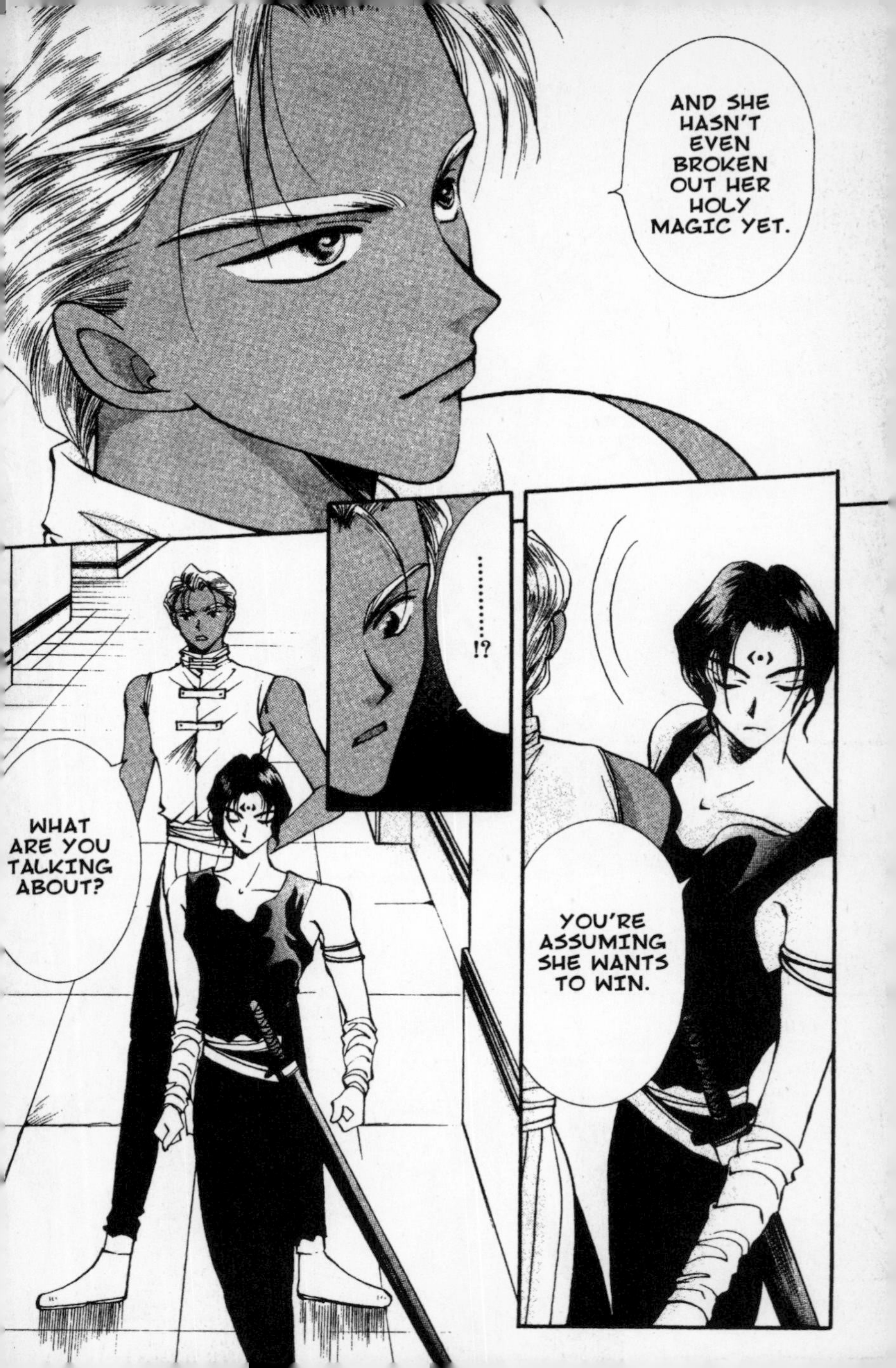
AND SHE HASN'T EVEN BROKEN OUT HER HOLY MAGIC YET.
YOU'RE ASSUMING SHE WANTS TO WIN.
......!?
WHAT ARE YOU TALKING ABOUT?

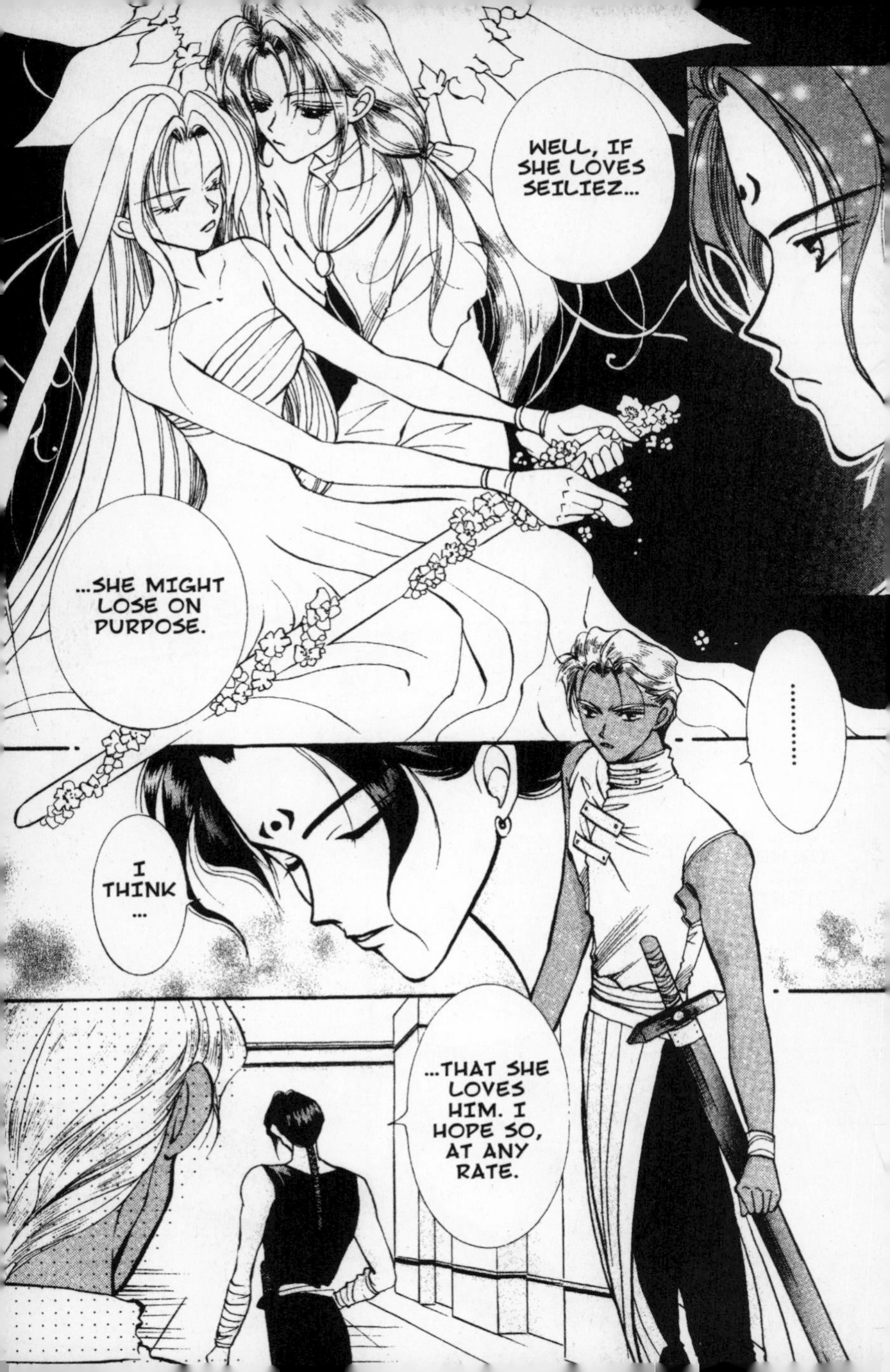
WELL, IF SHE LOVES SEILIEZ...
...SHE MIGHT LOSE ON PURPOSE.
......
I THINK ...
...THAT SHE LOVES HIM. I HOPE SO, AT ANY RATE.

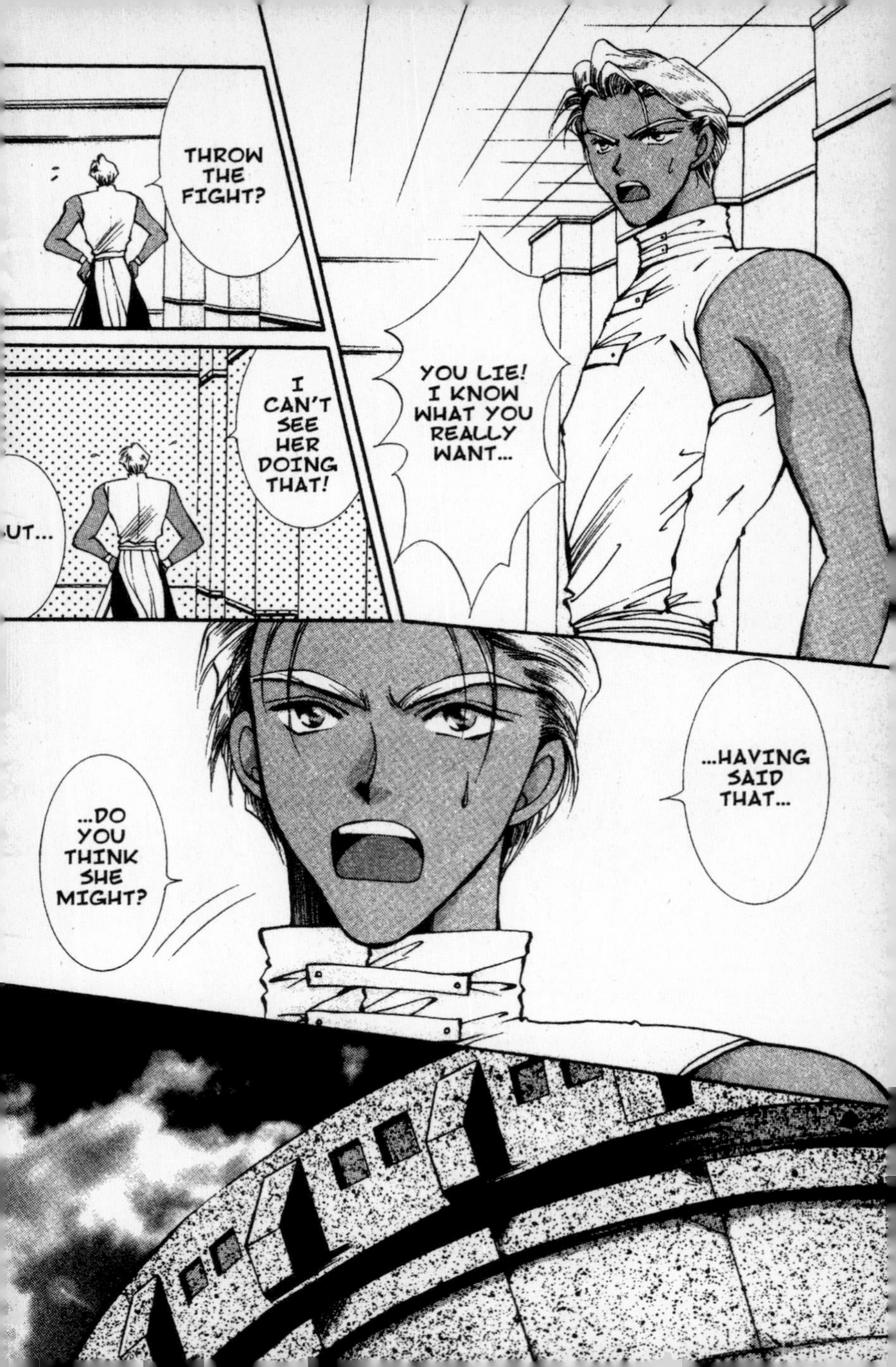
YOU LIE! I KNOW WHAT YOU REALLY WANT...
THROW THE FIGHT?
I CAN'T SEE HER DOING THAT!
UT...
...HAVING SAID THAT...
...DO YOU THINK SHE MIGHT?

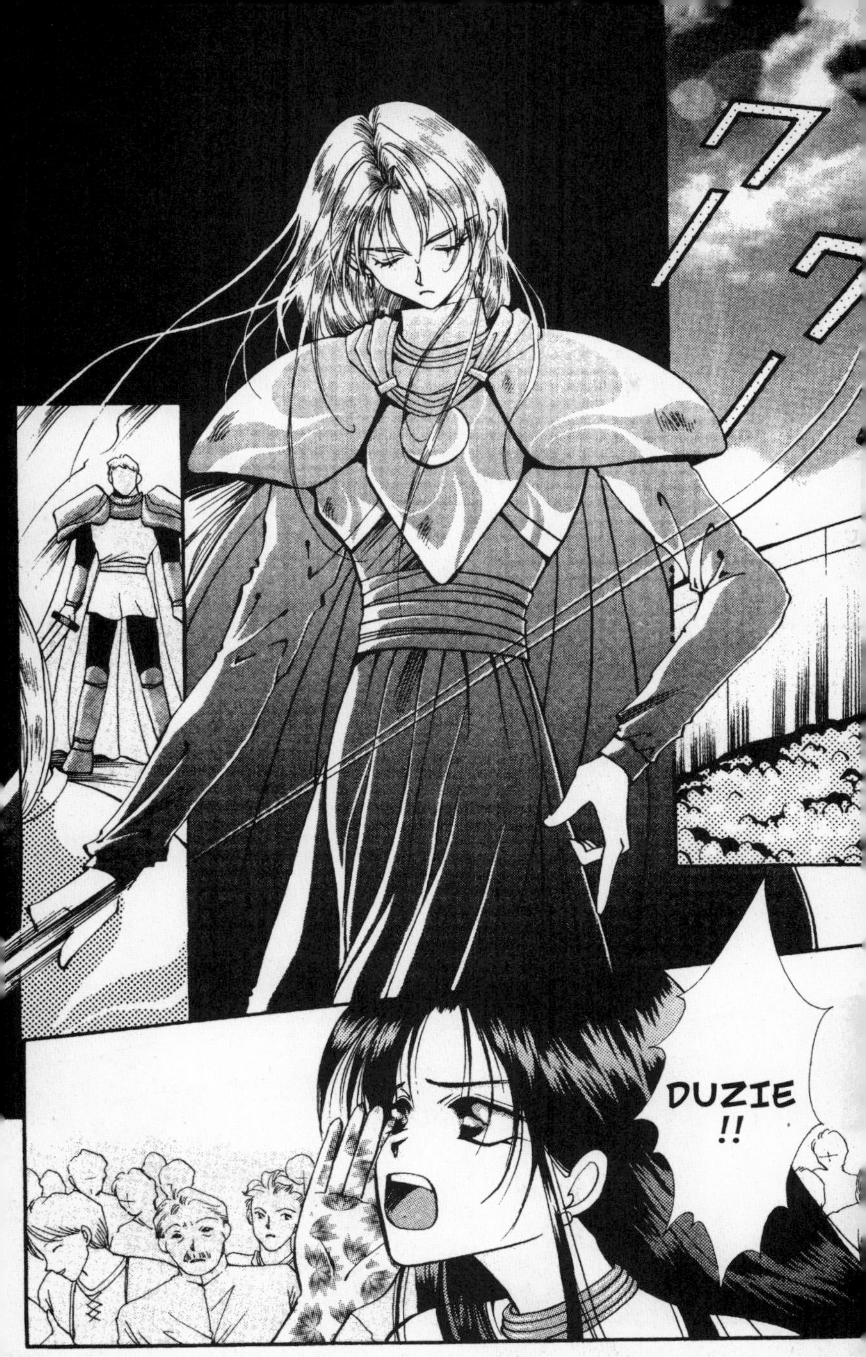
DUZIE !!

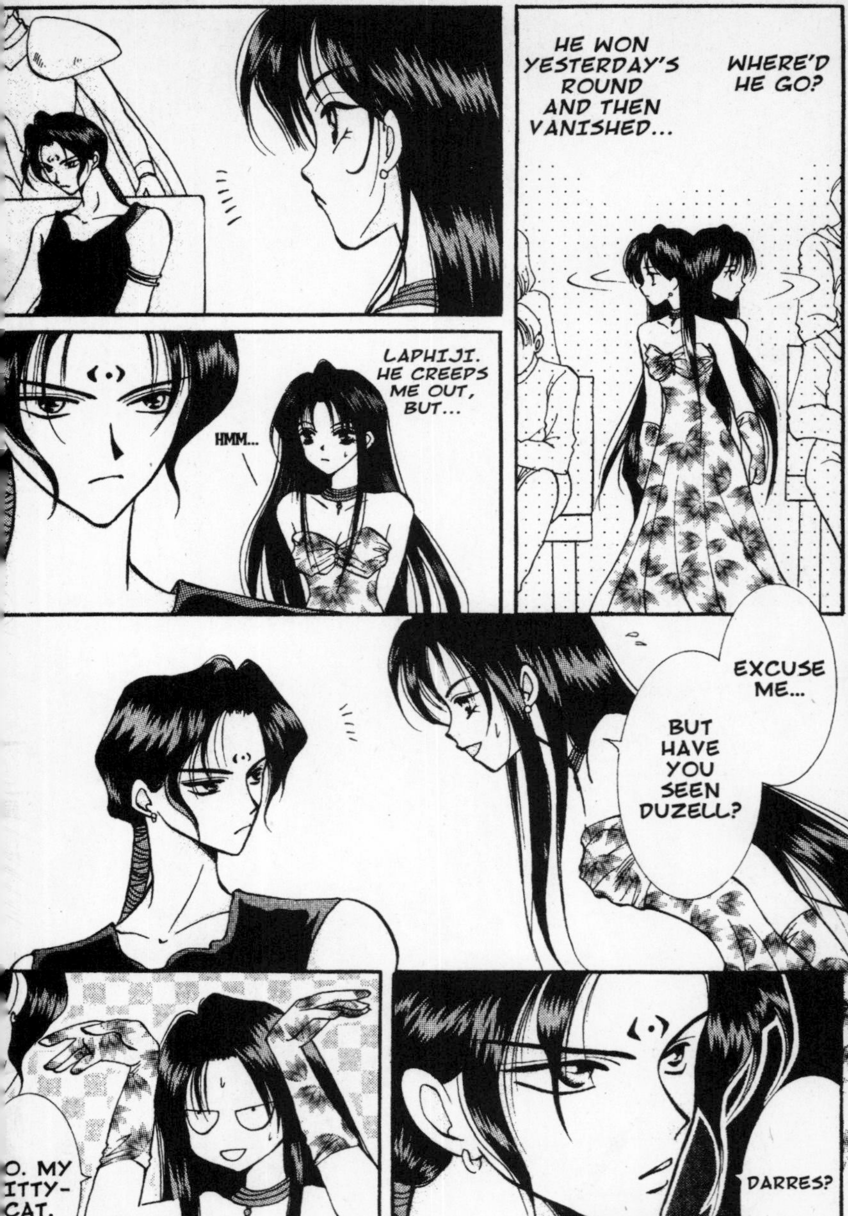
WHERE'D HE GO?
HE WON YESTERDAY'S ROUND AND THEN VANISHED...
LAPHIJI. HE CREEPS ME OUT, BUT...
HMM...
EXCUSE ME...
BUT HAVE YOU SEEN DUZELL?
DARRES?
O. MY ITTY-CAT.

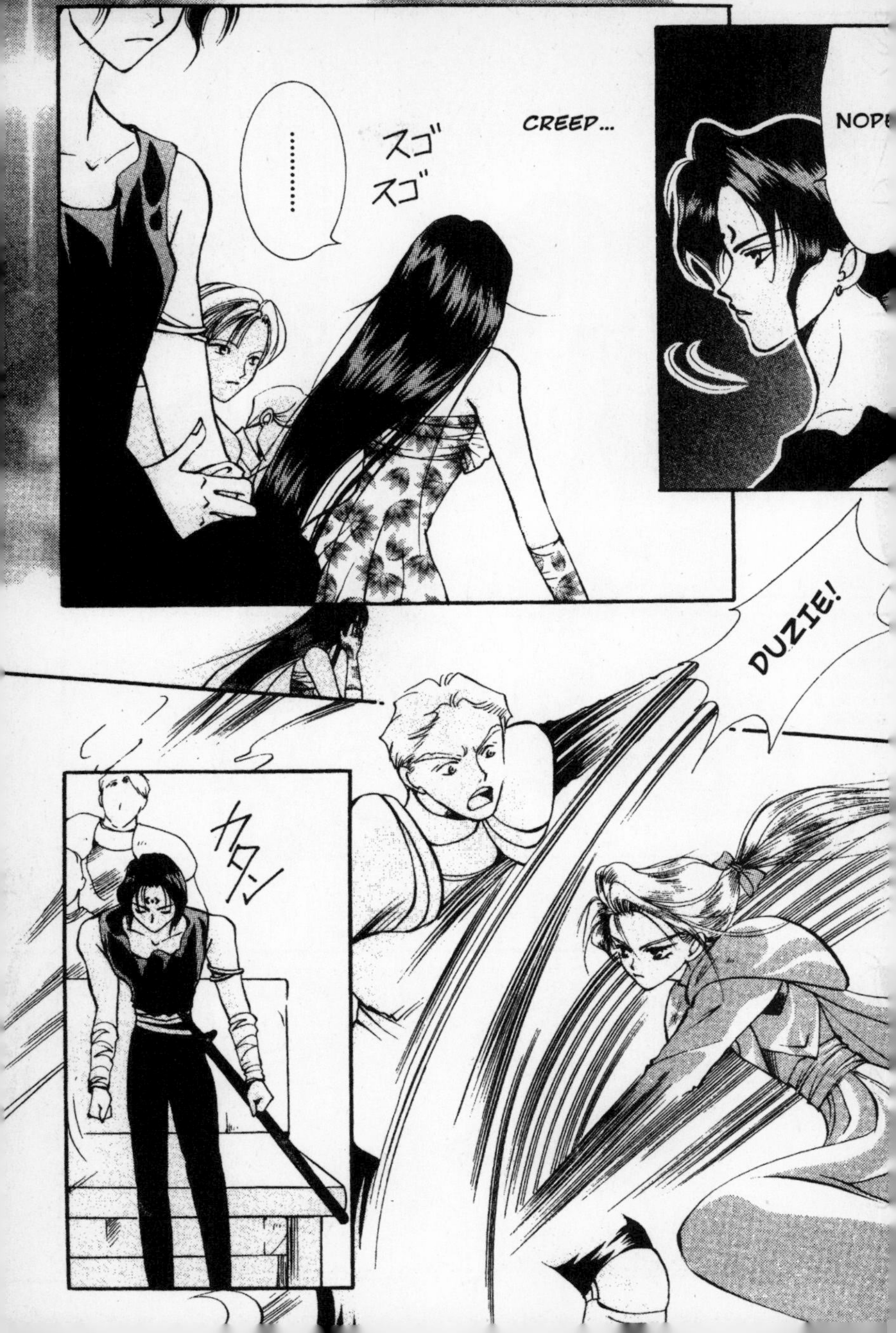
NOPE
CREEP...
スゴスゴ
....
DUZIE!
カタン

HOWEVER, PRINCESS, IF HE'S NEARBY, I KNOW A LITTLE MAGIC THAT'LL FIND HIM.

......!?

WANT ME TO TRY?

...KAY, SO ...AYBE MR. ...EEPSHOW ...AS HIS ...GOOD ...OINTS.

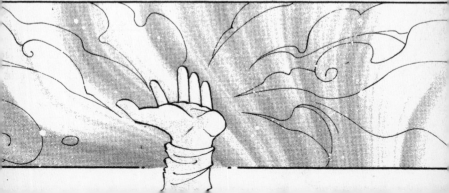

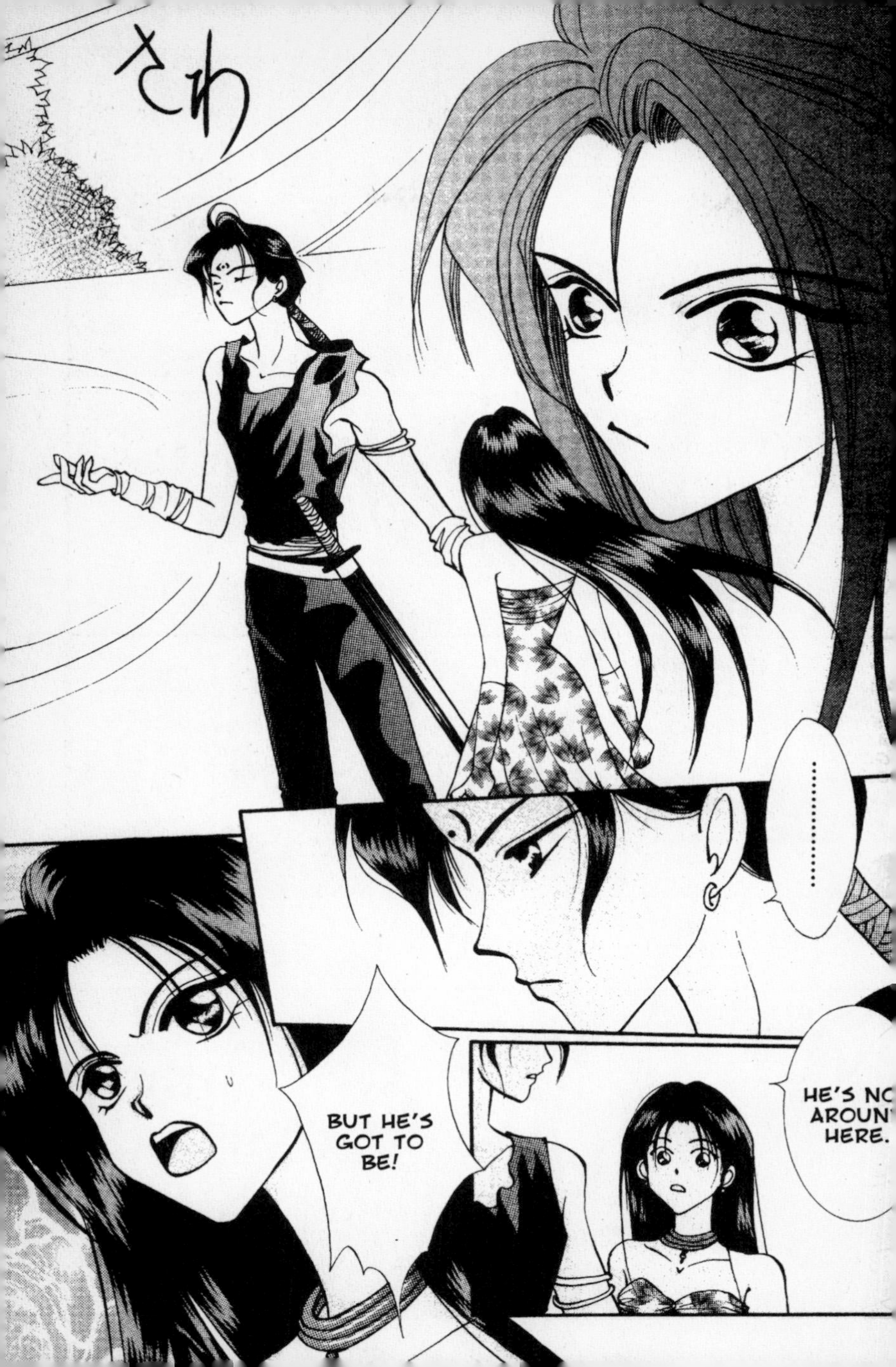
さわ
……
HE'S NO AROUN HERE.
BUT HE'S GOT TO BE!

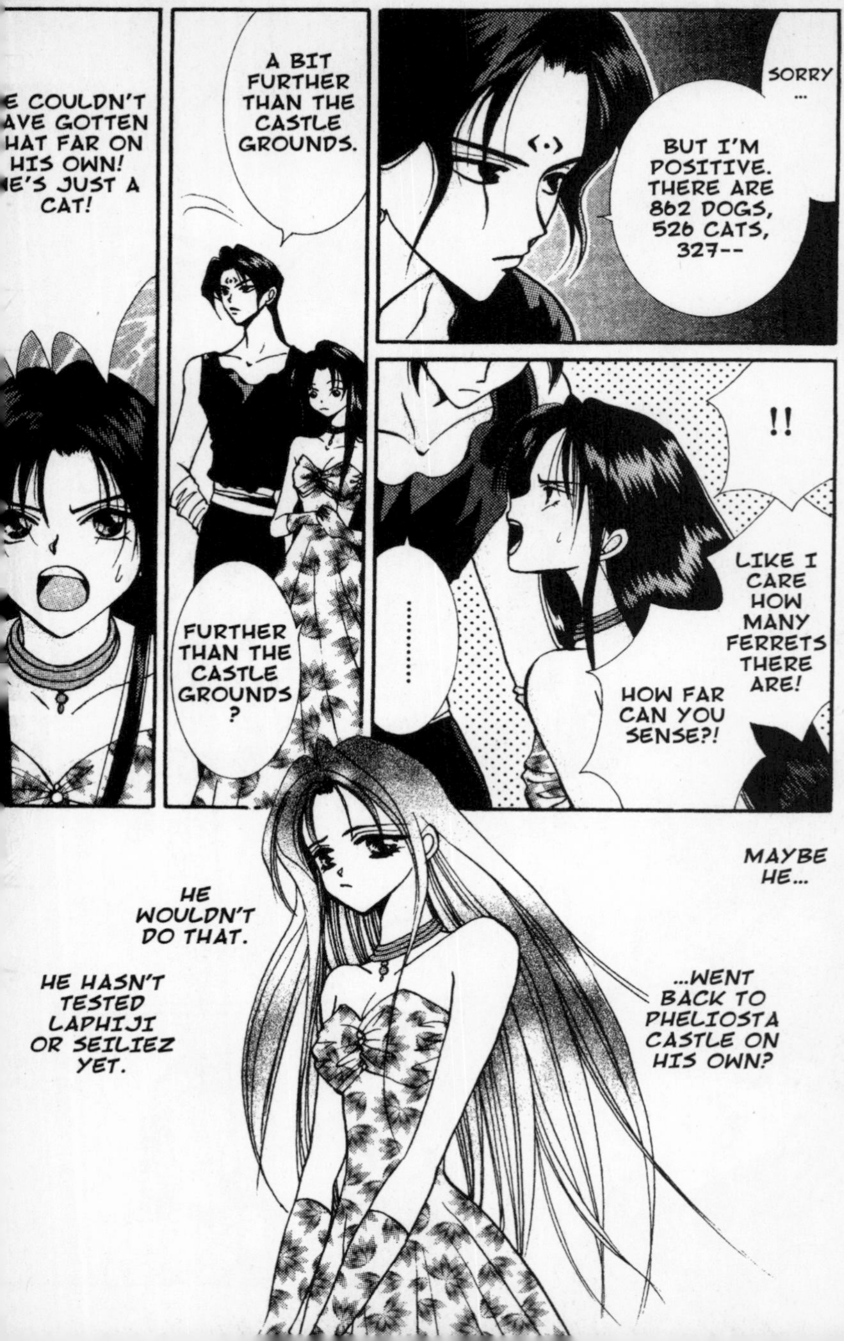
SORRY ...
BUT I'M POSITIVE. THERE ARE 862 DOGS, 526 CATS, 327--
!!
LIKE I CARE HOW MANY FERRETS THERE ARE!
HOW FAR CAN YOU SENSE?!
....
A BIT FURTHER THAN THE CASTLE GROUNDS.
FURTHER THAN THE CASTLE GROUNDS ?
E COULDN'T AVE GOTTEN HAT FAR ON HIS OWN! E'S JUST A CAT!
MAYBE HE...
...WENT BACK TO PHELIOSTA CASTLE ON HIS OWN?
HE WOULDN'T DO THAT.
HE HASN'T TESTED LAPHIJI OR SEILIEZ YET.

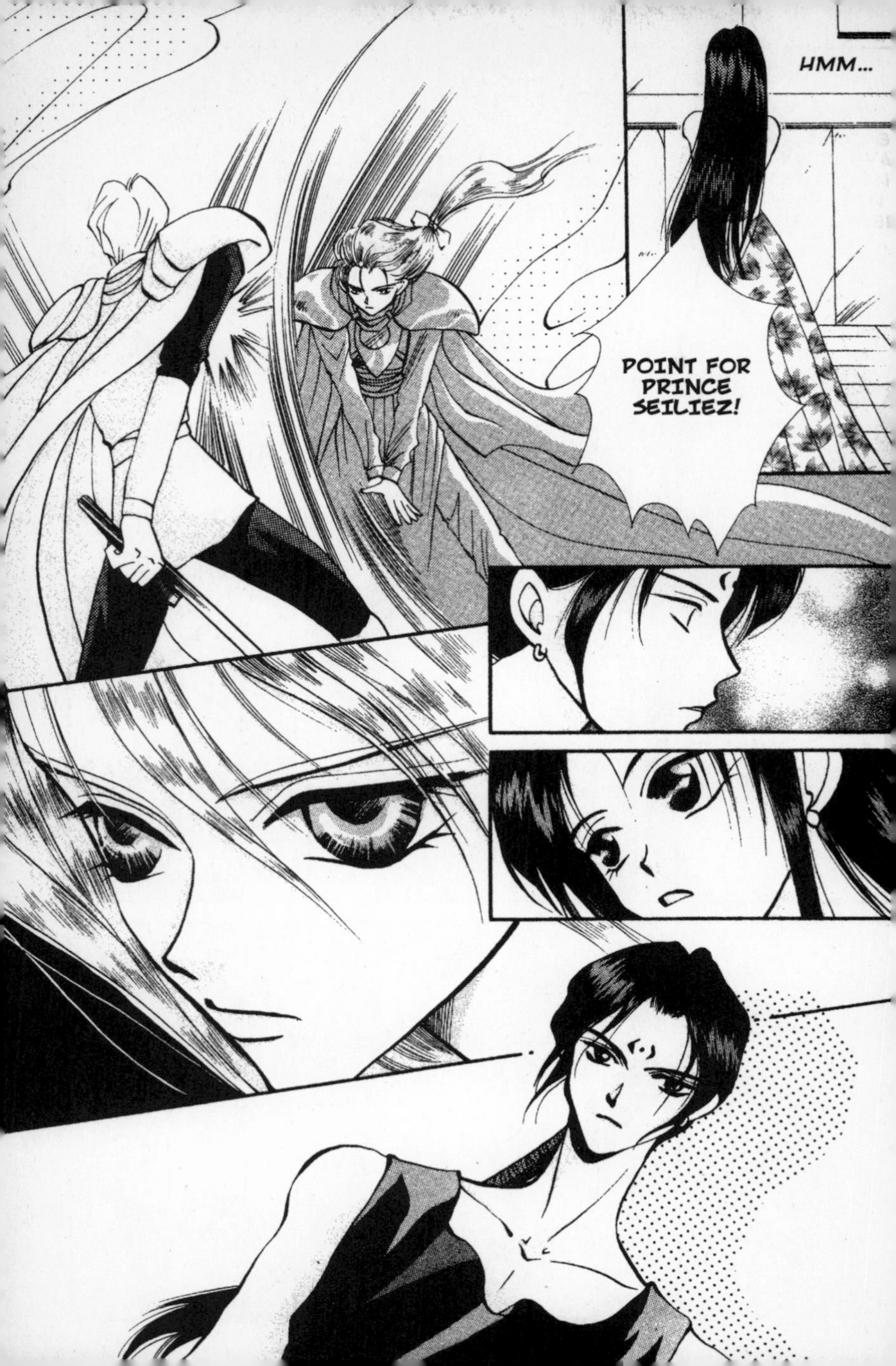
HMM...
POINT FOR PRINCE SEILIEZ!

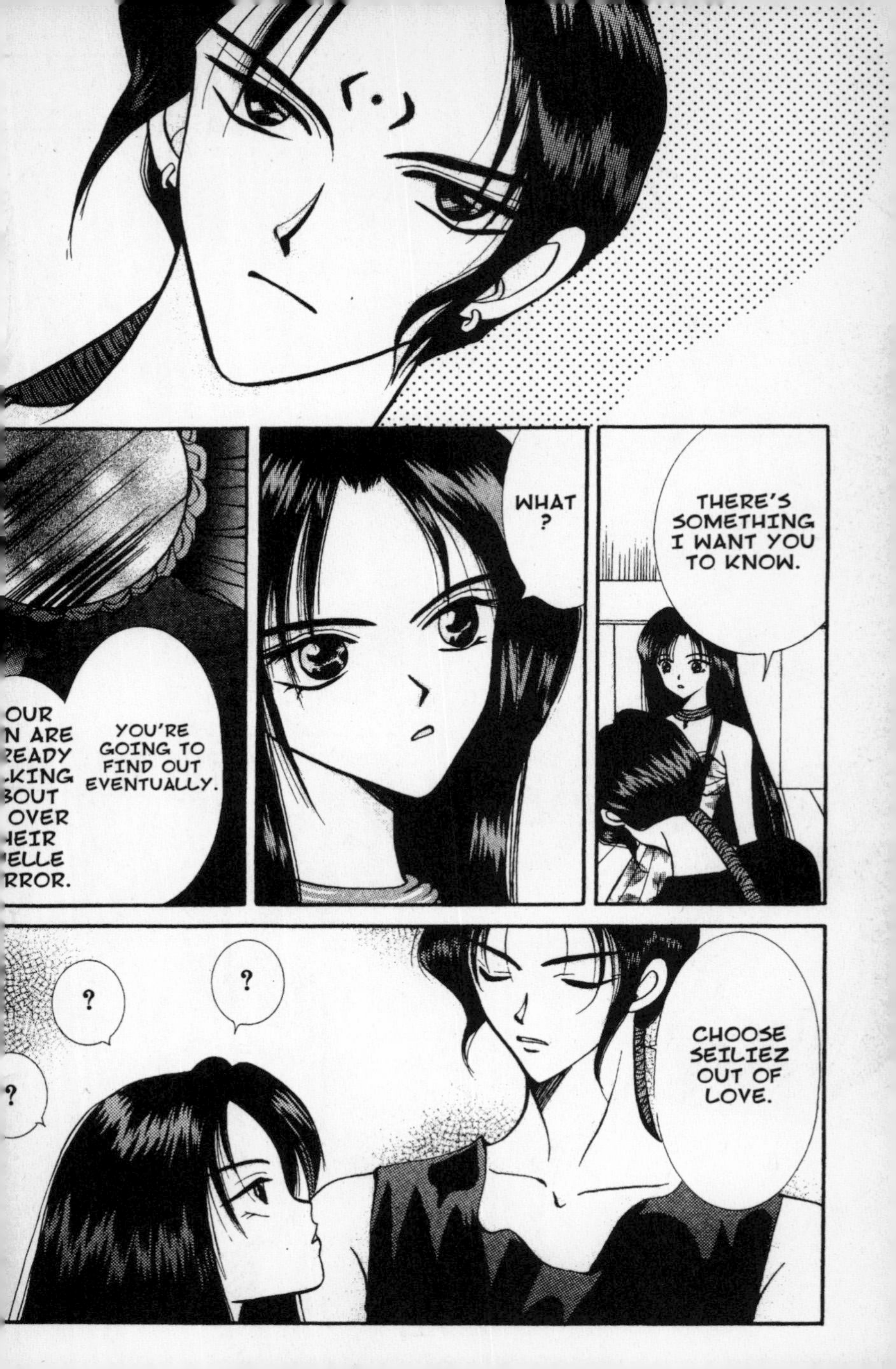
THERE'S SOMETHING I WANT YOU TO KNOW.
WHAT?
YOU'RE GOING TO FIND OUT EVENTUALLY.
CHOOSE SEILIEZ OUT OF LOVE.
?
?
?

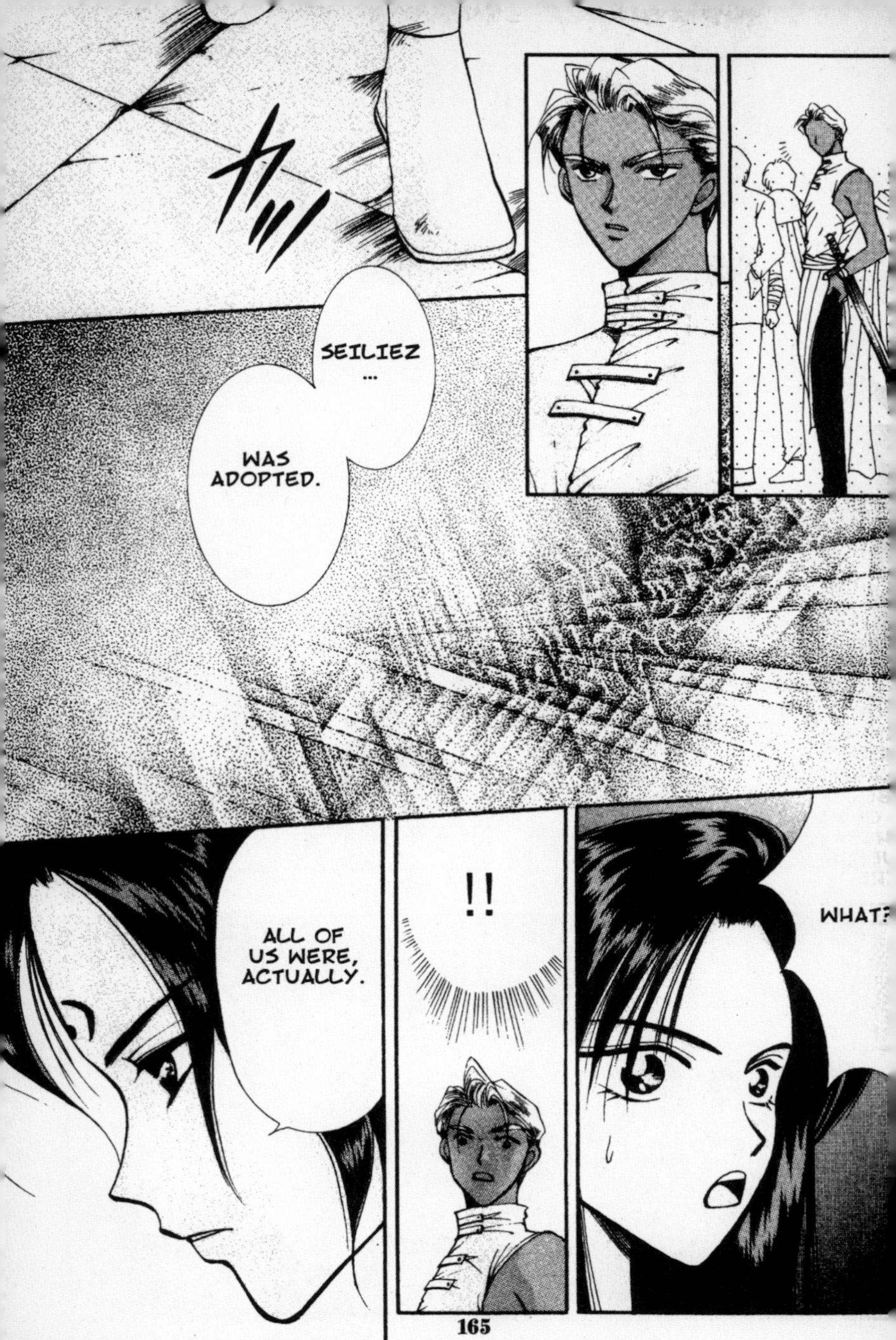
SEILIEZ ...
WAS ADOPTED.
WHAT?
!!
ALL OF US WERE, ACTUALLY.

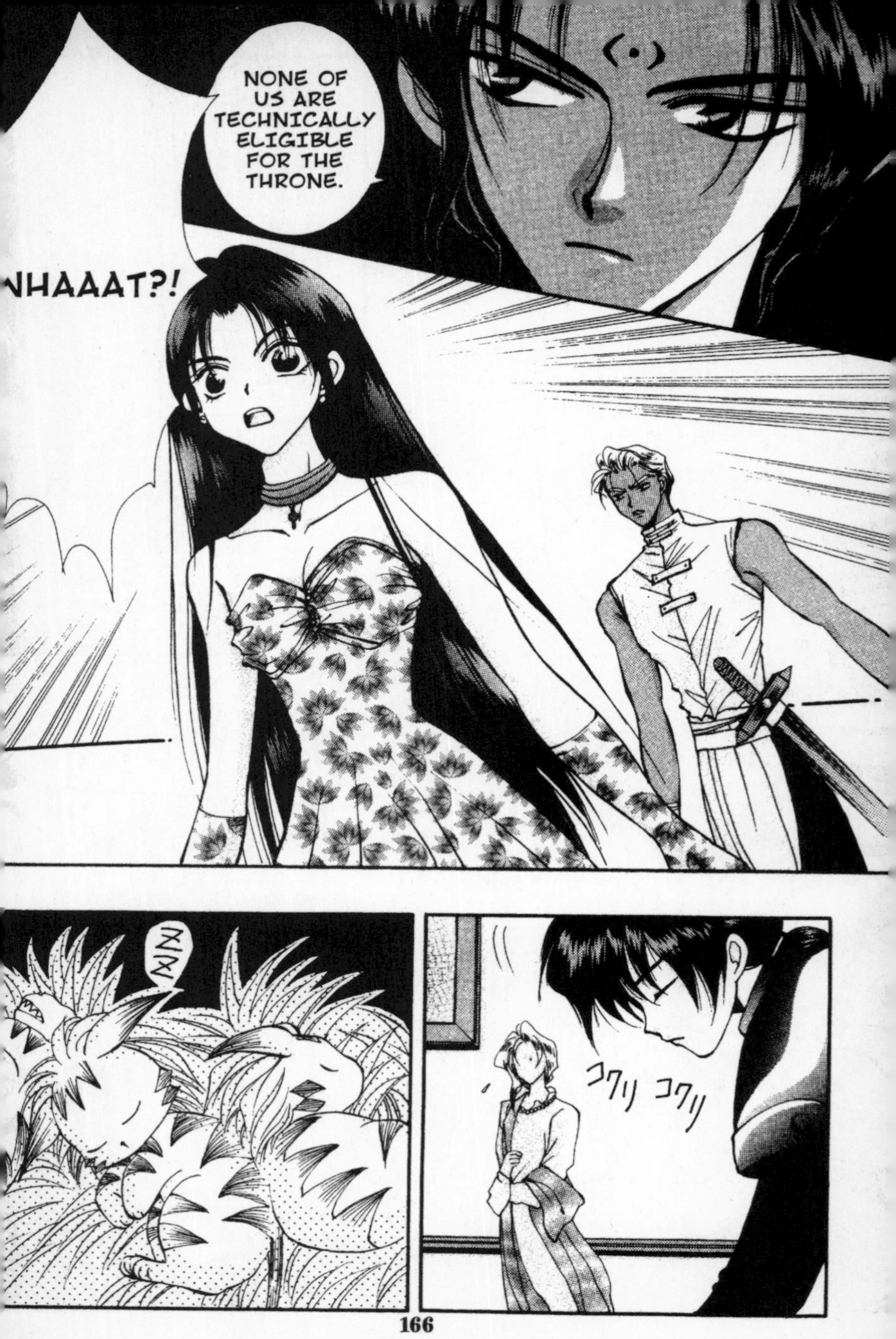
NONE OF US ARE TECHNICALLY ELIGIBLE FOR THE THRONE.
WHAAAT?!
コクリ コクリ

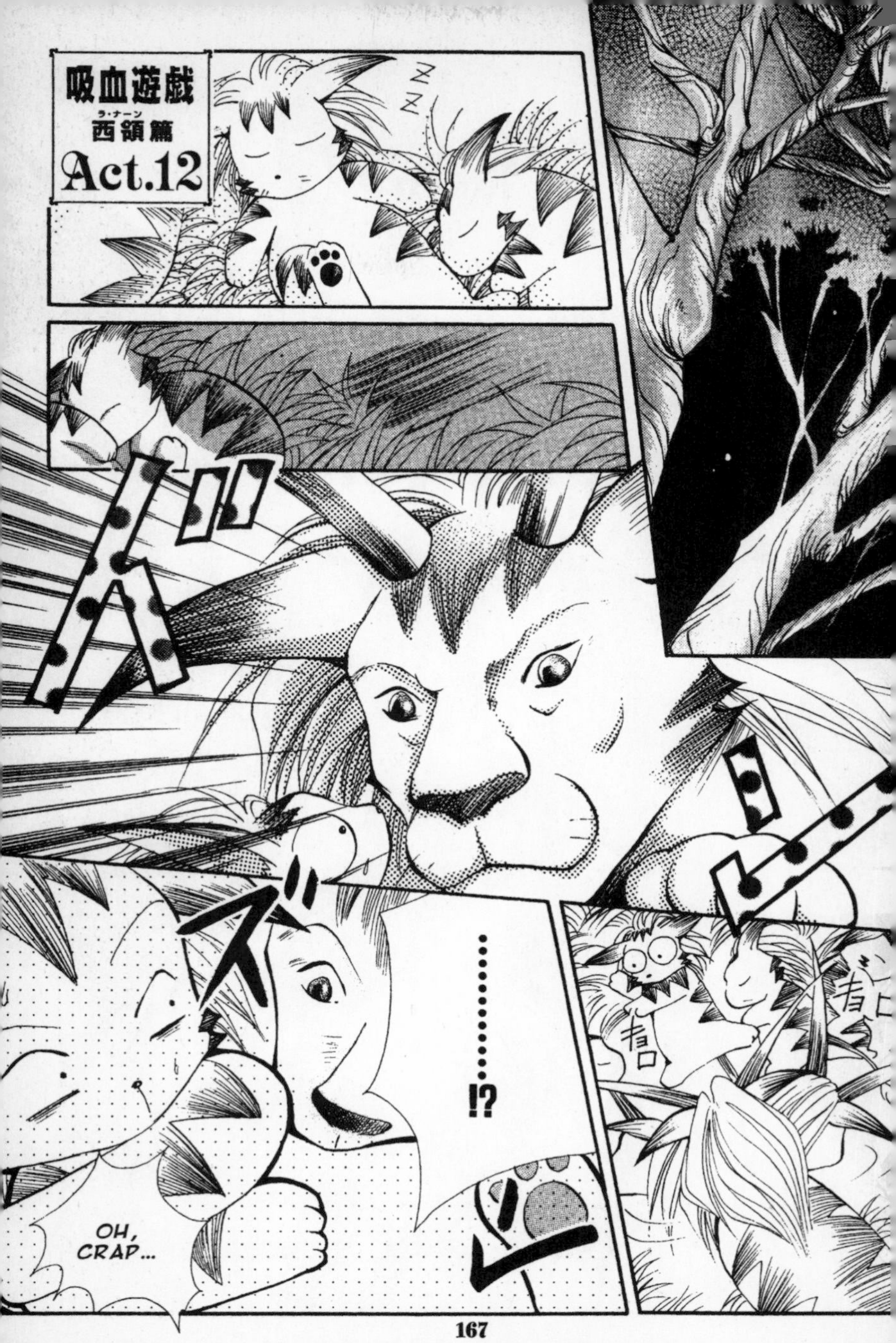
吸血遊戯
西領篇
ラ・ナーン
Act.12
ZZZ
......!?
OH, CRAP...

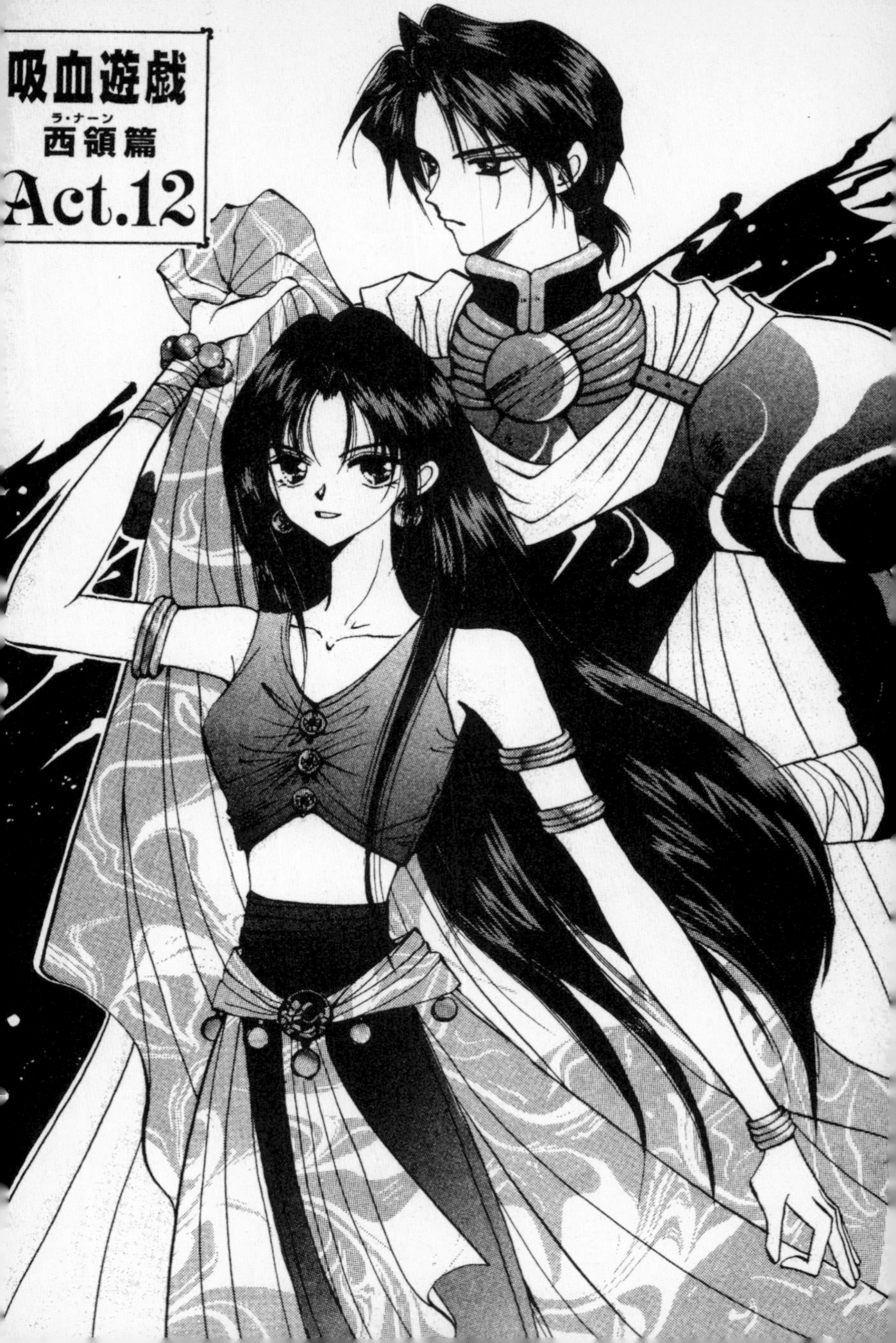
吸血遊戯
西領篇（ラ・ナーン）
Act.12

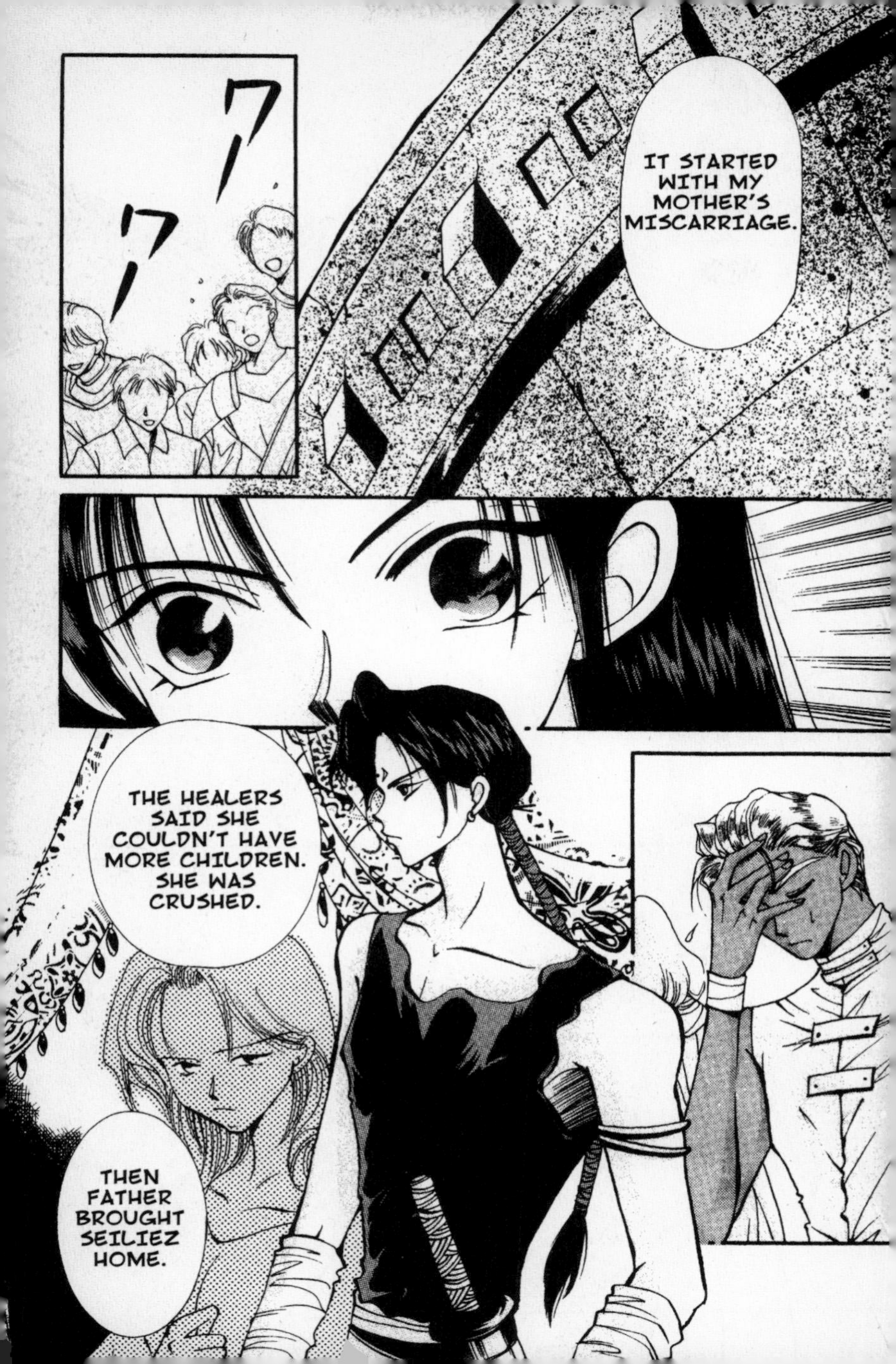
IT STARTED WITH MY MOTHER'S MISCARRIAGE.
THE HEALERS SAID SHE COULDN'T HAVE MORE CHILDREN. SHE WAS CRUSHED.
THEN FATHER BROUGHT SEILIEZ HOME.

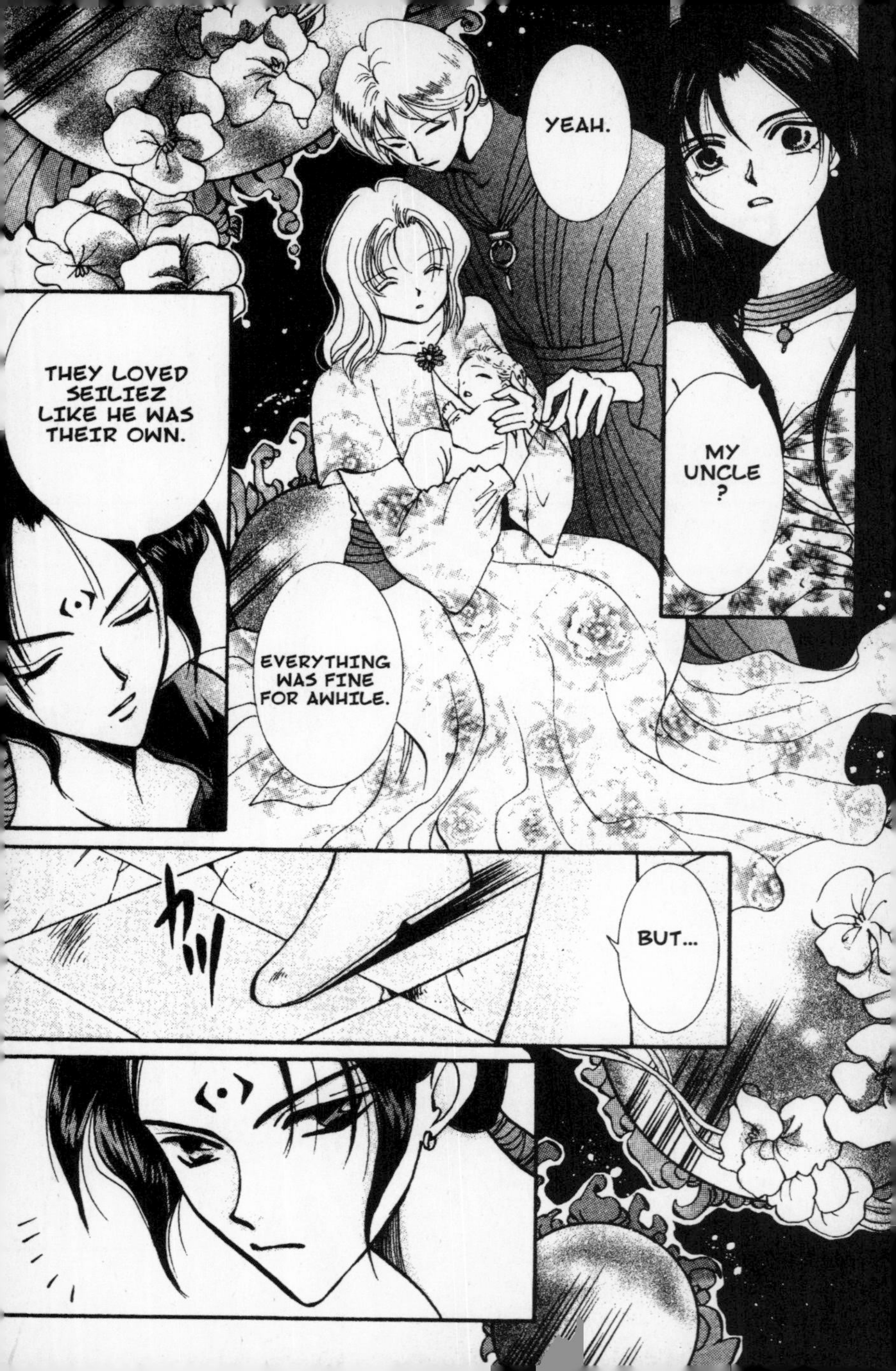
MY UNCLE ?
YEAH.
THEY LOVED SEILIEZ LIKE HE WAS THEIR OWN.
EVERYTHING WAS FINE FOR AWHILE.
BUT...
カッ

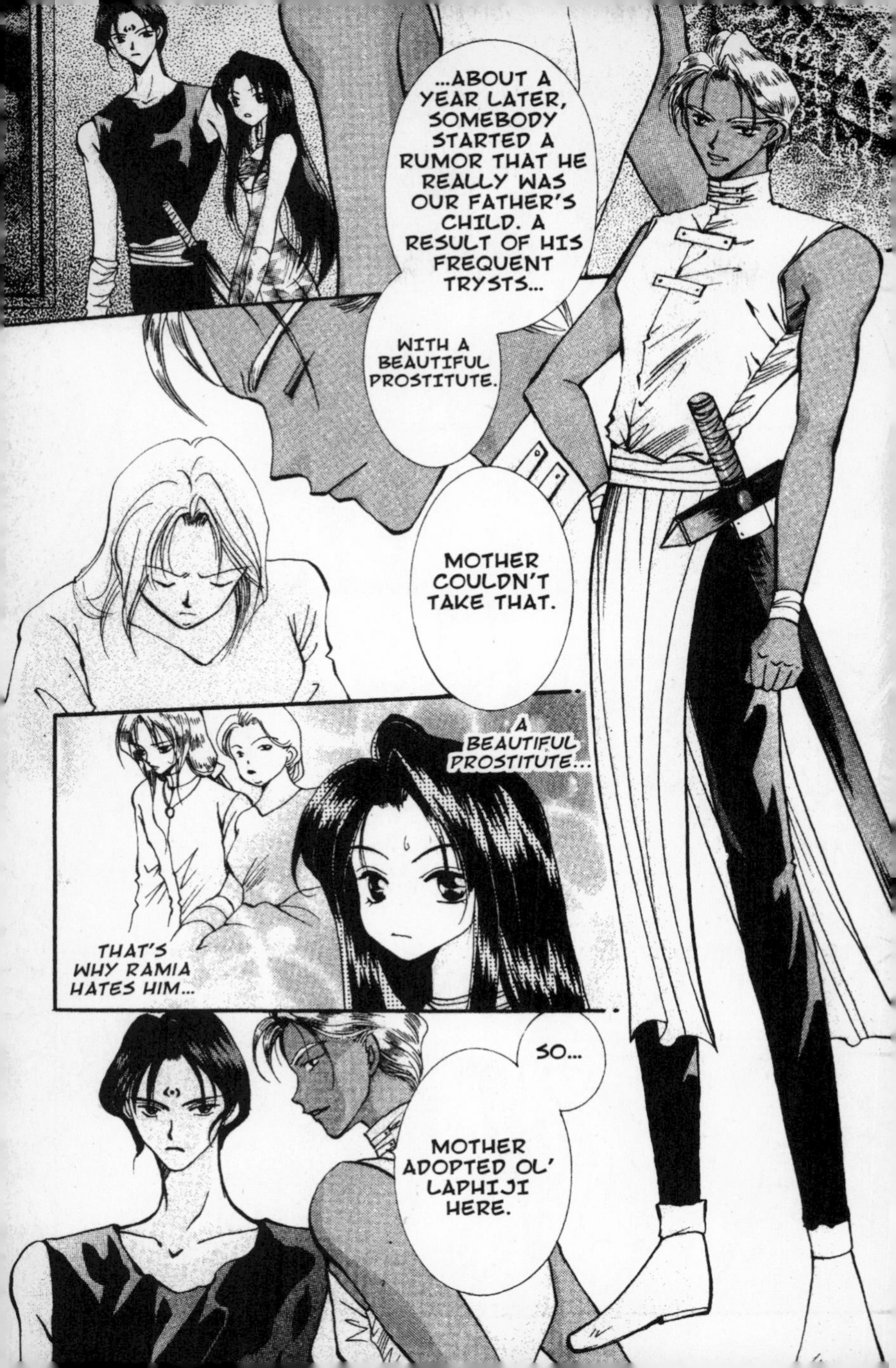
...ABOUT A YEAR LATER, SOMEBODY STARTED A RUMOR THAT HE REALLY WAS OUR FATHER'S CHILD. A RESULT OF HIS FREQUENT TRYSTS...
WITH A BEAUTIFUL PROSTITUTE.
MOTHER COULDN'T TAKE THAT.
A BEAUTIFUL PROSTITUTE...
THAT'S WHY RAMIA HATES HIM...
SO...
MOTHER ADOPTED OL' LAPHIJI HERE.

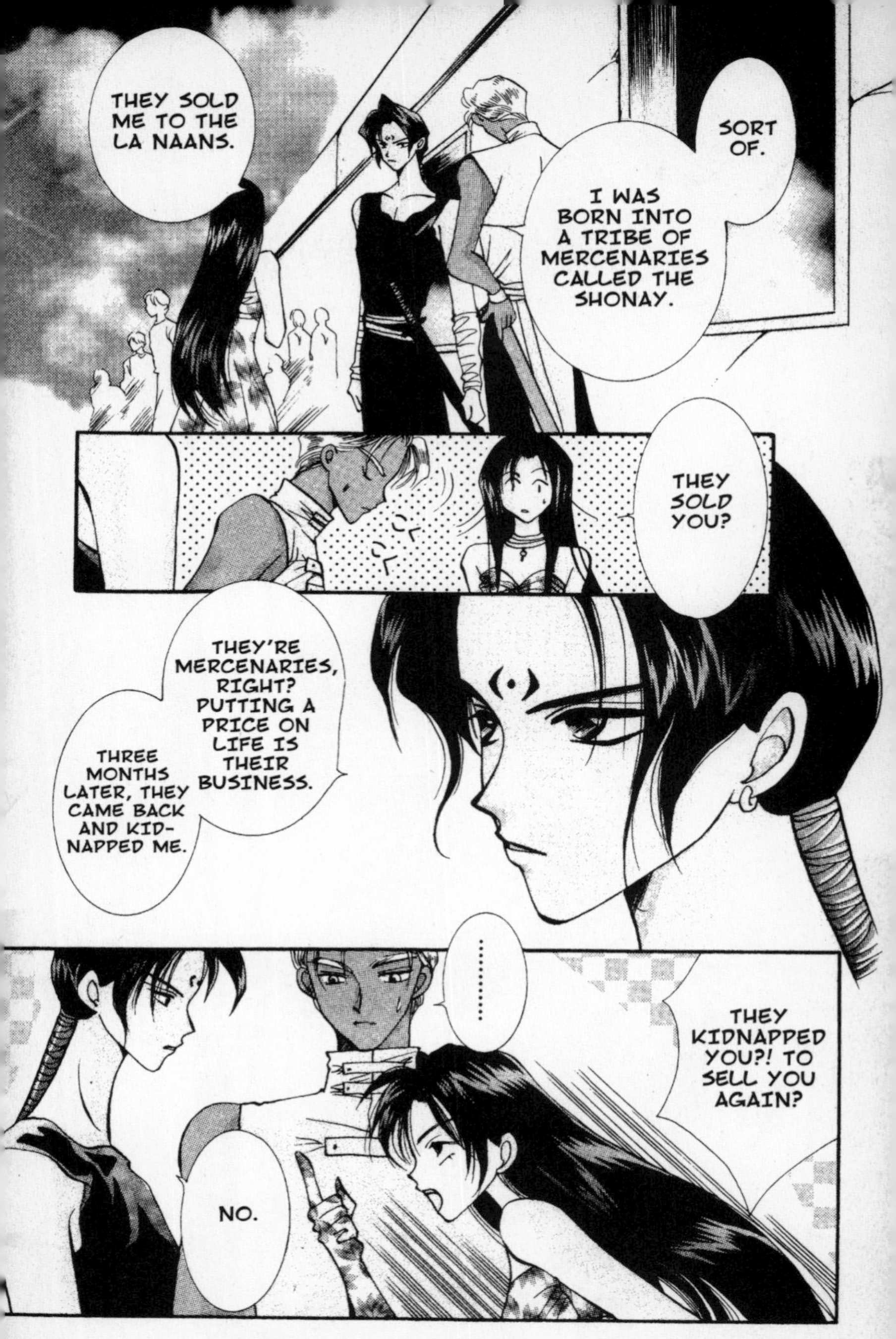
SORT OF.
I WAS BORN INTO A TRIBE OF MERCENARIES CALLED THE SHONAY.
THEY SOLD ME TO THE LA NAANS.
THEY SOLD YOU?
THEY'RE MERCENARIES, RIGHT? PUTTING A PRICE ON LIFE IS THEIR BUSINESS.
THREE MONTHS LATER, THEY CAME BACK AND KID-NAPPED ME.
THEY KIDNAPPED YOU?! TO SELL YOU AGAIN?
......
NO.

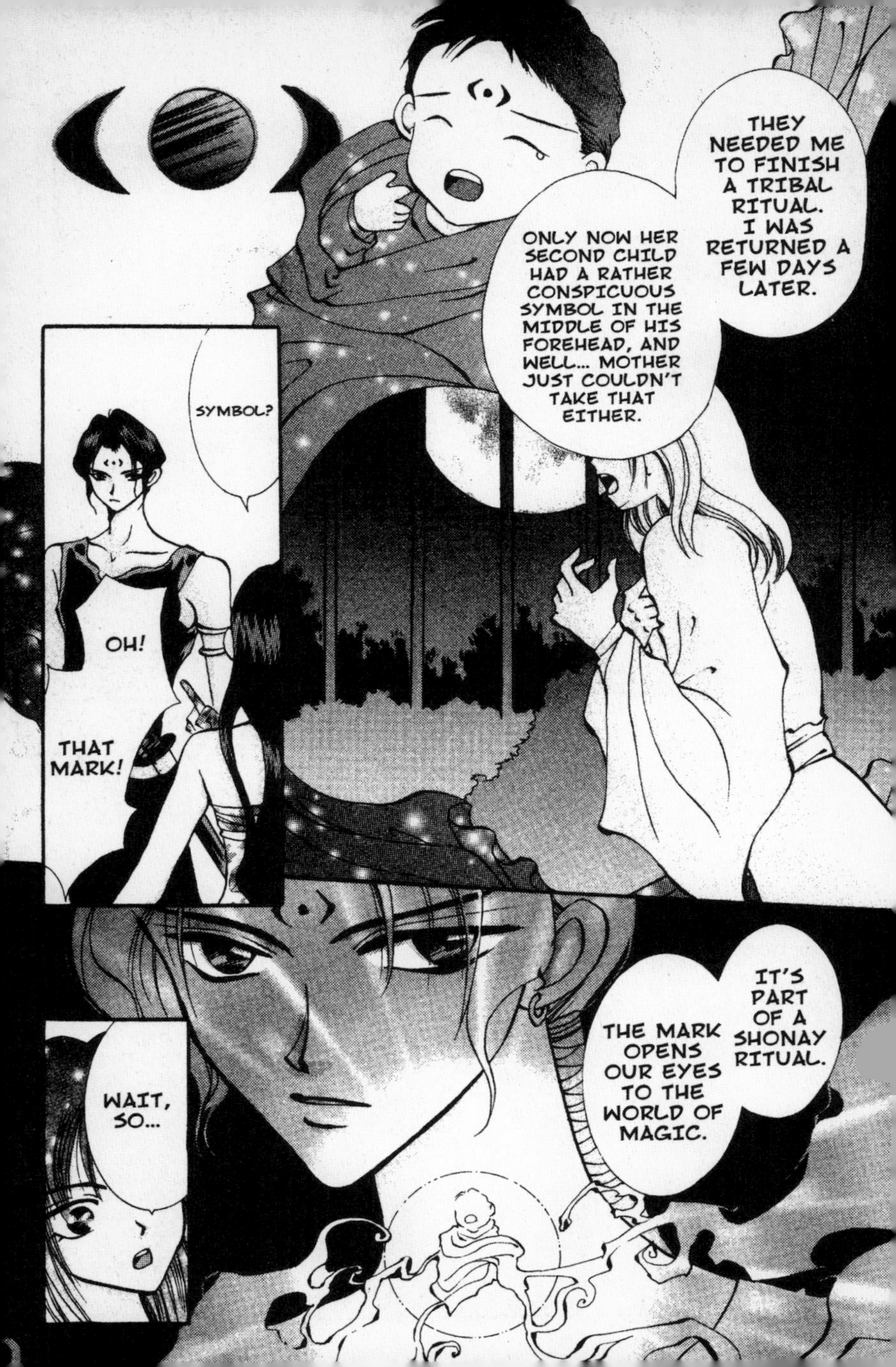
THEY NEEDED ME TO FINISH A TRIBAL RITUAL. I WAS RETURNED A FEW DAYS LATER.
ONLY NOW HER SECOND CHILD HAD A RATHER CONSPICUOUS SYMBOL IN THE MIDDLE OF HIS FOREHEAD, AND WELL... MOTHER JUST COULDN'T TAKE THAT EITHER.
SYMBOL?
OH!
THAT MARK!
IT'S PART OF A SHONAY RITUAL.
THE MARK OPENS OUR EYES TO THE WORLD OF MAGIC.
WAIT, SO...

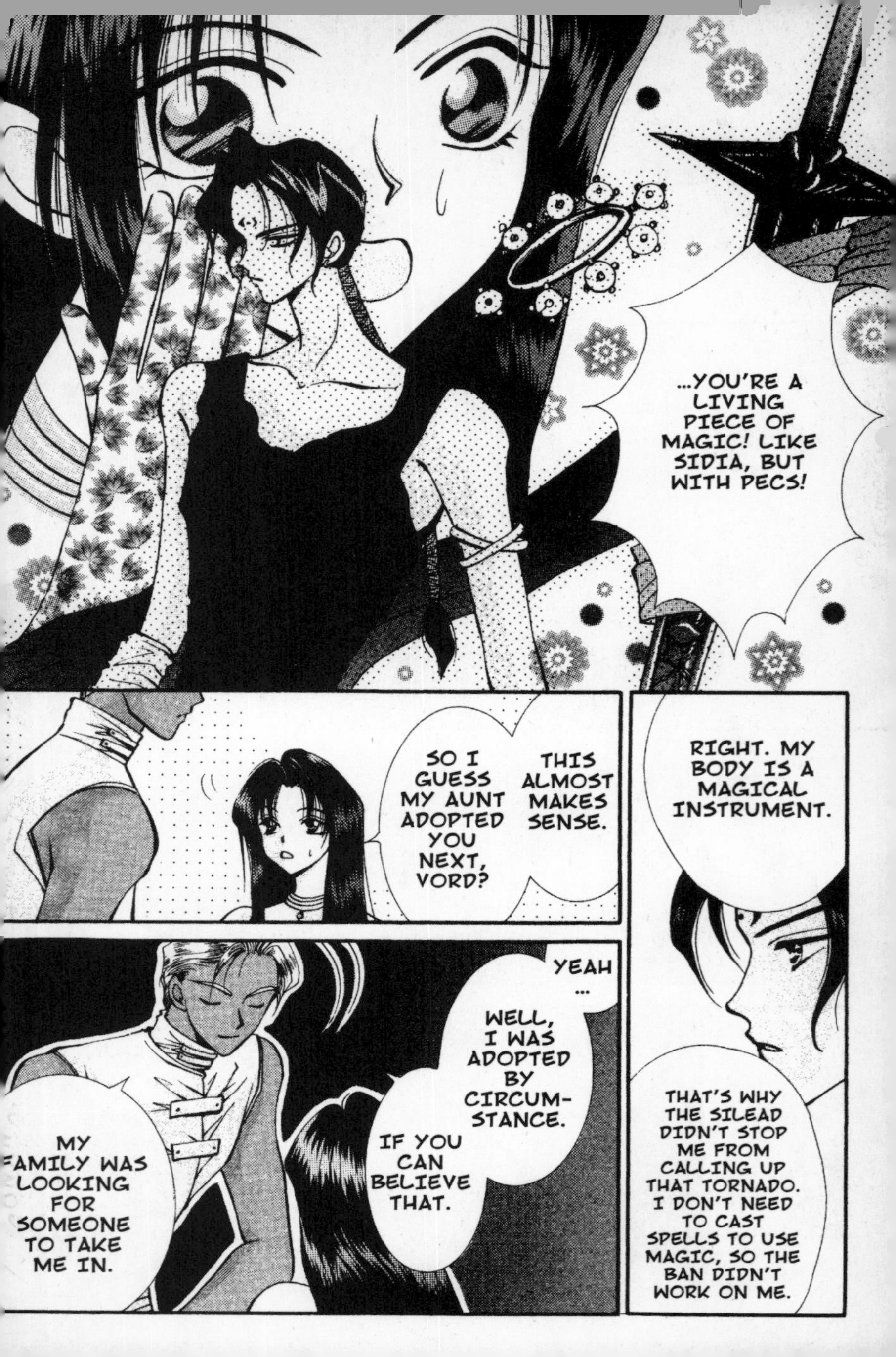
...YOU'RE A LIVING PIECE OF MAGIC! LIKE SIDIA, BUT WITH PECS!
RIGHT. MY BODY IS A MAGICAL INSTRUMENT.
THAT'S WHY THE SILEAD DIDN'T STOP ME FROM CALLING UP THAT TORNADO. I DON'T NEED TO CAST SPELLS TO USE MAGIC, SO THE BAN DIDN'T WORK ON ME.
THIS ALMOST MAKES SENSE.
SO I GUESS MY AUNT ADOPTED YOU NEXT, VORD?
YEAH ...
WELL, I WAS ADOPTED BY CIRCUM-STANCE.
IF YOU CAN BELIEVE THAT.
MY FAMILY WAS LOOKING FOR SOMEONE TO TAKE ME IN.

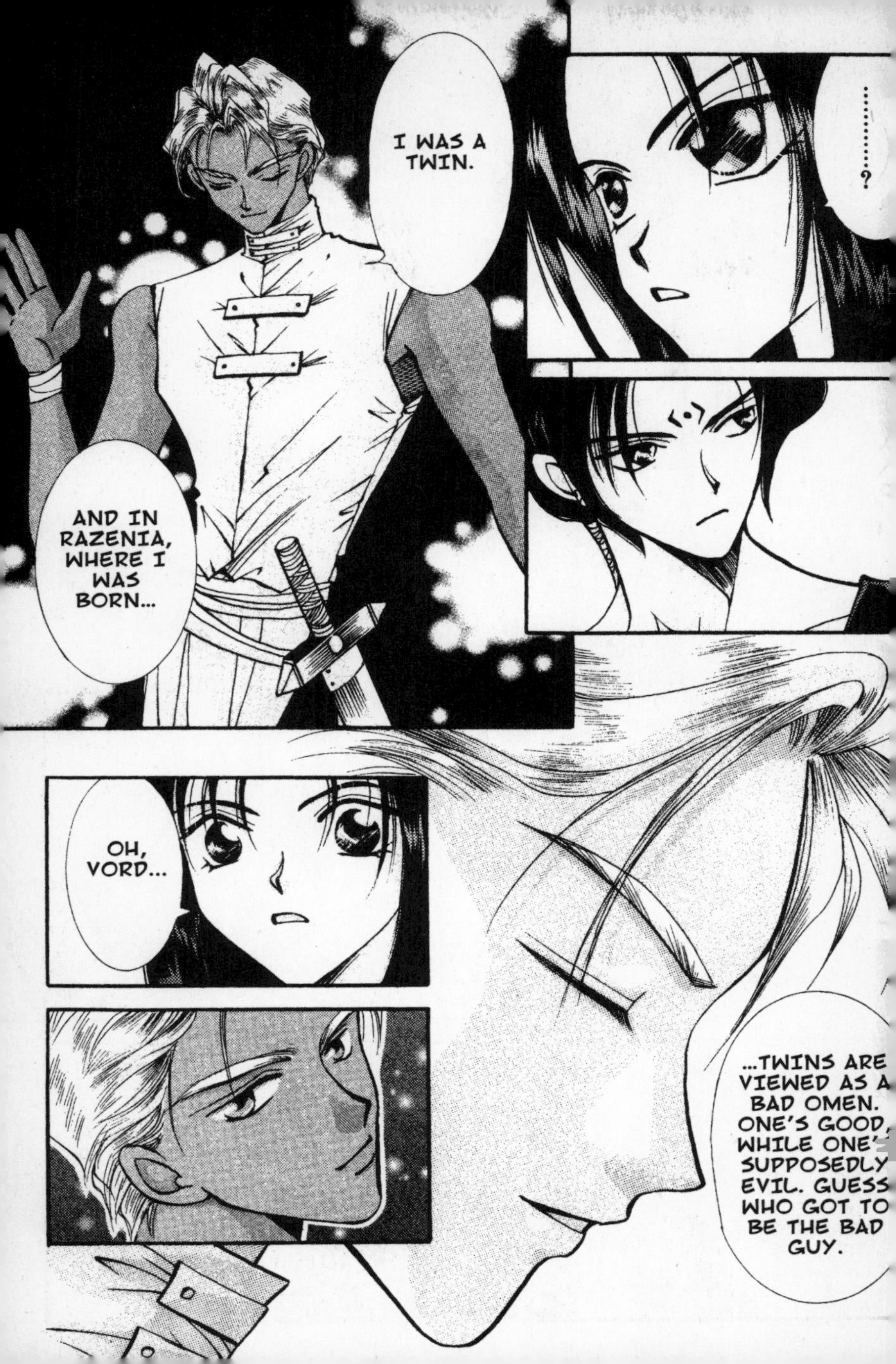

......?
I WAS A TWIN.
AND IN RAZENIA, WHERE I WAS BORN...
...TWINS ARE VIEWED AS A BAD OMEN. ONE'S GOOD, WHILE ONE'S SUPPOSEDLY EVIL. GUESS WHO GOT TO BE THE BAD GUY.
OH, VORD...

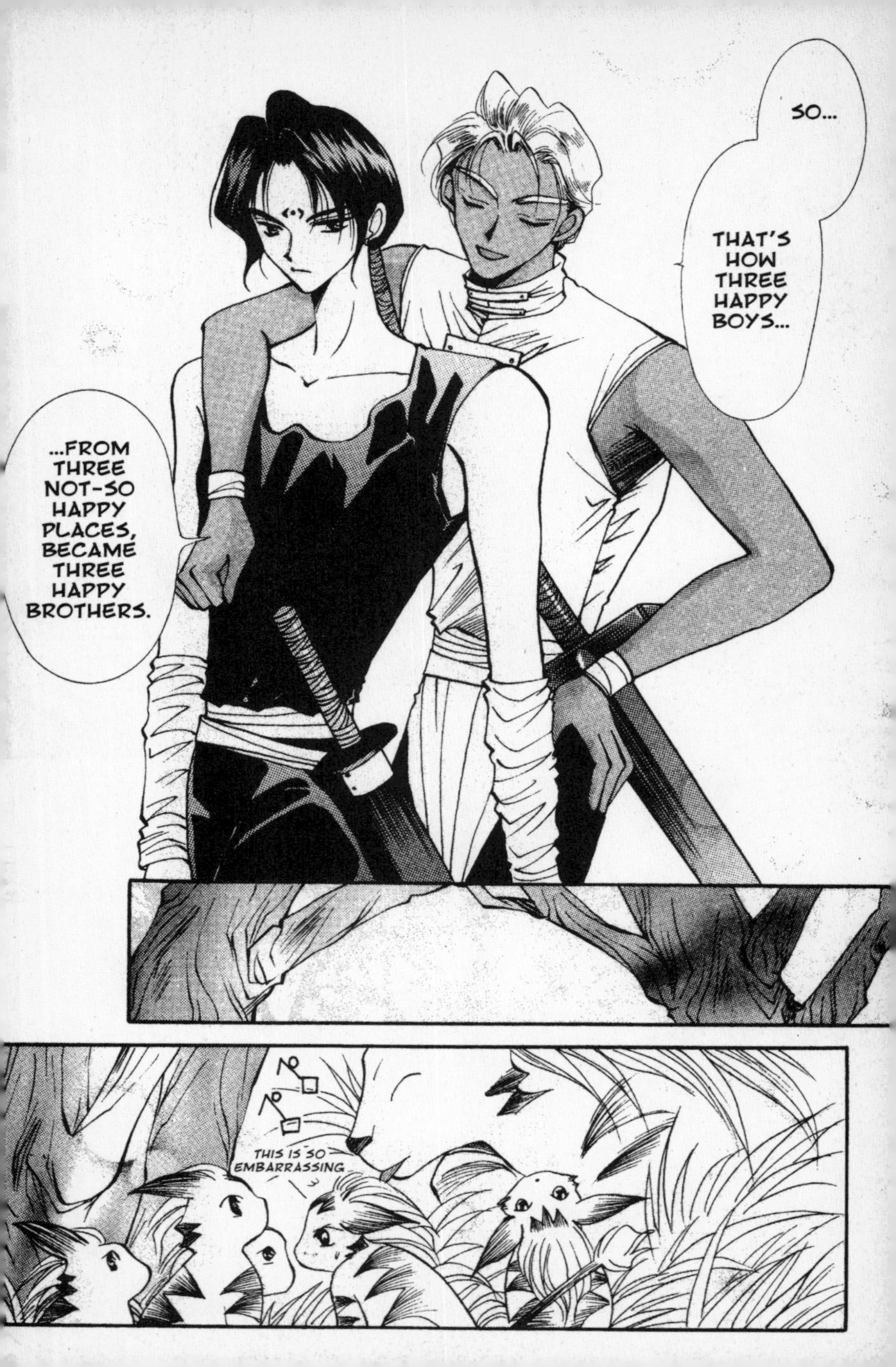
SO...
THAT'S HOW THREE HAPPY BOYS...
...FROM THREE NOT-SO HAPPY PLACES, BECAME THREE HAPPY BROTHERS.
THIS IS SO EMBARRASSING

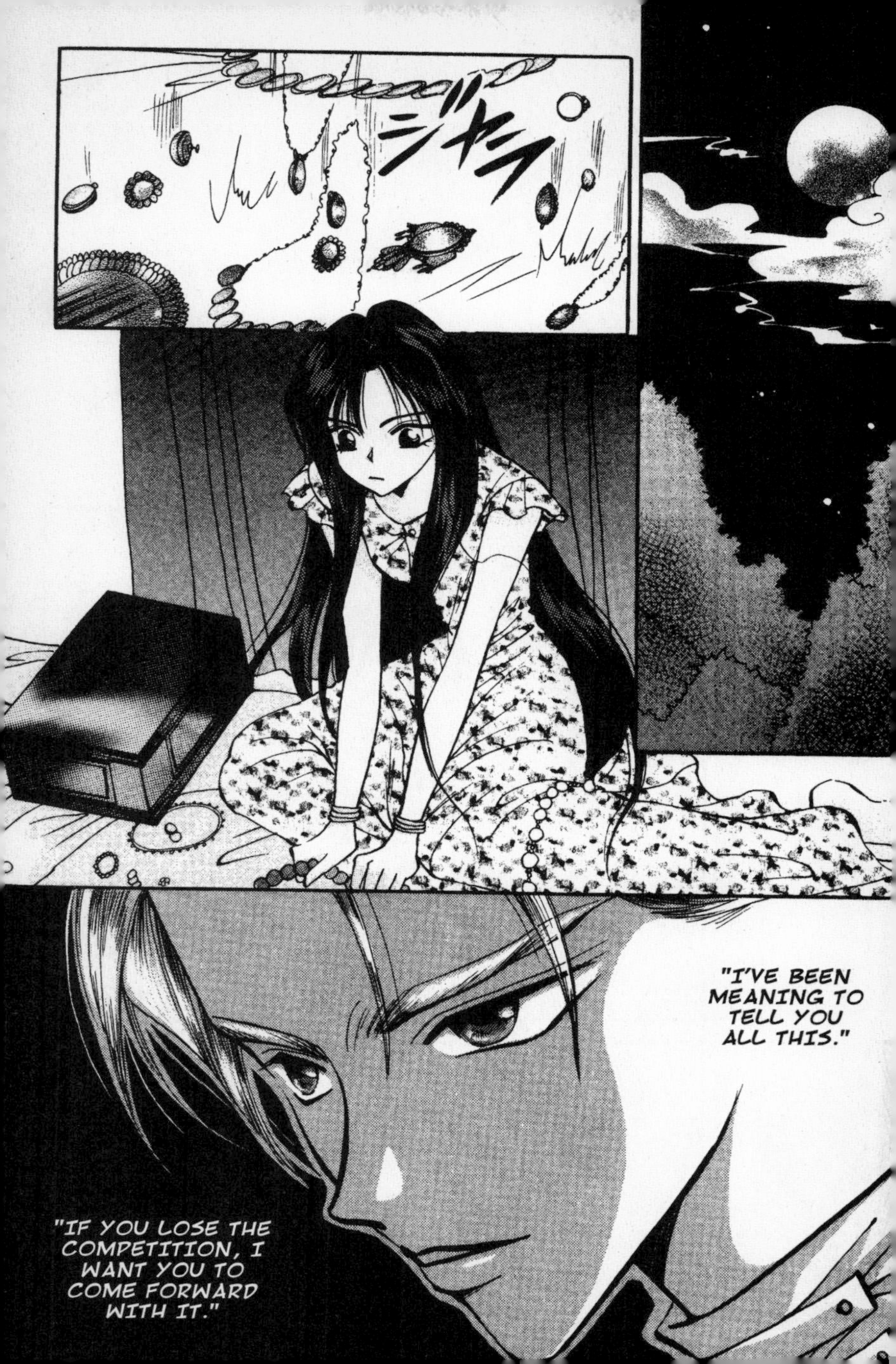
ジャラ
"I'VE BEEN MEANING TO TELL YOU ALL THIS."
"IF YOU LOSE THE COMPETITION, I WANT YOU TO COME FORWARD WITH IT."

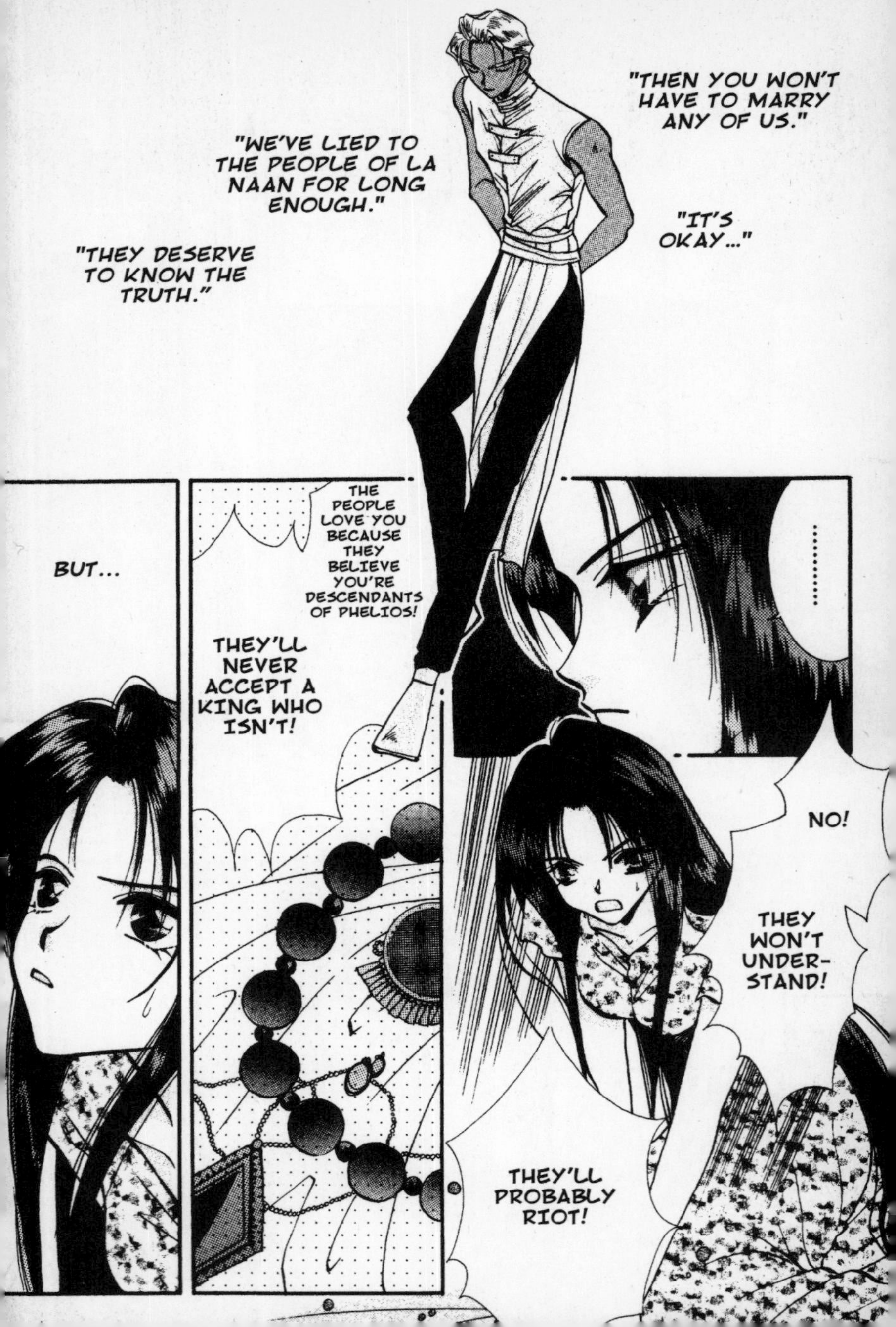
"THEN YOU WON'T HAVE TO MARRY ANY OF US."
"IT'S OKAY..."
"WE'VE LIED TO THE PEOPLE OF LA NAAN FOR LONG ENOUGH."
"THEY DESERVE TO KNOW THE TRUTH."
......
NO!
THEY WON'T UNDERSTAND!
THEY'LL PROBABLY RIOT!
THE PEOPLE LOVE YOU BECAUSE THEY BELIEVE YOU'RE DESCENDANTS OF PHELIOS!
THEY'LL NEVER ACCEPT A KING WHO ISN'T!
BUT...

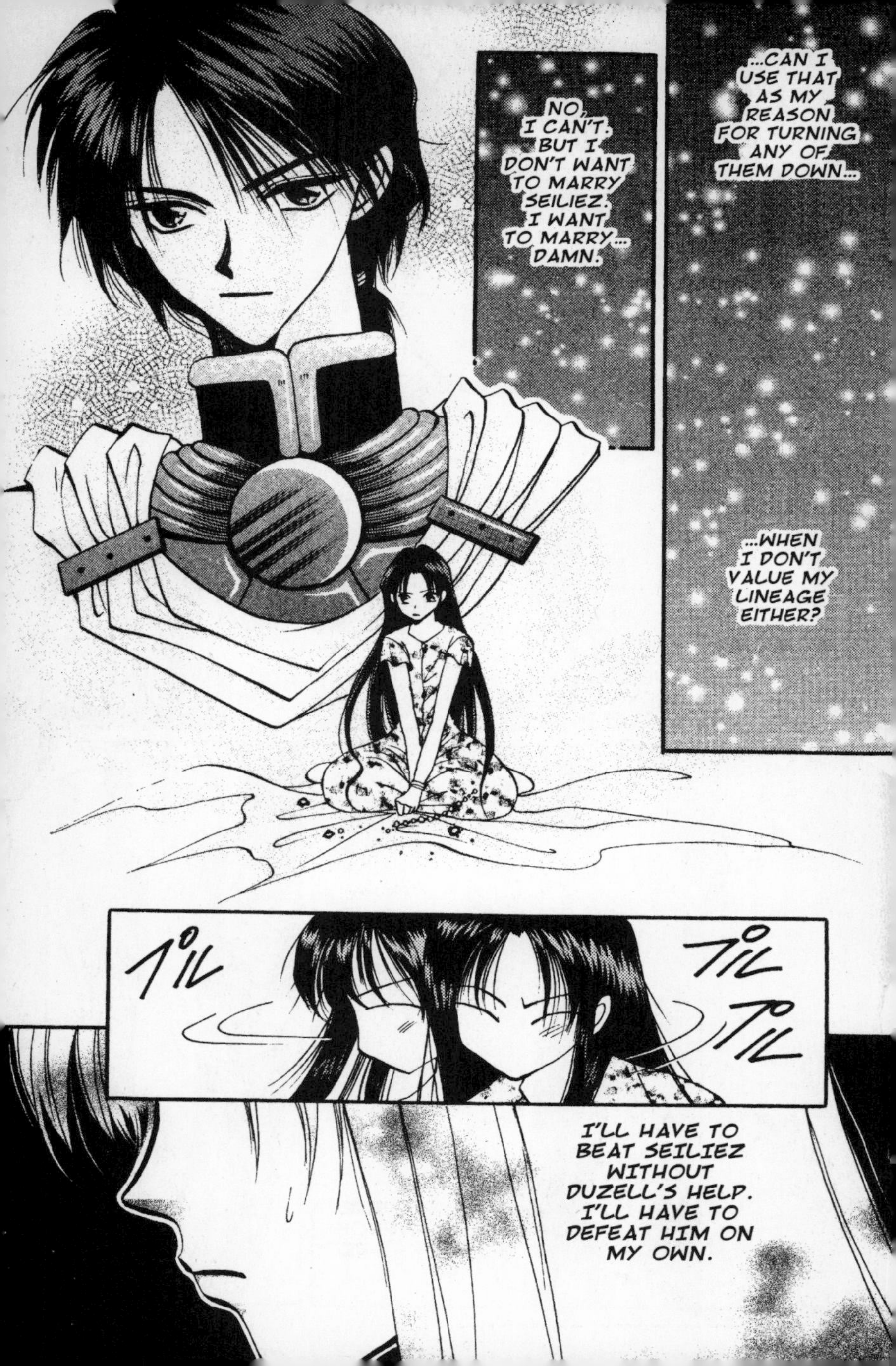
...CAN I USE THAT AS MY REASON FOR TURNING ANY OF THEM DOWN...
...WHEN I DON'T VALUE MY LINEAGE EITHER?
NO, I CAN'T. BUT I DON'T WANT TO MARRY SEILIEZ. I WANT TO MARRY... DAMN.
プル
プル
プル
I'LL HAVE TO BEAT SEILIEZ WITHOUT DUZELL'S HELP. I'LL HAVE TO DEFEAT HIM ON MY OWN.

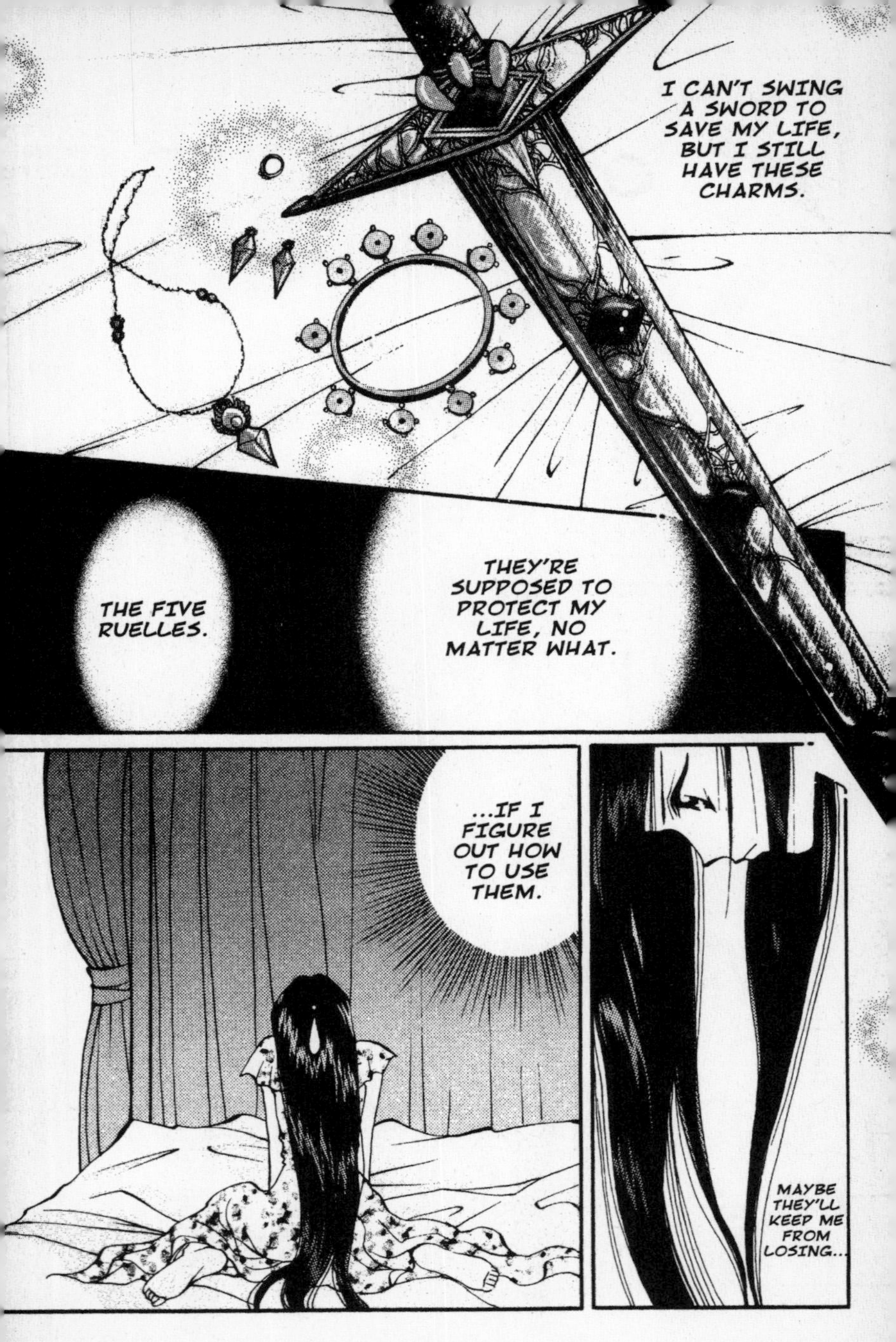
I CAN'T SWING A SWORD TO SAVE MY LIFE, BUT I STILL HAVE THESE CHARMS.
THEY'RE SUPPOSED TO PROTECT MY LIFE, NO MATTER WHAT.
THE FIVE RUELLES.
MAYBE THEY'LL KEEP ME FROM LOSING...
...IF I FIGURE OUT HOW TO USE THEM.

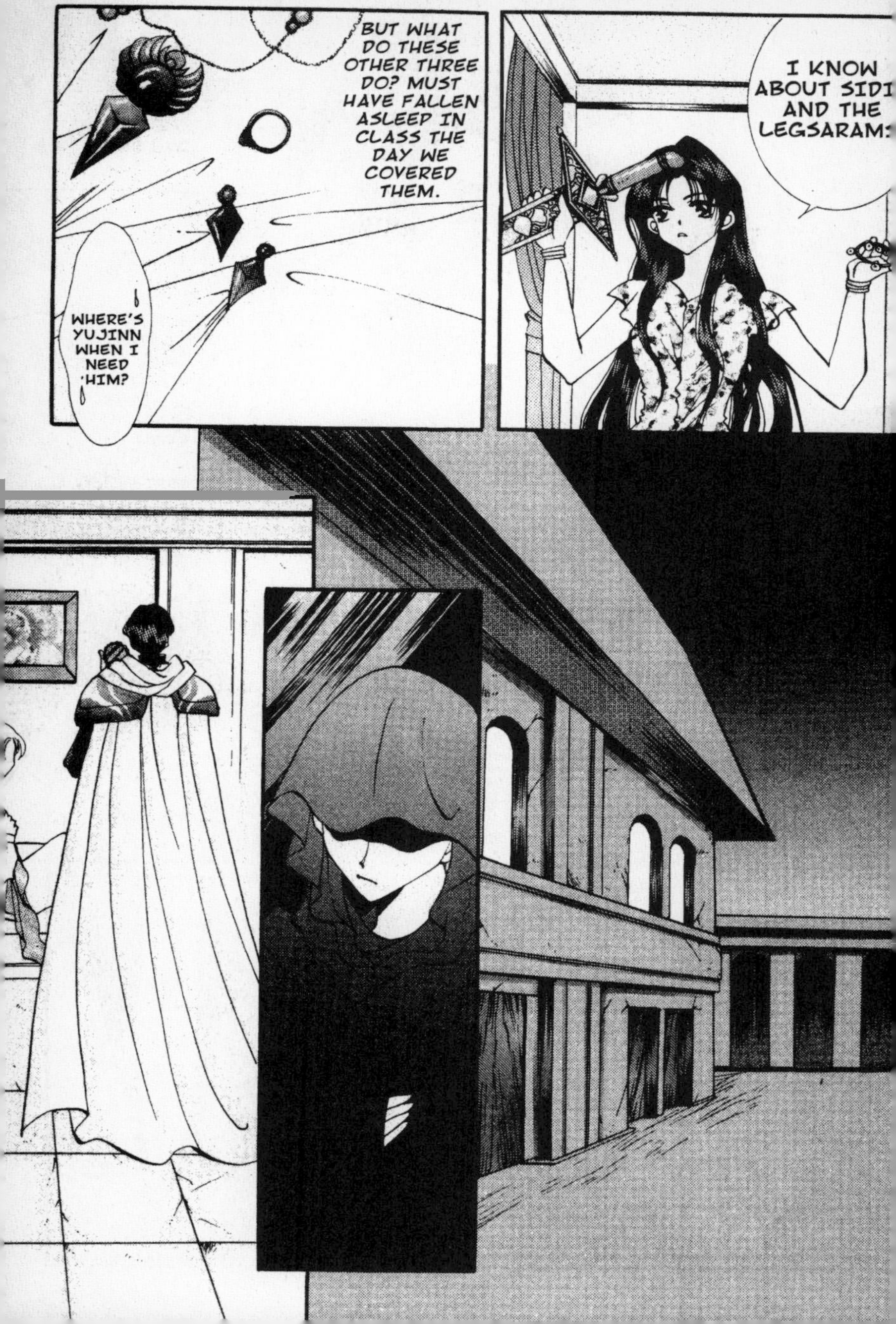
I KNOW ABOUT SIDI AND THE LEGSARAM:
BUT WHAT DO THESE OTHER THREE DO? MUST HAVE FALLEN ASLEEP IN CLASS THE DAY WE COVERED THEM.
WHERE'S YUJINN WHEN I NEED HIM?

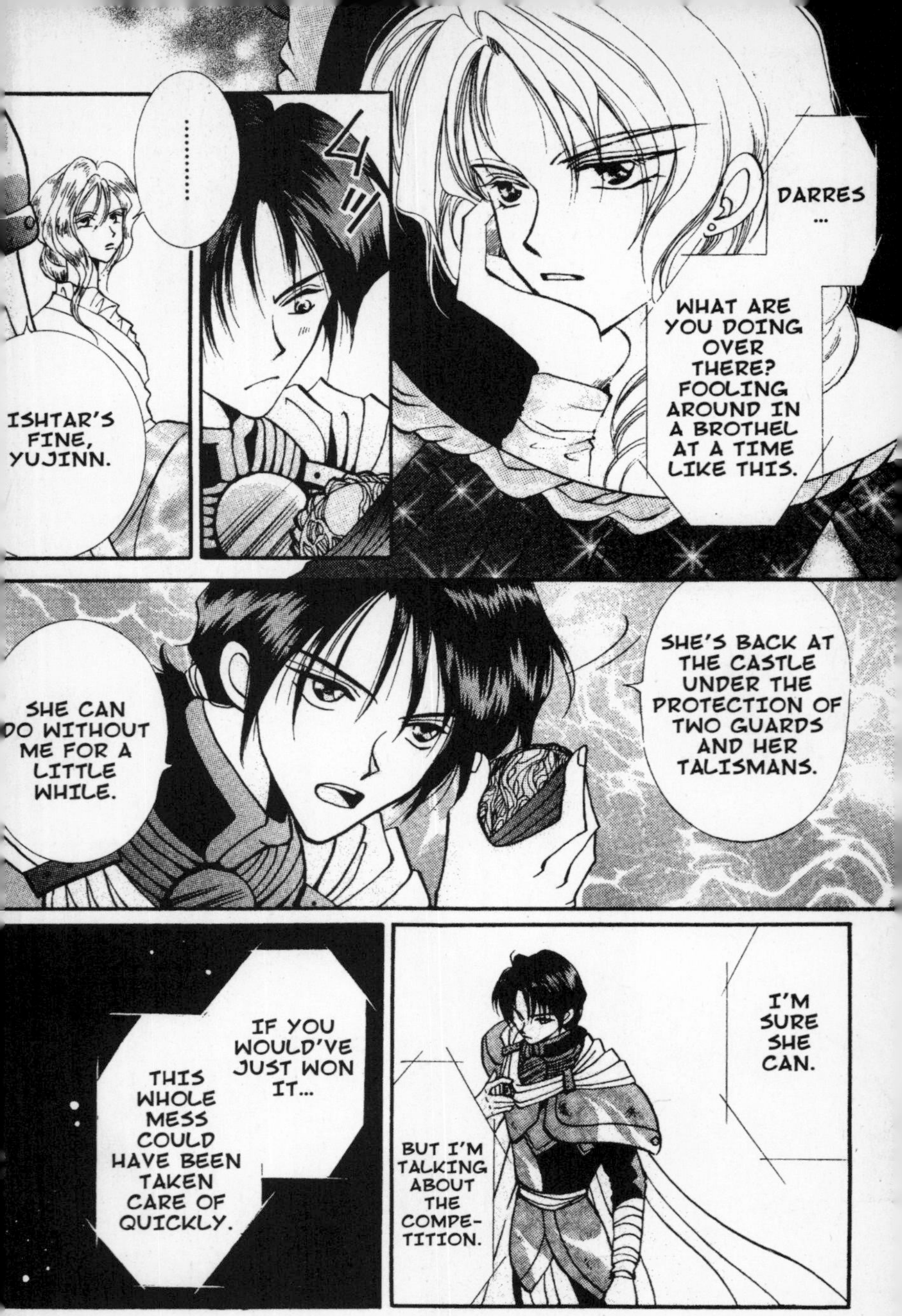

DARRES ...
WHAT ARE YOU DOING OVER THERE? FOOLING AROUND IN A BROTHEL AT A TIME LIKE THIS.
ムッ
....
ISHTAR'S FINE, YUJINN.
SHE'S BACK AT THE CASTLE UNDER THE PROTECTION OF TWO GUARDS AND HER TALISMANS.
SHE CAN DO WITHOUT ME FOR A LITTLE WHILE.
I'M SURE SHE CAN.
BUT I'M TALKING ABOUT THE COMPE-TITION.
IF YOU WOULD'VE JUST WON IT...
THIS WHOLE MESS COULD HAVE BEEN TAKEN CARE OF QUICKLY.

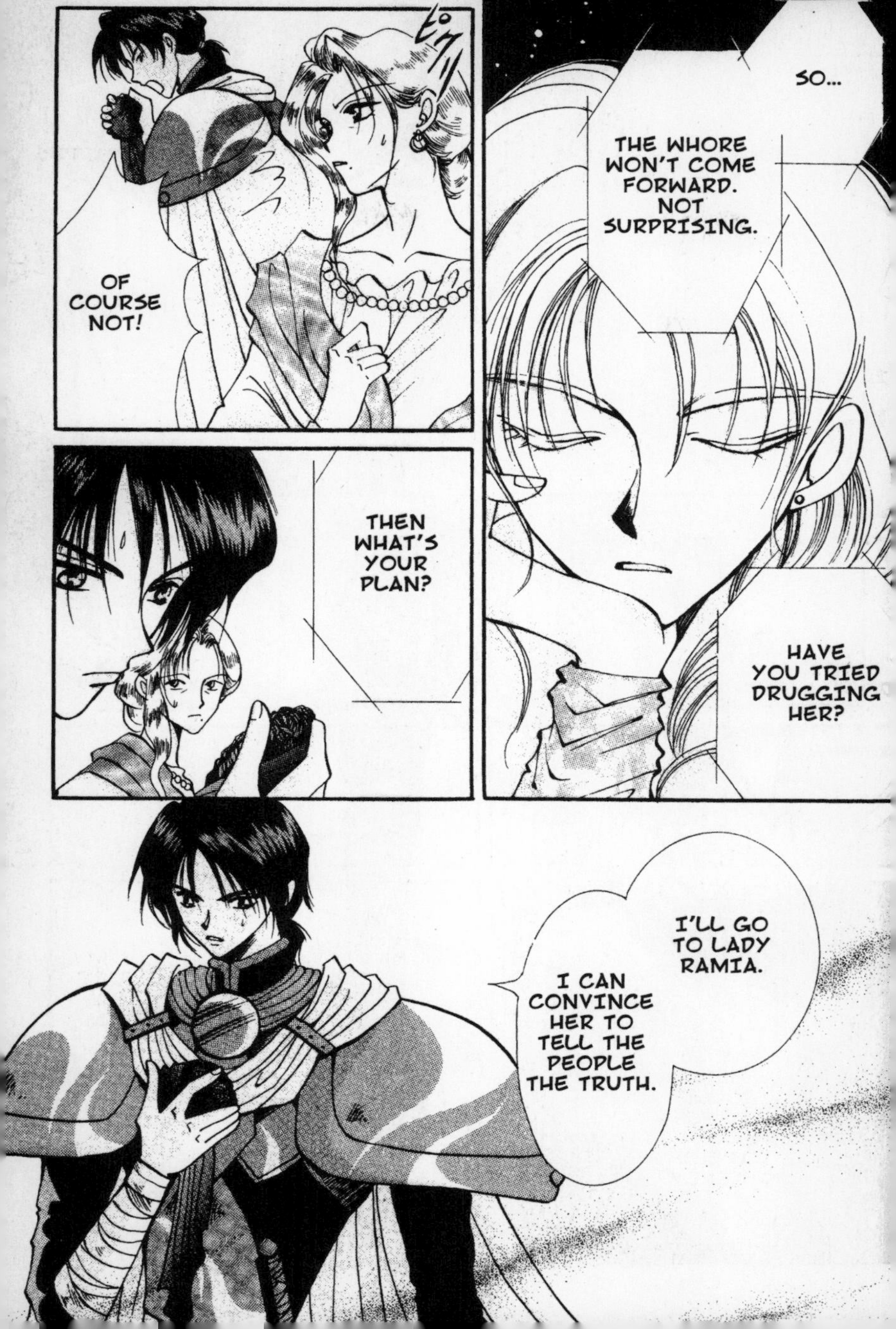
SO...
THE WHORE WON'T COME FORWARD. NOT SURPRISING.
HAVE YOU TRIED DRUGGING HER?
OF COURSE NOT!
THEN WHAT'S YOUR PLAN?
I'LL GO TO LADY RAMIA.
I CAN CONVINCE HER TO TELL THE PEOPLE THE TRUTH.

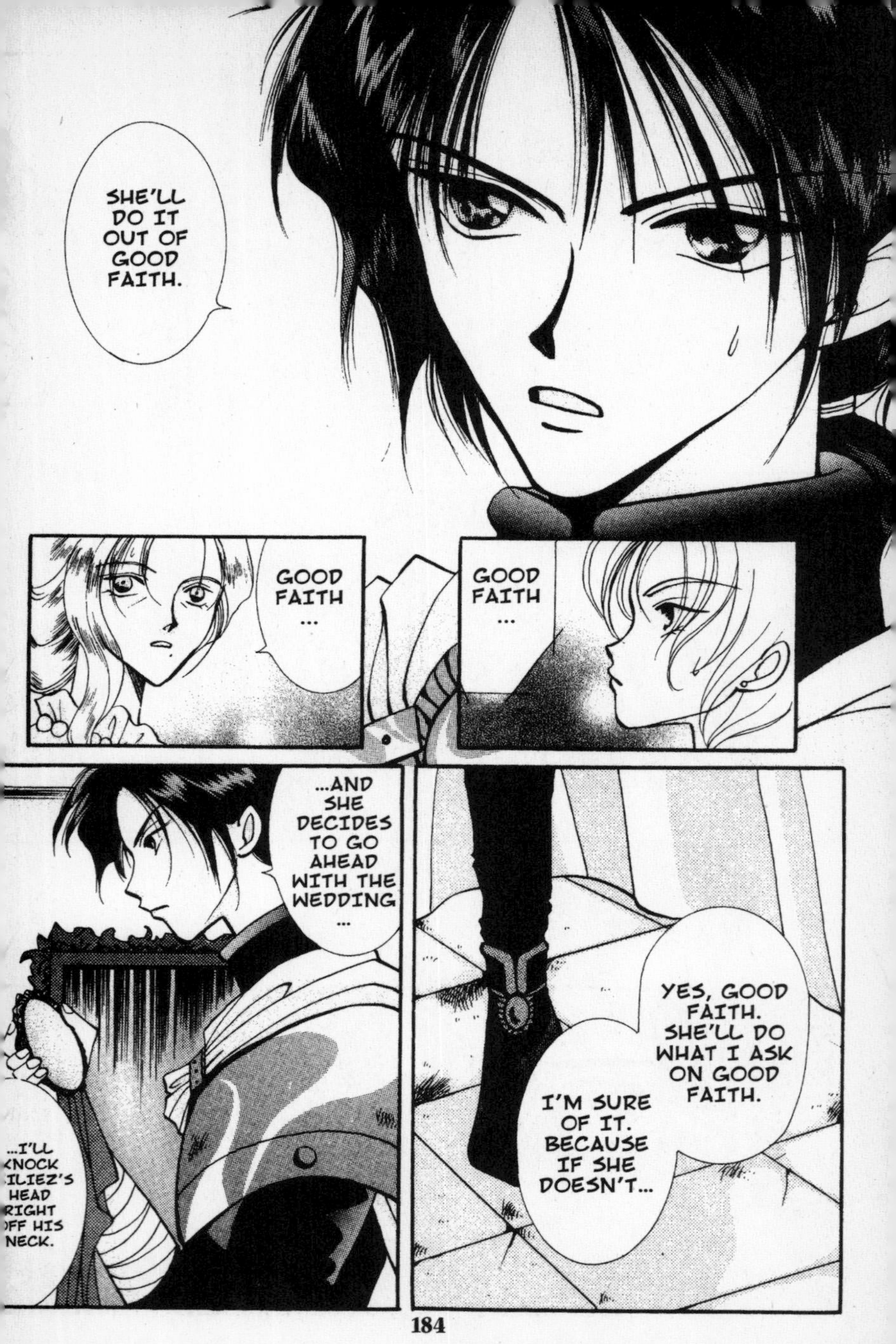
SHE'LL DO IT OUT OF GOOD FAITH.
GOOD FAITH ...
GOOD FAITH ...
YES, GOOD FAITH. SHE'LL DO WHAT I ASK ON GOOD FAITH.
I'M SURE OF IT. BECAUSE IF SHE DOESN'T...
...AND SHE DECIDES TO GO AHEAD WITH THE WEDDING ...
...I'LL KNOCK ILIEZ'S HEAD RIGHT OFF HIS NECK.

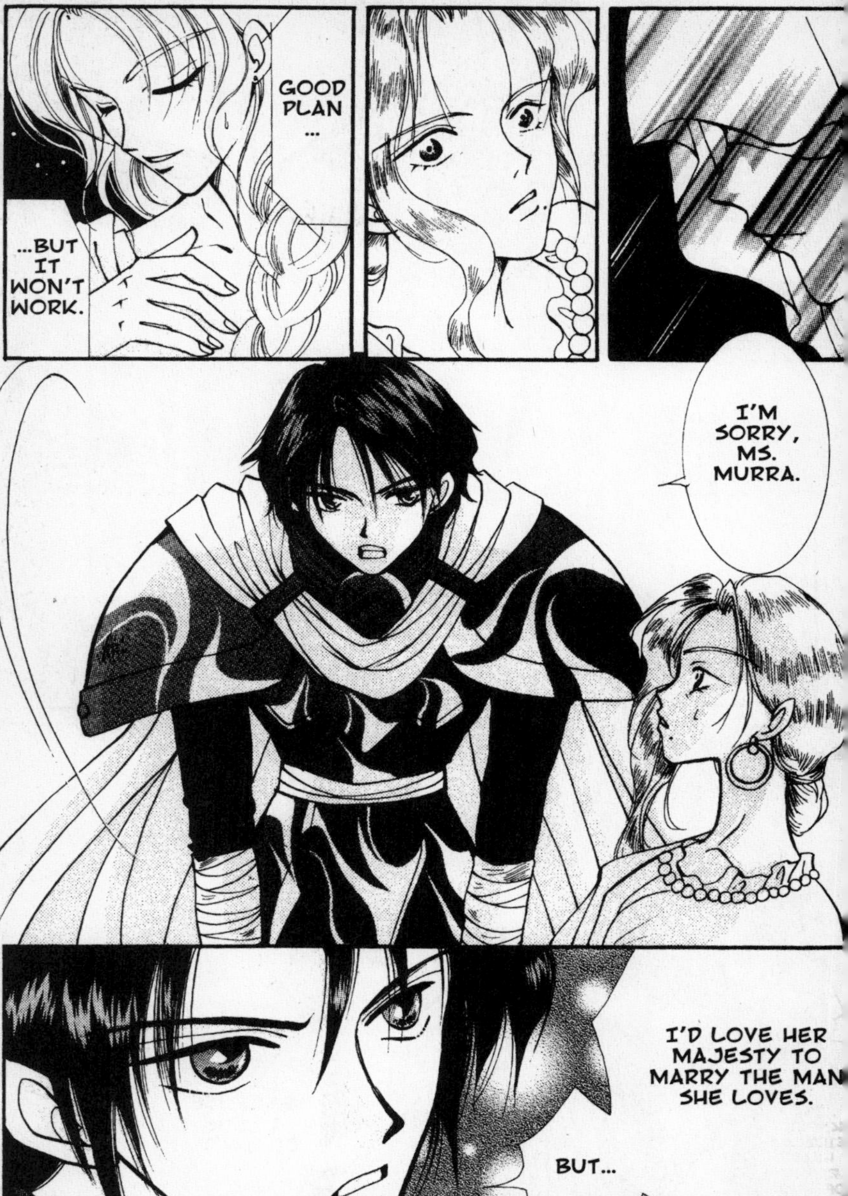
GOOD PLAN ...
...BUT IT WON'T WORK.
I'M SORRY, MS. MURRA.
I'D LOVE HER MAJESTY TO MARRY THE MAN SHE LOVES.
BUT...

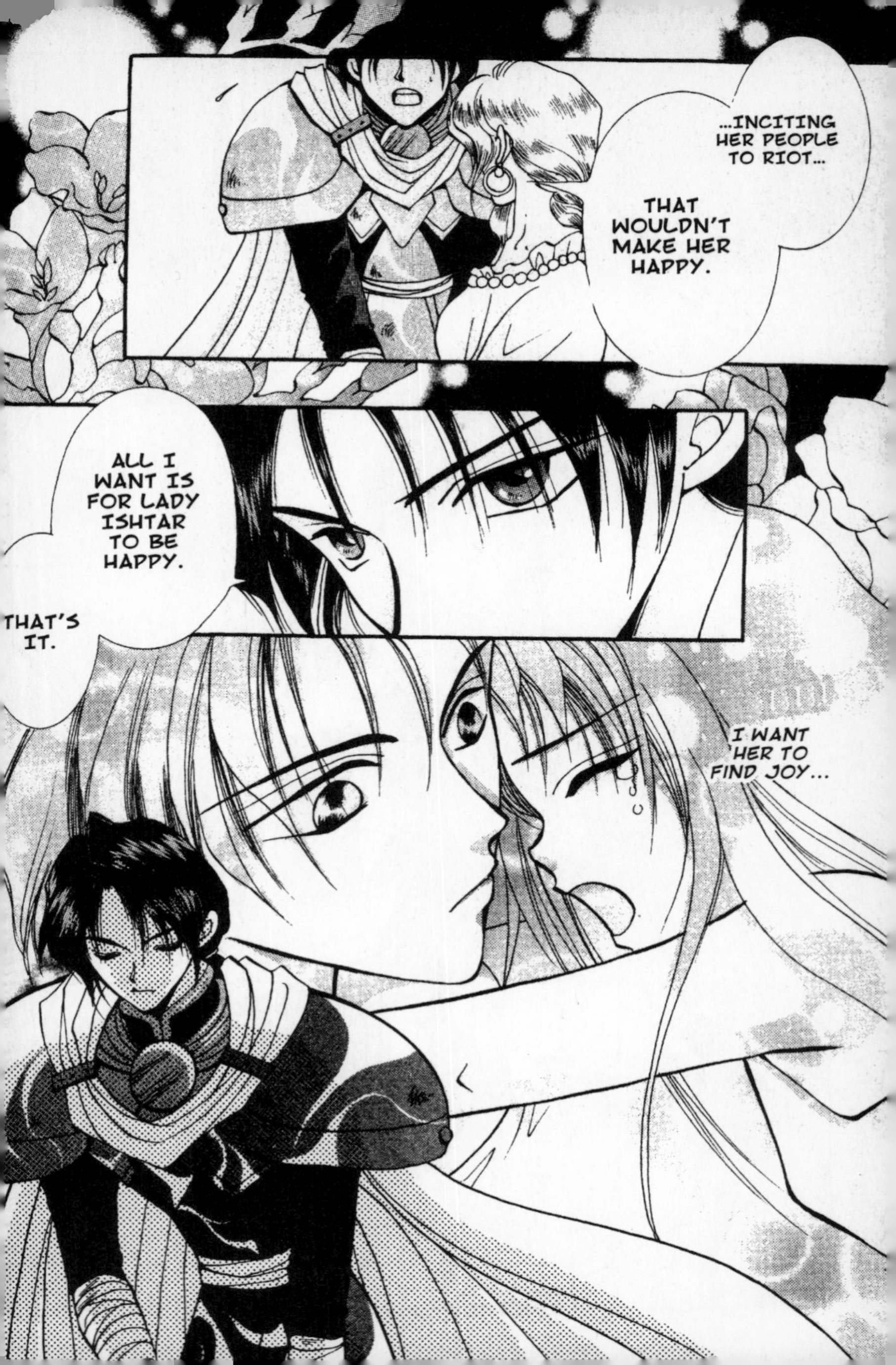
...INCITING HER PEOPLE TO RIOT...
THAT WOULDN'T MAKE HER HAPPY.
ALL I WANT IS FOR LADY ISHTAR TO BE HAPPY.
THAT'S IT.
I WANT HER TO FIND JOY...

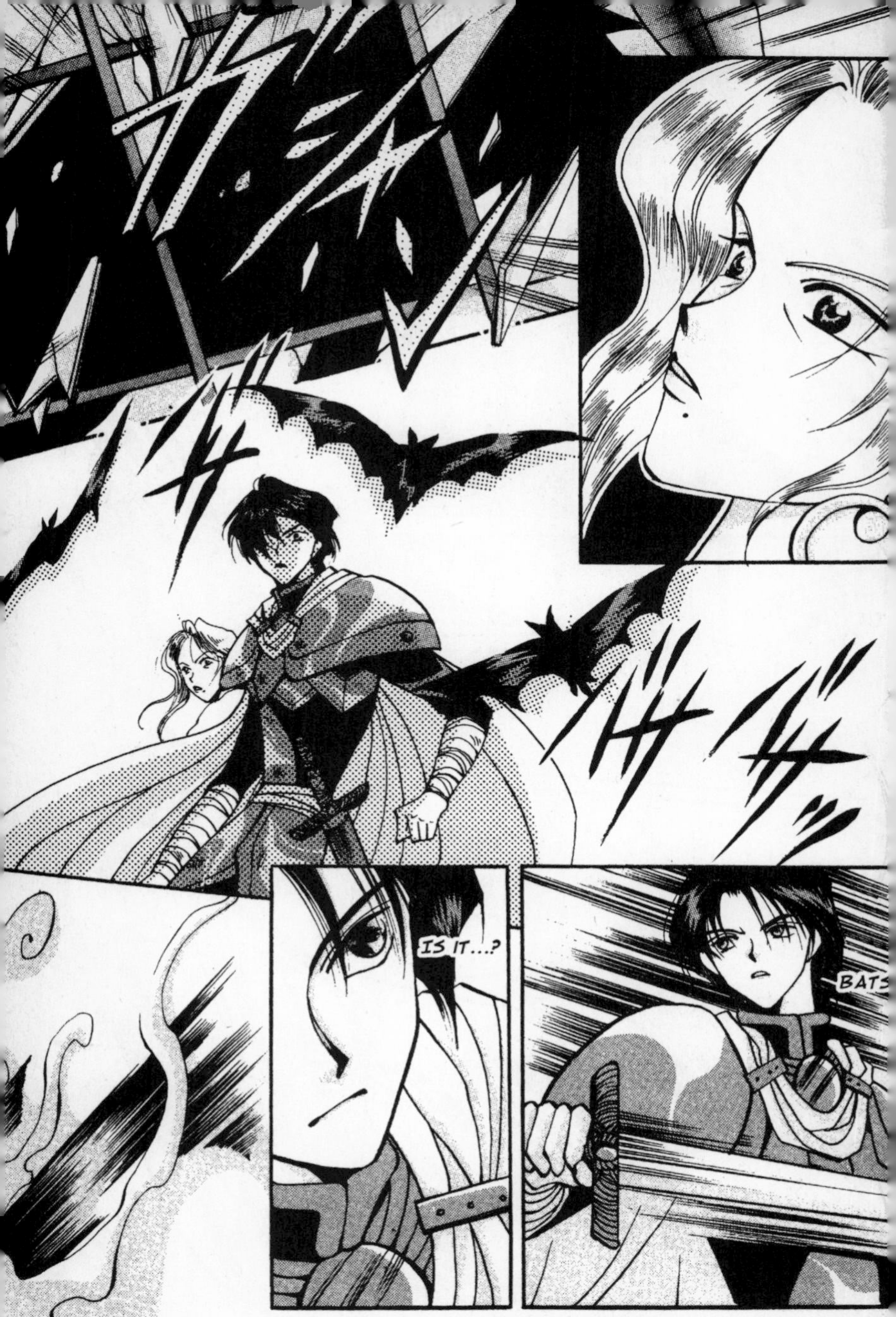
BATS
IS IT...?

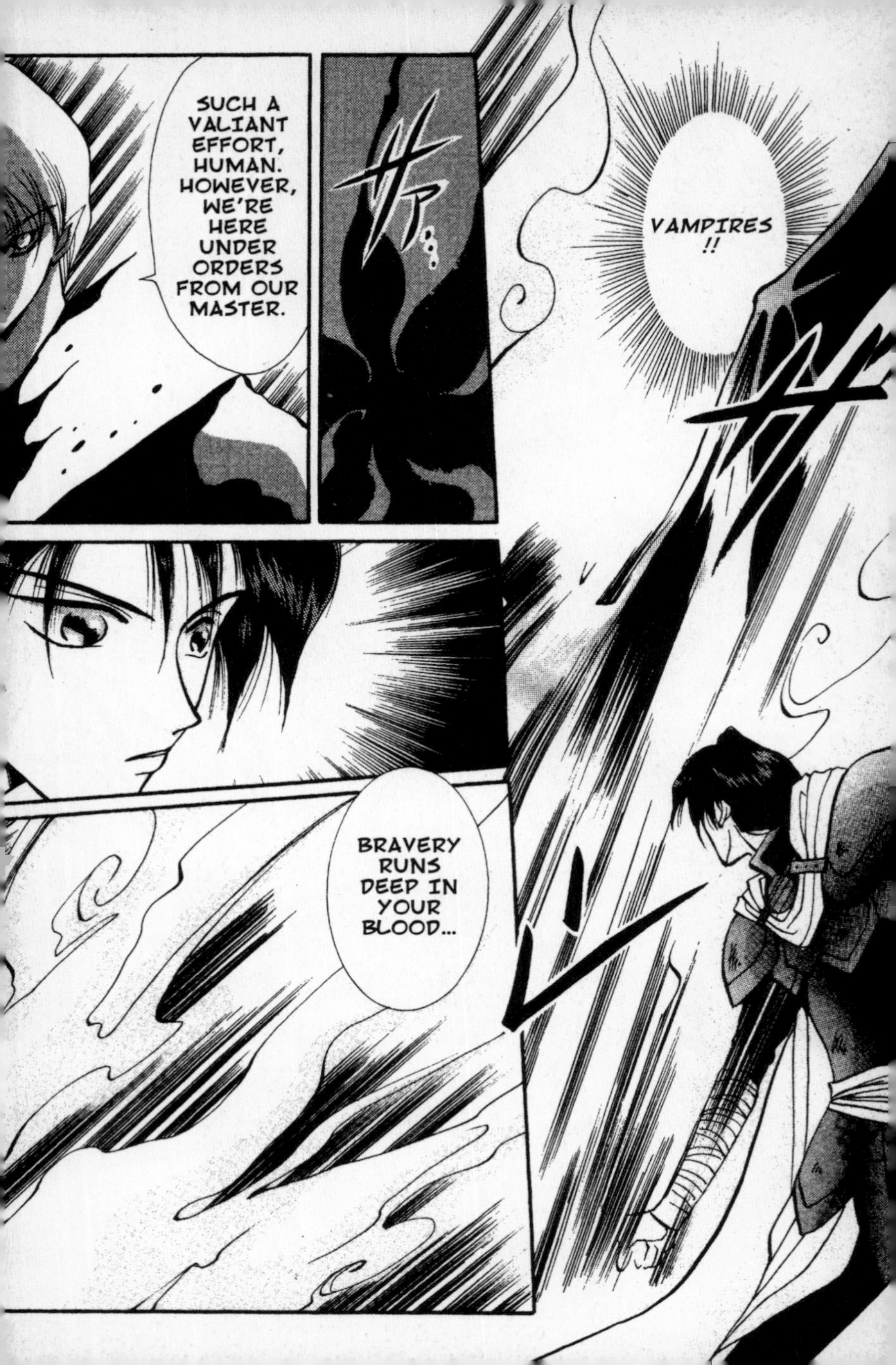
VAMPIRES !!
SUCH A VALIANT EFFORT, HUMAN. HOWEVER, WE'RE HERE UNDER ORDERS FROM OUR MASTER.
BRAVERY RUNS DEEP IN YOUR BLOOD...

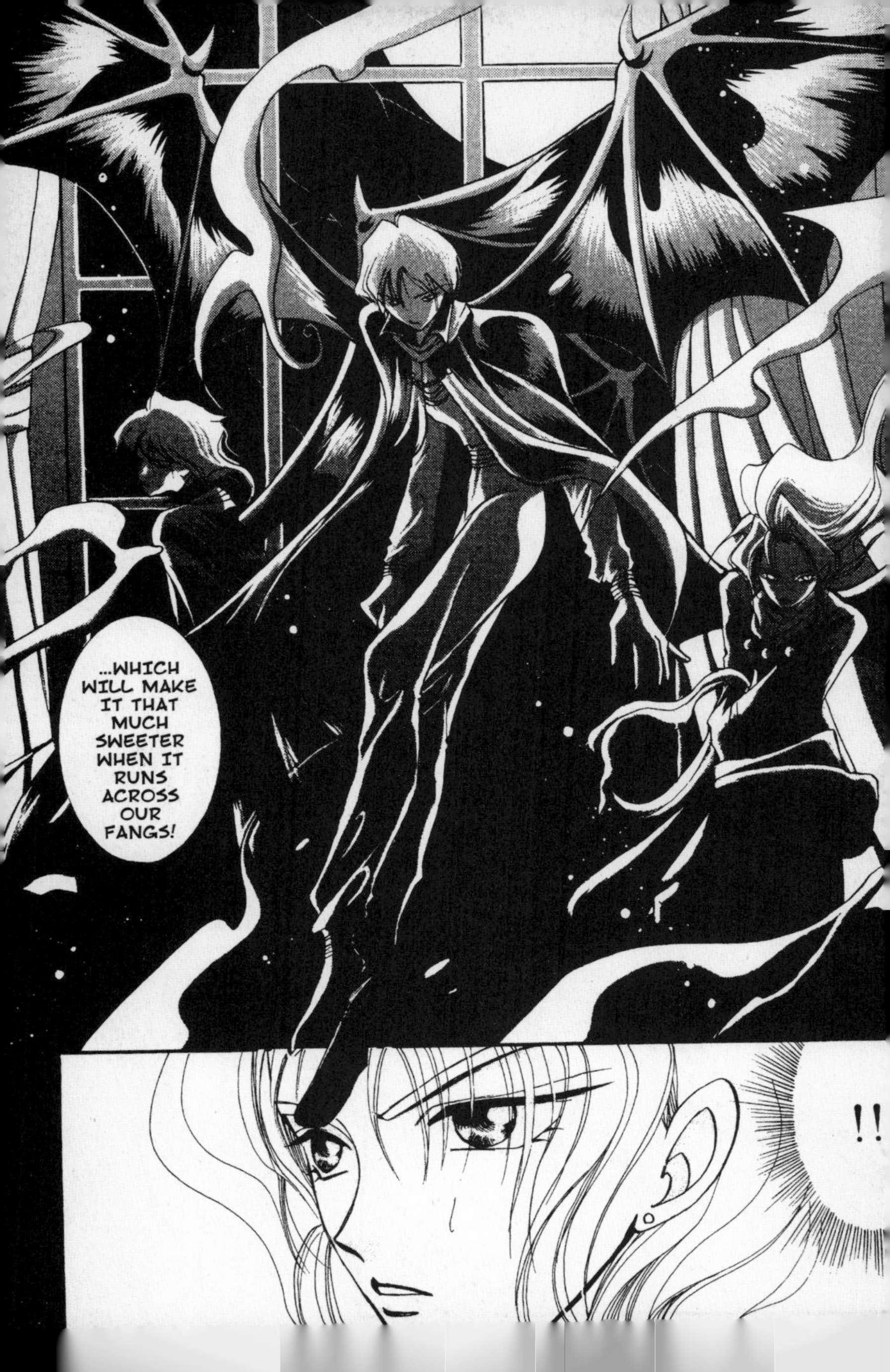
...WHICH WILL MAKE IT THAT MUCH SWEETER WHEN IT RUNS ACROSS OUR FANGS!
!!

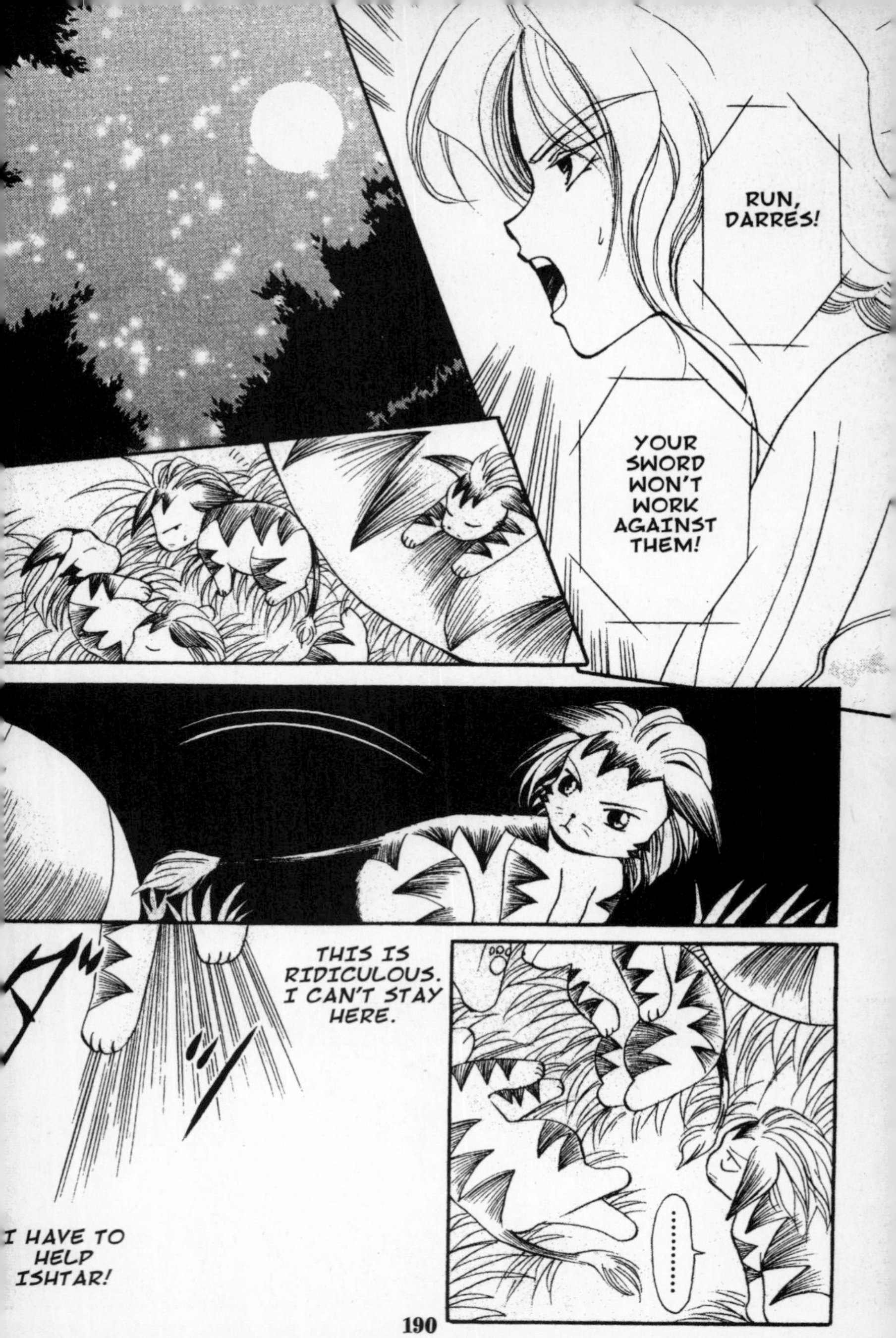
RUN, DARRES!
YOUR SWORD WON'T WORK AGAINST THEM!
......
THIS IS RIDICULOUS. I CAN'T STAY HERE.
I HAVE TO HELP ISHTAR!

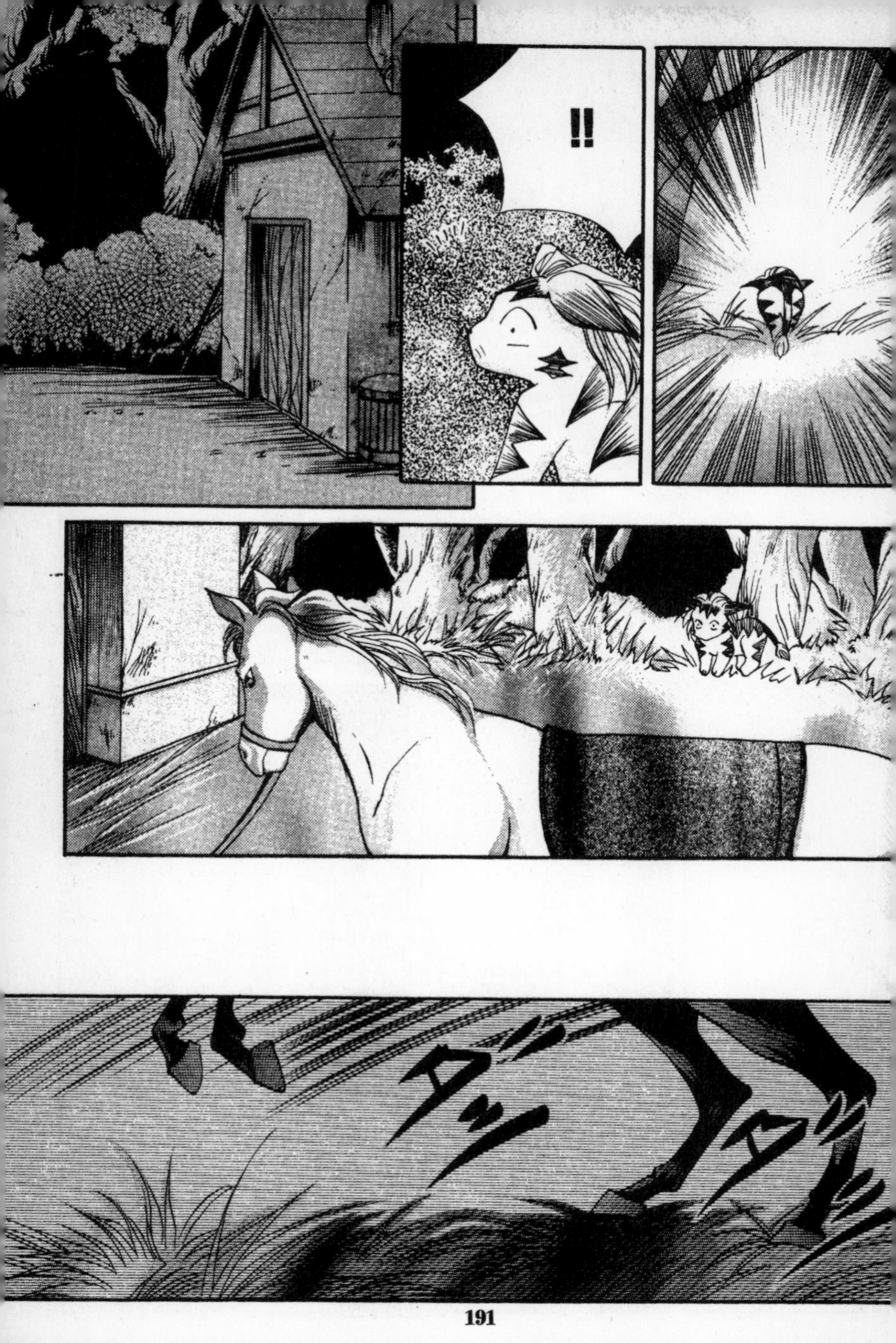
!!
タッ

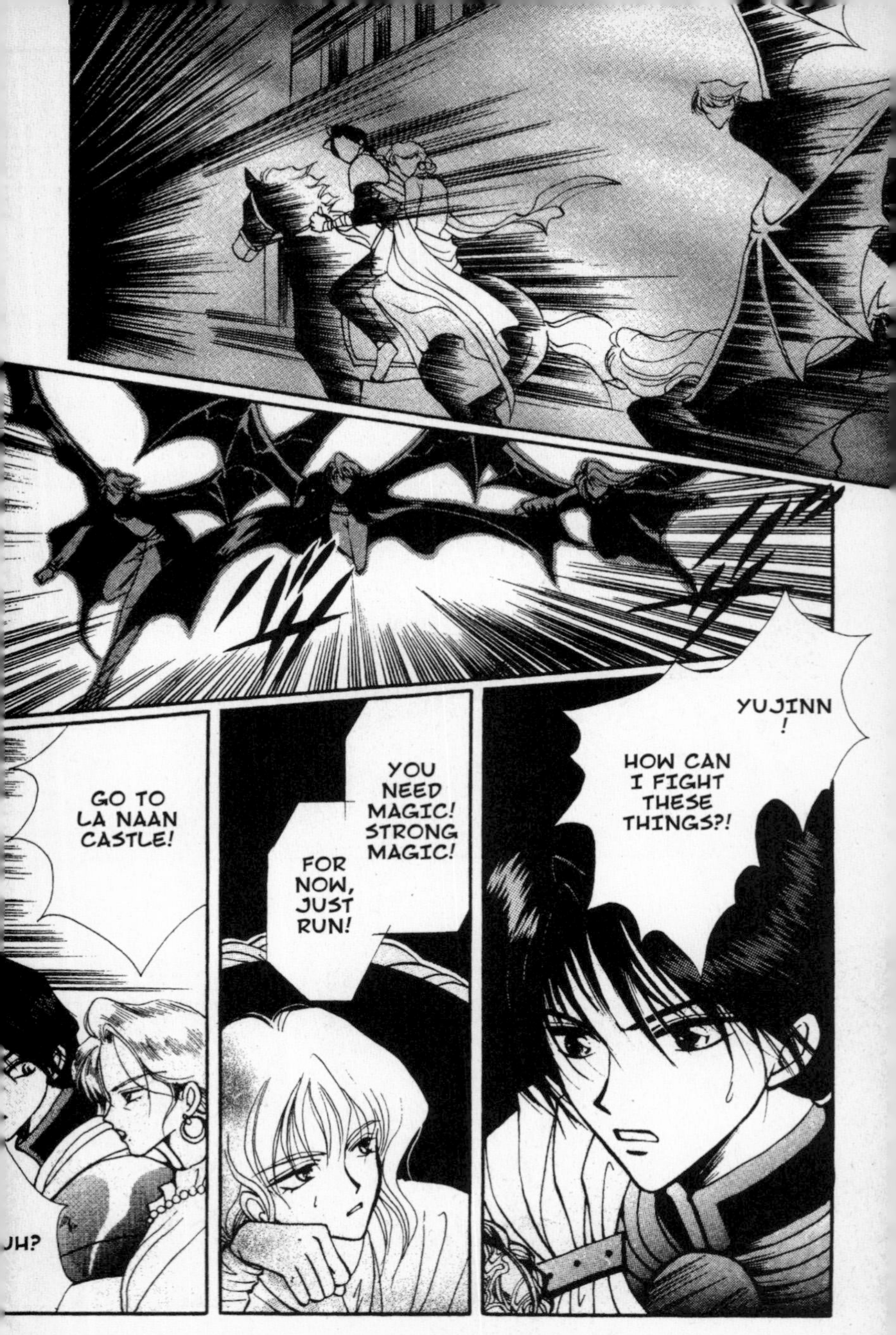
YUJINN!
HOW CAN I FIGHT THESE THINGS?!
YOU NEED MAGIC! STRONG MAGIC!
FOR NOW, JUST RUN!
GO TO LA NAAN CASTLE!
UH?

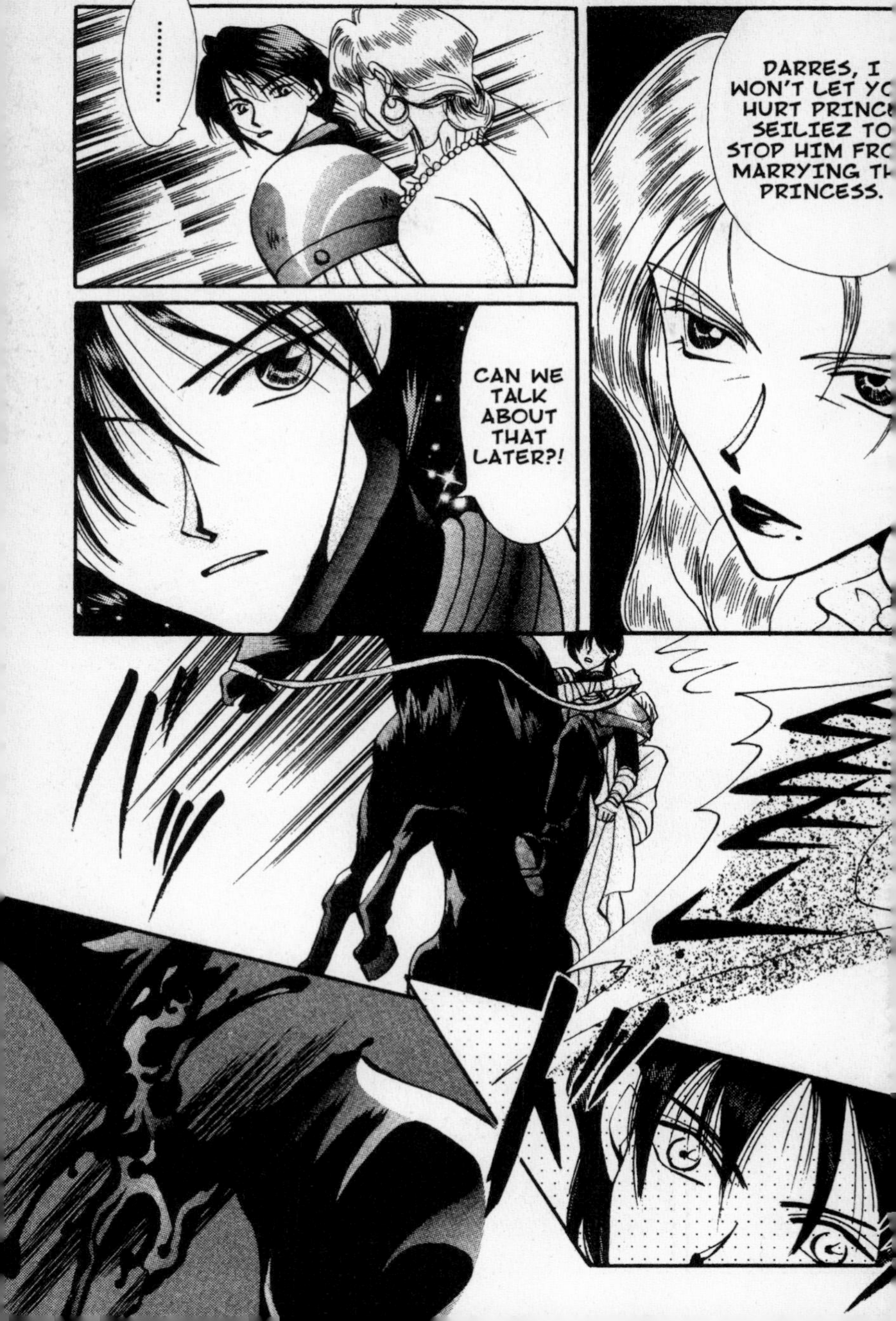
DARRES, I WON'T LET YO HURT PRINCE SEILIEZ TO STOP HIM FRO MARRYING TH PRINCESS.
......
CAN WE TALK ABOUT THAT LATER?!

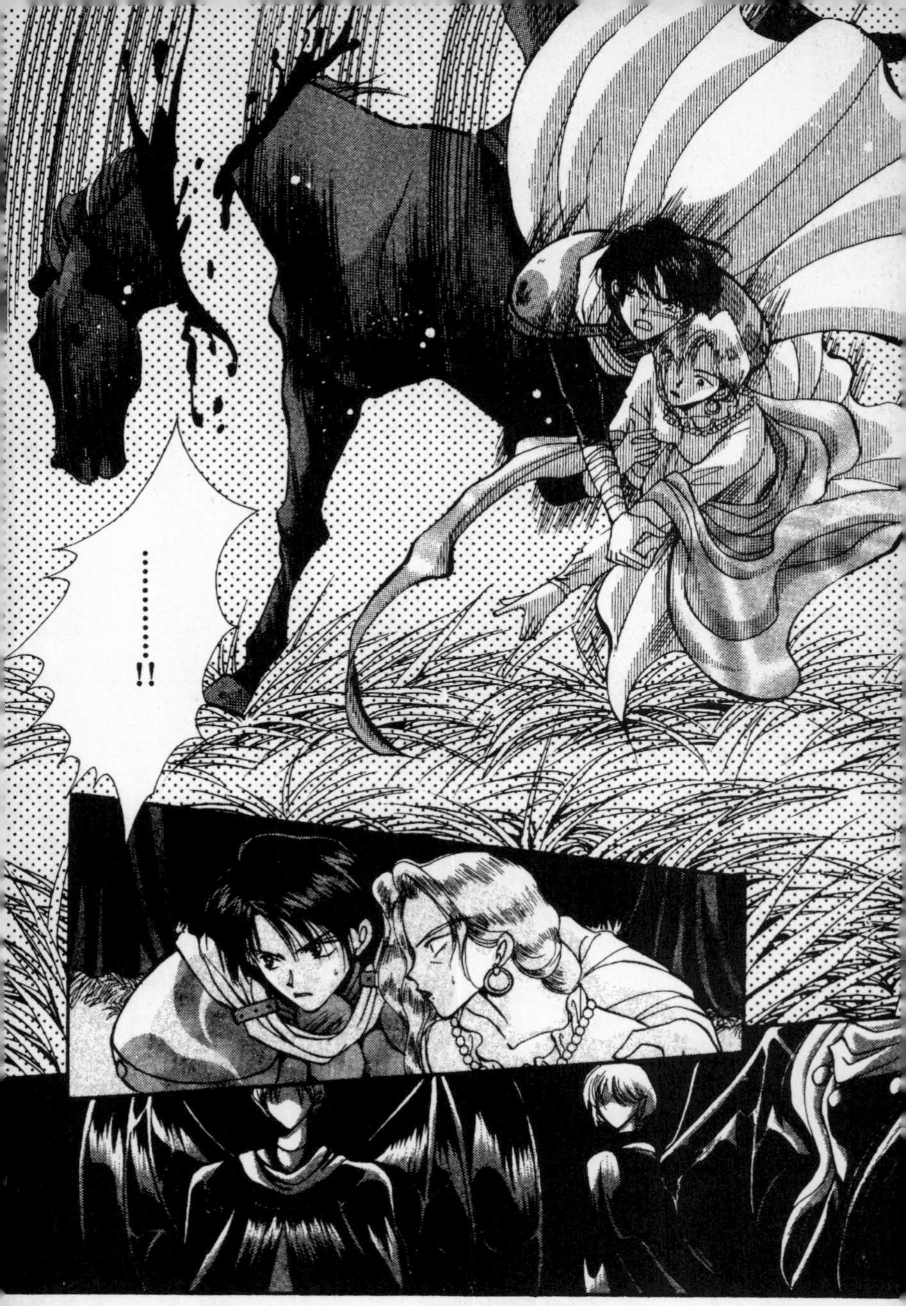
……!!

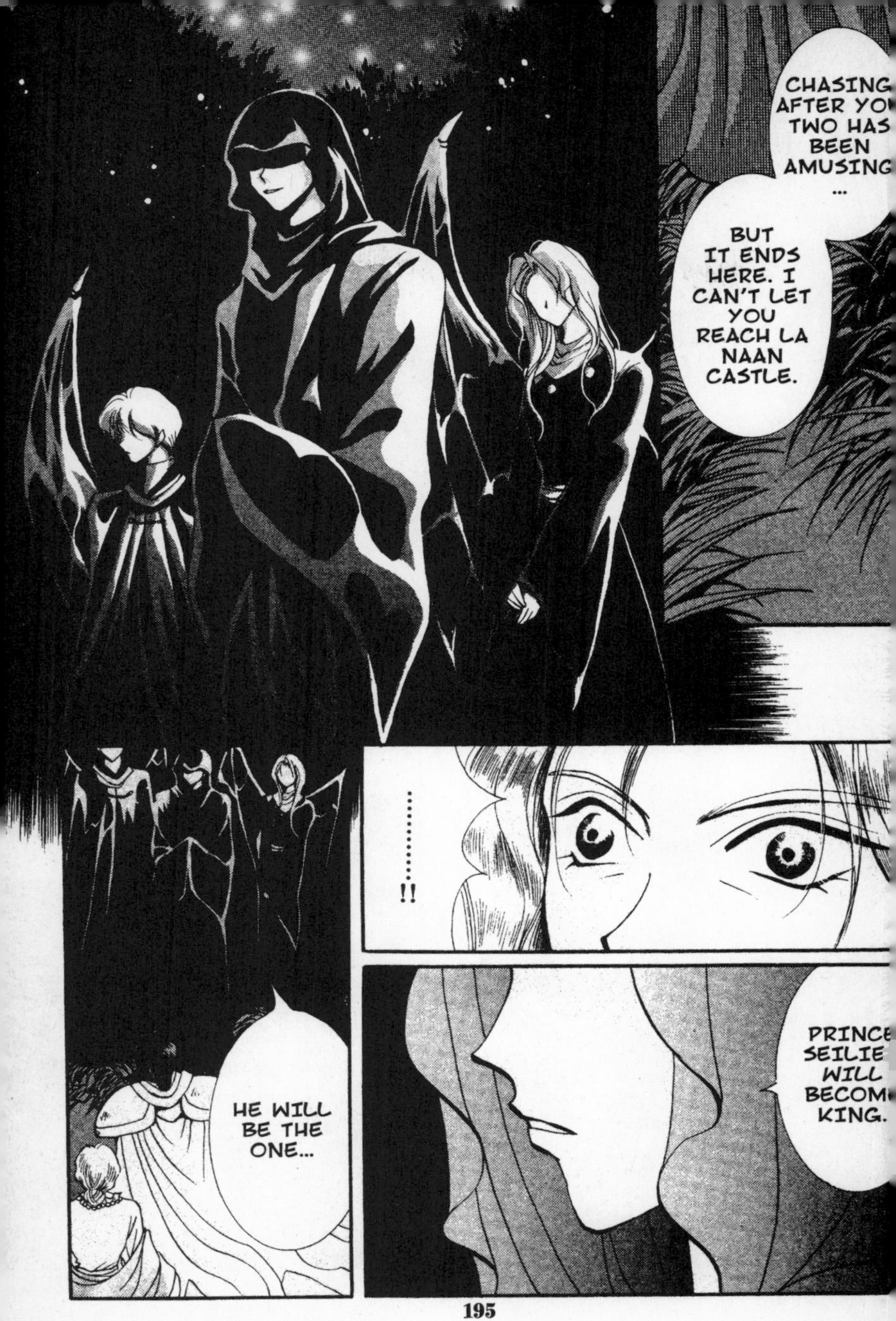
CHASING AFTER YOU TWO HAS BEEN AMUSING ...
BUT IT ENDS HERE. I CAN'T LET YOU REACH LA NAAN CASTLE.
......!!
PRINCE SEILIE WILL BECOME KING.
HE WILL BE THE ONE...

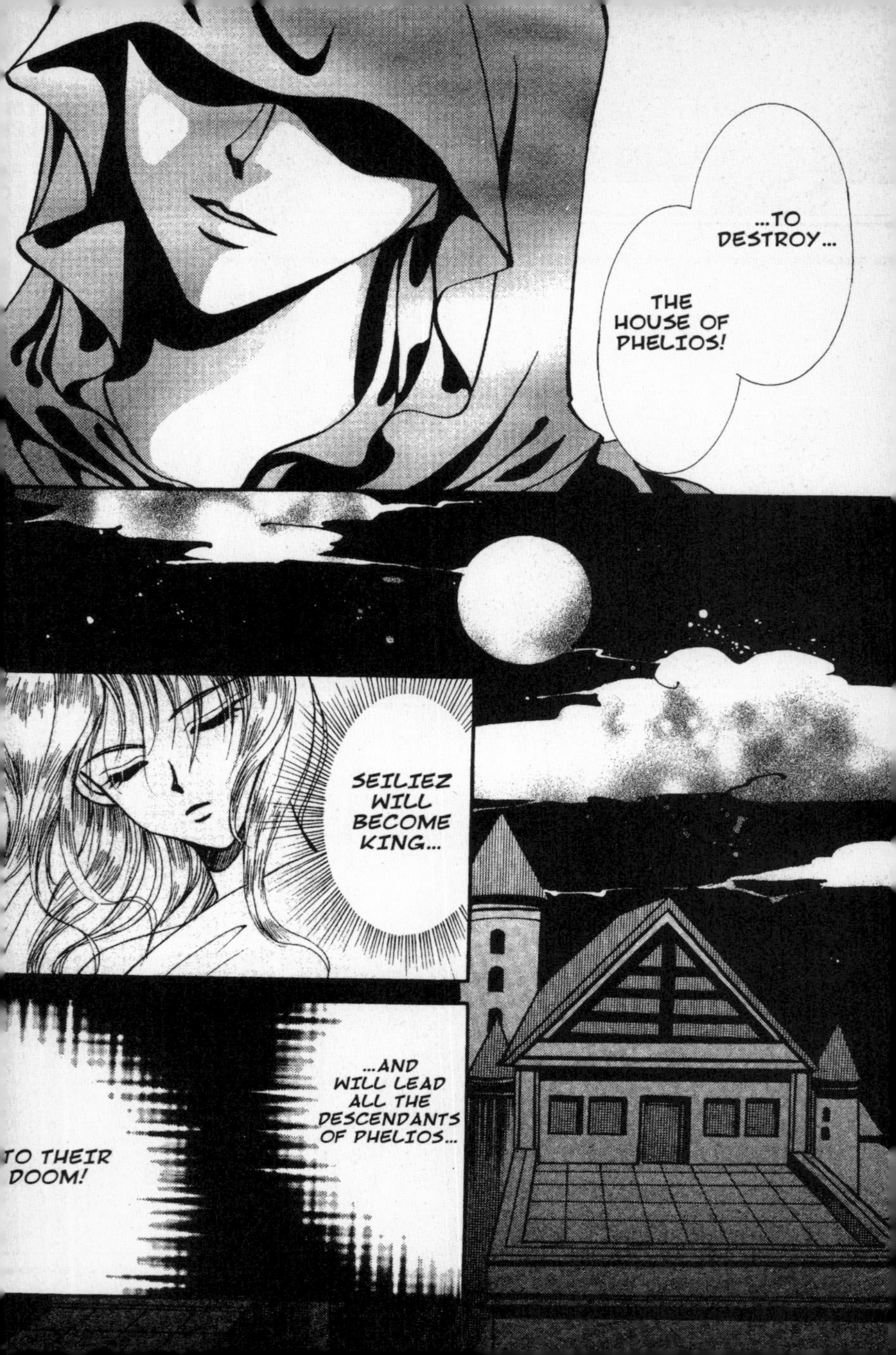
...TO DESTROY...
THE HOUSE OF PHELIOS!
SEILIEZ WILL BECOME KING...
...AND WILL LEAD ALL THE DESCENDANTS OF PHELIOS...
TO THEIR DOOM!

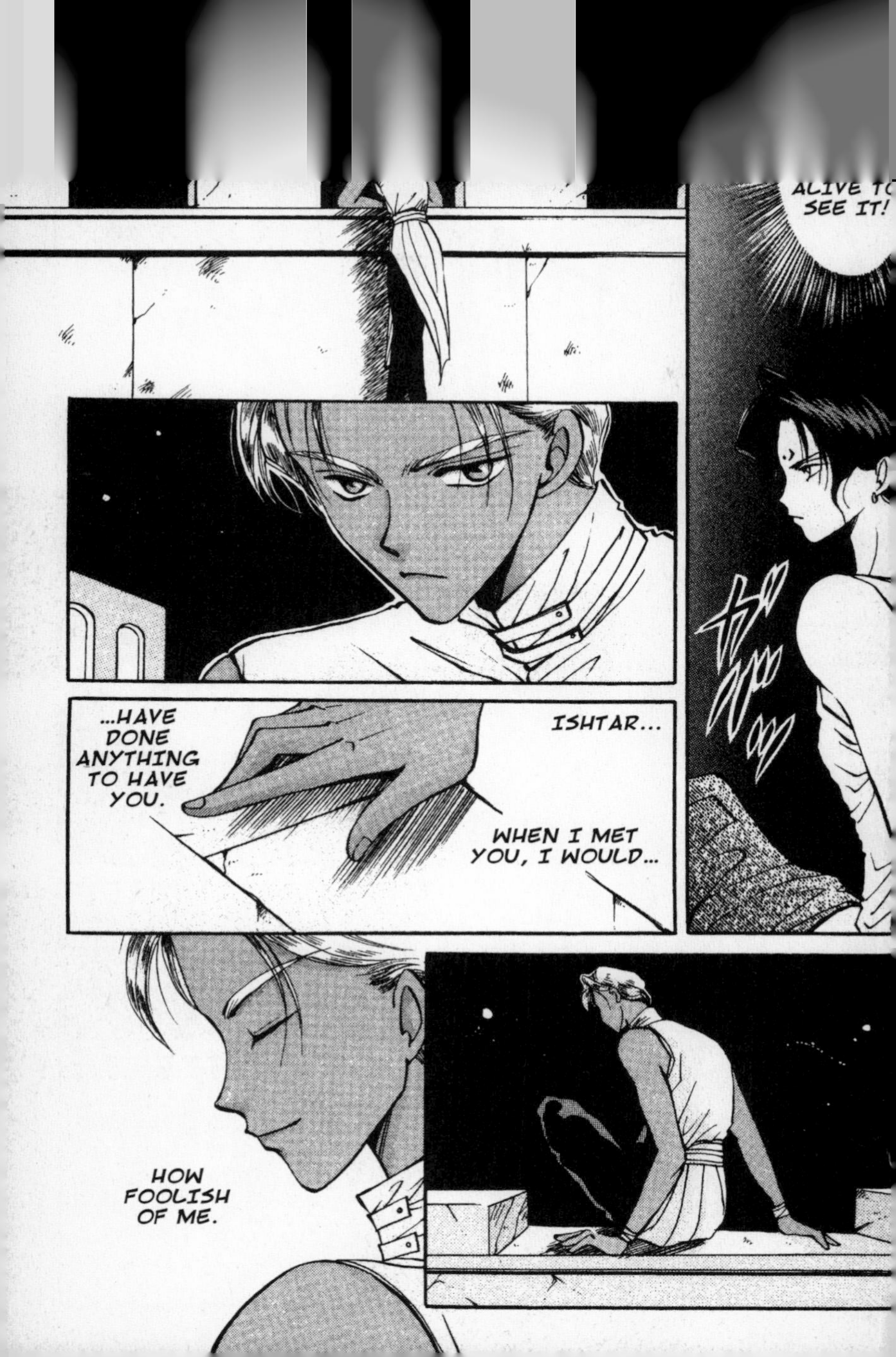

ALIVE TO SEE IT!
ISHTAR...
WHEN I MET YOU, I WOULD...
...HAVE DONE ANYTHING TO HAVE YOU.
HOW FOOLISH OF ME.

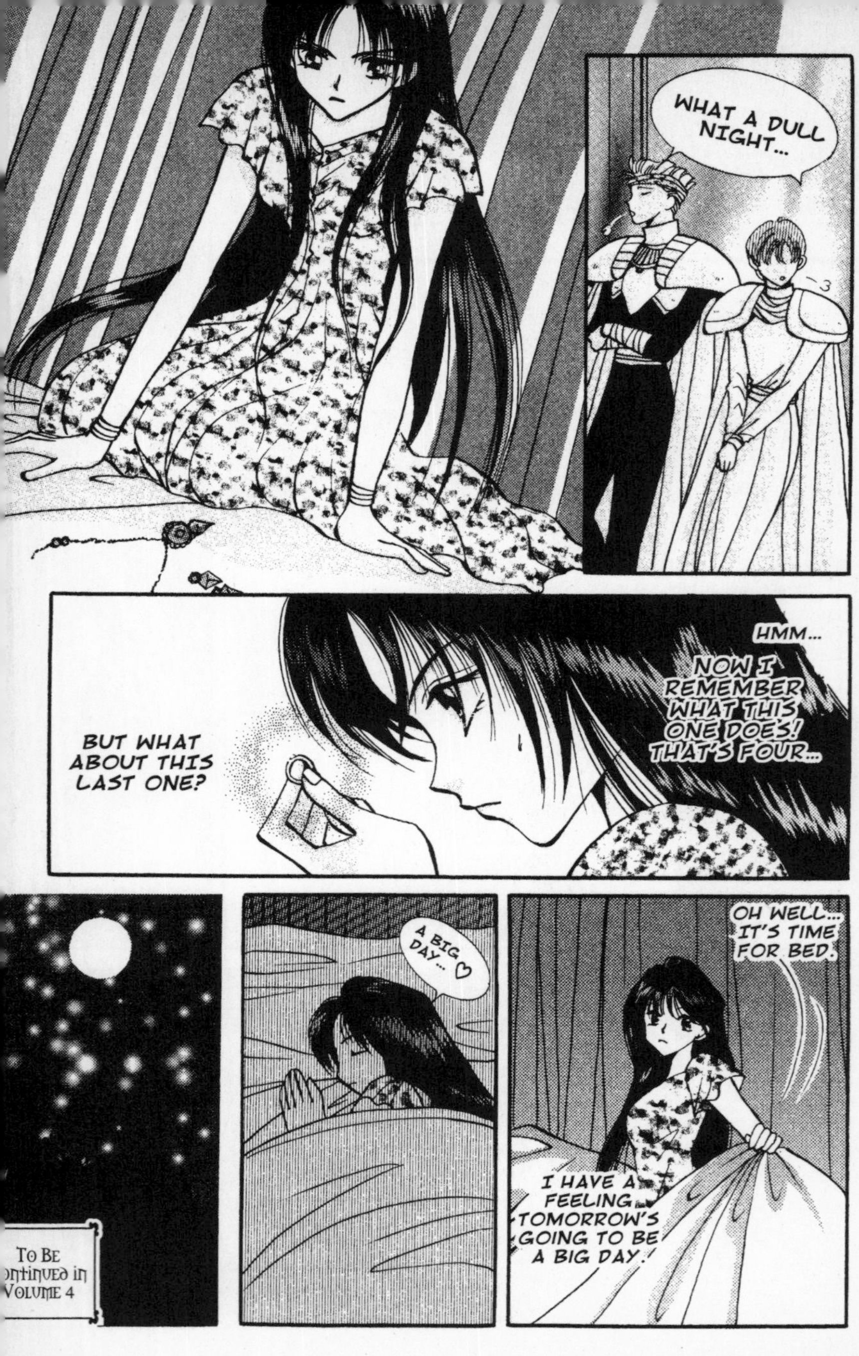
WHAT A DULL NIGHT...
HMM...
NOW I REMEMBER WHAT THIS ONE DOES! THAT'S FOUR...
BUT WHAT ABOUT THIS LAST ONE?
OH WELL... IT'S TIME FOR BED.
I HAVE A FEELING TOMORROW'S GOING TO BE A BIG DAY.
A BIG DAY... ♡
To Be
ontinued in
Volume 4

Postscript

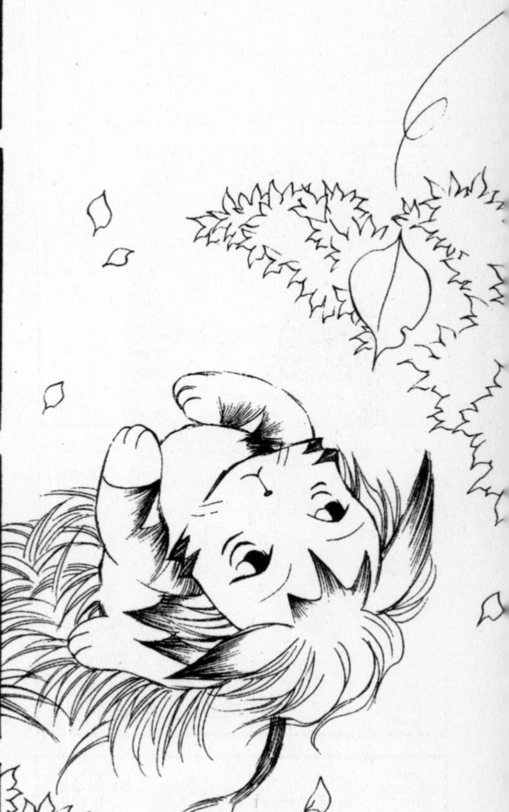

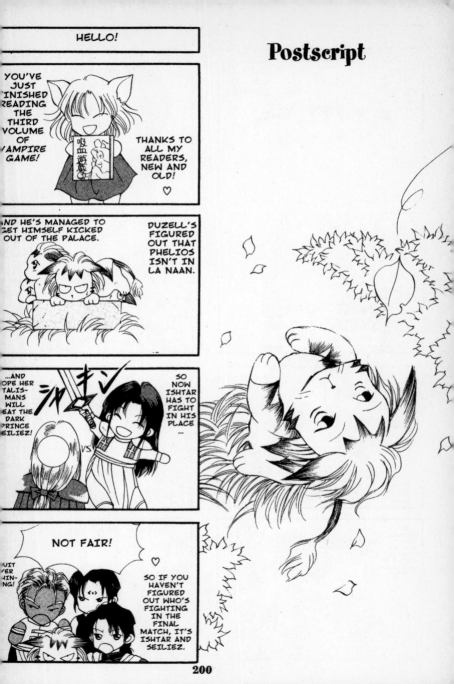

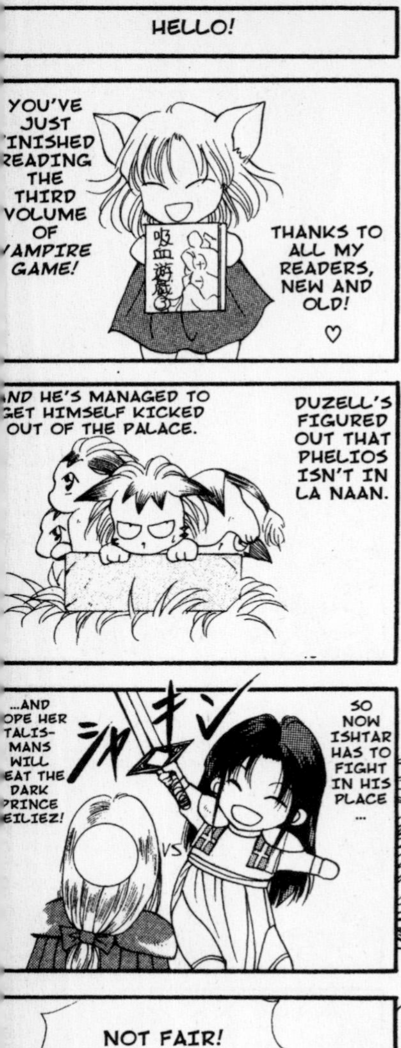
HELLO!
YOU'VE JUST INISHED READING THE THIRD VOLUME OF AMPIRE GAME!
吸血遊戯 3
THANKS TO ALL MY READERS, NEW AND OLD! ♡
DUZELL'S FIGURED OUT THAT PHELIOS ISN'T IN LA NAAN.
ND HE'S MANAGED TO GET HIMSELF KICKED OUT OF THE PALACE.
SO NOW ISHTAR HAS TO FIGHT IN HIS PLACE ...
シャキン
...AND OPE HER TALIS-MANS WILL EAT THE DARK PRINCE EILIEZ!
VS
NOT FAIR!
♡
SO IF YOU HAVEN'T FIGURED OUT WHO'S FIGHTING IN THE FINAL MATCH, IT'S ISHTAR AND SEILIEZ.

ABOUT ISHTAR

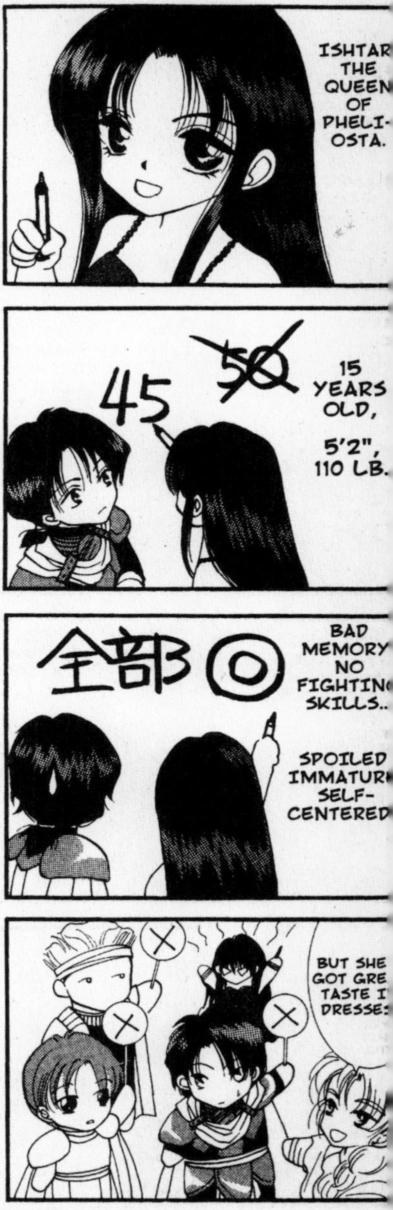
ISHTAR THE QUEEN OF PHELI-OSTA.
50
15 YEARS OLD,
5'2", 110 LB.
45
BAD MEMORY NO FIGHTIN SKILLS..
全部◎
SPOILED IMMATUR SELF-CENTERED
BUT SHE GOT GRE TASTE I DRESSE

ABOUT DUZELL

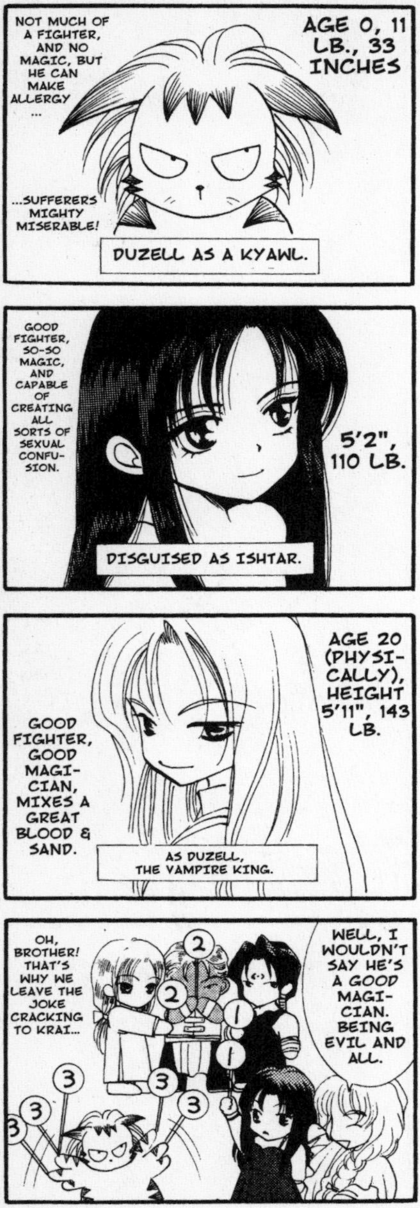
AGE 0, 11 LB., 33 INCHES
NOT MUCH OF A FIGHTER, AND NO MAGIC, BUT HE CAN MAKE ALLERGY ...
...SUFFERERS MIGHTY MISERABLE!
DUZELL AS A KYAWL.
5'2", 110 LB.
GOOD FIGHTER, SO-SO MAGIC, AND CAPABLE OF CREATING ALL SORTS OF SEXUAL CONFU-SION.
DISGUISED AS ISHTAR.
AGE 20 (PHYSI-CALLY), HEIGHT 5'11", 143 LB.
GOOD FIGHTER, GOOD MAGI-CIAN, MIXES A GREAT BLOOD & SAND.
AS DUZELL, THE VAMPIRE KING.
WELL, I WOULDN'T SAY HE'S A GOOD MAGI-CIAN. BEING EVIL AND ALL.
OH, BROTHER! THAT'S WHY WE LEAVE THE JOKE CRACKING TO KRAI...

ABOUT DARRES

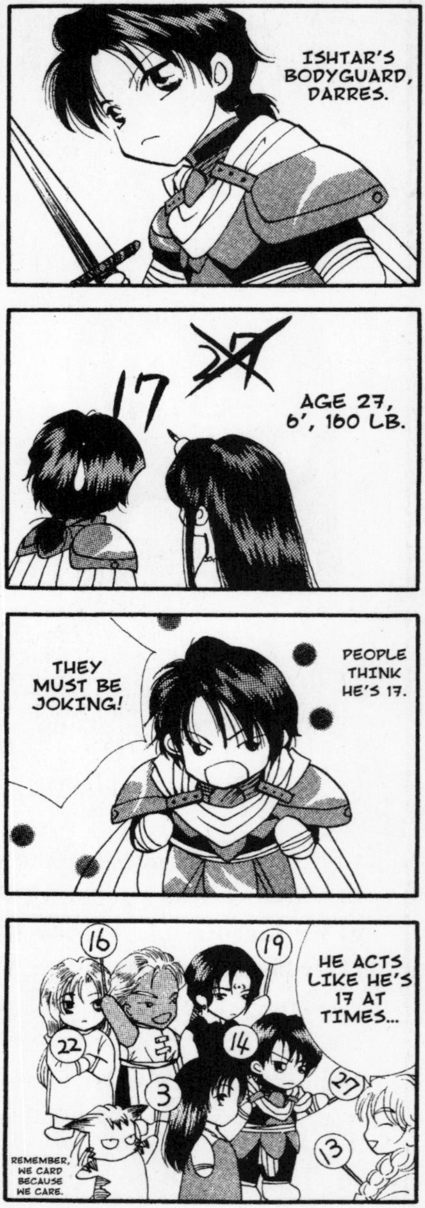
ISHTAR'S BODYGUARD, DARRES.
AGE 27, 6', 160 LB.
17
PEOPLE THINK HE'S 17.
THEY MUST BE JOKING!
HE ACTS LIKE HE'S 17 AT TIMES...
19
16
14
22
27
3
13
REMEMBER, WE CARD BECAUSE WE CARE.

CONCLUSION

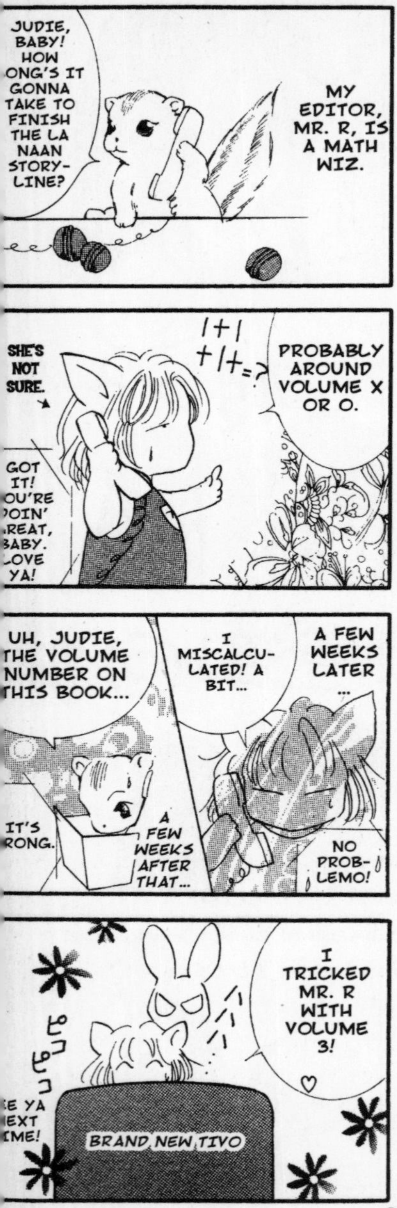
MY EDITOR, MR. R, IS A MATH WIZ.
JUDIE, BABY! HOW ONG'S IT GONNA TAKE TO FINISH THE LA NAAN STORY-LINE?
PROBABLY AROUND VOLUME X OR O.
1+1 +1+=?
SHE'S NOT SURE.
GOT IT! OU'RE OIN' REAT, ABY. LOVE YA!
A FEW WEEKS LATER ...
I MISCALCULATED! A BIT...
UH, JUDIE, THE VOLUME NUMBER ON HIS BOOK...
IT'S RONG.
A FEW WEEKS AFTER THAT...
NO PROBLEMO!
I TRICKED MR. R WITH VOLUME 3!
ピコピコ
BRAND NEW TIVO
EE YA EXT IME!

VAMPIRE GAME

Next issue...

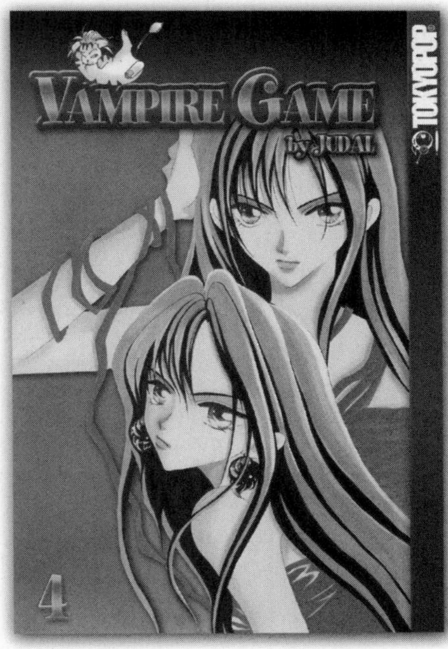
VAMPIRE GAME
by JUDAL
TOKYOPOP
4

Days of political intrigue (and decades of bad marriages) come to a head as Seiliez squares off against Ishtar in the final fight of the tournament. At stake is the Kingdom of Pheliosta, and likely the princess's wardrobe. Can the dashing Darres keep from becoming dinner long enough to help? Not likely, and with Duzell preoccupied with getting back to nature, things aren't looking good. So what's a girl to do? Find out as the La Naan arc comes to its exciting close!

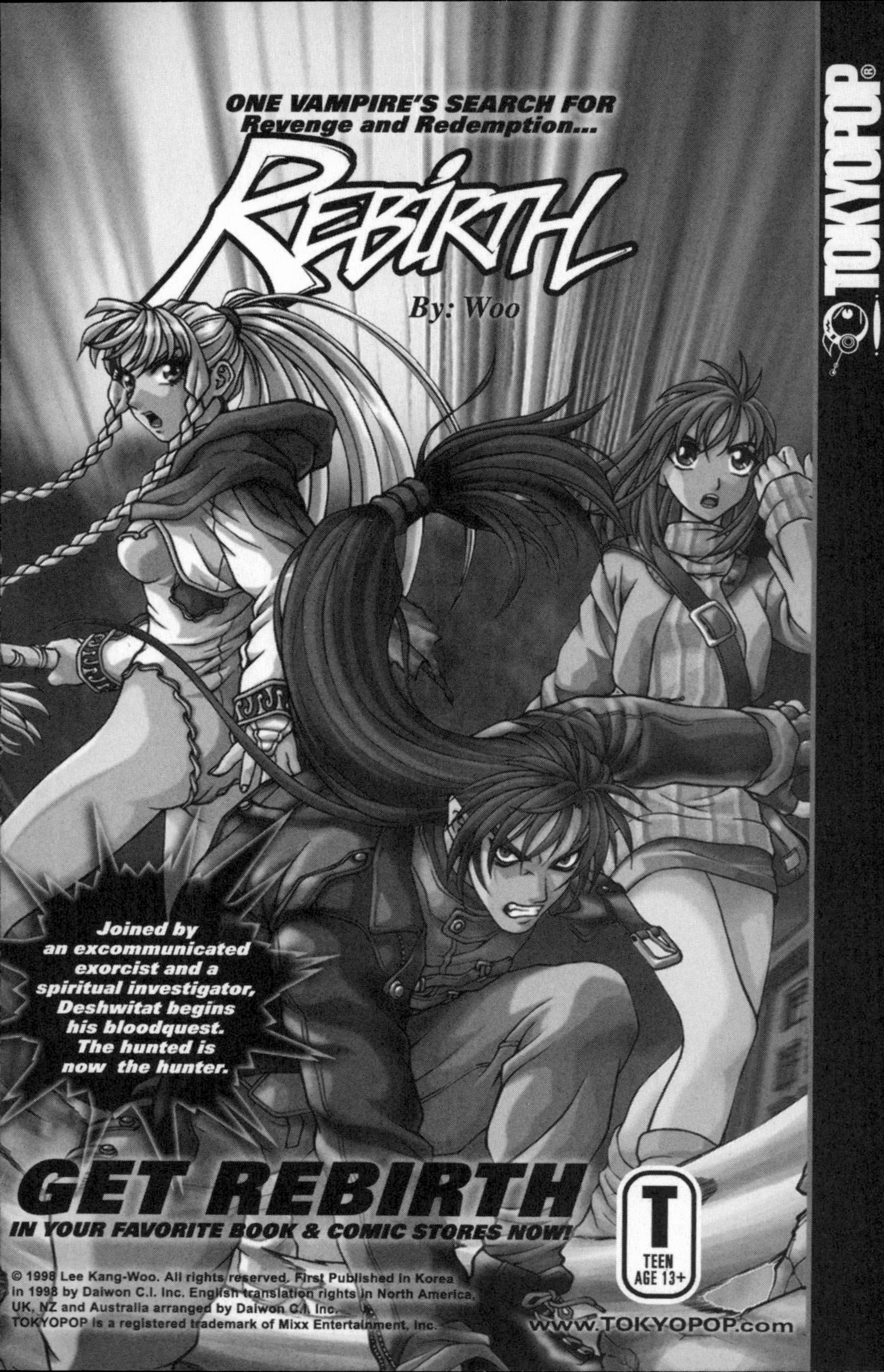

ONE VAMPIRE'S SEARCH FOR
Revenge and Redemption...
REBIRTH
By: Woo
Joined by an excommunicated exorcist and a spiritual investigator, Deshwitat begins his bloodquest. The hunted is now the hunter.
GET REBIRTH
IN YOUR FAVORITE BOOK & COMIC STORES NOW!
T
TEEN
AGE 13+
© 1998 Lee Kang-Woo. All rights reserved. First Published in Korea in 1998 by Daiwon C.I. Inc. English translation rights in North America, UK, NZ and Australia arranged by Daiwon C.I. Inc.
TOKYOPOP is a registered trademark of Mixx Entertainment, Inc.
www.TOKYOPOP.com
TOKYOPOP

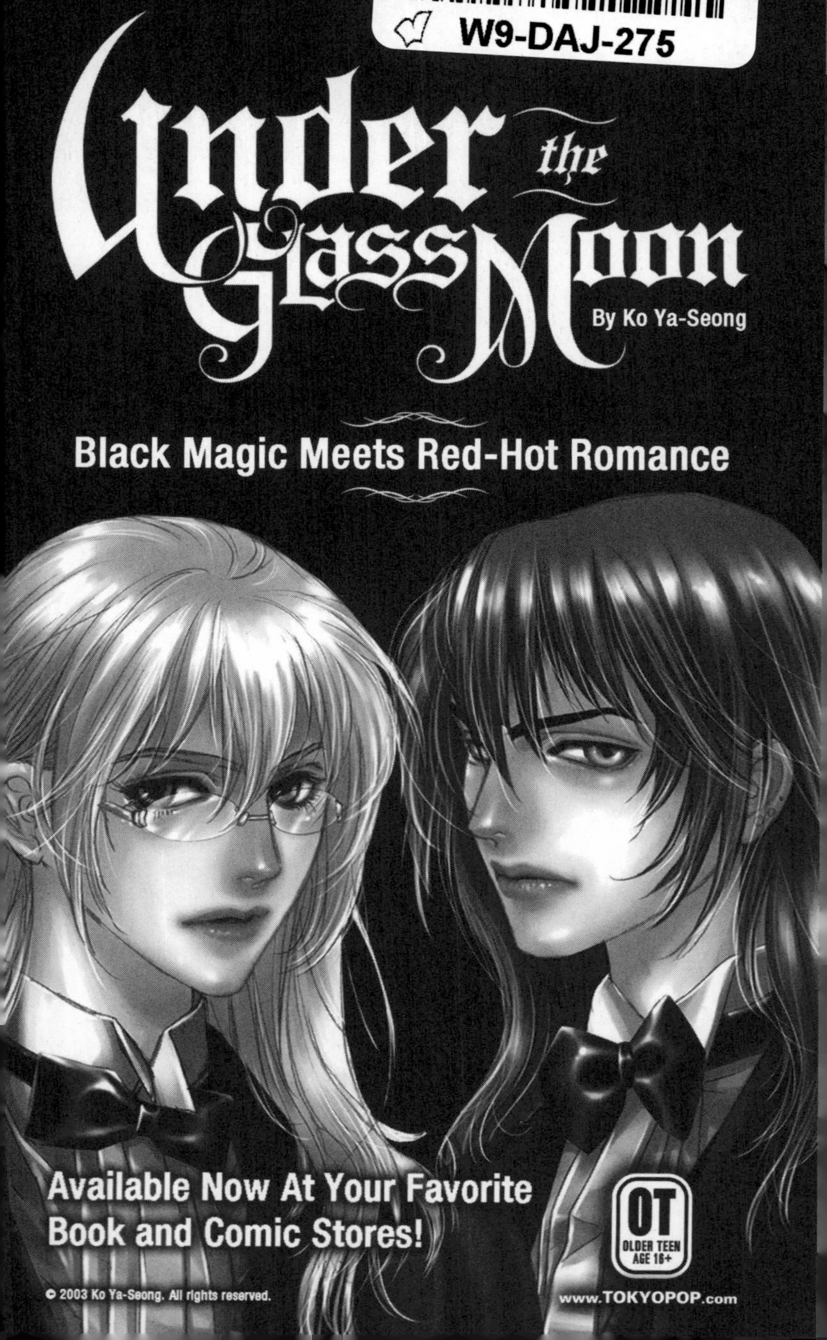
Under the Glass Moon
By Ko Ya-Seong
Black Magic Meets Red-Hot Romance
Available Now At Your Favorite Book and Comic Stores!
OT
OLDER TEEN AGE 16+
© 2003 Ko Ya-Seong. All rights reserved.
www.TOKYOPOP.com

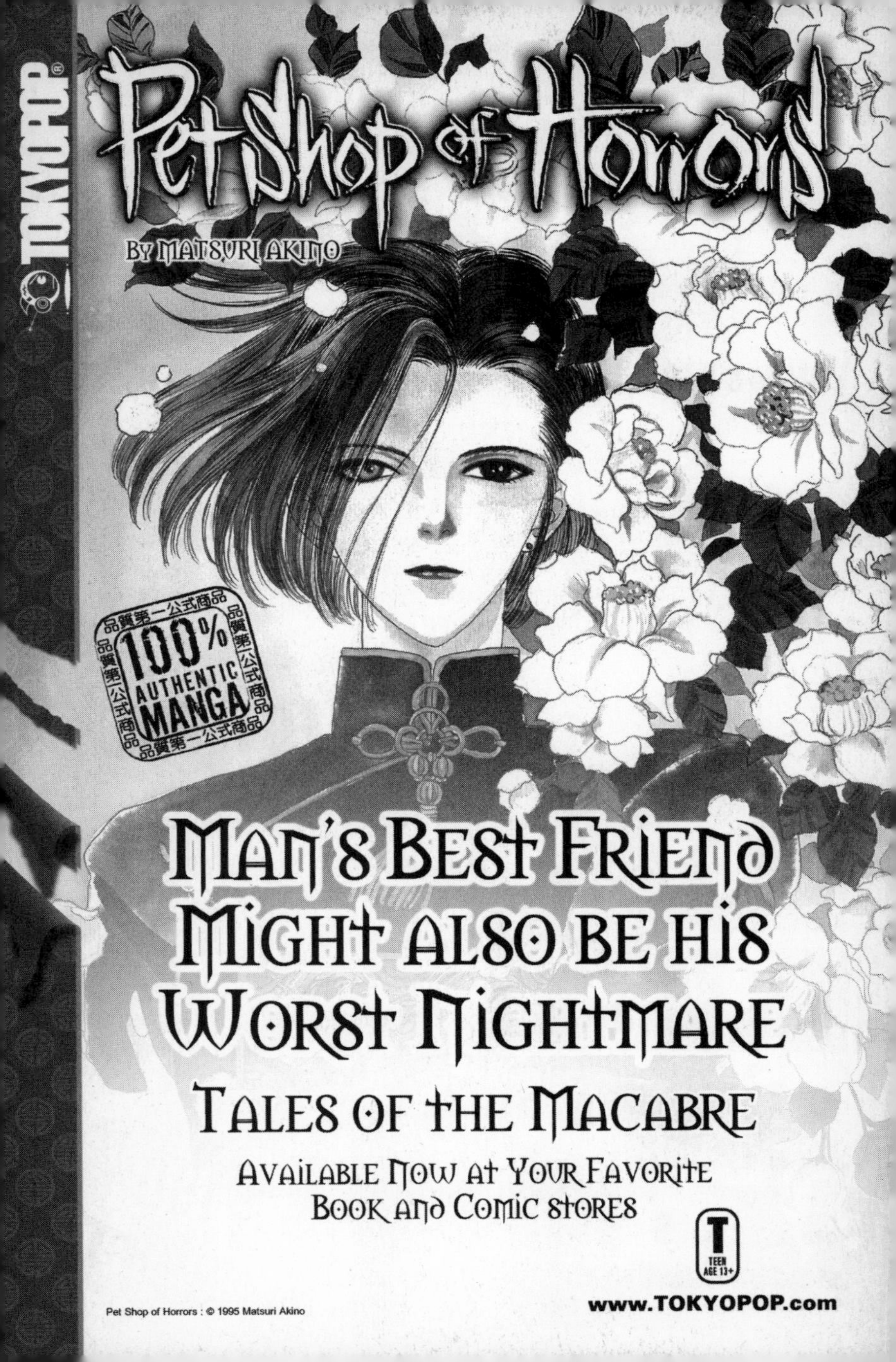
TOKYOPOP
Pet Shop of Horrors
By Matsuri Akino
品質第一公式商品
100% AUTHENTIC MANGA
Man's Best Friend Might Also Be His Worst Nightmare
Tales of the Macabre
Available Now at Your Favorite Book and Comic Stores
T TEEN AGE 13+
Pet Shop of Horrors : © 1995 Matsuri Akino
www.TOKYOPOP.com

STOP!

This is the back of the book.
You wouldn't want to spoil a great ending!

This book is printed "manga-style," in the authentic Japanese right-to-left format. Since none of the artwork has been flipped or altered, readers get to experience the story just as the creator intended. You've been asking for it, so TOKYOPOP® delivered: authentic, hot-off-the-press, and far more fun!

DIRECTIONS

If this is your first time reading manga-style, here's a quick guide to help you understand how it works.

It's easy... just start in the top right panel and follow the numbers. Have fun, and look for more 100% authentic manga from TOKYOPOP®!